SHARPE'S FURY

BOOKS BY BERNARD CORNWELL

The Saxon Novels

THE LAST KINGDOM
THE PALE HORSEMAN
THE LORDS OF THE NORTH

The Sharpe Novels (in chronological order)

SHARPE'S TIGER*
Richard Sharpe and the Siege of Seringapatam, 1799

SHARPE'S TRIUMPH*
Richard Sharpe and the Battle of Assaye,
September 1803

SHARPE'S FORTRESS*
Richard Sharpe and the Siege of Gawilghur,
December 1803

SHARPE'S TRAFALGAR*
Richard Sharpe and the Battle of Trafalgar,
21 October 1805

SHARPE'S PREY*
Richard Sharpe and the Expedition to
Copenhagen, 1807

SHARPE'S RIFLES
Richard Sharpe and the French Invasion of Galicia,
January 1809

SHARPE'S HAVOC*
Richard Sharpe and the Campaign in Northern
Portugal, Spring 1809

SHARPE'S EAGLE
Richard Sharpe and the Talavera Campaign,
July 1809

SHARPE'S GOLD
Richard Sharpe and the Destruction of Almeida,
August 1810

SHARPE'S ESCAPE*
Richard Sharpe and the Bussaco Campaign, 1810

SHARPE'S BATTLE*
Richard Sharpe and the Battle of Fuentes de Onoro,
May 1811

SHARPE'S COMPANY
Richard Sharpe and the Siege of Badajoz,
January to April 1812

SHARPE'S SWORD
Richard Sharpe and the Salamanca Campaign,
June and July 1812

SHARPE'S ENEMY
Richard Sharpe and the Defense of Portugal,
Christmas 1812

SHARPE'S HONOUR
Richard Sharpe and the Vitoria Campaign,
February to June 1813

SHARPE'S REGIMENT
Richard Sharpe and the Invasion of France,
June to November 1813

SHARPE'S SIEGE
Richard Sharpe and the Winter Campaign, 1814

SHARPE'S REVENGE
Richard Sharpe and the Peace of 1814

SHARPE'S WATERLOO
Richard Sharpe and the Waterloo Campaign,
15 June to 18 June 1815

SHARPE'S DEVIL★
Richard Sharpe and the Emperor, 1820–21

The Grail Quest Series
THE ARCHER'S TALE
VAGABOND
HERETIC

The Nathaniel Starbuck Chronicles
REBEL
COPPERHEAD
BATTLE FLAG
THE BLOODY GROUND

The Warlord Chronicles
THE WINTER KING
THE ENEMY OF GOD
EXCALIBUR

Other Novels
REDCOAT
A CROWNING MERCY
STORMCHILD
SCOUNDREL
GALLOWS THIEF
STONEHENGE, 2000 B.C.: A NOVEL

★Published by HarperCollins*Publishers*

SHARPE'S FURY

Richard Sharpe and
the Battle of Barrosa,
March 1811

Bernard Cornwell

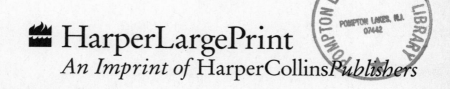

HarperLargePrint
An Imprint of HarperCollinsPublishers

HarperCollins books may be purchased for educational, business, or sales promotional use. For information, please write: Special Markets Department, Harper-Collins Publishers, 10 East 53rd Street, New York, NY 10022.

FIRST HARPER LARGE PRINT EDITION

Library of Congress Cataloging-in-Publication Data is available upon request.

ISBN-10: 0-06-123304-8
ISBN-13: 978-0-06-123304-3

06 07 08 09 10 BVG/RRD 10 9 8 7 6 5 4 3 2 1

This Large Print Book carries the
Seal of Approval of N.A.V.H.

Sharpe's Fury is for
Eric Sykes.

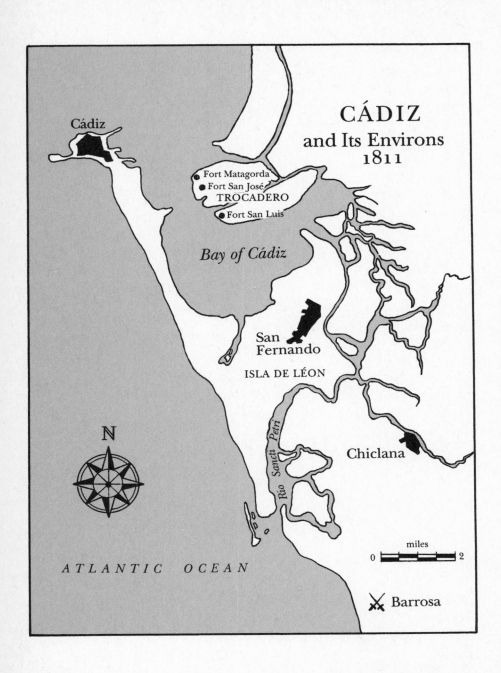

CÁDIZ
and Its Environs
1811

Cádiz

Fort Matagorda
Fort San José
TROCADERO
Fort San Luis

Bay of Cádiz

San
Fernando

ISLA DE LÉON

Río Sancti Petri

Chiclana

N

ATLANTIC OCEAN

miles
0 ⚊⚊⚊⚊ 2

Barrosa

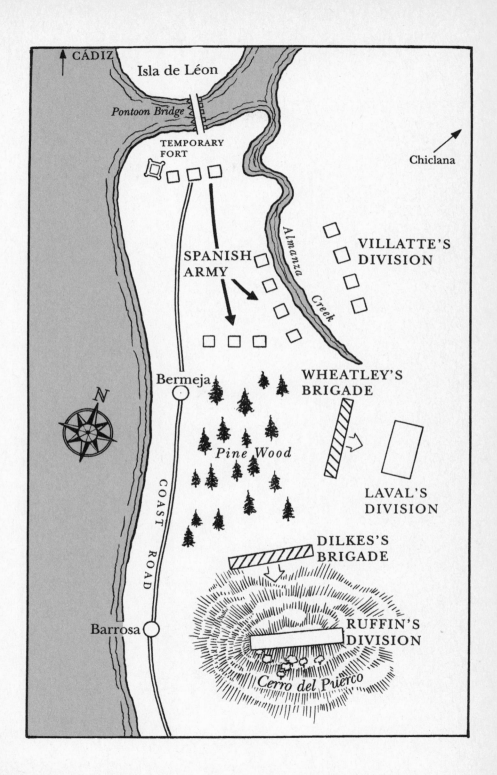

Part One
The River

Chapter 1

You were never far from the sea in Cádiz. The smell of it was always there, almost as powerful as the stink of sewage. On the city's southern side, when the wind was high and from the south, the waves would shatter on the sea wall and spray would rattle on shuttered windows. After the battle of Trafalgar storms had battered the city for a week and the winds had carried the sea spray to the cathedral and torn down scaffolding about its unfinished dome. Waves had besieged Cádiz and pieces of broken ship had clattered on the stones, and then the corpses had come. But that had been almost six years ago and now Spain fought on the same side as Britain, though Cádiz was all that was left of Spain. The rest of the country was either ruled by France or had no government at all. Guerrilleros haunted the hills, poverty ruled the streets, and Spain was sullen.

February 1811. Nighttime. Another storm beat at the city and monstrous waves shattered white against the sea wall. In the dark the watching man could see the explosions of foam and they reminded him of the powder smoke blasted from cannons. There was the same uncertainty about the violence. Just when he thought the waves had done their worst, another two or three would explode in sudden bursts, the white water would bloom above the wall like smoke, and the spray would be driven by the wind to spatter against the city's white walls like grapeshot.

The man was a priest. Father Salvador Montseny was dressed in a cassock, a cloak, and a wide black hat that he needed to hold against the wind's buffeting. He was a tall man, in his thirties, a fierce preacher of saturnine good looks, who now waited in the small shelter of an archway. He was a long way from home. Home was in the north where he had grown up as the unloved son of a widower lawyer who had sent Salvador to a church school. He had become a priest because he did not know what else he should be, but now he wished he had been a soldier. He thought he would have been a good soldier, but fate had made him a sailor instead. He had been a chaplain on board a Spanish ship captured at Trafalgar and in the darkness above him the sound of battle crashed again. The sound was the boom and snap of the great canvas sheets that protected the cathedral's half-built dome, but the wind made the huge tarpaulins sound like cannons. The canvas, he knew, had once been the sails of Spain's battle fleet, but after Trafalgar the sails had been stripped from the few ships that had limped home. Father Salvador Montseny had been in England then. Most Spanish prisoners had been put ashore swiftly, but Montseny was chaplain to an admiral and he had accompanied his master to the damp country house in Hampshire where he had watched the rain fall and the snow cover the pastures, and where he had learned to hate.

And he had also learned patience. He was being patient now. His hat and cloak were soaked through and he was cold, but he did not stir. He just waited. He had a pistol in his belt, but he reckoned the priming powder would be sodden. It did not matter. He had a knife. He touched the hilt, leaned on the wall, saw another wave break at the street's end, saw the spray dash past the dim light from an unshuttered window, and then heard the footsteps.

A man came running from the Calle Compania. Father Montseny waited, just a dark shadow in dark shadows, and saw the man go to the door opposite. It was unlocked. The man went through and the priest followed fast, pushing the door open as the man tried to close it. **"Gracias,"** Father Montseny said.

They were in an arched tunnel that led to the courtyard. A lantern flickered from an alcove and the man, seeing that Montseny was a priest, looked relieved. "You live here, Father?" he asked.

"Last rites," Father Montseny said, shaking water off his cassock.

"Ah, that poor woman upstairs," the man made the sign of the cross. "It's a dirty night," he said.

"We've had worse, my son, and this will pass."

"True," the man said. He went into the courtyard and climbed the stairs to the first-floor balcony. "You're Catalonian, Father?"

"How did you know?"

"Your accent, Father." The man took out his key and unlocked his front door and the priest appeared to edge past him toward the steps climbing to the second floor.

The man opened his door, then pitched forward as Father Montseny suddenly turned and gave him a push. The man sprawled on the floor. He had a knife and tried to draw it, but the priest kicked him hard under the chin. Then the front door swung shut and they were in the dark. Father Montseny knelt on the fallen man's chest and put his own knife at his victim's throat. "Say nothing, my son," he ordered. He felt under the trapped man's wet cloak and found the knife, which he drew and tossed up the passageway. "You will speak," he said, "only when I ask you questions. Your name is Gonzalo Jurado?"

"Yes." Jurado's voice was scarce above a breath.

"Do you have the whore's letters?"

"No," Jurado said, then squealed because Father Montseny's knife had cut through his skin to touch his jawbone.

"You will be hurt if you lie," the priest said. "Do you have the letters?"

"I have them, yes!"

"Then show them to me."

Father Montseny let Jurado rise. He stayed close as Jurado went into a room that overlooked the street where the priest had waited. Steel struck flint and a candle was lit. Jurado could see his assailant more clearly now and thought Montseny must be a soldier in disguise because his face did not have the look of a priest. It was a dark, lantern-jawed face without pity. "The letters are for sale," Jurado said, then gasped because Father Montseny had hit him in the belly.

"I said you will speak only when I question you," the priest said. "Show me the letters."

The room was small, but very comfortable. It was evident that Gonzalo Jurado liked his luxuries. Two couches faced an empty fireplace above which a gilt-framed mirror hung. There were rugs on the floor. Three paintings hung on the wall opposite the window, all showing naked women. A bureau stood under the window that looked onto the street and the frightened man unlocked one of its drawers and took out a bundle of letters tied with black string. He put them on the bureau and stepped back.

Father Montseny cut the string and spread the letters on the bureau's leather top. "Is this all of them?"

"All fifteen," Jurado said.

"And the whore?" Father Montseny asked. "She has some still?"

Jurado hesitated, then saw the knife blade reflect candlelight. "She has six."

"She kept them?"

"Yes, señor."

"Why?"

Jurado shrugged. "Fifteen are enough? Maybe she can sell the others later? Perhaps she is still fond of the man? Who knows? Who understands women? But . . ." He had been about to ask a question, then feared being hit for speaking out of turn.

"Go on," Father Montseny said, picking out a letter at random.

"How do you know about the letters? I told no one except the English."

"Your whore made confession," Father Montseny said.

"Caterina! She went to confession?"

"Once a year, she told me," Father Montseny said, scanning the letter, "always on her patron saint's name day. She came to the cathedral, told God about her many sins, and I granted her absolution on his behalf. How much do you want for the letters?"

"English guineas," Jurado said, "fifteen letters, twenty guineas each." He was feeling more confident now. He kept a loaded pistol in the bureau's bottom drawer. He tested the mainspring every day and changed the powder at least once a month. And his fear had subsided now that he understood Montseny really was a priest. A frightening priest, to be sure, but still a man of God. "If you prefer to pay Spanish money, Father," he went on, "then the letters are yours for thirteen hundred dollars."

"Thirteen hundred dollars?" Father Montseny responded absently. He was reading one of the letters. It was written in English, but that was no problem for he had learned the language in Hampshire. The letter's writer had been deeply in love and the fool had committed that love to paper. The fool had made promises, and the girl to whom he had made the promises had turned out to be a whore, and Jurado was her pimp, and now the pimp wanted to blackmail the letter writer.

"I have a reply." The pimp dared to speak without invitation.

"From the English?"

"Yes, Father. It's in here." Jurado gestured at the bureau's bottom drawer.

Father Montseny nodded his permission and Jurado opened the drawer, then yelped because a fist had struck him so hard that he reeled backward. He hit the door behind him, which gave way so that he fell on his back in the bedroom. Father Montseny took the pistol from the bureau drawer, opened the frizzen, blew out the powder, and tossed the now useless weapon onto one of the silk-covered couches. "You said you had received a reply?" he asked as though there had been no violence.

Jurado was shaking now. "They said they would pay."

"You have arranged the exchange?"

"Not yet." Jurado hesitated. "Are you with the English?"

"No, thank God. I am with the most holy Roman church. So how do you communicate with the English?"

"I am to leave a message at the Cinco Torres."

"Addressed to whom?"

"To a Señor Plummer."

The Cinco Torres was a coffeehouse on the Calle Ancha. "So in your next message," Father Montseny said, "you will tell this Plummer where to meet you? Where the exchange will take place?"

"Yes, Father."

"You have been very helpful, my son," Father Montseny said, then held out a hand as if to pull

Jurado to his feet. Jurado, grateful for the help, allowed himself to be pulled up, and only at the last second saw that he was being hauled onto the priest's knife that slashed into his throat. Father Montseny grimaced as he wrenched the blade sideways. It was harder than he had thought, but he gave a grunt as he slashed the sharpened steel through gullet and artery and muscle. The pimp collapsed, making a noise like water draining. Montseny held Jurado down as he died. It was messy, but the blood would not show on his black cloak. Some blood trickled through the floorboards where it would drip into the saddler's shop that occupied most of the building's ground floor. It took over a minute for the pimp to die, and all the while the blood dripped through the boards, but at last Jurado was dead and Father Montseny made the sign of the cross over the pimp's face and said a brief prayer for the departed soul. He sheathed his knife, wiped his hands on the dead man's cloak, and went back to the bureau. He found a great stack of money in one of the drawers and he pushed the folded notes into the top of his left boot and then he bundled the letters. He wrapped them in a cover he took from a cushion and then, to ensure they stayed dry, he put them next to his skin beneath his shirt. He poured a glass of sherry from a decanter and, as he sipped it, he thought about the girl to whom the letters had been written. She lived, he knew, just two streets away and she still had six letters, but he possessed fifteen. More than enough, he decided. Besides, the girl was almost certainly not at home, but servicing a client in one of Cádiz's more palatial bedrooms.

He blew out the candle and went back into the night where the waves broke white at the city's edge and the great sails boomed like guns in the wet dark. Father Salvador Montseny, killer, priest, and patriot, had just ensured the salvation of Spain.

It had all begun so well.

In the moonlit darkness the River Guadiana lay beneath the South Essex Light Company like a misted streak of molten silver pouring slow and massive between black hills. Fort Joseph, named for Napoleon's brother who was the French puppet on the throne of Spain, was on the hill closest to the company, while Fort Josephine, named after the emperor's discarded wife, lay at the top of a long slope on the far bank. Fort Joseph was in Portugal, Josephine was in Spain, and between the two forts was a bridge.

Six light companies had been sent from Lisbon under the command of Brigadier General Sir Barnaby Moon. A coming man, Brigadier Moon, a young thruster, an officer destined for higher things, and this was his first independent command. If he got this right, if the bridge was broken, then Sir Barnaby could look to a future as shining as the river that slid between the darkened hills.

And it had all begun so well. The six companies had been ferried across the Tagus in a misted dawn, then had marched across southern Portugal, which was supposedly French-held territory, but the partisans had assured the British that the French had withdrawn their few garrisons and so it proved. Now, just four days after leaving Lisbon, they had reached the river and the bridge. Dawn was close. The British troops were on the Guadiana's western bank where Fort Joseph had been built on a hill beside the river, and in the last of the night's darkness the ramparts of the fort were outlined by the glow of fires behind the firestep. The encroaching dawn was dimming that glow, but every now and then the silhouette of a man showed in one of the fort's embrasures.

The French were awake. The six British light companies knew that because they had heard the bugles calling the reveilles, first in distant Fort Josephine, then in Joseph, but just because the French were awake did not mean they were alert. If you wake men every day in the chill darkness before dawn, they soon learn to carry their dreams to the ramparts. They might look as though they are staring alertly into the dark, ready for a dawn attack, but in truth they are thinking of the women left in France, of the women still sleeping in the fort's barrack rooms, of the women they wished were sleeping in the fort, of the women they could only dream about, of women. They were dozy.

And the forts had been undisturbed all winter. It was true there were guerrilleros in these hills, but they rarely came close to the forts that had cannon in their embrasures, and peasants armed with muskets quickly learn they are no match for emplaced artillery. The Spanish and Portuguese partisans either ambushed the forage parties of the French troops besieging Badajoz thirty miles to the north or else harried the forces of Marshal

Victor who besieged Cádiz a hundred and fifty miles to the south.

There had once been five good stone bridges crossing the Guadiana between Badajoz and the sea, but they had all been blown up by the contending armies, and now there was only this one French pontoon bridge to provide a link between the emperor's siege forces. It was not used much. Travel in Portugal or Spain was dangerous for the French because the guerrilleros were merciless, but once every two or three weeks the pontoon bridge would creak under the weight of a battery of artillery, and every few days a dispatch rider would cross the river escorted by a regiment of dragoons. Not many local folk used the bridge, for very few could afford the toll and fewer still wanted to risk the animosity of the twin garrisons who were, as a result, mostly left in peace. The war seemed far away, which was why the defenders manning the ramparts in the early morning were dreaming of women rather than looking for the enemy troops who had followed a goat track from the darkened heights into the blackness of the valley to the west of Fort Joseph.

Captain Richard Sharpe, commander of the South Essex Light Company, was not in the valley. He was with his company on a hill to the north of the fort. He had the easiest job of the morning, which was to create a diversion, and that meant none of his men should die and none should even be wounded. Sharpe was glad of that, but he was also aware that he had not been given the easy job as a reward, but because Moon disliked him. The brigadier had made that plain when the six light companies had reported to him in Lisbon. "My name's Moon," the brigadier had said, "and you've got a reputation."

Sharpe, taken aback by the offhand greeting, had looked surprised. "I do, sir?"

"Don't be modest with me, man," Moon had said, stabbing a finger at the South Essex badge, which showed a chained eagle. Sharpe and his sergeant, Patrick Harper, had captured that eagle from the French at Talavera, and such a feat, as Moon had said, gave a man a reputation. "I don't want any damn heroics, Sharpe," the brigadier went on.

"No, sir."

"Good plain soldiering wins wars," Moon had said. "Doing mundane things well is what counts." That was undoubtedly true, but it was odd coming from Sir Barnaby Moon whose reputation was anything but mundane. He was young, only just a year over thirty, and he had been in Portugal for little more than a year, yet he had already made a name for himself. He had led his battalion at Bussaco where, on the ridge where the French had climbed and died, he had rescued two of his skirmishers by galloping through his men's ranks and killing the skirmishers' captors with his sword. "No damned frog will take my fusiliers!" he had announced, leading the two men back, and his soldiers had cheered him and he had taken off his cocked hat and bowed to them from the saddle. He was also said to be a gambler and a ruthless hunter of women and, because he was as wealthy as he was handsome, he was reckoned a most successful hunter. London, it was said, was a safer city now that Sir Barnaby was in Portugal, though doubtless there was a score or more of Lisbon ladies who might give birth to babies who would grow up to have Sir Barnaby's lean face, fair hair, and startling blue eyes. He was, in brief, anything but a plain soldier, yet that was what he required of Sharpe and Sharpe was happy to oblige. "You need make no reputation with me, Sharpe," Sir Barnaby had said.

"I'll try hard not to, sir," Sharpe had said, for which he had received a foul look, and ever since Moon had virtually ignored Sharpe. Jack Bullen, who was Sharpe's lieutenant, reckoned that the brigadier was jealous.

"Don't be daft, Jack," Sharpe had said when this was proposed.

"In any drama, sir," Bullen had persevered, "there is only room for one hero. The stage is too small for two."

"You're an expert on drama, Jack?"

"I am an expert on everything except for the things you know about," Bullen had said, making Sharpe laugh. The truth, Sharpe reckoned, was that Moon simply shared most officers' mistrust of men who had been promoted from the ranks. Sharpe had joined the army as a private, he had served as a sergeant, and now he was a captain, and that irritated some men who saw Sharpe's rise as an affront to the established order, which, Sharpe decided, was fine by him. He would create the diversion, let the other five companies do the fighting, then go back to Lisbon and so back to the battalion. In a month or two, as spring arrived in Portugal, they would march north from the Lines of Torres Vedras and pursue Marshal

Masséna's forces into Spain. There would be plenty enough fighting in the spring, even enough for upstarts.

"There's the light, sir," Harper said. He was lying flat beside Sharpe and staring into the valley.

"You're sure?"

"There it is again, sir. See it?"

The brigadier had a shielded lantern and, by raising one of its screens, could flash a dim light that would be hidden from the French. It glowed again, made faint by the dawn, and Sharpe called to his men. "Now, lads."

All they had to do was show themselves, not in ranks and files, but scattered across the hilltop so that they looked like partisans. The object was to make the French peer northward and so ignore the attack creeping from the west.

"That's all we do?" Harper asked. "We just piss around up here?"

"More or less," Sharpe said. "Stand up, lads! Let the Crapauds see you!" The light company was on the skyline, plainly visible, and there was just enough light to see that the French in Fort Joseph had registered their presence. Undoubtedly the garrison's officers would be training their telescopes on the hill, but Sharpe's men were in greatcoats so their uniforms, with their distinctive crossbelts, were not visible, and he had told them to take off their shakos so they did not look like soldiers.

"Can we give them a shot or two?" Harper asked.

"Don't want to get them excited," Sharpe said. "We just want them to watch us."

"But we can shoot when they wake up?"

"When they see the others, yes. We'll give them a greenjacket breakfast, eh?"

Sharpe's company was unique in that while most of its men wore the red coats of the British infantry, others were uniformed in the green jackets of the rifle battalions. It was all because of a mistake. Sharpe and his riflemen had been cut off from the retreat to Corunna, had made their way south to the forces in Lisbon, and there been temporarily attached to the redcoated South Essex and somehow they had never left. The greenjackets carried rifles. To most people a rifle looked like a short musket, but the difference was hidden inside the barrel. The Baker Rifle had seven grooves twisting the length of its barrel and those grooves gave the bullet a spin that made it lethally accurate. A musket was quick to load and fast to fire, but beyond sixty paces a man might as well shut his eyes rather than take aim. The rifle could kill at three times that range. The French had no rifles, which meant Sharpe's greenjackets could lie on the hill, shoot at the defenders, and know that none of the infantry inside Fort Joseph could answer their fire.

"There they go," Harper said.

The five light companies were advancing up the hill. Their red uniforms looked black in the half-light. Some carried short ladders. They had a nasty job, Sharpe thought. The fort had a dry ditch and from the bottom of the ditch to the top of the parapet was at least ten feet and the top of the parapet was protected by sharpened stakes. The redcoats had to cross the ditch, place the ladders between the stakes, climb into the musket fire of the defenders, and, worse, face cannon fire as well. The French cannons were undoubtedly loaded, but with what? Round shot or canister? If it was canister then Moon's troops could be hit hard by the first volley, while round shot would do much less damage. Not Sharpe's problem. He walked along the hilltop, making sure he was silhouetted against the lightening sky, and miraculously the French were still oblivious of the four hundred men approaching from the west. "Go on, boys," Harper muttered, not speaking to all of the attacking troops, but to the light company of the 88th, the Connaught Rangers, an Irish regiment.

Sharpe was not watching. He had suddenly been seized by the superstition that if he watched the attack, then it would fail. Instead he stared down at the river, counting the bridge's pontoons that were dark shadows in the mist that writhed just above the water. He decided he would count them and not look at Fort Joseph until the first shot was fired. Thirty-one, he reckoned, which meant there was one pontoon every ten feet, for the river was just over a hundred yards wide. The pontoons were big, clumsy, square-ended barges across which a timber roadway had been laid. The winter had been wet all across southern Spain and Portugal; the Guadiana was running high and he could see the water seething where it broke on the pontoons' bluff bows. Each boat had anchor chains running into the river and spring lines tensioned between the neighboring barges across which the heavy baulks ran to support the chesses, the planks that made the roadway. It probably weighed over a hundred tons, Sharpe reckoned, and this job would not be over until that long bridge was destroyed.

"They're dozy bastards," Harper said in wonderment, presumably speaking of Fort Joseph's defenders, but still Sharpe would not look. He was staring at Fort Josephine across the river where he could see men clustered about a cannon. They stepped away and the gun fired, belching a dirty smoke above the river's thinning mist. It had fired a round of canister. The tin can, crammed with bullets, tore itself apart as it left the cannon's muzzle and the half-inch balls whipped the air about Sharpe's hilltop. The boom of the cannon rolled and echoed up the river valley. "Anyone hit?" Sharpe called. No one answered.

The cannon's fire only made the defenders of the nearer fort stare at the hill more intently. They were aiming one of their own cannon now, trying to elevate it so that the canister would scrape the skyline. "Keep your heads down," Sharpe said. Then there was a dull rattle of musketry and he dared to look back at the attack.

It was almost over. There were redcoats in the ditch, more on ladders, and even as Sharpe watched he saw the redcoats surge over the parapet and carry bayonets at the blue-uniformed Frenchmen. There was no need of his rifles. "Get out of sight of that damned gun," he shouted, and his men hurried off the crest. A second cannon fired from the fort across the river. A musket ball plucked at the hem of Sharpe's greatcoat and another drove up a flurry of dew from the grass by his side, but then he was off the hilltop and hidden from the distant gunners.

No gun fired from Fort Joseph. The garrison had been taken utterly by surprise and there were redcoats in the center of the fort now. A panicked stream of Frenchmen was running from the eastern gate to cross the bridge to the safety of Fort Josephine on the river's Spanish bank. The musket fire was slowing. Maybe a dozen Frenchmen had been captured, the rest were fleeing, and there seemed to be scores of them running toward the bridge. The redcoats, screaming their war cries in the dawn, carried bayonets that encouraged the panicked flight. The French tricolor was hauled down before the last of the attacking troops had even crossed the ditch and wall. It had all been that quick.

"Our job's done," Sharpe said. "Down to the fort."

"That was easy," Bullen said happily.

"Not over yet, Jack."

"The bridge, you mean?"

"Got to be destroyed."

"The hard bit's done, anyway."

"That's true," Sharpe said. He liked young Jack Bullen, a bluff Essex boy who was uncomplaining and hardworking. The men liked Bullen too. He treated them fairly, with the confidence that came from privilege, but it was a privilege that was always tempered by cheerfulness. A good officer, Sharpe reckoned.

They filed down the hill, across the rocky valley, over a small stream that fell cold from the hills and so up the next hill to the fort where the ladders were still propped against the parapet. Every now and then a petulant gun fired from Fort Josephine, but the balls were wasted against the earth-filled wicker baskets that topped the parapet. "Ah, you're here, Sharpe." Brigadier Moon greeted him. He was suddenly affable, his dislike of Sharpe washed away by the elation of victory.

"Congratulations, sir."

"What? Oh, thank you. That's generous of you." Moon did seem touched by Sharpe's praise. "It went better than I dared hope. There's tea on the boil over there. Let your lads have some."

The French prisoners were sitting in the fort's center. A dozen horses had been found in the stables and they were now being saddled, presumably because Moon, who had marched from the Tagus, reckoned he had earned the privilege of riding back. A captured officer was standing beside the well, disconsolately watching the victorious British troops who were gleefully searching the French packs captured in the barracks. "Fresh bread!" Major Gillespie, one of Moon's aides, tossed Sharpe a loaf. "Still warm. The bastards live well, don't they?"

"I thought they were supposed to be starving."

"Not here they're not. Land of milk and honey, this place."

Moon climbed to the eastern firestep, which faced the bridge, and began looking into the ready magazines beside the guns. The artillerymen in Fort Josephine saw his red coat and opened fire. They were using canister and their shots rattled on the parapet and whistled overhead. Moon ignored the balls. "Sharpe!" he called, then waited as the rifleman climbed to the rampart. "Time you earned your wages,

Sharpe," he said. Sharpe said nothing, just watched as the brigadier peered into a magazine. "Round shot," Moon announced, "common shell and grapeshot."

"Not canister, sir?"

"Grapeshot, definitely grapeshot. Naval stores, I suspect. Bastards haven't got any ships left so they've sent their grapeshot here." He let the magazine lid drop and stared down at the bridge. "Common shell won't break that brute, will it? There are a score of women down below. In the barracks. Have some of your fellows escort them over the bridge, will you? Deliver them to the French with my compliments. The rest of your men can help Sturridge. He says he'll have to blow the far end."

Lieutenant Sturridge was a Royal Engineer whose job was to destroy the bridge. He was a nervous young man who seemed terrified of Moon. "The far end?" Sharpe asked, wanting to be sure he had heard correctly.

Moon looked exasperated. "If we break the bridge at this end, Sharpe," he explained with exaggerated patience as though he were speaking to a young and not very bright child, "the damn thing will float downstream, but will still be attached to the far bank. The French can then salvage the pontoons. Not much point in coming all this way and leaving the French with a serviceable pontoon bridge that they can rebuild, is there? But if we break it at the Spanish end, the pontoons should end up on this bank and we can burn them." A barrel load of canister or grapeshot hissed overhead and the brigadier threw Fort Josephine an irritated glance. "Get on with it," he said to Sharpe. "I want to be away by tomorrow's dawn."

A picquet from the 74th's light company guarded the eighteen women. Six were officers' wives and they stood apart from the rest, trying to look brave. "You'll take them over," Sharpe told Jack Bullen.

"I will, sir?"

"You like women, don't you?"

"Of course, sir."

"And you speak some of their horrible language, don't you?"

"Incredibly well, sir."

"So take the ladies over the bridge and up to that other fort."

While Lieutenant Bullen persuaded the women that no harm would come to them and that they must gather their luggage and be ready to cross the river, Sharpe looked for Sturridge and found the engineer in the fort's main magazine. "Powder," said Sturridge as he greeted Sharpe. He had prised the lid from a barrel and now tasted the gunpowder. "Bloody awful powder," he spat it out with a grimace. "Bloody French powder. Nothing but bloody dust. Damp, too."

"Will it work?"

"It should go bang," Sturridge said gloomily.

"I'm taking you over the bridge," Sharpe told him.

"There's a handcart outside," Sturridge said, "and we'll need it. Five barrels should be enough, even of this rubbish."

"You've got fuse?"

Sturridge unbuttoned his blue jacket and showed that he had several yards of slow match coiled around his waist. "You just thought I was portly, didn't you? Why doesn't he just blow the bridge at this end? Or in the middle?"

"So the French can't rebuild it."

"They couldn't anyway. Takes a lot of skill to make one of those bridges. Doesn't take much to undo one, but making a pontoon bridge isn't a job for amateurs." Sturridge hammered the lid back onto the opened powder barrel. "The French aren't going to like us being over there, are they?"

"I wouldn't think so."

"So is this where I die for England?"

"That's why I'm there. To make sure you don't."

"That is a consolation," Sturridge said. He glanced across at Sharpe who was leaning, arms folded, against the wall. Sharpe's face was shadowed by his shako's peak, but his eyes were bright in the shadow. The face was scarred, hard, watchful, and thin. "Actually it is a consolation," Sturridge said, then flinched because the brigadier was bellowing in the courtyard, demanding to know where Sturridge was and why the damned bridge was still intact. "Bloody man," Sturridge said.

Sharpe went back to the sunlight where Moon was exercising the captured horse, showing off to the French wives who had gathered by the eastern gate where Jack Bullen had commandeered the handcart for their luggage. Sharpe ordered the bags off and the cart to the main magazine where Harper and a half dozen men loaded it with gunpowder. Then the women's luggage was placed on top. "It'll disguise the powder barrels," Sharpe explained to Harper.

"Disguise it, sir?"

"If the Crapauds see us crossing the bridge with powder, what do you think they'll do?"

"They won't be happy, sir."

"No, Pat, they won't. They'll use us for target practice."

It was mid-morning before everything was ready. The French in Fort Josephine had abandoned their desultory cannon fire. Sharpe had half expected the enemy to send an envoy across the river to inquire about the women, but none had come. "Three of the officers' wives are from the 8th, sir," Jack Bullen told Sharpe.

"They're what?" Sharpe asked.

"French regiment, sir. The 8th. They've been at Cádiz, but they were sent to reinforce the troops besieging Badajoz. They're across the river, sir, but some of the officers and their wives slept here last night. Better quarters, see?" Bullen paused, evidently expecting some reaction from Sharpe. "Don't you see, sir? There's a whole French battalion over there. The 8th. Not just the garrison, but a fighting battalion. Oh, dear God." This last was because two women had detached themselves from the rest and were haranguing him in Spanish. Bullen calmed them with a smile. "They say they're Spanish, sir," he explained to Sharpe, "and say they don't want to go to the other fort."

"What are they doing here in the first place?"

The women talked to Sharpe, both at the same time, both urgently, and he thought he understood that they were claiming to have been captured by the French and forced to live with a pair of soldiers. That might be true, he thought. "So where do you want to go?" he asked them in bad Spanish.

They both spoke again, pointing across the river and southward, claiming that was where they had come from. Sharpe hushed them. "They can go wherever they bloody like, Jack."

The fort's gate was thrown open and Bullen led the way through, holding his arms wide to show the French across the river that he meant no harm. The women followed. The track down to the river was rough and stony and the women went slowly until they reached the wooden roadway laid across the pontoons. Sharpe and his men brought up the rear. Harper, his seven-barreled gun slung next to his rifle, nodded across the river. "There's a reception party, sir," he said, referring to three mounted French officers who had just appeared outside Fort Josephine. They were waiting there, watching the approaching women and soldiers.

A dozen of Sharpe's men were manhandling the cart. Lieutenant Sturridge, the engineer, was with them and he kept flinching because the cart had a skewed axle and constantly lurched to the left. It went more smoothly once they were on the bridge, though the women were nervous of crossing because the whole roadway of planked chesses was vibrating from the pressure of the winter-swollen river as it forced its way between the bargelike pontoons. Dead branches and flotsam were jammed on the upstream side, increasing the pressure and making the water break white about the bluff bows. Each of the big pontoons was held against the current by a pair of thick anchor chains and Sharpe hoped that five barrels of damp powder would prove sufficient to shatter the massive construction. "Are you thinking what I'm thinking?" Harper asked.

"Porto?"

"All those poor bastards," Harper said, remembering the awful moment when the pontoon bridge across the Douro had snapped. The roadway had been crowded with folk fleeing the invading French, and hundreds of them had drowned. Sharpe still saw the children in his dreams.

The three French officers were riding down to the bridge's far end now. They waited there and

Sharpe hurried past the women. "Jack," he called to Bullen, "I need you to translate."

Sharpe and Bullen led the way to the Spanish bank. The women followed hesitantly. The three French officers waited and, as Sharpe drew near, one of them took off his cocked hat in salute. "My name is Lecroix," he said as he introduced himself. He spoke in English. Lecroix was a young man, exquisitely uniformed, with a lean handsome face and very white teeth. "Captain Lecroix of the 8th," he added.

"Captain Sharpe."

Lecroix's eyes widened slightly, perhaps because Sharpe did not look like a captain. His uniform was torn and dirty and, though he wore a sword, as officers did, the blade was a Heavy Cavalry trooper's weapon, which was a huge and unwieldy blade better suited for butchering. He carried a rifle too, and officers did not usually carry longarms. Then there was his face, tanned and scarred, a face you might meet in some fetid alley, not in a salon. It was a frightening face and Lecroix, who was no coward, almost recoiled from the hostility in Sharpe's eyes. "Colonel Vandal," he said, putting the stress on the name's second syllable, "sends his compliments, monsieur, and requests that you permit us to recover our wounded"—he paused, glancing at the handcart that had been stripped of the women's luggage, thus revealing the powder kegs—"before you attempt to destroy the bridge."

"Attempt?" Sharpe asked.

Lecroix ignored the scorn. "Or do you intend to leave our wounded for the amusements of the Portuguese?"

Sharpe was tempted to say that any French wounded deserved whatever they got from the Portuguese, but he resisted the urge. The request, he reckoned, was fair enough and so he drew Jack Bullen away far enough so that the French officers could not overhear him. "Go and see the brigadier," he told the lieutenant, "and tell him these buggers want to fetch their wounded over the river before we destroy the bridge."

Bullen set off back across the bridge while two of the French officers started back toward Fort Josephine, followed by all the women except the two Spaniards who, barefooted and ragged, hurried south down the river's bank. Lecroix watched them go. "Those two didn't want to stay with us?" He sounded surprised.

"They said you captured them."

"We probably did." He took out a leather case of long thin cigars and offered one to Sharpe. Sharpe shook his head, then waited as Lecroix laboriously struck a light with his tinderbox. "You did well this morning," the Frenchman said once the cigar was alight.

"Your garrison was asleep," Sharpe said.

Lecroix shrugged. "Garrison troops. No good. Old and sick and tired men." He spat out a shred of tobacco. "But I think you have done all the damage you will do today. You will not break the bridge."

"We won't?"

"Cannon," Lecroix said laconically, gesturing at Fort Josephine, "and my colonel is determined to preserve the bridge, and what my colonel wants, he gets."

"Colonel Vandal?"

"Vandal," Lecroix corrected Sharpe's pronunciation, "Colonel Vandal of the 8th of the Line. You have heard of him?"

"Never."

"You should educate yourself, Captain," Lecroix said with a smile. "Read the accounts of Austerlitz and be astonished by Colonel Vandal's bravery."

"Austerlitz?" Sharpe asked. "What was that?"

Lecroix just shrugged. The women's luggage was dropped at the bridge's end and Sharpe sent the men back, then followed them until he reached Lieutenant Sturridge who was kicking at the planks on the foredeck of the fourth pontoon from the bank. The timber was rotten and he had managed to make a hole there. The stench of stagnant water came from the hole. "If we widen it," Sturridge said, "then we should be able to blow this one to hell and beyond."

"Sir!" Harper called. Sharpe turned eastward and saw French infantry coming from Fort Josephine. They were fixing bayonets and forming ranks just outside the fort, but he had no doubt they were coming to the bridge. It was a big company, at least a hundred men. French battalions were divided into six companies, unlike the British who had ten, and this company looked formidable with fixed bayonets. Bloody hell, Sharpe thought, but if the frogs wanted to make a fight of it, then they had better hurry because Sturridge, helped by a half dozen of Sharpe's men, was prising off the pontoon's foredeck and Harper was carrying the first powder barrel toward the widening hole.

There was a thunderous sound from the Portuguese side of the bridge and Sharpe saw the

brigadier, accompanied by two officers, galloping onto the roadway. More redcoats were coming from the fort, doubling down the stony
track, evidently to reinforce Sharpe's men. The
brigadier's commandeered stallion was nervous
of the vibrating roadway, but Moon was a superb
horseman and kept the beast under control. He
curbed the horse close to Sharpe. "What the
devil's going on?"

"They said they wanted to fetch their
wounded, sir."

"So what are those bloody men doing?" Moon
looked at the French infantry.

"I reckon they want to stop us blowing the
bridge, sir."

"Damn them to hell," Moon said, throwing
Sharpe an angry look as if it was Sharpe's fault.
"Either they're talking to us or they're fighting
us. They can't do both at the same time! There
are some bloody rules in war!" He spurred on.
Major Gillespie, the brigadier's aide, followed
him after giving Sharpe a sympathetic glance.
The third horseman was Jack Bullen. "Come on,
Bullen!" Moon shouted. "You can interpret for
me. My frog ain't up to scratch."

Harper was filling the bows of the fourth pontoon with the barrels and Sturridge had taken off

his jacket and was unwinding the slow match coiled about his waist. There was nothing there for Sharpe to do, so he went to where the brigadier was snarling at Lecroix. The immediate cause of the brigadier's anger was that the French infantry company had advanced halfway down the hill and were now arrayed in line facing the bridge. They were no more than a hundred paces away, and were accompanied by three mounted officers. "You can't talk to us about recovering your wounded and make threatening movements at the same time!" Moon snapped.

"I believe, monsieur, those men merely come to collect the wounded," Lecroix said soothingly.

"Not carrying weapons, they don't," Moon said, "and not without my permission! And why the hell have they got fixed bayonets?"

"A misunderstanding, I'm sure," Lecroix said emolliently. "Perhaps you would do us the honor of discussing the matter with my colonel?" He gestured toward the horsemen waiting behind the French infantry.

But Moon was not going to be summoned by some French colonel. "Tell him to come here," he insisted.

"Or you will send an emissary, perhaps?"

Lecroix suggested smoothly, ignoring the brigadier's direct order.

"Oh, for God's sake," Moon snarled. "Major Gillespie? Go and talk sense to the damned man. Tell him he can send one officer and twenty soldiers to recover their wounded. They're not to bring any weapons, but the officer may carry sidearms. Lieutenant?" The brigadier looked at Bullen. "Go and translate."

Gillespie and Bullen rode uphill with Lecroix. Meanwhile the light company of the 88th had arrived on the French side of the bridge that was now crowded with soldiers. Sharpe was worried. His own company was on the roadway, guarding Sturridge, and now the 88th's light company had joined them, and they all made a prime target for the French company that was in a line of three ranks. Then there were the French gunners watching from the ramparts of Fort Josephine who doubtless had their barrels loaded with grapeshot. Moon had ordered the 88th down to the bridge, but now seemed to realize that they were an embarrassment rather than a reinforcement. "Take your men back to the other side," he called to their captain, then turned around because a single Frenchman was now riding toward the bridge. Gillespie and Bullen, meanwhile, were with the other French officers behind the enemy company.

The French officer curbed his horse twenty paces away and Sharpe assumed this was the renowned Colonel Vandal, the 8th's commanding officer, for he had two heavy gold epaulettes on his blue coat and his cocked hat was crowned with a white pom-pom, which seemed a frivolous decoration for a man who looked so baleful. He had a savagely unfriendly face with a narrow black moustache. He appeared to be about Sharpe's age, in his middle thirties, and had a force that came from an arrogant confidence. He spoke good English in a clipped, harsh voice. "You will withdraw to the far bank," he said without any preamble.

"And who the devil are you?" Moon demanded.

"Colonel Henri Vandal," the Frenchman said, "and you will withdraw to the far bank and leave the bridge undamaged." He took a watch from his coat pocket, clicked open the lid, and showed the face to the brigadier. "I shall give you one minute before I open fire."

"This is no way to behave," Moon said loftily.

"If you wish to fight, Colonel, then you will have the courtesy to return my envoys first."

"Your envoys?" Vandal seemed amused by the word. "I saw no flag of truce."

"Your fellow didn't carry one either!" Moon protested.

"And Captain Lecroix reports that you brought your gunpowder with our women. I could not stop you, of course, without killing women. You risked the women's lives, I did not, so I assume you have abandoned the rules of civilized warfare. I shall, however, return your officers when you withdraw from the undamaged bridge. You have one minute, **monsieur.**" And with those words Vandal turned his horse and spurred it back up the track.

"Are you holding my men prisoners?" Moon shouted.

"I am!" Vandal called back carelessly.

"There are rules of warfare!" Moon shouted at the retreating colonel.

"Rules?" Vandal turned his horse, and his handsome, arrogant face showed disdain. "You think there are rules in war? You think it is like your English game of cricket?"

"Your fellow asked us to send an emissary,"

Moon said hotly. "We did. There are rules governing such matters. Even you French should know that."

"We French," Vandal said, amused. "I shall tell you the rules, monsieur. I have orders to cross the bridge with a battery of artillery. If there is no bridge, I cannot cross the river. So my rule is that I shall preserve the bridge. In short, monsieur, there is only one rule in warfare, and that is to win. Other than that, monsieur, we French have no rules." He turned his horse and spurred uphill. "You have one minute," he called back carelessly.

"Good God incarnate," Moon said, staring after the retreating Frenchman. The brigadier was plainly puzzled, even astonished by Vandal's ruthlessness. "There are rules!" he protested into thin air.

"Blow the bridge, sir?" Sharpe asked stolidly.

Moon was still gazing after Vandal. "They invited us to talk! The bloody man invited us to talk! They can't do this. There are rules!"

"You want us to blow the bridge, sir?" Sharpe asked again.

Moon appeared not to hear. "He has to return Gillespie and your lieutenant," he said. "God damn it, there are rules!"

"He's not going to return them, sir," Sharpe said.

Moon frowned from the saddle. He appeared puzzled, as if he did not know how he was to deal with Vandal's treachery. "He can't keep them prisoner!" he protested.

"He's going to keep them, sir, unless you tell me to leave the bridge intact."

Moon hesitated, but then recalled that his future career, with all its dazzling rewards, depended on the bridge's destruction. "Blow the bridge," he said harshly.

"Back!" Sharpe turned and shouted at his men. "Get back! Mister Sturridge! Light the fuse!"

"Bloody hell!" The brigadier suddenly realized he was on the wrong side of a bridge that was crowded with men, and that in about half a minute the French planned to open fire. So he turned his horse and spurred it back along the roadway. The riflemen and redcoats were running and Sharpe followed them, walking backward, keeping his eye on the French, the rifle in his hands. He reckoned he was safe enough. The French company was a long musket shot away and so far they had made no attempt to close the range, but then Sharpe saw Vandal turn and wave to the fort.

"Bloody hell." Sharpe echoed the brigadier, and then the world shook to the sound of six guns emptying their barrels of grapeshot. Dark smoke whipped the sky, the balls screamed around Sharpe, slapping onto the bridge and slashing into men and churning the river into foam. Sharpe heard a scream behind him, then saw the French company running toward the bridge. There was an odd silence after the guns fired. No muskets had been used yet. The river settled from the strike of the grapeshot and Sharpe heard another scream and snatched a look behind him to see Moon's stallion rearing, blood seething from its neck, and then the brigadier fell into a knot of men.

Sturridge was dead. Sharpe found him some twenty paces beyond the powder barrels. The engineer, struck in the head by a piece of grapeshot, was lying beside the slow match that had not been lit and now the French were almost at the bridge and Sharpe snatched up Sturridge's tinderbox and ran toward the powder barrels. He shortened the slow match by tearing it apart just a couple of paces from the charge, then struck the flint on the steel. The spark flew and died. He struck again, and this time a scrap of dried linen caught the spark and he blew on it gently and the tinder flared up and he put the flame to the fuse and saw the powder begin to spark and fizz. The first Frenchmen were obstructed by the women's abandoned luggage, but they kicked it aside and ran onto the bridge where they knelt and aimed their muskets. Sharpe watched the fuse. It was burning so damn slowly! He heard rifles fire, their sound crisper than muskets, and a Frenchman slowly toppled with a look of indignation on his face and a bright stab of blood on his white crossbelt. Then the French pulled their triggers and the balls flew close around him. The damned fuse was slower than slow! The French were just yards away. Then Sharpe heard more rifles firing, heard a French officer screaming at his men, and Sharpe tore the fuse again, much closer to the powder barrels, and he used the burning end to light the new stub. That new stub was just inches from the barrel, and to make sure it burned fiercely, he blew on it, then turned and ran toward the western bank.

Moon was wounded, but a pair of men from the 88th had picked the brigadier off the roadway and were carrying him. "Come on, sir!" Harper shouted. Sharpe could hear the Frenchmen's boots on the roadway. Then Harper was beside him and leveled the seven-barrel gun. It was a naval weapon, one that had never really worked well. It was supposed to be carried in the fighting tops where its seven bunched barrels could launch a small volley of half-inch balls at marksmen in the enemy rigging, but the recoil of the volley gun was so violent that few men were strong enough to wield it. Patrick Harper was strong enough. "Down, sir!" he shouted, and Sharpe dropped flat as the sergeant pulled the trigger. The noise deafened Sharpe, and the leading rank of Frenchmen was blown apart by the seven balls, but one sergeant survived and he ran to where the fizzing fuse sparked and smoked at the barrel's top. Sharpe was still sprawled on the roadway, but he wrenched the rifle clear of his body. He had no time to aim, just point the muzzle and pull the trigger, and he saw, through the sudden powder smoke, the French sergeant's face turn to a blossom of blood and red mist. The sergeant was hurled backward, the fuse still smoking, and then the world exploded.

Flame, smoke, and timbers erupted into the air, though the chief effect of the exploding powder was to drive the pontoon down into the river. The roadway buckled under the strain, planks snapping free. The French were thrown back, some dead, some burned, some stunned, and then the shattered pontoon violently reared up from the water and its anchor chains snapped from the recoil. The bridge jerked downstream, throwing Harper off his feet. He and Sharpe clung to the planks. The bridge was shuddering now, the river foaming and pushing at the broken gap as scraps of burning timber flamed on the roadway. Sharpe had been half dazed by the explosion and now found it hard to stand, but he staggered toward the British-held shore. The pontoon anchor chains began to snap, one after the other, and the more that parted, the more pressure was put on the remaining chains. The French cannon fired again and the air was filled with screaming grapeshot. One of the men carrying Brigadier Moon jerked forward with blood staining the back of his red coat. The man vomited blood and the brigadier bellowed in agony as he was dropped. The bridge began to shake like a bough in the wind and Sharpe had to fall to his knees and hold on to a plank to stop being thrown into the water. Musket balls were coming from the French company, but the range was too long for accuracy. The brigadier's wounded horse was in the river, blood swirling as it struggled against the inevitable drowning.

A shell struck the bridge's far end. Sharpe decided the French gunners were trying to hold the British fugitives on the breaking bridge where they could be flayed by grapeshot. The French infantry had retreated to the eastern bank from where they fired musket volleys. Smoke was filling the valley. Water splashed across the pontoon where Sharpe and Harper clung. Then it shook again and the roadway splintered. Sharpe feared the remnants of the bridge would overturn. A bullet slammed into a plank by his side. Another shell exploded at the bridge's far end, leaving a puff of dirty smoke that drifted upstream where white birds flew in panic.

Then suddenly the bridge quivered and went still. The central portion of six pontoons had broken free and was drifting down the river. There was a tug as a last anchor chain snapped. Then the six pontoons were circling and floating as a barrel load of grapeshot churned the water just behind them. Sharpe could kneel now. He loaded the rifle, aimed at the French infantry, and fired. Harper slung his empty volley gun and shot with his rifle instead. Rifleman Slattery and Rifleman Harris came to join them and sent two more bullets, both aimed at the

French officers on horseback, but when the rifle smoke cleared the officers were still mounted. The pontoons were traveling fast in the current, accompanied by broken and charred timbers. Brigadier Moon was lying on his back, trying to prop himself up on his elbows. "What happened?"

"We're floating free, sir," Sharpe said. There were six men of the 88th on the makeshift raft and five of Sharpe's riflemen from the South Essex. The rest of his company had either escaped the bridge before it broke or else were in the river. So now, with Sharpe and the brigadier, there were thirteen men floating downstream and over a hundred Frenchmen running down the bank, keeping level with them. Sharpe hoped that thirteen was not unlucky.

"See if you can paddle to the western bank," Moon ordered. Some British officers, using captured horses, were on that bank and were trying to catch up with the raft.

Sharpe had the men use their rifle and musket butts as paddles, but the pontoons were monstrously heavy and their efforts were futile. The raft drifted on southward. A last shell plunged harmlessly into the river, its fuse extinguished instantly by the water. "Paddle, for God's sake!" Moon snapped.

"They're doing their best, sir," Sharpe said. "Broken leg, sir?"

"Calf bone," Moon said, wincing. "Heard it snap when the horse fell."

"We'll straighten it up in a minute, sir," Sharpe said soothingly.

"You'll do no such bloody thing, man! You'll get me to a doctor."

Sharpe was not certain how he was going to get Moon anywhere except straight down the river, which was curving now about a great rock bluff on the Spanish bank. That bluff, at least, would check the French pursuit. He used his rifle as a paddle, but the raft defiantly took its own path. Once past the bluff the river widened, swung back to the west, and the current slowed a little.

The French pursuers were left behind and the British were finding the going hard on the Portuguese bank. The French cannon were still firing, but they could no longer see the raft so they had to be shooting at the British forces on that western bank. Sharpe tried to steer with a length of scorched, broken plank, not because he thought it would do any good, but to prevent Moon complaining. The makeshift rudder had no effect. The raft stubbornly stayed close to the Spanish bank. Sharpe thought about Bullen and felt a pulse of pure anger at the way in which the lieutenant had been taken prisoner. "I'm going to kill that bastard," he said aloud.

"You're going to do what?" Moon demanded.

"I'm going to kill that bastard Frenchman, sir. Colonel Vandal."

"You're going to get me to the other bank, Sharpe, that's what you're going to do, and you're going to do it quickly."

At which point, with a shudder and a lurch, the pontoons ran aground.

The crypt lay beneath the cathedral. It was a labyrinth hacked from the rock on which Cádiz defied the sea, and in deeper holes beneath the crypt's flagged floor, the dead bishops of Cádiz waited for the resurrection.

Two flights of stone steps descended to the crypt, emerging into a large chapel that was a round chamber twice the height of a man and thirty paces wide. If a man stood in the chamber's center and clapped his hands once, the noise would sound fifteen times. It was a crypt of echoes.

Five caverns opened from the chapel. One led to a smaller round chapel at the farthest end of the labyrinth, while the other four flanked the big chamber. The four were deep and dark, and they were connected to one another by a hidden passageway that circled the whole crypt. None of the caverns was decorated. The cathedral above might glitter with candlelight and shine with marble and have painted saints and monstrances of silver and candlesticks of gold, but the crypt was plain stone. Only the altars had color. In the smaller chapel a virgin gazed sadly down the long passage to where, across the wider chamber, her son hung on a silver cross in never-ending pain.

It was deep night. The cathedral was empty. The last priest had folded his scapular and gone home. The women who haunted the altars had been ushered out, the floor had been swept, and the doors locked. Candles still burned, and the red light of the eternal presence glowed under the scaffolding that ringed the crossing where the transept met the nave. The cathedral was unfinished. The sanctuary with its high altar had yet to be built, the dome was half made, and the bell towers not even started.

Father Montseny had a key to one of the eastern doors. The key scraped in the lock and the door hinges squealed when he pushed it open. He came with six men. Two of them stayed close to the unlocked cathedral door. They stood in shadow, hidden, both with loaded muskets and with orders to use them only if things became desperate. "This is a night for knives," Montseny told the men.

"In the cathedral?" one of the men asked nervously.

"I will give you absolution for any sins," Montseny said, "and the men who must die here are heretics. They are Protestants, English. God will be gladdened by their deaths."

He took the remaining four men to the crypt and, once in the main chamber, he placed candles on the floor and lit them. The light flickered on the shallow-domed ceiling. He put two men in one of the chambers to the east while he, with the remaining pair, waited in the darkness of the chamber opposite. "No noise now!" he warned them. "We wait."

The English came early as Father Montseny had supposed they would. He heard the distant squeal of the hinges as they pushed open the unlocked door. He heard their footsteps coming down the cathedral's long nave and he knew that the two men he had left by the door would have bolted it now and would be following the English toward the crypt.

Three men appeared on the western steps. They came slowly, cautiously. One of them, the tallest, had a bag. That man peered into the big round chamber and saw no one. "Hello!" he shouted.

Father Montseny tossed a packet into the chamber. It was a thick packet, tied with string. "What you will do," he said in the English he had learned as a prisoner, "is bring the money, put it beside the letters, take the letters, and go."

The man looked at the black archways leading from the big candlelit chamber. He was trying to decide where Montseny's voice had come from. "You think I'm a fool?" he asked. "I must see the letters first." He was a big man, red-faced, with a bulbous nose and thick black eyebrows.

"You may examine them, Captain," Montseny said. He knew the man was called Plummer and that he had been a captain in the British army, and now he was a functionary in the British embassy. Plummer's job was to make certain the embassy's servants did not steal, that the gratings on the windows were secure, and that the shutters were locked at night. Plummer was, in Montseny's opinion, a nonentity, a failed soldier, a man who now came anxiously into the ring of candles and squatted by the package. The string was tough and knotted tight and Plummer could not undo it. He felt in his pocket, presumably looking for a knife.

"Show me the gold," Montseny ordered.

Plummer scowled at the peremptory tone, but obliged by opening the bag he had placed beside the package. He took out a cloth bag that he unlaced, then brought out a handful of golden guineas. "Three hundred," he said, "as we agreed." His voice echoed back and forth, confusing him.

"Now," Montseny said, and his men appeared from the dark with leveled muskets. The two men Plummer had left on the steps staggered forward as Montseny's last two men came down the stairs behind them.

"What the hell are you . . ." Plummer began, then saw the priest was carrying a pistol. "You're a priest?"

"I thought we should all examine the merchandise," Montseny said, ignoring the question.

He had the three men surrounded now. "You will lie flat while I count the coins."

"The devil I will," Plummer said.

"On the floor," Montseny spoke in Spanish, and his men, all of whom had served in the Spanish navy and had muscles hardened by years of grueling work, easily subdued the three and put them facedown on the crypt floor. Montseny picked up the string-bound package and put it in his pocket, then pushed the gold aside with his foot. "Kill them," he said.

The two men accompanying Plummer were Spaniards themselves, embassy servants, and they protested when they heard Montseny's order. Plummer resisted, heaving up from the floor, but Montseny killed him easily, sliding a knife up into his ribs and letting Plummer heave against the blade as it sought his heart. The other two died just as quickly. It was done with remarkably little noise.

Montseny gave his men five golden guineas apiece, a generous reward. "The English," he explained to them, "secretly plan to keep Cádiz for themselves. They call themselves our allies, but they will betray Spain. Tonight you have fought for your king, for your country, and for the holy church. The admiral will be pleased with you, and God will reward you." He searched the bodies, found a few coins and a bone-handled knife. Plummer had a pistol under his cloak, but it was a crude, heavy weapon and Montseny let one of the sailors keep it.

The three corpses were dragged up the steps, down the nave, and then carried to the nearby seawall. There Father Montseny said a prayer for their souls and his men heaved the dead over the stony edge. The bodies smacked down into the rocks where the Atlantic sucked and broke white. Father Montseny locked the cathedral and went home.

The next day the blood was found in the crypt and on the stairs and in the nave, and at first no one could explain it until some of the women who prayed in the cathedral every day declared that it must be the blood of Saint Servando, one of Cádiz's patron saints whose body had once lain in the city, but had been taken to Seville, which was now occupied by the French. The blood, the women insisted, was proof that the saint had miraculously spurned the French-held city and returned home, and the discovery of three bodies being buffeted by the waves on the rocks below the seawall would not dissuade them. It was a miracle, they said, and the rumor of the miracle spread.

Captain Plummer was recognized and his body was carried to the embassy. There was a makeshift chapel inside and a hurried funeral service was read and the captain was then buried in the sands of the isthmus that connected Cádiz to the Isla de León. The next day Montseny wrote to the British ambassador, claiming that Plummer had tried to keep the gold and take the letters, and his regrettable death had thus been inevitable, but that the British could still have the letters back, only now they would cost a great deal more. He did not sign the letter, but enclosed one bloodstained guinea. It was an investment, he thought, that would bring back a fortune, and the fortune would pay for Father Montseny's dreams: dreams of Spain, glorious again and free of foreigners. The English would pay for their own defeat.

Chapter 2

"Now what?" Brigadier Moon demanded.

"We're stuck, sir."

"Good God incarnate, man, can't you do anything right?"

Sharpe said nothing. Instead he and Harper stripped off their cartridge boxes and jumped overboard to find themselves in four feet of water. They heaved on the pontoon, but it was like trying to push the Rock of Gibraltar. It was immovable and they were stranded fifty or sixty feet from the eastern bank on which the French pursued them, and over a hundred and fifty yards from the British-held bank. Sharpe ordered the other soldiers to get in the river and push, but it did no good. The big pontoons had grounded hard on a shingle bank and evidently intended to stay there.

"If we can cut one of the buggers free, sir," Harper suggested. It was a good suggestion. If one of the pontoons could be loosed from the others then they would have a boat light enough to be forced off the shingle, but the big barges were connected by ropes and by stout timber beams that had carried the plank roadway.

"It'll take us half a day to do it," Sharpe said, "and I don't think the Crapauds will be happy."

"What the devil are you doing, Sharpe?" Moon demanded from the raft.

"Going ashore, sir," Sharpe decided, "all of us."

"For God's sake, why?"

"Because, sir," Sharpe said, forcing himself to stay patient, "the French will be here in half an hour and if we're in the river, sir, they'll either shoot us down like dogs or else take us prisoner."

"So your intentions?"

"Go up that hill, sir, hide there, and wait for the enemy to leave. And when they've gone, sir, we'll cut one of the pontoons free." Though how he would do that with no tools he was not sure, but he would have to try.

Moon plainly wanted to suggest another course of action, but none came to his mind so he submitted to being carried ashore by

Sergeant Harper. The rest of the men followed, carrying their weapons and cartridge boxes over their heads. Once ashore they made a makeshift stretcher from a pair of muskets threaded through the sleeves of two red coats, then Harris and Slattery carried the brigadier up the steep hill. Sharpe, before leaving the riverbank, collected a few short sticks and a scrappy piece of fishing net, all of which had been washed onto the rocks, then he followed the others up to the first crest and saw, looking to his left, that the French had climbed to the top of the bluff. They were nearly half a mile away, which did not stop one of them loosing off his musket. The ball must have fallen into the intervening valley and the report, when it came, was muffled.

"This is far enough," Moon announced. The jolting of the crude stretcher was giving him agony and he looked pale.

"To the top," Sharpe said, nodding to where rocks crowned the bare hill.

"For God's sake, man," Moon began.

"French are coming, sir," Sharpe interrupted the brigadier. "If you want, sir, I can leave you for them, sir? They must have a surgeon in the fort."

Moon looked tempted for a few seconds, but

understood that high-ranking prisoners were rarely exchanged. It was possible that a French brigadier might be captured soon and after prolonged negotiations would be exchanged for Moon, but it would take weeks if not months, and all the while his career would be stalled and other men promoted over him. "Up the hill if you must," he said grudgingly, "but what are your plans after that?"

"Wait for the French to go, sir, detach a pontoon, cross the river, get you home."

"And why the devil are you carrying firewood?"

The brigadier discovered why at the top of the hill. Private Geoghegan, one of the men from the 88th, claimed his mother had been a bonesetter and said he had often helped her as a child. "What you do, sir," he explained, "is pull the bone."

"Pull it?" Sharpe asked.

"Give it a good swift tug, sir, and he'll like as not squeal like a piglet, and I straightens it then and we bind it up. Would the gentleman be a Protestant, would he, sir?"

"I should think so."

"Then we don't need the holy water, sir, and

we'll do without the two prayers as well, but he'll be straight enough when we're done."

The brigadier protested. Why not wait till they were across the river, he wanted to know, and blanched when Sharpe said that could be two days. "Soonest done, soonest mended, sir," Private Geoghegan said, "and if we don't mend it soon, sir, it'll set crooked as can be. And I'll have to cut your trouser off, sir, sorry, sir."

"You'll not damned well cut them!" Moon protested hotly. "They're Willoughby's best! There isn't a finer tailor in London."

"Then you'll have to take them off yourself, sir, you will," Geoghegan said. He looked as wild as any of the Connaught men, but had a soft, sympathetic voice and a confidence that somewhat allayed the brigadier's apprehensions, yet even so it took twenty minutes to persuade Moon that he should allow his leg to be straightened. It was the thought that he would have to spend the rest of his life with a crooked limb that really convinced him. He saw himself limping into salons, unable to dance, awkward in the saddle, and his vanity at last overcame his fear. Sharpe, meanwhile, watched the French. Forty men had worked their way over the bluff and now they were walking toward the stranded pontoons.

"Buggers are going to salvage them," Harper said.

"Take the riflemen halfway down the hill," Sharpe said, "and stop them."

Harper left, taking Slattery, Harris, Hagman, and Perkins with him. They were the only men from Sharpe's company stranded on the pontoons, but it was a consolation that they were all good riflemen. There was no better soldier than Sergeant Patrick Harper, the huge Ulsterman who hated the British rule of his homeland, but still fought like a hero. Slattery was from County Wicklow and was quiet, soft-spoken, and capable. Harris had been a schoolmaster once and was clever, well-read, and too fond of gin, which was why he was now a soldier, but he was amusing and loyal. Dan Hagman was the oldest, well over forty, and he had been a poacher in Cheshire before the law caught him and condemned him to the army's ranks. There was no better marksman in any rifle company. Perkins was the youngest, young enough to be Hagman's grandson, and he had been a street urchin in London as Sharpe had once been, but he was learning to be a good soldier. He was learning that discipline tied to savagery was unbeatable. They were all good men and Sharpe was glad to have them, and just then the brigadier gave a yelp that he managed to stifle, though he could not contain a long moan. Geoghegan had eased off the brigadier's boots, which must have hurt like hell, and somehow managed to take down Moon's trousers, and now he placed two of Sharpe's sticks alongside the broken calf and wrapped one of the brigadier's trouser legs about the limb so that it gripped the sticks. He tightened the pressure by winding the trouser leg as though he wrung water from the material. He tightened it until the brigadier gave a hiss of protest. Then Geoghegan grinned at Sharpe. "Would you help me, sir? Just take the general's ankle, will you, sir? And when I tell you, sir, give it a good smart pull."

"For God's sake," the brigadier managed to say.

"As brave a man as ever I saw, sir, so you are," Geoghegan said, and he smiled reassuringly at Sharpe. "Are you ready, sir?"

"How hard do I pull?"

"A good tug, sir, just like pulling a lamb that doesn't want to be born. Are you ready? Take firm hold, sir, both hands! Now!"

Sharpe pulled, the brigadier gave a high-pitched cry, Geoghegan screwed the material even tighter, and Sharpe distinctly heard the bone grate into place. Geoghegan was stroking the brigadier's leg now. "And that's just good as can be, sir, good as new, sir." Moon did not respond and Sharpe realized the brigadier had either fainted or was in such shock that he could not speak.

Geoghegan splinted the leg with the sticks and the net. "He can't walk on it, not for a while, but we'll make him crutches, we will, and he'll be dancing like a pony soon enough."

The rifles sounded and Sharpe turned and ran down the hill to where his greenjackets were kneeling on the turf. They were about a hundred and fifty yards from the river and sixty feet above it, and the French were crouching in the water. They had been trying to haul the big barges off the shingle, but the bullets had ended that effort and now the men were using the pontoon hulls as protection. An officer ran into the shallow water, probably shouting at the men to get to their feet and try again, and Sharpe aimed at the officer, pulled the trigger, and the rifle banged into his shoulder as an errant spark from the flint stung his right eye. When the smoke cleared he saw the panicked officer running back to the bank, holding his scabbarded sword clear of the water in one hand and clutching his hat in the other. Slattery fired a second time and a splinter smacked up from one of the pontoons. Then Harper's next shot threw a man into the river and there was a swirl of blood in which the man thrashed as he drifted away. Harris fired and most of the French waded away from the pontoons to take shelter behind some boulders on the bank.

"Just keep them there," Sharpe said. "As soon as they try to shift those barges, kill them."

He climbed back up the hill. The brigadier was propped against a rock now. "What's happening?" he asked.

"Frogs are trying to salvage the barges, sir. We're stopping them."

The boom of the French guns in Fort Josephine echoed down the river valley. "Why are they firing?" the brigadier asked irritably.

"My guess, sir," Sharpe said, "is that some of our boys are trying to use a pontoon as a boat to look for us. And the frogs are shooting at them."

"Bloody hell," Moon said. He closed his eyes and grimaced. "You wouldn't, I suppose, have any brandy?"

"No, sir, sorry, sir." Sharpe would have bet a penny against the crown jewels that at least one of his men had brandy or rum in their canteen, but he would be damned before he took it away from them for the brigadier. "I've got water, sir," he said, offering his canteen.

"Damn your water."

Sharpe reckoned he could trust his riflemen to behave sensibly until they managed to recross the river, but the six fugitives from the 88th were another matter. The 88th were the Connaught Rangers and some men reckoned them the most fearsome regiment in the whole army, but they also had a reputation for wild indiscipline. The six rangers were led by a toothless sergeant and Sharpe, knowing that if the sergeant was on his side then the other men would probably cause no trouble, crossed to him. "What's your name, Sergeant?" Sharpe asked him.

"Noolan, sir."

"I want you to watch over there," Sharpe said, pointing north to the crest of the hill above the bluff. "I'm expecting a battalion of bloody frogs to come over that hill, and when they do, sing out."

"I'll sing right enough, sir," Noolan promised, "sing like a choir, I will."

"If they do come," Sharpe said, "we'll have to go south. I know the 88th is good, but I don't think there's quite enough of you to fight off a whole French battalion."

Sergeant Noolan looked at his five men, considered Sharpe's statement, then nodded gravely. "Not quite enough of us, sir, you're right. And what are you thinking of doing, sir, if you don't mind my asking?"

"What I'm hoping," Sharpe said, "is that the frogs will get tired of us and bugger off. Then we can try to float one of those pontoons and get across the river. Tell your men that, Sergeant. I want to get them home, and the best way home is to be patient."

A sudden rattle of rifle fire drew Sharpe back to Harper's position. The French were making another attempt to free the pontoons, and this time they had made a rope by linking their musket slings together and three men were bravely fastening the line to one of the samsom posts. One man had been hit and was limping back to the shore. Sharpe began reloading his rifle, but before he had rammed the leather-wrapped ball down the barrel, the remaining Frenchmen sprinted back to their shelter, taking the line with them. Sharpe saw the rope come dripping from the river as men hauled on it. The line straightened and tightened and he guessed that nearly all the French were tugging on it, but he could do nothing about it for they were hidden by the big boulder. The line quivered and Sharpe thought he saw the pontoons shift slightly, or perhaps that was his imagination, and then the rope snapped and Sharpe's riflemen jeered loudly.

Sharpe looked upriver. When the bridge had broken there had been seven or eight pontoons left on the British side and he was sure someone had thought to use one as a rescue craft, but no such boat appeared and by now he suspected the French cannons had either holed those pontoons or else driven the work parties away from the shore. That suggested rescue was a remote hope, leaving him with the need to salvage one of the six stranded barges.

"Does this remind you of anything?" Harper asked him.

"I was trying not to think about it," Sharpe said.

"What were those other rivers called?"

"The Douro and the Tagus."

"And there were no bloody boats on those either, sir," Harper said cheerfully.

"We found boats in the end," Sharpe said. Two years ago his company had been trapped on the wrong side of the Douro. Then, a year later, he and Harper had been stranded on the Tagus. But both times they had found their way back to the army, and he would again now, but he wished the damned French would leave. Instead the troops hidden beneath him sent a messenger back to Fort Josephine. The man scrambled up the hill and all the riflemen turned to aim at him, hauling back the flints of their weapons, but the man kept looking back, dodging and ducking, and his fear was palpable and somehow funny so that none of them pulled their triggers.

"He was too far away," Harper said. Hagman might have dropped the man, but in truth all the riflemen had felt sorry for the Frenchman who had shown bravery in risking the rifle fire.

"He's gone to fetch help," Sharpe said.

Nothing happened then for a long time. Sharpe lay on his back watching a hawk slide in the high sky. Sometimes a Frenchman would peer round the rocks below, see the riflemen were still there, and duck back. After an hour or so a man waved at them, then stepped cautiously out from the boulder and mimed unbuttoning his breeches. "Bugger wants a pee, sir," Harris said.

"Let him," Sharpe said and they raised the rifles so the barrels pointed at the sky. A succession of Frenchmen went to stand by the river and all politely waved their thanks when they were done. Harper waved back. Sharpe went from man to man and found they had nothing but three pieces of biscuit between them. He made one of Sergeant Noolan's men soften the biscuit with water and divide it equally, but it was a miserable dinner.

"We can't go without food, Sharpe," Moon complained. The brigadier had watched the division of the biscuits with a glittering eye and Sharpe had been certain he was planning to claim a larger share for himself, so Sharpe had loudly announced that every man got exactly the same portion. Moon was now in a filthier mood than usual. "How do you propose feeding us?" he demanded.

"We may have to go hungry till morning, sir."

"Good God incarnate," Moon muttered.

"Sir!" Sergeant Noolan called and Sharpe turned to see that two companies of the French had appeared by the bluff. They were in skirmish order to make themselves a more difficult target for the rifles.

"Pat!" Sharpe called down the slope. "We're pulling back! Up you come!"

They went south, carrying the brigadier again, struggling over the steep slopes to keep the river in sight. The French pursued for an hour, then seemed content merely to have driven the fugitives away from the stranded pontoons.

"Now what?" Moon demanded.

"We wait here, sir," Sharpe said. They were on a hilltop, sheltered by rocks and with a fine view in every direction. The river ran empty to the west while, off to the east, Sharpe could see a road winding through the hills.

"How long do we wait?" Moon asked snidely.

"Till nightfall, sir. Then I'll go and see if the pontoons are still there."

"Of course they won't be," Moon said, implying that Sharpe was a fool to believe otherwise, "but I suppose you'd better look."

Sharpe need not have bothered because, in the dusk, he saw the smoke rising above the river and when dark fell there was a glow across the side of the hill. He went north, taking Sergeant Noolan and two men of the 88th, and they saw that the French had failed to free the pontoons, so instead had ensured they were useless. The barges were burning. "That is a pity," Sharpe said.

"The brigadier will not be happy, sir," Sergeant Noolan said cheerfully.

"No, he won't," Sharpe agreed.

Noolan spoke to his men in Gaelic, presumably sharing his thoughts of the brigadier's unhappiness. "Don't they speak English?" Sharpe asked.

"Fergal doesn't," Noolan said, nodding at one of the men, "and Padraig will if you shout at him, sir, but if you don't shout he won't have a word of it."

"Tell them I'm glad you're with us," Sharpe said.

"You are?" Noolan sounded surprised.

"We were next to you on the ridge at Bussaco," Sharpe said.

Noolan grinned in the dark. "That was a fight, eh? They kept coming and we kept killing them."

"And now, Sergeant," Sharpe went on, "it seems that you and I are stuck with each other for a few days."

"So it does, sir," Noolan agreed.

"So you need to know my rules."

"You have rules, do you, sir?" Noolan asked cautiously.

"You don't steal from civilians unless you're starving, you don't get drunk without my permission, and you fight like the devil himself was at your back."

Noolan thought about it. "What happens if we break the rules?" he asked.

"You don't, Sergeant," Sharpe said bleakly, "you just don't."

They went back to make the brigadier unhappy.

Sometime in the night the brigadier sent Harris to wake Sharpe who was half awake anyway because he was cold. Sharpe had given his greatcoat to the brigadier who, being coatless, had demanded that one of the men yield him a covering. "Is there trouble?" Sharpe asked Harris.

"Don't know, sir. His Excellency just wants you, sir."

"I've been thinking, Sharpe," the brigadier announced when Sharpe arrived.

"Yes, sir?"

"I don't like those men speaking Irish. You'll tell them to use English. You hear me?"

"Yes, sir," Sharpe said, and paused. The brigadier had woken him to tell him that? "I'll tell them, sir, but some of them don't speak English, sir."

"Then they can bloody well learn," the brigadier snapped. He was sleepless through pain and now wanted to spread his misery. "You can't trust them, Sharpe. They brew mischief."

Sharpe paused, wondering how to put sense into Moon's head, but before he could speak Rifleman Harris intervened. "You'll forgive me, sir?" Harris said respectfully.

"Are you talking to me, rifleman?" the brigadier asked in astonishment.

"Begging your pardon, sir, I am. If I might, sir, with respect?"

"Go on, man."

"It's just, sir, as Mister Sharpe says, sir, that they don't speak English, being benighted papists, sir, and they were only discussing whether it might be possible to build a boat or a raft, sir, and they do that best in their own language, sir, because they have the words, if you follow me, sir."

The brigadier, thoroughly buttered by Harris, thought about it. "You speak their wretched language?" he asked.

"I do, sir," Harris said, "and French, sir, and Portuguese and Spanish, sir, and some Latin."

"Good God incarnate," the brigadier said, after staring at Harris for a few heartbeats, "but you are English?"

"Oh yes, sir. And proud of it."

"Quite right. Then I can depend on you to tell me if the teagues brew trouble?"

"The teagues, sir? Oh, the Irish! Yes, sir, of course, sir, a pleasure, sir," Harris said enthusiastically.

Just before dawn there came the sound of explosions from upriver. Sharpe stared north but could see nothing. At first light he could see thick smoke above the river valley, but he had no way of knowing what had caused that smoke, so he sent Noolan and two of his men to discover what had happened. "Stay on the hilltops," he told the 88th's sergeant, "and keep a lookout for Crapaud patrols."

"That was a damn fool decision," the brigadier said when the three rangers had gone.

"It was, sir?"

"You'll not see those men again, will you?"

"I think we will, sir," Sharpe said mildly.

"Damn it, man, I know the teagues. My first commission was with the 18th. I managed to escape to the fusiliers when I became a captain." Meaning, Sharpe thought, that the brigadier had purchased out of the Irish 18th to the more congenial fusiliers of his home county.

"I think you'll see Sergeant Noolan soon, sir," Sharpe said stubbornly, "and while we're waiting I'm going south. I'll be looking for food, sir."

Sharpe took Harris and the two of them walked the high ground above the river. "How much Gaelic do you speak, Harris?" Sharpe asked.

"About three words, sir," Harris said, "and none of them repeatable in high company." Sharpe laughed. "So what do we do, sir?" Harris went on.

"Cross the bloody river," Sharpe said.

"How, sir?"

"Don't know."

"And if we can't?"

"Keep going south, I suppose," Sharpe said. He tried to remember the maps he had seen of southern Spain and had an idea that the Guadiana joined the sea well to the west of Cádiz. There was no point in trying to reach Cádiz by road, for that great port was under French siege, but once at the river's mouth he could find a ship to carry them north to Lisbon. The only ships off the coast were allied vessels, and he reckoned that the Royal Navy patrolled the shore. It would take time, he knew, but once they reached the sea they would be as good as home. "But if we have to walk to the sea," he added, "I'd rather do it on the far bank."

"Because it's Portugal?"

"Because it's Portugal," Sharpe said, "and they're friendlier than the Spanish, and because there are more frogs on this side."

Sharpe's hopes of crossing the river rose after a couple of miles when they came to a place where the hill dropped to a wide basin where the Guadiana broadened so that it looked like a lake. A smaller river flowed from the east, and in the basin where the two rivers joined, there was a small town of white houses. Two bell towers broke the tiled roofs. "There has to be a ferry there," Harris said, "or fishing boats."

"Unless the frogs burned everything."

"Then we float over on a table," Harris said, "and at least we'll find food down there, sir, and His Lordship will like that."

"You mean Brigadier Moon will like that," Sharpe said in mild reproof.

"And he'll like that place too, won't he?" Harris said, pointing to a large house with stables that stood just to the north of the small town. The house was of two stories, was painted white, and had a dozen windows on each floor, while at its eastern end was an ancient castle tower, now in ruins. Smoke drifted from the house's chimneys.

Sharpe took out his telescope and examined the house. The windows were shuttered and the only signs of life were some men repairing a terrace wall in one of the many vineyards that covered the nearby slopes and another man bending over a furrow in a kitchen garden that lay beside the Guadiana. He edged the glass sideways and saw what looked like a boathouse on the riverbank. Sharpe gave the telescope to Harris. "I'd rather go to the town," he said.

"Why's that, sir?" Harris asked, staring at the house through Sharpe's glass.

"Because that house hasn't been plundered, has it? Kitchen garden all nice and tidy. What does that suggest?"

"The owner has shaken hands with the French?"

"Like as not."

Harris thought about that. "If they're friends with the Crapauds, sir, then perhaps there's a boat in that shed by the river?"

"Perhaps," Sharpe said dubiously. A door in the courtyard by the old castle ruin opened and he saw someone emerge into the sunlight. He nudged Harris, pointed, and the rifleman swung the telescope.

"Just a frow hanging out the washing," Harris said.

"We can get our shirts laundered," Sharpe said. "Come on, let's fetch the brigadier."

They walked back across the high hills to find Moon in a triumphant mood because Sergeant Noolan and his men had failed to return.

"I told you, Sharpe!" Moon said. "You can't trust them. That sergeant looked decidedly shifty."

"How's your leg, sir?"

"Bloody painful. Can't be helped, eh? So you say there's a decent-sized town?"

"Large village anyway, sir. Two churches."

"Let's hope they have a doctor who knows his business. He can look at this damned leg, and the sooner the better. Let's get on the march, Sharpe. We're wasting time."

But just then Sergeant Noolan reappeared to the north and the brigadier had no choice but to wait as the three men from the 88th rejoined. Noolan, his long face more lugubrious than ever, brought grim news. "They blew up the fort, sir," he told Sharpe.

"Talk to me, man, talk to me!" Moon insisted. "I command here."

"Sorry, your honor," Noolan said, snatching off his battered shako. "Our lot, sir, blew up the fort, sir, and they've gone."

"Fort Joseph, you mean?" Moon asked.

"Is that what it's called, sir? The one on the other side of the river, sir, they blew it up proper, they did! Guns tipped over the parapet and nothing left on the hill but smitherings."

"Nothing but what?"

Noolan cast a helpless look at Sharpe. "Scraps, sir," the sergeant tried again. "Bits and pieces, sir."

"And you say our fellows are gone? How the hell do you know they've gone?"

"Because the Crapauds are over there, sir, so they are. Using a boat. Going back and forth, they are, sir, back and forth, and we watched them."

"Good God incarnate," Moon said in disgust.

"You did well, Noolan," Sharpe said.

"Thank you, sir."

"And we're buggered," the brigadier said irritably, "because our forces have buggered off and left us here."

"In that case, sir," Sharpe suggested, "the

sooner we get to the town and find some food, the better."

Harper, because he was the strongest man, carried the front end of the brigadier's stretcher while the tallest of the Connaught Rangers took the rear. It took three hours to go the short distance and it was late morning by the time they reached the long hill above the big house and the small town. "That's where we'll go," Moon announced the moment he saw the house.

"I think they might be **anfrancesados,** sir," Sharpe said.

"Talk English, man, talk English."

"I think they're sympathetic to the French, sir."

"How can you possibly tell?"

"Because the house hasn't been plundered, sir."

"You can't surmise that," the brigadier said, though without much conviction. Sharpe's words had given him pause, but still the house drew him like a magnet. It promised comfort and the company of gentle folk. "There's only one way to find out, though, isn't there?" he proclaimed. "That's to go there! So let's be moving."

"I think we should go to the town, sir," Sharpe persisted.

"And I think you should keep quiet, Sharpe, and obey my orders."

So Sharpe kept quiet as they went down the hill, through the upper vineyards and then beneath the pale leaves of an olive grove. They maneuvered the brigadier's stretcher over a low stone wall and approached the house through wide gardens of cypress, orange trees, and fallow flower beds. There was a large pond, full of brown leaves and stagnant water, and then an avenue of statues. The statues were all of saints writhing in their death agonies. Sebastian clutched at the stub of an arrow piercing his ribs, Agnes stared serenely heavenward despite the sword in her throat, while next to her Andrew hung upside down on his cross. There were men being burned, women being disemboweled, and all of them preserved in white marble streaked with lichen and bird droppings. The ragged soldiers stared wide-eyed and the Catholics among them made the sign of the cross while Sharpe looked for any sign of life in the house. The windows remained shuttered, but smoke still drifted from a chimney, and then the big door that opened onto a balustraded terrace was thrown open and a man, dressed in black, stepped into the sunlight and waited as though he had been expecting them. "We had best observe the proprieties," Moon said.

"Sir?" Sharpe asked.

"For God's sake, Sharpe, gentry live here! They don't want their drawing room filled with common soldiers, do they? You and I can go in, but the men have to find the servants' quarters."

"Do they drop your stretcher outside, sir?" Sharpe asked innocently, and thought he heard a slight snort from Harper.

"Don't be ridiculous, Sharpe," the brigadier said. "They can carry me in first."

"Yes, sir."

Sharpe left the men on the terrace as he accompanied the brigadier into a vast room filled with dark furniture and hung with gloomy pictures, most showing scenes of martyrdom. More saints burned here, or else gazed in rapture as soldiers skewered them, while over the mantel was a life-size painting of the crucifixion. Christ's pale body was laced with blood while behind him a great thunderstorm unleashed lightning on a cowering city. A crucifix made of a wood so dark it was almost black hung at the other end of the room and beneath it was a private shrine draped in black on which a saber lay between two unlit candles.

The man who had greeted them was a servant who informed the brigadier that the Marquesa would join him very soon, and was there anything that his guests needed? Sharpe did his best to translate, using more Portuguese with the servant than Spanish. "Tell him I need breakfast, Sharpe," the brigadier commanded, "and a doctor."

Sharpe passed on the requests, then added that his men needed food and water. The servant bowed and said he would take the soldiers to the kitchen. He left Sharpe alone with Moon who was now lying on a couch. "Damned uncomfortable furniture," the brigadier said. He grimaced from a stab of pain in his leg, then looked up at the paintings. "How do they live with this gloom?"

"I suppose they're religious, sir."

"We're all bloody religious, man, but that doesn't mean we hang paintings of torture on our walls! Good God incarnate. Nothing wrong with a few decent landscapes and some family portraits. Did he say there was a Marquesa here?"

"Yes, sir."

"Well let's hope she's easier on the eye than her damned paintings, eh?"

"I think I ought to make sure the men are properly settled, sir," Sharpe said.

"Good idea," Moon said, subtly insinuating that Sharpe would be happier in the servants' quarters. "Do take your time, Sharpe. That fellow understood I need a doctor?"

"He did, sir."

"And food?"

"He knows that too, sir."

"Pray God he gets both here before sundown. Oh, and Sharpe, send that bright young fellow, the one who speaks the languages, to translate for me. But tell him to smarten himself up first." The brigadier jerked his head, dismissing Sharpe who went back onto the terrace and found his way through an alley, across the stable yard, and so to a whitewashed kitchen hung with hams and smelling of wood smoke, cheese, and baking bread. A crucifix hung above the huge fireplace where two cooks were busy at a blackened stove. A third woman pounded a mass of dough on a long scrubbed table.

Harper grinned at Sharpe, then gestured at the cheeses, hams, and the two fat wine barrels on their stands. "You wouldn't think there was a war going on, sir, would you now?"

"You've forgotten something, Sergeant."

"And what would that be, sir?"

"There's a battalion of French infantry within half a day's march."

"So there is."

Sharpe walked to the twin wine barrels and rapped the nearest. "You know the rules," he told the watching soldiers. "If any of you get drunk I'll make you wish you hadn't been born." They stared at him solemnly. What he should do, he knew, was take the two barrels outside and stave them in, but if they wanted to get drunk they would still find liquor in a house this size. Put a British soldier in a wilderness and he would soon discover a taproom. "We might have to get out of here fast," he explained, "so I don't want you drunk. When we get to Lisbon, I promise I'll fill you all so full of rum that you won't be able to stand for a week. But today, lads? Today you stay sober."

They nodded and he slung his rifle on his shoulder. "I'm going to stand watch until you've eaten," he told Harper. "Then you and two others take over from me. You saw that old castle tower?"

"Couldn't miss it, sir."

"That's where I'll be. And Harris? You're to be an interpreter for the brigadier."

Harris shuddered. "Do I have to, sir?"

"Yes, you bloody do. And you're to smarten yourself up first."

"Three bags full, sir," Harris said.

"And Harris!" Sergeant Harper called.

"Sergeant?"

"Make sure to tell His Lordship if us teagues are causing trouble."

"I'll do that, Sergeant, I promise."

Sharpe went to the tower that formed the eastern end of the stable yard. He climbed to the parapet that was some forty feet above the ground and from there he had a good view of the road that ran eastward along the smaller river. It was the road the French would use if they decided to come here. Would they come? They knew a handful of British troops was stranded on the Spanish bank of the river, but would they bother to pursue? Or perhaps they might just send a forage party. It was evident that this large house had been spared the usual French cruelties and that was doubtless because the Marquesa was **anfrancesado,** and that meant she must be supplying the French garrisons with provisions. So had the French refrained from plundering the town as well? If so, was there a boat? And if there was, then they could cross the river as soon as the brigadier had seen a doctor, if any doctor was available. Though once across the river, what then? The brigadier's troops had blown up Fort Joseph and were withdrawing westward, going back to the Tagus, and as long as Moon had a broken leg there was no hope of catching them. Sharpe worried for a moment, then decided it was not his problem. Brigadier Moon was the senior officer, so all Sharpe had to do was wait for orders. In the meantime he would have his men make some crutches for the brigadier.

He stared eastward. The sides of the valley were thick with grapevines and a few men worked there, shoring up one of the stone walls holding the terraces in place. A horseman ambled eastward and a child drove two goats down the road, but otherwise nothing moved except a hawk that glided across the cloudless sky. It was winter still, but the sun had a surprising warmth. By turning around he could just see a sliver of the river beyond the house and, on the Guadiana's far side, the Portuguese hills.

Harper relieved him, bringing Hagman and Slattery. "Harris is back, sir. Seems the lady speaks English so he isn't needed. Is anything happening?"

"Nothing. The lady?"

"The Marquesa, sir. An old biddy."

"I think the brigadier was hoping for something young and luscious."

"We were all hoping for that, sir. So what do we do if we see a Frenchie?"

"We get down to the river," Sharpe said. He gazed eastward. "If the bastards come," he said, "this is the road they'll use, and at least we'll see them a couple of miles away."

"Let's hope they're not coming."

"And let's hope no one's drunk if they do," Sharpe said.

Harper threw a puzzled look at Sharpe, then understood. "You needn't worry about the Connaught men, sir. They'll do what you tell them."

"They will?"

"I had a word with Sergeant Noolan, so I did, and said you weren't entirely bad unless you were crossed, and then you were a proper devil. And I told him you had an Irish father, which might be true, might it not?"

"So I'm one of you now, am I?" Sharpe asked, amused.

"Oh no, sir. You're not handsome enough."

Sharpe went back to the kitchen where he discovered Geoghegan pounding the dough and two more of Noolan's men stacking firewood beside the stove. "They'll make you eggs and ham," Sergeant Noolan told him, "and we've shown them how to make proper tea."

Sharpe contented himself with a piece of newly baked bread and a hunk of hard cheese. "Have any of your men got razors?" he asked Noolan.

"I'm sure Liam has," Noolan said, nodding at one of the men stacking firewood. "Keeps himself looking smart, he does, for the ladies."

"Then I want every man shaved," Sharpe said, "and no one's to leave the stable yard. If the bloody frogs come we don't want to be searching for lost men. And Harris? Look around the stables. See if you can find some wood to make the brigadier crutches."

Harris grinned. "He's already got crutches, sir. The lady had some that belonged to her husband."

"The Marquesa?"

"She's a crone, sir, a widow, and hell, has she got a bloody tongue on her!"

"Has the brigadier been given food?"

"He has, sir, and there's a doctor on his way."

"He doesn't need a doctor," Sharpe grumbled. "Private Geoghegan did a good job on that leg."

Geoghegan grinned. "I did, sir."

"I'm going to have a look about," Sharpe said, "so if the bloody frogs come you must get the brigadier down to the river." He was not sure what they could do beside the river with the French on their heels, but maybe some escape would offer itself.

"You think they will come, sir?" Noolan asked.

"God knows what the bastards will do."

Sharpe went back outside, then crossed the terrace and down into the kitchen garden. Two men worked there now, setting out plants in newly turned furrows, and they straightened up and watched him with suspicion as he walked to the boathouse. It was a wooden building on a stone foundation and had a padlocked door. It was an old ball-padlock, the size of a cooking apple, and Sharpe did not even bother trying to pick it, but just put its shackle against the door, then rapped the lock's base with the brass butt of his rifle. He heard the bolts shear inside, pulled the shackle free, and swung the door outward.

And there was the boat.

The perfect boat. It looked like an admiral's barge with six rowing benches and a wide stern thwart and a dozen long oars laid neatly up its center line. It floated between two walkways and there was hardly a drop of water in its bilges, suggesting that the boat was watertight. The gunwales, transom, and stern thwart had been painted white once, but the paint was peeling now and there was dust everywhere and cobwebs between the thwarts. A scrabble in the dark beneath the walkways betrayed rats.

He heard the footsteps behind and turned to see that one of the gardeners had come to the boathouse. The man was holding a fowling piece that he trained at Sharpe and then spoke in a harsh voice. He jerked his head and twitched the gun, ordering Sharpe away from the boat.

Sharpe shrugged. The fowling piece had a barrel at least five feet long. It looked ancient, but that did not mean it would not work. The man was tall, well-built, in his forties, and he held the old gun confidently. He ordered Sharpe out of the boathouse again and Sharpe meekly obeyed. The man was reprimanding him, but so fast that Sharpe could hardly understand one word in ten, but he understood well enough when the man emphasized his words by poking his gun barrel into Sharpe's waist. Sharpe seized the gun with his left hand and hit the man with his right. Then he kicked him between the legs and took the fowling piece away. "You don't poke guns at British officers," Sharpe said, though he doubted the man understood him, or even heard him for that matter, for he was crouching in agony and making a mewing sound. Sharpe blew the last remnants of powder from the gun's pan so it could not fire, then he banged the muzzle against a stone until the shot and powder came tumbling out. He scuffed the powder into the earth and then, just to make sure the weapon could not fire, he wrenched the doghead away from the lock and threw it into the river. "You're lucky to be alive," he told the man. He tossed the fowling piece onto the man's belly and resisted the urge to kick him again. He had not realized how angry he was. The second gardener backed away, bowing.

Sharpe found the brigadier propped up on the couch with a towel wrapped about his neck. A young manservant was shaving him. "There you are, Sharpe," Moon greeted him. "You'll be pleased to know I've discovered the secret of a good shave."

"You have, sir?"

"Add some lime juice to the shaving water. Very clever, don't you think?"

Sharpe was not sure what to say to that. "We've posted sentries, sir. The men are cleaning themselves up and I've found a boat."

"What use is a boat now?" Moon asked.

"Cross the river, sir. We can make a horse swim behind sir, if we've got the cash to buy one, and if you ride, sir, we've a chance to catch up with our lads." Sharpe doubted there was any chance of catching the six light companies who retreated from Fort Joseph, but he had to give the brigadier hope.

Moon paused as the manservant rinsed his face, then patted it dry with a hot towel. "We're not going anywhere, Sharpe," the brigadier said, "until a doctor has seen this leg. The Marquesa says the fellow in the town is perfectly adequate for broken bones. She's a damned bitter old hag, but she's being helpful enough, and I assume her physician is better than some teague soldier, don't you think?"

"I think, sir, that the sooner we're away from here, the better."

"Not before a proper doctor has seen this leg," the brigadier said firmly. "The fellow's been summoned and should be here soon. We can go after that. Have the men ready."

Sharpe sent Noolan and his men down to the boathouse. "Guard the damn boat," he told them, then he climbed the tower and joined Harper, Hagman, and Slattery, who kept watch from the tower's top. Harper told Sharpe that nothing moved on the road leading eastward. "Be ready to go, Pat," Sharpe said. "I've got a boat. We're just waiting for the brigadier now."

"You've found a boat? Easy as that?"

"Easy as that."

"So what do we do with it?"

Sharpe thought for a second. "I doubt we can catch the others," he said, "so probably the best thing is to go downriver. Find a British ship on the coast. We'll be in Lisbon in five days, and back with the battalion in six."

"Now that would be nice," Harper said fervently.

Sharpe smiled. "Joana?" he asked. Joana was a Portuguese girl whom Harper had rescued in Coimbra and who now shared the sergeant's quarters.

"I'm fond of the girl," Harper admitted airily. "And she's a good lass. She can cook, mend, works hard."

"Is that all she does?" Sharpe asked.

"She's a good girl," Harper insisted.

"You should marry her then," Sharpe said.

"There's no call for that, sir," Harper said, sounding alarmed.

"I'll ask Colonel Lawford when we're back," Sharpe said. Officially only six wives were allowed with the men of each company, but the colonel could give permission to add another to the strength.

Harper looked at Sharpe a long time, trying to work out whether he was being serious or not, but Sharpe's face gave away nothing. "The colonel's got enough to worry about, sir, so he does," Harper said.

"What's he got to worry about? We do all the work."

"But he's a colonel, sir. He's got to worry."

"And I worry about you, Pat. I worry that you're a sinner. It worries me that you'll be going to hell when you die."

"At least I can keep you company there, sir."

Sharpe laughed at that. "That's true, so maybe I won't ask the colonel."

"You escaped, Sergeant," Slattery said, amused.

"But it all depends on Moon, doesn't it?"

Sharpe said. "If he wants to cross the river and try to catch the others, that's what we'll have to do. If he wants to go downriver we go downriver, but one way or another we should get you back to Joana in a week." He saw a horseman appear on the northern hill from which he had first glimpsed the house and town, and he took out his telescope, but by the time he had trained it the man had gone. Probably a hunter, he told himself. "So be ready to move, Pat. And you'll have to fetch the brigadier. He's got crutches now, but if the bloody frogs show we'll need to get him down to the river fast so you'll have to carry him."

"There's a wheelbarrow in the stable yard, sir," Hagman said. "A dung barrow."

"I'll put it on the terrace," Sharpe said.

He found the barrow behind a heap of horse manure and wheeled it to the terrace and parked it beside the door. He had done all he could now. He had a boat, it was guarded, the men were ready, and all now depended on Moon giving the orders.

He sat outside the brigadier's door and took off his hat so the winter sun could warm his face. He closed his eyes in tiredness and within seconds he was asleep, his head tipped back onto the house wall beside the door. He was dreaming, and he was aware it was a good dream, and then someone hit him hard across the head, and that was no dream. He scrambled sideways, reaching for his rifle, and was hit again. "Impudent puppy!" a voice shrieked, and then she hit him again. She was an old woman, older than Sharpe could imagine, with a brown face like sun-dried mud, all cracks and wrinkles and malevolence and bitterness. She was dressed in black with a black widow's veil pinned to her white hair. Sharpe stood up, rubbing his head where she had hit him with one of the brigadier's borrowed crutches. "You dare attack one of my servants?" she shrieked. "You insolent cur!"

"Ma'am," Sharpe said for want of anything else to say.

"You break into my boathouse?" she said in a grating voice. "You assault my servant? If the world were respectable you would be whipped. My husband would have whipped you."

"Your husband, ma'am?"

"He was the Marquis de Cardenas and he had the misfortune to be ambassador to the Court of St. James for eleven sad years. We lived in London. A horrid city. A vile city. Why did you attack my gardener?"

"Because he attacked me, ma'am."

"He says not."

"If the world were a respectable place, ma'am, then an officer's word would be preferred to a servant's."

"You impudent puppy! I feed you, I shelter you, and you reward me with barbarism and lies. Now you wish to steal my son's boat?"

"Borrow it, ma'am."

"You can't," she snapped. "It belongs to my son."

"He's here, ma'am?"

"He is not, nor should you be. What you will do is march away from here once the doctor has seen your brigadier. You may take the crutches, nothing else."

"Yes, ma'am."

"Yes, ma'am," she mimicked him, "so humble." A bell sounded deep in the house and she turned away. **"El médico,"** she muttered.

Private Geoghegan appeared then, running up from the kitchen garden. "Sir," he panted, "there are men there."

"Men where?"

"Boathouse, sir. A dozen of them. All got guns. I think they came from the town, sir. Sergeant Noolan told me to tell you and ask what's to be done, sir?"

"They're guarding the boat?"

"That's it, sir, that's just what they're doing. They're stopping us getting to the boathouse, sir. Just that, sir. Jesus, what was that?"

The brigadier had given a sudden yelp, presumably as the doctor explored the makeshift splint. "Tell Sergeant Noolan," Sharpe said, "that's he's to do nothing. Just watch the men and make sure they don't take the boat away."

"Not to take the boat away, sir. And if they try?"

"You bloody stop them. You fix swords"—he paused, then corrected himself because only the rifles talked about fixing swords—"you fix bayonets and you walk slowly toward them and you point the bayonets at their crotches and they'll run."

"Aye, sir, yes, sir," Geoghegan grinned. "But really, sir, we're to do nothing else?"

"It's usually best."

"Oh, the poor man!" Geoghegan glanced at the door. "And if he'd left it alone it would have been fine. Thank you, sir."

Sharpe swore silently when Geoghegan was gone. It had all seemed so simple when he had discovered the boat, but he should have known nothing was ever that easy. And if the Marquesa had summoned men from the town, then there was a chance of bloodshed, and though Sharpe had no doubt that his soldiers would brush the townsmen away, he also feared that he would take two or three more casualties. "Bloody hell," he said aloud, and, because there was nothing else to do, he went back to the kitchen and rousted Harris from the table. "You're to stand outside the brigadier's room," he told him, "and let me know when the doctor's finished."

He went up to the tower where Harper still stood guard. "Nothing moving, sir," Harper said, "except I thought I saw a horseman up there a half hour ago"—he pointed to the northern heights—"but he's gone."

"I thought I saw the same thing."

"He's not there now, sir."

"We're just waiting for the doctor to finish with the brigadier," Sharpe said, "then we'll go." He said nothing about the men guarding the boathouse. He would deal with them when the time came. "That's a sour old bitch who lives here," he said.

"The Marquesa?"

"A shriveled old bitch. She bloody hit me!"

"There's some good in the woman then?" Harper suggested and, when Sharpe glowered, hurried on. "It's funny, though, isn't it, that the frogs haven't ruined this place? I mean there's food enough here for a battalion! And their foraging parties must have found this place months ago."

"She's made her peace with the bloody frogs," Sharpe said. "She probably sells them food and they leave her alone. She's not on our side, that's for sure. She hates us."

"So has she told the Crapauds we're here?"

"That worries me," Sharpe said. "She might have told them because she's a wicked old bitch, that's what she is." He gazed down the road. Something felt wrong. Everything was too peaceful. Perhaps, he thought, it was the news that the Marquesa was trying to protect the boat that had unsettled him, and the thought of a boat reminded him of what Sergeant Noolan had told the brigadier that morning. The French had crossed the river. Either they had fashioned a usable boat out of one of the undamaged pontoons, or else they had kept a boat in Fort Josephine, but if the French had a boat, any boat, then this road was not their only approach. "Bloody hell," he said softly.

"What, sir?"

"They're coming downriver."

"There's that fellow again," Slattery said, pointing to the northern hill where, silhouetted against the sky, the horseman had reappeared. The man was standing in his stirrups now and waving his arms extravagantly.

"Let's go!" Sharpe said.

The horseman must have been watching them all day, but his job was not just to watch, but to tell Colonel Vandal when the forces on the river were close to the house. Then the rest of the 8th would advance. Trapped, Sharpe thought. Some Frenchmen were coming by boat, others by road, and he was between them and then he was running down the crumbling staircase and shouting for the rest of his men who were lolling outside the kitchen to get down to the river. "We'll fetch the brigadier!" he told Harper.

The Marquesa was in the brigadier's room, watching as the doctor wrapped a bandage about a new splint that replaced Sharpe's makeshift contraption. She saw the alarm on Sharpe's face and gave a cackle. "So the French are coming," she taunted him, "the French are coming."

"We're going, sir," Sharpe said, ignoring her.

"He can't finish this?" The brigadier gestured at the half-wrapped bandage.

"We're going!" Sharpe insisted. "Sergeant!"

Harper pushed the doctor aside and lifted the brigadier. "My saber!" the brigadier protested. "The crutches!"

"Out!" Sharpe ordered.

"My saber!"

"The French are coming!" the Marquesa mocked.

"You sent for them, you sour old bitch," Sharpe said, and he was tempted to hammer her malevolent face, but instead went outside where Harper had unceremoniously dumped Moon into the wheelbarrow.

"My saber!" the brigadier pleaded.

"Slattery, push the barrow," Sharpe said. "Pat, get that volley gun ready." The seven-barrel gun, more than anything, would frighten the men guarding the boat. "Hurry!" he shouted.

Moon was still complaining about his lost saber, but Sharpe had no time for the man. He ran ahead with Harper, through the bushes. Then he was in the kitchen garden and he could see the knot of townsmen standing guard on the boathouse. "Sergeant Noolan!"

"Sir!" That was Harris. "There, sir."

Bloody hell. Two pontoons, crammed with French troops, drifting downstream. "Shoot at them, Harris! Sergeant Noolan!"

"Sir?"

"Forward march." Sharpe joined the small rank of Connaught men. They were outnumbered by the townsmen, but the redcoats had bayonets and Harper had joined them with his volley gun. Rifles fired from the upstream bank and French muskets cracked from the pontoons. A bullet struck the boathouse roof and the townsmen flinched. **"Váyase,"** Sharpe said, hoping his Spanish was understandable, **"yo le mataré."**

"What does that mean, sir?" Sergeant Noolan asked.

"Go away or we kill them."

Another French musket ball hit the boathouse and it was that, more perhaps than the threat of the advancing bayonets, that took the last shred of courage from the civilians. They fled, and Sharpe breathed a sigh of relief. Slattery arrived, pushing the brigadier, as Sharpe hauled the door open. "Get the brigadier in the boat!" he told Slattery, then ran to where Harris and three other riflemen were crouching by the bank. The two French boats, both salvaged pontoons being driven by crude paddles, were coming fast and he put the rifle to his shoulder, cocked it, and fired. The smoke hid the nearest French boat. He started to reload, then decided there was no time. "To the boat!" he called, and he ran back with the other riflemen. They threw themselves into the precious boat. Noolan had already cut the mooring lines and they shoved the boat out into the stream as they untangled the oars. A volley came from the French boats and one of Noolan's men gave a grunt and fell sideways. Other musket balls thumped into the gunwales. The brigadier was in the bows. Men were scrambling into thwarts, but Harper already had two of the long oars in their rowlocks and, standing up, was hauling on the shafts. The current caught them and turned them downstream. Another shot came from the nearest French boat and Sharpe waded over the men amidships and snatched up Harper's volley gun. He fired it at the French pontoon and the huge noise of the gun echoed back from the Portuguese hills as at last they began to outstrip their pursuers.

"Jesus Christ," Sharpe said in pure relief for their narrow escape.

"I think he's dying, sir," Noolan said.

"Who?"

"Conor, poor boy." The man who had been shot was coughing up blood that frothed pink at his lips.

"You left my saber!" Moon complained.

"Sorry about that, sir."

"It was one of Bennett's best!"

"I said I'm sorry, sir."

"And there was dung in that wheelbarrow."

Sharpe just looked into the brigadier's eyes and said nothing. The brigadier gave way first. "Did well to get away," he said grudgingly.

Sharpe turned to the men on the benches. "Geoghegan? Tie up the brigadier's splint. Well done, lads! Well done. That was a bit too close."

They were out of musket range now and the two ponderous French pontoons had given up the chase and turned for the bank. But ahead of them, where the smaller river joined the Guadiana, a knot of French horsemen appeared. Sharpe guessed they were the 8th's officers who had galloped ahead of the battalion. So now those men must watch their prey vanish downriver, but then he saw that some of the horsemen had muskets and he turned toward the stern. "Steer away from the bank!" he told Noolan who had taken the tiller ropes.

Sharpe reloaded the rifle. He could see that four of the horsemen had dismounted and were kneeling at the river's edge, aiming their muskets. The range was close, no more than thirty yards. "Rifles!" he called. He aimed his own. He saw Vandal. The French colonel was one of the officers kneeling by the river. He had a musket at his shoulder and he seemed to be aiming directly at Sharpe. You bastard, Sharpe thought, and he shifted the rifle, pointing it straight at Vandal's chest. The boat lurched, his aim wandered, he corrected it, and now he would teach the bastard the advantages of a rifle. He started to pull the trigger, keeping the foresight dead on the Frenchman's chest, and just then he saw the smoke billow from the musket muzzles and there was an instant when his whole head seemed filled with light, a searing white light that turned bloodred. There was pain like a lightning strike in his brain and then, like blood congealing on a corpse, the light went black and he could see and feel nothing at all. Nothing.

Chapter 3

Two men, both tall, walked side by side on Cádiz's ramparts. Those defenses were huge, ringing the city to protect it against enemies and the sea. The firestep facing the bay was wide, so wide that three coaches and horses could travel abreast, and it was a popular place for folk to take the air, but no one disturbed the two men. Three of the taller man's servants walked ahead to part the crowds, and three more walked on either side and still more walked behind to prevent any stranger disturbing their master.

The taller man, and he was very tall, was dressed in the uniform of a Spanish admiral. He had one white silk stocking, red knee breeches, a red sash, and a dark blue tailcoat with an elaborate red collar trimmed with gold lace. His straight sword was scabbarded in black fishskin and had a hilt of gold. His face was drawn, distinguished, and aloof, a face etched by pain and made harsh by disappointment. The admiral's left calf and foot were missing, so his lower leg was made of ebony, as was the gold-topped cane he used to help him walk.

His companion was Father Salvador Montseny. The priest was in a cassock and had a silver crucifix hanging on his breast. The admiral had been his companion in imprisonment in England after Trafalgar and sometimes, if they did not wish to be understood by nearby folk, they spoke English together. Not today. "So the girl confessed to you?" the admiral asked, amused.

"She makes confession once a year," Montseny said, "on her saint's day. January thirteenth."

"She is called Veronica?"

"Caterina Veronica Blazquez," Montseny said, "and God brought her to me. There were seven other priests hearing confession in the cathedral that day, but she was guided to me."

"So you killed her pimp, then you kill the Englishman and his servants. I trust God will forgive you for that, Father."

Montseny had no doubts about God's opinions. "What God wants, my lord, is a holy and a powerful Spain. He wants our flag spread across South America, he wants a Catholic king in Madrid, and he wants his glory to be reflected in our people. I do God's work."

"Do you enjoy it?"

"Yes."

"Good," the admiral said, then paused beside a cannon that faced the bay. "I need more money," he said.

"You will have it, my lord."

"Money," the admiral said in a tone of disgust. He was the Marquis de Cardenas. He had been born to money, and he had made more money, but there was never enough money. He tapped the cannon with the tip of his cane. "I need money for bribes," he said sourly, "because there is no courage in these men. They are lawyers, Father. Lawyers and politicians. They are scum." The scum of whom the admiral spoke were the deputies to the Cortes, the Spanish parliament, which now met in Cádiz where its chief business was to construct a new constitution for Spain. Some men, the **liberales,** wanted a Spain governed by the Cortes, a Spain in which citizens would have a say in their own destiny and such men spoke of liberty and democracy and the admiral hated them. He wanted a Spain like the old Spain, a Spain led by king and church, a Spain devoted to God and to glory. He wanted a Spain free of foreigners, a Spain without Frenchmen and without Britons, and to get it he would have to bribe members of the Cortes and he would have to make an offer to the French emperor. Leave Spain, the offer would say, and we shall help you conquer the British in Portugal. It was an offer, the admiral knew, that the French would accept because Napoleon was desperate. He wanted an end to the war in Spain. To the world's eyes it looked as if the French had won. They had occupied Madrid and taken Seville so that now the Spanish government, such as it was, clung to the land's edge at Cádiz. Yet to hold Spain meant keeping hundreds of thousands of Frenchmen in fortresses, and whenever those men left their walls they were harried by partisans. If Bonaparte could make peace with an amenable Spanish government then those garrisons would be freed to fight elsewhere.

"How much money do you need?" Montseny asked.

"With ten thousand dollars," the admiral said, "I can buy the Cortes." He watched a British frigate sail past the end of the long mole that protected Cádiz's harbor from the open Atlantic. He saw the great ensign ripple at the frigate's stern and felt a pulse of pure loathing. He had watched Nelson's ships sail toward him off Cape Trafalgar. He had breathed the powder smoke and listened to the screams of men dying aboard his ship. He had been felled by a piece of grapeshot that had shattered his left leg, but the admiral had stayed on the quarterdeck, shouting at his men to fight, to kill, to resist. Then he had watched as a crowd of yelling British sailors, ugly as apes, swarmed across his deck, and he had wept when Spain's ensign was lowered and the British flag hoisted. He had surrendered his sword, and then been a prisoner in England, and now he was the limping admiral of a broken country that had no battle fleet. He hated the British. "But the English," he said, still watching the frigate, "will never pay ten thousand dollars for the letters."

"I think they will pay a great deal," Father Montseny said, "if we frighten them."

"How?"

"I shall publish one letter. I shall change it, of course. And the implicit threat will be that we shall publish them all." Father Montseny paused, giving the admiral time to object to his proposal, but the admiral stayed silent. "I need a writer to make the changes," Montseny went on.

"A writer?" the admiral asked in a sour tone. "Why can't you make the changes yourself?"

"I can," Montseny said, "but once the letters are changed, the English will proclaim them forgeries. We cannot present the originals to anyone, because the originals will prove the English correct. So we must make new copies, in English, in an English hand, which we shall claim as the originals. I need a man who can write perfect English. My English is good, but not good enough." He fingered his crucifix, thinking. "The new letters need only persuade the Cortes, and most deputies will want to believe them, but the changes must still be convincing. The grammar, the spelling, must all be accurate. So I need a writer who can achieve that."

The admiral made a dismissive gesture. "I know a man. A horrid creature. He writes well, though, and has a passion for English books. He'll do, but how do you publish the letters?"

"**El Correo de Cádiz,**" Father Montseny said, naming the one newspaper that opposed the **liberales.** "I shall print one letter and I shall say in it that the English plan to take Cádiz and make it a second Gibraltar. The English will deny it, of course, but we will have a new letter with a forged signature."

"They'll do more than make denials," the admiral said vigorously, "they'll persuade the Regency to close the paper down!" The Regency was the council which ruled what was left of Spain, and ruled it with the help of British gold, which was why they were eager to keep the British friendly. A new constitution, though, could mean a new Regency, one which the admiral could lead.

"The Regency will be powerless if the letter is unsigned," Montseny pointed out dryly. "The English will not dare own to its authorship, will they? And rumor can do its work for us. Within a day all Cádiz will know that their ambassador wrote the letter."

The letters had been written by the British ambassador to Spain and they were pathetic outpourings of love. There was even a proposal of marriage in one letter, a proposal made to a girl who was a whore called Caterina Veronica Blazquez. She was an expensive whore, to be sure, but still a whore.

"The owner of the **Correo** is a man named Nuñez, yes?" the admiral asked.

"He is."

"And he will publish the letter?"

"There is an advantage to being a priest," Montseny said. "The secrets of the confessional, or course, are sacred, but gossip persists. We priests talk, my lord, and I know things about Nuñez that he does not want the world to know. He will publish."

"Suppose the English try to destroy the press?" the admiral suggested.

"They probably will," Montseny said dismissively, "but for a small sum I can turn the building into a fortress, and your men can help protect it. Then the British will be forced to buy the remaining letters. I'm sure, once we have published one, they will pay very generously."

"What utter fools men make themselves over women," the admiral said. He took a long black cigar from a pocket and bit the end off. Then he just stood, waiting until a couple of small boys saw the cigar and came running. Each lad held a length of thick hemp rope that smoldered at one end. The admiral indicated one of the boys who slapped his rope twice on the ground to revive its fire, then held it up so the admiral could light the cigar. He waved the boy toward the men who followed him and one of them tossed a coin. "It would be best," the admiral said, "if we possessed both the letters and the gold." He watched the British frigate that was now near the rocks that lay off the bastion of San Felipe and he prayed she would run aground. He wanted to see her masts lurch forward as the hull struck the rocks, he wanted to see her canted and sinking, and he wanted to see her sailors floundering in the heaving seas, but of course she sailed serenely past the danger.

"It would be best," Father Montseny said, "if we had the English gold and published the letters."

"It would be treacherous, of course," the admiral observed mildly.

"God wants Spain great again, my lord," Montseny said fervently. "It is never treachery to do God's work."

A sudden boom of a gun sounded flat across the bay and both men turned to see a far white cloud of smoke. It had come from one of the giant mortars the French had placed in their forts on the Trocadero Peninsula and the admiral hoped the shell had been aimed at the British frigate. Instead the missile fell on the city's waterfront a half mile to the east. The admiral waited for the shell to explode, then drew on his cigar. "If we publish the letters," he said, "then the Cortes will turn against the British. The bribes will make that certain, and then we can approach the French. You would be willing to go to them?"

"Very willing, my lord."

"I shall give you a letter of introduction, of course." The admiral had already made his proposals to Paris. That had been easy. He was known to hate the British and a French agent in Cádiz had spoken to him, but the reply from the emperor was simple. Deliver the votes in the Cortes and the Spanish king, now a prisoner in France, would be returned. France would make peace and Spain would be free. All the French demanded in return was the right to send troops across Spanish roads to complete the conquest of Portugal and so drive Lord Wellington's British army into the sea. As an earnest of their goodwill the French had given orders that the admiral's estates on the Guadiana should not be plundered and now, in return, the admiral must deliver the votes and so sever the alliance with Britain. "By summer, Father," he said.

"Summer?"

"It will be done. We shall have our king. We shall be free."

"Under God."

"Under God," the admiral agreed. "Find the money, Father, and make the English look like fools."

"It is God's will," Montseny said, "so it will happen."

And the British would go to hell.

Everything was easy after the shot felled Sharpe.

The boat drifted down the ever widening Guadiana into the night. A hazed moon silvered the hills and lit the long water that shuddered under the small wind. Sharpe lay in the boat's bilges, senseless, his head broken and bloodied and bandaged, and the brigadier sat in the stern, his leg splinted and his hands on the tiller ropes, and he wondered what he should do. The dawn found them between low hills without a house in sight. Egrets and herons stalked the river's edge. "He needs a doctor, sir," Harper said, and the brigadier heard the anguish in the Irishman's voice. "He's dying, sir."

"He's breathing, isn't he?" the brigadier asked.

"He is, sir," Harper said, "but he needs a doctor, sir."

"Good God incarnate, man, I'm not a conjuror! I can't find a doctor in a wilderness, can I?" The brigadier was in pain and spoke more sharply than he intended and he saw the flare of hostility on Harper's face and felt a stab of fear. Sir Barnaby Moon reckoned himself a good officer, but he was not comfortable dealing with the ranks. "If we come to a town," he said, trying to mollify the big sergeant, "we'll look for a physician."

"Yes, sir, thank you, sir."

The brigadier hoped they would find a town. They needed food and he wanted to find a doctor who could look at his broken leg that throbbed like the devil. "Row!" he snarled at the men, but they made a poor job of it. The painted blades clashed with every stroke, and the more they rowed, the less headway they seemed to make, and the brigadier realized that they were fighting an incoming tide. They must be miles from the sea, yet the tide was flooding against them and there was still no town or village anywhere in sight.

"Your honor!" Sergeant Noolan shouted from the bows, and the brigadier saw another boat had appeared about a bend in the wide river. She was a rowing boat, about the size of his own commandeered launch, and she was crammed with men who knew how to use their oars, and she had other men with muskets, and the brigadier hauled on the tiller to point the boat toward the Portuguese bank. "Row!" he shouted, then cursed as the oars tangled again. "Dear God," he said, because the strange boat was coming fast. She was expertly manned and being carried on the flooding tide, and Brigadier Moon cursed a second time just before the man commanding the approaching boat stood and hailed him.

The shout was in English. The officer commanding the boat wore naval blue and had come from a British sloop that patrolled the Guadiana's long tidal reach. The sloop rescued them, lifted Sharpe from the bottom boards, fed them, and then carried them out to sea where they were rowed to HMS **Thornside,** a thirty-six-gun frigate, and Sharpe knew none of it. There was just pain.

Pain and darkness, and a creaking sound so that Sharpe dreamed he was back on HMS **Pucelle,** sailing endlessly across the Indian Ocean, and Lady Grace was with him, and in his delirium he was happy again, but then he would half wake and know she was dead and he wanted to weep for that. The creaking went on and the world swayed and there was pain and darkness and a sudden flash of agonizing brilliance, then darkness again.

"I think he blinked," a voice said.

Sharpe opened his eyes and the pain in his skull was like white-hot embers. "Sweet Jesus," he hissed.

"No, it's just me, sir, Patrick Harper, sir." The sergeant loomed over him. There was a wooden ceiling partially lit by narrow shafts of sunlight that stabbed through a small grating. Sharpe closed his eyes. "Are you still there, sir?" Harper asked.

"Where am I?"

"HMS **Thornside,** sir. A frigate, sir."

"Jesus Christ," Sharpe groaned.

"He's had a few prayers this last day and a half, so he has."

"Here," another voice said and a hand went beneath Sharpe's shoulders to lift him so that the pain stabbed into his skull and he gasped. "Drink this," the voice said.

The liquid was bitter and Sharpe half choked on it, but whatever it was made him sleep and he dreamed again, and woke again, and this time it was night and a lantern in the passageway outside his diminutive cabin swung with the ship's motion so that the shadows careered all over the canvas walls and dizzied him.

He slept again, half aware of the sounds of a ship, of the bare feet on the planking overhead, the creak of a thousand timbers, the rush of water, and the intermittent clangor of the bell. Soon after dawn he woke and discovered his head was swathed in thick bandages. The pain was still gouging his skull, but it was no longer intense and so he swung his feet out of the cot and was immediately dizzy. He sat on the cot's swaying edge with his head in his hands. He wanted to vomit except there was nothing but bile in his stomach. His boots were on the floor, while his uniform, rifle, and sword were swaying from a wooden peg on the door. He closed his eyes. He remembered Colonel Vandal firing the musket. He thought of Jack Bullen, poor Jack Bullen.

The door opened. "What the hell are you doing?" Harper asked cheerfully.

"I want to go on deck."

"The surgeon says you must rest."

Sharpe told Harper what the surgeon could do. "Help me dress," he said. He did not bother with boots or sword, just pulled on his French cavalry overalls and his ragged green coat, then held on to Harper's strong arm as they walked out of the cabin. The sergeant then hauled Sharpe up a steep companionway to the frigate's deck where he clung to the hammock netting.

A brisk wind was blowing and it felt good. Sharpe saw that the frigate was sliding past a low dull coast dotted with watchtowers. "I'll get you a chair, sir," Harper said.

"Don't need a chair," Sharpe said. "Where are the men?"

"We're all snug up front, sir."

"You're improperly dressed, Sharpe." A voice interrupted and Sharpe turned his head to see Brigadier Moon enthroned near the frigate's wheel. He was sitting in a chair with his splinted leg propped on a cannon. "You haven't got boots on," the brigadier observed.

"Much better to go barefoot on deck," a cheerful voice said, "and what are you doing on your bare feet anyway? I gave orders that you were to stay below." A plump, cheerful man in civilian clothes smiled at Sharpe. "I'm Jethro McCann, surgeon to this scow." He introduced himself and held up a closed fist. "How many fingers am I showing you?"

"None."

"Now?"

"Two."

"The Sweeps can count," McCann said. "I'm impressed." The Sweeps were the Riflemen, so called because their dark green uniforms often looked black as a chimney sweep's rags. "Can you walk?" McCann asked and Sharpe managed a few paces before a gust of wind lurched the frigate and drove him back to the hammock netting. "You're walking well enough," McCann said. "Are you in pain?"

"It's getting better," Sharpe lied.

"You're a lucky bastard, Mister Sharpe, if you'll forgive me. Lucky as hell. You were hit by a musket ball. Glancing shot, which is why you're still here, but it depressed a piece of your skull. I fished it back into place." McCann grinned proudly.

"Fished it back into place?" Sharpe asked.

"Oh, it's not difficult," the surgeon said airily, "no more difficult than scarfing a sliver of wood." In truth it had been appallingly difficult. It had taken the doctor an hour and a half's work under inadequate lantern light as he teased at the wedge of bone with probe and forceps. His fingers had kept slipping in blood and slime, and he had thought he would never manage to free the bone without tearing the brain tissue, but at last he had succeeded in gripping the splintered edge and pulling the sliver back into place. "And here you are," McCann went on, "sprightly as a two-year-old. And the good news is that you've got a brain." He saw Sharpe's puzzlement and nodded vigorously. "You do! Honest! I saw it with my own eyes, thus disproving the navy's stubborn contention that soldiers have nothing whatsoever inside their skulls. I shall write a paper for the **Review.** I'll be famous! Brain discovered in a soldier."

Sharpe tried to smile in the pretense that he was amused, but only succeeded in a grimace. He touched the bandage. "Will the pain go?"

"We know almost nothing about head wounds," McCann said, "except that they bleed a lot, but in my professional opinion, Mister Sharpe, you'll either drop down dead or be right as rain."

"That is a comfort," Sharpe said. He perched on a cannon and stared at the distant land beneath the far clouds. "How long till we reach Lisbon?"

"Lisbon? We're sailing to Cádiz!"

"Cádiz?"

"That's our station," McCann said, "but

you'll find a boat going to Lisbon quick enough. Ah! Captain Pullifer's on deck. Straighten up."

The captain was a thin, narrow-faced, and grim-looking man, a scarecrow figure who, Sharpe noticed, was barefooted. Indeed, if it had not been for his coat with its salt-encrusted gilt, Sharpe might have mistaken Pullifer for an ordinary seaman. The captain spoke briefly with the brigadier, then strode down the deck and introduced himself to Sharpe. "Glad you're on your feet," he said morosely. He had a broad Devon accent.

"So am I, sir."

"We'll have you in Cádiz soon enough and a proper doctor can look at your skull. McCann, if you want to steal my coffee you'll find it on the cabin table."

"Aye aye, sir," the doctor said. McCann was evidently amused by his captain's insult, which suggested to Sharpe that Pullifer was not the grim beast he appeared to be. "Can you walk, Sharpe?" Captain Pullifer asked gruffly.

"I seem to be all right, sir," Sharpe said, and Pullifer jerked his head, indicating that the rifleman should go with him to the stern rail. Moon watched Sharpe pass by.

"Had supper with your brigadier last night,"

Pullifer said when he was alone with Sharpe beneath the great mizzen sail. He paused, but Sharpe said nothing. "And I spoke with your sergeant this morning," Pullifer went on. "It's strange, isn't it, how stories differ?"

"Differ, sir?"

Pullifer, who had been staring at the **Thornside**'s wake, turned to look at Sharpe. "Moon says it was all your fault."

"He says what?" Sharpe was not certain he had heard right. His head was filled with a pulsing pain. He tried closing his eyes, but it did not help so he opened them again.

"He says you were ordered to blow a bridge, but you hid the powder under women's luggage, which is against the rules of war, and then you dillydallied and the frogs took advantage, and he finishes up with a dead horse, a broken leg, and no saber. And the saber was Bennett's best, he tells me."

Sharpe said nothing, just stared at a white bird skimming the broken sea.

"You broke the rules of war," Pullifer said sourly, "but as far as I know the only rule in bloody war is to win. You broke the bridge, didn't you?"

"Yes, sir."

"But you lost one of Bennett's best sabers"—Pullifer sounded amused—"so your brigadier borrowed pen and paper off me this morning to write a report for Lord Wellington. It's going to be poisonous about you. Do you wonder why I'm telling you?"

"I'm glad you're telling me," Sharpe said.

"Because you're like me, Sharpe. You came up the hawse hole. I started as a pressed man. I was fifteen and had spent eight years catching mackerel off Dawlish. That was thirty years ago. I couldn't read, couldn't write, and didn't know a sextant from an arsehole, but now I'm a captain."

"Up the hawse hole," Sharpe said, relishing the navy's slang for a man promoted from the ranks into the officer's mess. "But they never let you forget, do they?"

"It's not so bad in the navy," Pullifer said grudgingly. "They value seamanship more than gentle birth. But thirty years at sea teaches you a thing or two about men, and I have a notion that your sergeant was telling the truth."

"He bloody was," Sharpe said hotly.

"So I'm warning you, that's all. If I were you I'd write my own report and muddy the water a little." Pullifer glanced up at the sails, found nothing to criticize, and shrugged. "We'll catch a few mortar rounds going into Cádiz, but they haven't hit us yet."

In the afternoon the west wind turned soft so that the **Thornside** slowed and wallowed in the long Atlantic swells. Cádiz came slowly into sight, a city of gleaming white towers that seemed to float on the ocean. By dusk the wind had died to a whisper that did nothing except fret the frigate's sails and Pullifer was content to wait till morning to make his approach. A big merchantman was much closer to land and she was ghosting into harbor on the last dying breaths of wind. Pullifer gazed at her through a big telescope. "She's the **Santa Catalina,**" he announced. "We saw her in the Azores a year ago." He collapsed the glass. "I hope she's getting more wind than we are. Otherwise she'll never make the southern part of the harbor."

"Does it matter?" Sharpe asked.

"The bloody frogs will use her for target practice."

It seemed the captain was right for just after dark Sharpe heard the muffled sound of heavy guns like thunder far away. They were the French mortars firing from the mainland and Sharpe watched their monstrous flashes from the

Thornside's forecastle. Each flash was like sheet lightning, silhouetting a mile of shoreline, gone in a heartbeat, the sudden brilliance confused by the lingering smoke beneath the stars. A sailor was playing a sad tune on a fiddle and a small wash of lantern light showed from the aft cabin's companionway where the brigadier was dining again with Captain Pullifer. "Were you not invited, sir?" Harper asked. Sharpe's riflemen and the Connaught Rangers were lounging around a long-barreled nine-pounder on the forecastle.

"I was invited," Sharpe said, "but the captain reckoned I might be happier eating with the wardroom."

"They made a plum duff up here," Harper said.

"It was good," Harris added, "really good."

"We had the same."

"I sometimes think I should have joined the navy," Harper said.

"You do?" Sharpe was surprised.

"Plum duff and rum."

"Not many women."

"That's true.

"How's your head, sir?" Daniel Hagman asked.

"Still there, Dan."

"Is it hurting?"

"It hurts," Sharpe admitted.

"Vinegar and brown paper, sir," Hagman said earnestly. "It always works."

"I had an uncle that was knocked on the head," Harper said. The Ulsterman had an endless supply of relatives who had suffered various misfortunes. "He was butted by a nanny goat, so he was, and you could have filled Lough Crockatrillen with his blood! Jesus, it was everywhere. My auntie thought he was dead!"

Sharpe, like the Riflemen and Rangers, waited. "So was he?" he asked after a while.

"Good God, no! He was milking the cows again that night, but the poor goat was never the same. So what do we do in Cádiz, sir?"

Sharpe shrugged. "We'll get a boat to Lisbon. There must be dozens of boats going to Lisbon." He turned as two reports rumbled across the water, but there was nothing to see. The far flashes had already faded and the mortar shells gave no light when they landed. Intermittent lamplight glimmered across the city's white walls, but otherwise the shoreline was dark. Black water lapped against the frigate's flanks and the sails shivered in the small wind.

By dawn the wind had freshened and the

Thornside stood southwest toward the entrance to the Bay of Cádiz. The city was closer now and Sharpe could see the massive gray ramparts above which the houses glowed white, their walls studded with squat watchtowers and church belfries through which smoke drifted. Lights flashed from the towers and at first Sharpe was puzzled by the glints. Then he realized that they were the sun reflecting from the telescopes that watched the **Thornside**'s approach. A pilot boat cut across the frigate's course, her captain waving his arms to show he had a pilot who was available to come aboard the frigate, but Pullifer had run this treacherous approach often enough to need no guide. Gulls wheeled about the frigate's masts and sails as she slid past the heave and wash of broken water that marked the Diamante Rock and then the bay opened before her bows. The **Thornside** turned due south, heading into the bay and watched by a crowd on the city ramparts. It was evident now that the smoke above the city was not just from cooking fires, but mostly from a merchantman that burned in the harbor. It was the **Santa Catalina,** her hull crammed with tobacco and sugar. A French mortar shell had plunged between her foremast and mainmast, pierced a hatch cover, and ex-

ploded a few feet below the deck. The crew had
rigged a pump and poured water onto the fire. It
seemed they must have mastered the blaze, but
somewhere an ember had lodged deep among
the bales and it grew sullenly. The hidden fire
spread secretly, its smoke disguised by the steam
from the pump's water. Then, just aft of the
mainmast, the deck burst into new flames, sudden and bright, and the blaze caught the tarred
rigging so that the whole intricate web of hal-
liards, masts, and sheets was outlined in fire.
Smoke boiled across the city's skyline above
which the white gulls keened and the dark smoke
drifted.

The **Thornside** ran within a quarter mile of
the burning merchantman. The rest of Cádiz
harbor, placid under a gentle wind, seemed un-
concerned with the burning ship. A whole fleet
of British warships was moored to the south,
and Pullifer ordered a salute fired to the admiral. The French mortars were firing at the
Thornside now, but the massive shells fell
harmlessly on either side, each throwing up a
fountain of spray. There were three French forts
on the marshy mainland, all with mortars just
capable of reaching the waterfront of Cádiz that

sat on its isthmus like a clenched fist protecting the bay. Lieutenant Theobald, the **Thornside**'s second lieutenant, was busy with a sextant, though instead of holding it vertically, as a man would when shooting the sun or trying to snare a star in the instrument's mirrors, he was using it horizontally. He lowered the sextant and frowned. His lips moved as he made some half-articulated calculations, then he crossed to where Sharpe and Harper leaned on the midships rail. "From the burning ship to the fort," Theobald announced, "is a distance of three thousand six hundred and forty yards."

"Bloody hell," Sharpe said, impressed. If the lieutenant was right, then the mortar's shell had traveled more than two miles.

"I won't vouch for the forty yards," Theobald said.

Another mortar fired from the Trocadero Peninsula. The shell vanished in the low clouds as the smoke of the mortar hung above the fort, which was a low, dark mass on the marsh-fringed headland. Then a white splash showed very close to the city's shore. "Even farther!" Theobald said in astonishment. "Must be close to three thousand seven hundred yards!" That was a thousand yards farther than any British mortar could reach. "The shells are huge too! Couple of feet across!"

Sharpe wondered about that. "Biggest French mortar I've ever seen," he said, "is a twelve-inch."

"Which is big enough, God knows," Harper put in.

"They had these specially cast in Seville," Theobald said, "or so prisoners tell us. Big bastards, anyway. They must use twenty pounds of powder to throw a ball that far. Thank God they're not accurate."

"Tell that to those poor bastards," Sharpe said, nodding to where the **Santa Catalina**'s crew were climbing into a longboat.

"A lucky shot," Theobald said. "How's your skull today?"

"Hurts."

"Nothing a woman's touch won't heal," Theobald said.

A mortar shell landed off the **Thornside**'s port quarter, splashing the deck with water and leaving the faintest gray trail from its smoking fuse lingering in the small wind. The next shot was a good hundred yards away, and the one after that even farther, and then the guns stopped firing as it became obvious that the frigate had sailed out of range.

Thornside anchored well south of the city, close to the other British warships and the host of small merchantmen. Brigadier Moon stumped toward Sharpe on crutches that the ship's carpenter had made. "You'll stay on board for the moment, Sharpe."

"Yes, sir."

"Officially British troops aren't permitted into the city so if we can't find a ship leaving today or tomorrow, I'll arrange quarters for you on the Isla de León." He gestured toward the low land south of the anchorage. "In the meantime I'm going to pay my respects at the embassy."

"The embassy, sir?"

Moon gave Sharpe a look of exasperation. "You are looking," he said, "at what is left of sovereign Spain. The French have the rest of the bloody country except for a handful of fortresses, so our embassy is now here in Cádiz instead of in Madrid or Seville. I'll send you orders."

Those orders arrived just after midday, sending Sharpe and his men to the Isla de León where they were to wait until a northbound transport left the harbor. The longboat carrying them ashore threaded the anchored fleet, most of which were merchantmen. "Rumor says they're taking an army south," the midshipman commanding the longboat told Sharpe.

"South?"

"They want to land somewhere down the coast," the midshipman said, "march on the French, and attack the siege lines. Bloody hell, they smell!" He pointed to four great prison hulks that stank like open sewers. The hulks had once been warships, but now they were mastless and their open gunports were protected by iron bars through which men watched the small boat pass. "Prison hulks, sir," the midshipman said, "full of frogs."

"I remember that one," the bosun put in, nodding at the nearest hulk. "She were at Trafalgar. We beat her to splinters. There was blood pouring down her side. Never seen the like."

"The dons were on the wrong side of that one," the midshipman said.

"They're on our side now," Sharpe said.

"We hope they are, sir. We do hope that. Here you are, sir, safe and sound, and I hope your eggshell mends."

The Isla de León was home to five thousand British and Portuguese soldiers who helped defend Cádiz from the French besiegers. Desultory cannon fire sounded from the siege lines that were some miles eastward. The small town of San Fernando was on the island and Sharpe reported there to a harassed major who seemed bemused that a handful of vagrants from the 88th and the South Essex had landed in his lap. "Your fellows can find space in the tent lines," the major said, "but you'll be billeted in San Fernando, of course, with the other officers. Dear God, what's free?" He looked through the billeting lists.

"It's only for a night or so," Sharpe said.

"Depends on the wind, doesn't it? So long as it blows northwest you aren't going anywhere near Lisbon. Here we are. You can share a house with Major Duncan. He's an artilleryman, so he's not particular. He's not there now. He's off hunting with Sir Thomas."

"Sir Thomas?"

"Sir Thomas Graham. Commands here. Mad about cricket. Cricket and hunting. Of course there aren't any bloody foxes so they chase after stray dogs instead. They do it between the lines and the French are good enough not to interfere. You'll want space for your servant, I assume?"

Sharpe had never had a servant, but decided

this was the moment to indulge himself. "Harris!"

"Sir?"

"You're my servant now."

"What joy, sir."

"San Fernando's a decent little place in winter," the major said. "Too many bloody mosquitoes in the summer, but nice enough at this time of year. Plenty of taverns, a couple with good bordellos. There are worse places to spend the war."

The wind did not change that night, nor the next. Sharpe gave his and Sergeant Noolan's men a make-and-mend day. They cleaned and repaired uniforms and weapons, and for every moment of the day Sharpe prayed that the wind would go south or east. He found a regimental surgeon who reckoned that inspecting Sharpe's wound would do more harm than good. "If that naval fellow fished the bone back into place," the man said, "then he did all that modern medicine can possibly do. Keep the bandage tight, Captain, keep it wet, say your prayers, and take rum for the pain."

Major Duncan, whose quarters Sharpe now shared, proved to be an affable Scot. He said there were at least a half dozen ships waiting to make passage to Lisbon. "So you'll be home in four or five days," he went on, "just as soon as the wind goes round." Duncan had invited Sharpe to the nearest tavern, insisting the food was adequate and ignoring Sharpe's plea that he had no cash. "The dons eat damn late," Duncan said, "so we're forced to drink until the cook wakes up. It's a hard life." He ordered a jug of red wine, and no sooner had it appeared than a slender young officer in cavalry uniform appeared at the tavern door.

"Willie!" Duncan greeted the cavalryman with evident pleasure. "Are you drinking with us?"

"I am searching for Captain Richard Sharpe, and I assume that you, sir, are he?" He smiled at Sharpe and held out a hand. "Willie Russell, aide to Sir Thomas."

"Lord William Russell," Duncan said.

"But Willie suffices," Lord William put in hastily. "You are Captain Sharpe? In which case, sir, you are summoned. I have a horse for you and we must ride like the very wind."

"Summoned?"

"To the embassy, Captain! To meet His Majesty's Minister Plenipotentiary and Envoy Extraordinary to the Court of Spain. Good lord, that is rotgut!" He had tried some of Duncan's wine. "Did someone piss in it? Are you ready, Sharpe?"

"I'm wanted at the embassy?" Sharpe asked, confused.

"You are, and you're late. This is the third tavern I've tried and I had to have a drink in each one, didn't I? **Noblesse oblige** and all that." He drew Sharpe out of the tavern. "I must say I'm honored to meet you!" Lord William spoke generously, then saw Sharpe's disbelief. "No, truly. I was at Talavera. I got cut up there, but you took an eagle! That was one in the eye for Boney, wasn't it? Here we are, your horse."

"Do I really have to go?" Sharpe asked.

Lord William Russell looked thoughtful for a second. "I think you do," he said seriously, "because it's not every day that envoys extraordinary and ministers plenipotentiary send a summons for a captain. And he's not a bad fellow for an ambassador. You can ride?"

"Badly."

"How's your skull?"

"Hurts."

"It would, wouldn't it? I fell off a horse once and bashed my head against a tree stump and I couldn't think for a month! Not sure I'm cured yet, to be honest. Up you get."

Sharpe settled himself in the saddle and followed Lord William Russell out of the town and onto the sandy isthmus. "How far is it?" he asked.

"Just over six miles. It's a nice ride! At low tide we use the beach, but tonight we'll have to jog along the road instead. You'll meet Sir Thomas at the embassy. He's a splendid fellow. You'll like him. Everyone does."

"And Moon?"

"I'm afraid he's there too. Man's a brute, isn't he? Mind you, he's been very civil to me, probably because my father's a duke."

"A duke?"

"Of Bedford," Lord William said, grinning. "But don't worry, I'm not the heir, not even the one after the heir. I'm the one who has to die for king and country. Moon doesn't like you, does he?"

"So I hear."

"He's been blaming you for all his ills. Says you lost his saber. One of Bennetts's eh?"

"Never heard of Bennetts," Sharpe said.

"Cutler in St. James's, fearfully good, and awfully pricy. They say you can shave yourself on one of Bennetts's sabers, not that I've tried."

"Is that why they sent for me? To complain?"

"Good Lord, no! It was the ambassador who sent for you. He wants to get you drunk, I expect."

The isthmus narrowed. Off to Sharpe's left was the wide Atlantic, while to the right lay the Bay of Cádiz. The edge of the bay looked white in the dusk, and the whiteness was interrupted by hundreds of shining pyramids. "Salt," Lord William explained. "Big industry here, lots of salt."

Sharpe suddenly felt ashamed of his ragged uniform. "I thought British soldiers weren't allowed in the city?"

"Officers are, but only officers. The Spaniards are terrified that if we put a garrison into the city we'd never leave. They think we'd turn the place into another Gibraltar. Oh, there is one rather important thing you ought to know, Sharpe."

"What's that, my lord?"

"Call me Willie, for God's sake, everyone else does. And the one absolutely important thing, the one never-to-be-forgotten thing, and do not break this rule even if you're drunk to the roof beams, is never ever mention the ambassador's wife."

Sharpe looked at the ebullient Lord William with bemusement. "Why would I?" he asked.

"You mustn't," Lord William said energetically, "because it would be in the most frightfully bad taste. She's called Charlotte and she ran away. Charlotte the Harlot. She scampered off with Harry Paget. It was awful really. A horrible scandal. If you spend any time in the city you're going to see a few of these"—he fished in a pocket and brought out a brooch. "There," Lord William said, tossing the object to Sharpe.

The brooch was a cheap little thing made of bone. It showed a pair of horns. Sharpe looked at it and shrugged. "Cow horns?"

"The horns of the cuckold, Sharpe. That's what they call the ambassador, **el Cornudo.** Our political enemies wear that badge to mock him, poor man. He takes it well, but I'm sure it hurts. So, for God's sake, don't ask about Charlotte the Harlot, there's a good fellow."

"I'm not likely to, am I?" Sharpe asked. "I don't even know the man."

"But of course you do!" Lord William said cheerfully. "He knows you."

"Me? How?"

"You really don't know who His Brittanic Majesty's Envoy Extraordinary to Spain is?"

"Of course I don't know!"

"Youngest brother to the foreign secretary?" Lord William said, and saw that Sharpe still did not know who he meant. "He's also Arthur Wellesley's little brother."

"Arthur Wellesley's . . . you mean Lord Wellington?"

"Lord Wellington's brother indeed," Lord William said, "and it gets worse. Charlotte ran off with the ghastly Paget and Henry got a divorce, which meant he had to have an act of Parliament passed and that, believe me, was a deal of trouble, so then Henry comes here and meets this damnably attractive girl. He thought she was respectable and she absolutely wasn't, and he wrote her some letters. Poor Henry. And she's a pretty thing, terrifically pretty! Much prettier than Charlotte the Harlot, but the whole thing is completely embarrassing and we all pretend none of it has ever happened. So say nothing, Sharpe, absolutely nothing. Soul of discretion, Sharpe, that's the thing to be. Soul of discretion." He fell silent because they had come to the massive gates and huge bastions that guarded the city's southern entrance. There were sentries, muskets, bayonets, and long-muzzled cannons in embrasures. Lord William had to produce a pass. Only then did the vast gates crash open and Sharpe could thread the walls and arches and tunnels of the ramparts until he found himself in the narrow streets of the sea-bound city. He had come to Cádiz.

Sharpe, to his surprise, liked Henry Wellesley. He was a slender man in his late thirties and handsome like his elder brother, though his nose was less hooked and his chin was broader. He had none of Lord Wellington's cold arrogance. Instead he seemed diffident and even gentle. He stood as Sharpe came into the embassy's dining room and appeared to be genuinely pleased to see the rifleman. "My dear fellow," he said, "have a seat here. You know the brigadier, of course?"

"I do, sir."

Moon gave Sharpe a very cold look and not so much as a nod.

"And allow me to name Sir Thomas Graham," Henry Wellesley said. "Lieutenant General Sir Thomas Graham who commands our garrison on the Isla de León."

"Honored to make your acquaintance, Sharpe," Sir Thomas said. He was a tall, well-built Scotsman with white hair, a sun-beaten face, and very shrewd eyes.

"And I believe you already know William Pumphrey," Wellesley said as he introduced the last man at the table.

"Good lord," Sharpe said involuntarily. He did know Lord Pumphrey, but was still astonished to see him. Lord Pumphrey, meanwhile, blew Sharpe a kiss off the tips of his fingers.

"Don't embarrass our guest, Pumps," Henry Wellesley said, though too late because Sharpe was already embarrassed. Lord Pumphrey had that effect on him, and on a good number of other men too. He was Foreign Office, that much Sharpe knew, and Sharpe had met his lordship in Copenhagen and then in northern Portugal, and Pumphrey was still as outrageous as ever. This night he was dressed in a lilac-colored coat embroidered with silver thread, and on his thin cheek was a black velvet beauty patch. "William is our principal secretary here," Henry Wellesley explained.

"Actually, Richard, I was posted here to astonish the natives," Lord Pumphrey said languidly.

"At which you're bloody successful," Sir Thomas said.

"You are too kind, Sir Thomas," Lord Pumphrey said, giving the Scotsman an inclination of his head, "altogether too kind."

Henry Wellesley sat and pushed a dish toward Sharpe. "Do try the crab claws," he urged. "They're a local delicacy, collected from the marshes. You crack them and suck the flesh out."

"I'm sorry I'm late, sir," Sharpe said. It was plain from the wreckage on the table that the dinner was over, and equally obvious that Henry Wellesley had eaten nothing. He saw Sharpe glance at his clean plate.

"I have a formal dinner to attend, Sharpe," the ambassador explained, "and Spanish dinners start extraordinarily late, and I really can't eat two dinners every night. Still, that crab does tempt me." He took a claw and used a nutcracker to open the shell. Sharpe realized that the ambassador had only split the claw to show him how it was done, and he gratefully picked up a pair of nutcrackers himself. "So how is your head, Sharpe?" Henry Wellesley asked.

"Mending, sir, thank you."

"Nasty things, head wounds," the ambassador said. "I had an assistant in India who cracked his head open and I thought the poor fellow was dead. But he was up and about, quite cured, in a week."

"You were in India, sir?" Sharpe asked.

"Twice," Henry Wellesley said. "On the civil side, of course. I liked the place."

"I did too, sir," Sharpe said. He was ravenous and cracked open another claw, which he dipped into a bowl of melted butter. Lord William Russell, thankfully, was just as hungry and the two of them shared the dish as the other men took cigars.

It was February, but warm enough for the windows to be open. Brigadier Moon said nothing, content to glower at Sharpe while Sir Thomas Graham complained bitterly about his Spanish allies. "The extra ships haven't come from the Balearics," he grumbled, "and I've not seen any of the maps they promised."

"I'm sure both will come," Henry Wellesley said.

"And the ships we've already got are threatened by fire rafts. The French are building five of the things."

"I'm certain you and Admiral Keats will be delighted to deal with the fire rafts," Henry Wellesley said firmly, then changed the topic by looking at Sharpe. "Brigadier Moon tells me you got rid of the bridge over the Guadiana?"

"We did, sir."

"That's a relief. All in all, Sir Barnaby"—Wellesley looked at the brigadier—"a most successful operation."

Moon shifted in his chair, then winced as pain stabbed at his leg. "It could have gone better, Your Excellency."

"How so?"

"You'd need to be a soldier to understand," Moon said abruptly. Sir Thomas frowned in disapproval of the brigadier's rudeness, but Moon would not yield an inch. "At best," he went on, "it was only a flawed success. A very flawed success."

"I served in the 40th Foot," Henry Wellesley said. "It was not, perhaps, my finest hour, but I am not ignorant of soldiering. So tell me why it was flawed, Sir Barnaby?"

"Things could have gone better," Moon said as though that closed the matter.

The ambassador took a cut cigar from a servant, then bent to light it from the proffered taper. "And there I was," he said, "inviting you to tell us of your triumph. You're as reticent as my brother, Sir Barnaby."

"I'm flattered to be compared with Lord Wellington, Your Excellency," Moon said stiffly.

"Mind you, Arthur did once tell me of an exploit of his," Henry Wellesley said, "and it's not one from which he emerges with very much credit." The ambassador blew a plume of smoke toward the crystal chandelier. Sir Thomas and Lord Pumphrey were sitting very still, as if they knew something was brewing in the room, while Sharpe, sensing the strained atmosphere, left the crab claws alone. "He was unhorsed at Assaye," the ambassador went on. "I think that's the name of the place. Whatever, he was pitched into the enemy ranks, and everyone else had galloped on and Arthur told me he knew he was going to die. He was surrounded by the enemy, all of them fierce as thieves, and then from nowhere a British sergeant appears. From nowhere, he says!" Henry Wellesley waved the cigar as though he were a magician who had suddenly made it appear. "And what followed, Arthur says, was the finest piece of soldiering he ever witnessed. He reckons that sergeant put down five men. At least five men, he told me. The fellow slaughtered them! All on his own."

"Five men!" Lord Pumphrey said in unfeigned admiration.

"At least five," the ambassador said.

"Recollection of battle," Moon said, "can be very confusing."

"Oh! You think Arthur embellished the tale?" Henry Wellesley asked with exaggerated politeness.

"One man against five?" Moon suggested. "I'd be very surprised, Your Excellency."

"Then let us ask the sergeant who fought against them," Henry Wellesley said, springing his trap. "How many men do you remember, Sharpe?"

Moon looked as if he had been stung by a wasp while Sharpe, embarrassed again, just shrugged.

"Well, Sharpe?" Sir Thomas Graham prompted him.

"There were a few, sir," Sharpe said uncomfortably. "But of course the general was fighting beside me, sir."

"Arthur told me he was dazed," Henry Wellesley said. "He told me he was quite incapable of defending himself."

"Fighting away, sir, he was," Sharpe said. In truth Sharpe had pushed a dizzied Sir Arthur Wellesley under one of the Indian cannons and had sheltered him there. Was it truly five men?

He could not remember. "And help came very fast, sir," he went on hurriedly, "very fast."

"But as you say, Sir Barnaby"—Henry Wellesley's voice was silky now—"recollections of battle can be very confusing. I would take it as a favor if you would permit me to see the report on your great triumph at Fort Joseph."

"Of course, Your Excellency," Moon said, and Sharpe understood then what had happened. His Majesty's Envoy Extraordinary and Minister Plenipotentiary had intervened on Sharpe's behalf, letting Moon know that Lord Wellington was beholden to Sharpe and that it would be sensible if the brigadier were to change his report accordingly. That was a favor, and it was a generous one, but Sharpe knew that favors were given so that other favors could be returned.

A clock on the mantelpiece struck ten and Henry Wellesley sighed. "I must put on fancy dress for our allies," he said. There was a scraping of chairs as the guests stood. "Do finish the port and the cigars," the ambassador said as he moved toward the door where he paused. "Mister Sharpe? Might I have a word?"

Sharpe followed Henry Wellesley down the passage and into a small room lit by candles. A coal fire burned in the hearth, books lined the walls, and a leather-topped desk stood under the window that the ambassador pushed open. "The Spanish servants insist on keeping me warm," he said. "I tell them I prefer cold air, but they don't believe me. Did I embarrass you back there?"

"No, sir."

"It was for Brigadier Moon's benefit. He told me you had let him down, which I somehow doubt. He is a man who is unable to share credit, I think." The ambassador opened a cupboard and took out a dark bottle. "Port, Sharpe. It's Taylor's best and you won't get finer this side of paradise. May I pour you a glass?"

"Thank you, sir."

"And there are cigars in the silver box. You should have one. My doctor says they're good for the wind." Henry Wellesley poured a single glass of port, which he handed to Sharpe. Then he walked to an elegant round table that served as a chess board. He stared at the pieces, which were in midgame. "I think I'm in trouble," he said. "Do you play?"

"No, sir."

"I play with Duff. He was consul here and he's rather good." The ambassador touched a black castle with a tentative finger, then abandoned the game to sit behind his desk from where he gave the rifleman a shrewd inspection. "I doubt my brother ever thanked you adequately for saving his life." He waited for an answer, but Sharpe was silent. "Obviously not. That sounds like Arthur."

"He gave me a very fine telescope, sir," Sharpe said.

"Doubtless one that had been given to him," Henry Wellesley suggested, "and that he didn't want?"

"I'm sure that's not true, sir," Sharpe said.

Wellesley smiled. "My brother has many virtues, but the ability to express sentiment is not among them. If it is any consolation, Sharpe, he has frequently expressed his admiration of your qualities."

"Thank you, sir," Sharpe said awkwardly.

The ambassador sighed, suggesting that the pleasantest part of the conversation was now done. He hesitated, as if looking for words, then opened a drawer and found a small object that he tossed across the desk's leather top. It was one of the horned brooches. "Know what that is, Sharpe?"

"I'm afraid I do, sir."

"I rather thought Willie Russell would tell you. And how about this?" He pushed a newspaper across the desk. Sharpe picked it up, saw it was called **El Correo de Cádiz,** but the light was too dark and the print too small to attempt to read the ill-printed sheet. He put the paper down. "Have you seen that?" the ambassador asked.

"No, sir."

"It appeared on the streets today and it purports to print a letter I am supposed to have sent to a lady. In the letter I tell her that the British plan to annex Cádiz and make it into a second Gibraltar. It does not name me, but in a city as small as Cádiz it hardly needs to. And I need hardly tell you that His Majesty's government has no designs on Cádiz either."

"So the letter's a forgery, sir?" Sharpe asked.

Henry Wellesley paused. "Not entirely," he said cautiously. He was not looking at Sharpe now, but had twisted in his chair to stare into the dark garden. He drew on his cigar. "I imagine Willie Russell told you of my circumstances?"

"Yes, sir."

"So I shall not describe them further except to say that some months ago I met a lady here and was persuaded that she was of gentle birth. She came from the Spanish colonies and assured me her father was wealthy, respectable indeed, but he was not. And before I discovered that truth I was foolish enough to express my sentiments in letters." He paused, still staring through the open window, waiting for Sharpe to speak, but Sharpe was silent. "The letters were stolen from her," the ambassador went on, "and it was not her fault." He turned and gazed at Sharpe defiantly, as if he half expected Sharpe to disbelieve him.

"And the thief, sir, tried to blackmail you?"

"Exactly," Henry Wellesley said. "The wretch made an arrangement to sell the letters to me, but my envoy was murdered. He and his two companions. The money, of course, vanished and the letters are now in the hands of our political enemies." Wellesley spoke bitterly and gave the newspaper a blow with his hand. "You must understand, Sharpe, that there are men in Cádiz who believe, quite sincerely, that Spain's future would be a great deal brighter if they were to make peace with Napoleon. They believe that Britain is the more formidable enemy. They think we are intent on destroying Spain's colonies and on taking her Atlantic trade. They do not believe that my brother can expel the French from Portugal, let alone from Spain, and they are working diligently to fashion a political future that does not include a British alliance. My job is to persuade them otherwise, and those letters are going to make the task much harder. It may even make it impossible." Again he paused as if inviting some comment from Sharpe, but the rifleman sat very still and silent. "Lord Pumphrey tells me you are an able man," the ambassador said quietly.

"He's very kind, sir," Sharpe said woodenly.

"And he says you have a piquant past."

"Not sure what that is, sir."

Henry Wellesley half smiled. "Forgive me if I'm wrong and believe my assurance that I am not trying to give offense, but Lord Pumphrey tells me you were once a thief?"

"I was, sir," Sharpe admitted.

"What else?"

Sharpe hesitated, then decided the ambassador had been honest with him so he would return the compliment. "Thief, murderer, soldier, sergeant, rifleman," he said the list flatly, though Henry Wellesley detected pride in the words.

"Our enemies, Sharpe," Wellesley said, "have printed one letter, but say they are willing to sell the rest to me. The price, I have no doubt, will be extortionate, but they have intimated that they will publish no more if I pay their price. Lord

Pumphrey is negotiating on my behalf. If an agreement is reached, then I would be most grateful if you would serve as his escort and his protector when the letters are exchanged for the money."

Sharpe thought about it. "You say that your previous fellow was murdered, sir?"

"He was called Plummer. The thieves claimed he tried to take the letters without surrendering the gold, and I have to say that sounds plausible. Captain Plummer was a belligerent man, God rest his soul. They knifed him and his two companions in the cathedral, then threw their bodies over the seawall."

"What's to say they won't do it again, sir?"

Wellesley shrugged. "Captain Plummer may have antagonized them. And he certainly wasn't an accredited diplomat. Lord Pumphrey is. Murdering Lord Pumphrey, I can assure you, would invoke a most vigorous response. And your presence, I dare say, might deter them."

Sharpe ignored that compliment. "One other question, sir. You mentioned I was a thief. What's that to do with keeping Lord Pumphrey alive?"

Henry Wellesley looked embarrassed. "If Lord Pumphrey fails to reach an agreement I was hoping the letters could be stolen back."

"You know where they are, sir?"

"I assume at the place where the newspaper is printed."

It seemed a huge assumption to Sharpe, but he let it go. "How many letters are there, sir?"

"They have fifteen."

"There are more?"

"I wrote more, I fear, but they only stole fifteen."

"So the girl has more, sir?"

"I'm sure she doesn't," Henry Wellesley said stiffly. "Perhaps only fifteen survived."

Sharpe was aware that something was not being said, but he reckoned that pushing the ambassador would not reveal it. "Thieving's a skilled trade, sir," he said instead, "and blackmail's a nasty one. I need men. We're dealing with killers, sir, so I need my own killers."

"I have no men to offer," the ambassador said, shrugging, "with Plummer dead."

"I've five riflemen with me, sir, and they'll do. But they need to be here, in the city, and they need civilian clothes, and they need a letter from you to Lord Wellington saying that they're here on duty. I need that most of all, sir."

"All agreed," Henry Wellesley said with relief in his voice.

"And I need to speak to the lady, sir. No point in stealing one set of letters if there's another lot waiting."

"I'm afraid I don't know where she is," the ambassador said. "If I knew then I would, of course, tell you. She appears to have hidden herself."

"I still need her name, sir."

"Caterina," Henry Wellesley said wistfully. "Caterina Blazquez." He rubbed his face with a hand. "I feel very foolish telling you all this."

"We've all made fools of ourselves over women, sir," Sharpe said. "We wouldn't be alive if we hadn't."

Wellesley smiled ruefully at that. "But if Lord Pumphrey negotiates successfully," he said, "then it will all be over. A lesson learned."

"And if he doesn't, sir, then you want me to steal the letters?"

"I hope it doesn't come to that," Wellesley said. He stood and spun his cigar into the night where it hit the dark lawn with a shower of sparks. "I really must get dressed. Full court uniform, sword and all. But one last thing, Sharpe."

"Sir?" Sharpe asked. He knew he should call the ambassador "Your Excellency," but he kept forgetting and Wellesley did not seem to mind.

"We live, breathe, and have our very being in this city by permission of the Spanish. That is as it should be. So whatever you do, Sharpe, do it carefully. And please don't mention this to anyone but Lord Pumphrey. He alone is privy to the negotiations." That was not true. There was another man who might help, who would help, though Henry Wellesley doubted that he would succeed. Which left him dependent on this scarred and bandaged rogue.

"I won't mention it, sir," Sharpe said.

"Then good night, Sharpe."

"Good night, sir."

Lord Pumphrey, smelling faintly of violets, was waiting in the hall. "Well, Richard?"

"It seems I've got a job here."

"I'm so pleased. Shall we talk?" Lord Pumphrey led Sharpe down the candlelit corridor. "Was it really five men, Richard? Be truthful. Five?"

"Seven," Sharpe said, though he could not remember. Nor did it matter. He was a thief, he was a murderer, he was a soldier, and now he had a blackmailer to settle.

Part Two
The City

Chapter 4

Sharpe was given a room in the embassy's attic. The roof was flat and it had leaked badly at some time for a great patch of plaster was missing and the rest was dangerously cracked. A jug of water stood on a small table and a chamber pot lay beneath the bed. Lord Pumphrey had apologized for the accommodation. "The consul here in Cádiz rented the premises for us. Six houses in all. I have one of them, but I think you'd be happier staying in the embassy itself."

"I would," Sharpe had said hurriedly.

"I thought as much. Then I shall meet you at five tomorrow evening."

"And I need some civilian clothes," Sharpe had told His Lordship, and when he went to bed he found a pair of trousers, a shirt, and a coat laid out for him. He suspected the clothes had belonged to the unfortunate Plummer. They were black, too big, stiff, and slightly damp, as if they had never dried properly after being washed.

He left the embassy at six in the morning. He knew that because a score of church bells rang the hour, their sound cacophonous in the rising wind. He carried neither sword nor rifle, for both weapons were conspicuous, though he had borrowed a pistol from the embassy. "You won't need it," Lord Pumphrey had said the previous night.

"Don't like being unarmed," Sharpe had retorted.

"You know best, I'm sure," Pumphrey had said, "but for God's sake don't startle the natives. They mistrust us enough as it is."

"I'm just exploring," Sharpe had said. There was nothing else for him to do. Lord Pumphrey was waiting for a message from the blackmailers. Who those blackmailers were, no one knew, but the appearance of the letter in the newspaper pointed to the political faction most desperate to break the British alliance. "If your negotiations fail," Sharpe had said, "then that newspaper is where we start."

"My negotiations never fail," Lord Pumphrey averred grandly.

"I'll still have a look at the newspaper," Sharpe insisted, and so he had left in the early morning and, though he had been given careful directions, was soon lost. Cádiz was a maze of narrow dark alleys and high buildings. No one could use a carriage here for few streets were wide enough so the wealthy either rode, were carried in sedan chairs, or walked.

The sun had not yet risen and the city was asleep. The few folk awake had probably not yet gone to bed or else were servants sweeping courtyards or carrying firewood. A cat writhed about Sharpe's ankles and he stooped to pet it, then headed down another cobbled alleyway at the end of which he found what he wanted outside a church. A beggar slept on the steps, and he woke the man and gave him a whole guinea along with Plummer's cloak and hat. In return he got the beggar's cloak and wide-brimmed hat. Both were greasy and matted with filth.

He walked toward his few glimpses of the dawn and found himself on the city rampart. Its outer face fell steeply to the harbor wharves, but the firestep was almost on the same level as the city's streets. He walked along the wide top where dark cannons hunched behind embrasures. A spark of light showed across the water on the Trocadero Peninsula where the French had their giant mortars. A company of Spanish soldiers was posted on the wall, but at least half were snoring. Dogs foraged along the rampart's edge.

The whole world, like the city, seemed asleep, but then an explosion of light ripped the eastern horizon in two. The light spread flat, like a disk, sudden and white to silhouette the few ships anchored near the wharves, and then the light faded, the last of it writhing in a great blossom of smoke that billowed above one of the French forts, and then the noise came. A thunder rolled over the bay, startling sleeping sentries awake as the shell landed just across the ramparts, a quarter mile ahead of Sharpe. There was a brief silence before the missile exploded. A wavering trace of smoke, left by the burning fuse, hung in the first daylight. The shell had blown itself apart inside a small grove of orange trees and Sharpe, when he reached the spot, could smell the powder smoke. He kicked a shard of broken casing that skittered down the rampart. Then he jumped down to the scorched grass and crossed the grove into a dark street. The house walls were a dirty white now as dawn glowed in the east.

He was lost, but he was at the city's northern edge where he wanted to be. By exploring the narrow streets he at last found the church with the red-painted crucifix on its outer wall. Lord Pumphrey had told him the crucifix had been brought from Venezuela and it was believed that on the Feast of Saint Vincent the red paint turned to blood. Sharpe wondered when the saint's feast day was. He would like to see paint turn to blood.

He squatted on the bottom step of the church entrance. The filthy cloak swathed him and the wide hat hid his face. The street here was just five paces wide, and almost opposite him was a four-storied house marked by a stone scallop shell cemented into the white facade. An alley ran down the side of the house that had an ornate front door flanked by two windows. The windows were shuttered on the inside while outside the glass were thick black-painted grilles. The upper floors had three windows apiece facing onto narrow balconies. This, Pumphrey had assured him, was where **El Correo de Cádiz** was printed.

"The house belongs to a man called Nuñez, who owns the newspaper. He lives above the printing premises."

No one stirred in the Nuñez house. Sharpe squatted, unmoving, with a wooden bowl taken from the embassy kitchen beside him on the step. He had put a handful of coins in the bowl, remembering that that was the way to encourage generosity, though as the street stayed empty there was no generosity to encourage. He thought about the beggars of his childhood. Blind Michael, who could see like a hawk, and Ragged Kate, who hired babies for tuppence an hour and plucked at the shawls of well-dressed women in the Strand. She had carried a hat pin to make the babies cry and on a good day she had sometimes made two or three pounds that she would drink away in an evening. There had been Stinking Moses who claimed to have been a parson before he fell into debt. He would tell folks' fortunes for a shilling. "Always tell them they'll be lucky in love, boy," he had advised Sharpe, " 'cuz they'd rather be lucky in bed than get to heaven."

It was oddly restful. Sharpe squatted and, when the first pedestrians appeared, he mumbled the words Pumphrey had suggested. **"Por**

favor, Madre de Dios." He said the words over
and over, occasionally muttering thanks when a
copper coin rattled into the bowl. And all the
time he watched the house with the scallop shell,
and he noted that the big front door was never
used and that the shutters behind the heavy window grilles were never opened even though the
other houses in the street opened their shutters
to take advantage of what small light found its
way between the high buildings. Six men came
to the house and all used a side door down the
alley. Late in the morning Sharpe moved there,
muttering his incantation as he went, and he
squatted again, this time just inside the alley's
mouth, and watched a man go to the side door
and knock. A hatch slid open, a question was
asked, it was evidently answered satisfactorily,
and the door opened. In the next hour three
porters delivered crates and a woman brought a
bundle of laundry. The same hatch was slid open
each time before the visitors were allowed inside.
The laundress dropped a coin in Sharpe's bowl.
"Gracias," he said.

Around midmorning a priest came out of the
alley door. He was tall and lantern-jawed. He
dropped a coin in Sharpe's bowl and at the same
time gave a command that Sharpe did not un-

derstand, but the priest pointed to the church and Sharpe assumed he had been ordered to move out of the alleyway. He picked up his bowl and shuffled toward the church, and there saw trouble waiting.

Three beggars had taken his place on the steps. All were men. At least half the male beggars in Cádiz were cripples, survivors of battles against the British or the French. They were limbless, scarred, and ulcerous. Some wore placards with the names of the battles where they had been wounded, while others proudly wore the remnants of their uniforms, but none of the three waiting men was crippled or wore uniforms, and all three were watching Sharpe.

He had trespassed. The beggars in London were as organized as any battalion. If a man took post where other beggars had their usual pitches, then the man would be warned, and if he did not heed the warning, the beggar-lords would be summoned from their lairs. Stinking Moses had always worked the church of St. Martins in the Fields, and he had once been robbed by two sailors who had kicked him across the street to the door of the workhouse, where they had taken his coins, then taken his place on the church steps. Next morning Stinking Moses was back at the church and two corpses were found in Moons Yard.

These three men were on a similar mission. They said nothing as Sharpe emerged from the alley, but just surrounded him. One took his bowl and the remaining two held his elbows and hurried him westward until they reached a shadowed archway. "**Madre de Dios,**" Sharpe mumbled. He was still crouching as though he had a wounded spine.

The man holding the bowl demanded to know who Sharpe was. Sharpe did not understand the man's fast and colloquial Spanish, but guessed that was what the man wanted to know, just as he guessed what was coming next. It was a knife that came from under the man's ragged cloak and flashed up toward Sharpe's throat. At that moment the apparently crippled beggar turned into a soldier. Sharpe seized the man's wrist and kept the knife moving upward, but now toward its owner, and Sharpe was smiling as the blade slid easily into the soft flesh under the man's chin. He gave the wrist one last jerk so that the knife went through the man's tongue into his palate. The man made a mewling noise as blood spilled from his lips. Sharpe, who had easily freed his right arm, now pulled his left free as the man on that side launched a massive kick and Sharpe seized the boot and pushed it upward so that the man flew back, to fall hard on the cobbles, his skull making a sound like a musket butt dropped on stone. Sharpe elbowed the third man between the eyes. It had taken seconds. The first man was staring with wide eyes at Sharpe, who now drew his pistol. The man who had fallen was now on his knees, groggy. The second man had blood pouring from his nose and the pistol was pointing at the leader's groin. Sharpe cocked the gun and, in the archway, the sound was ominous.

The man, with his own knife still pinning his mouth shut, put down the bowl. He held his hands out as if to ward off trouble. "Bugger off," Sharpe said in English and, though they did not understand, they obeyed. They backed away slowly until Sharpe leveled the pistol, and then they ran.

"Bugger," Sharpe said. His head was throbbing. He touched the bandage and flinched from the pain. He crouched and scooped up the coins. When he stood, there was a heartbeat and he felt faint, so he leaned at the archway's side and looked up, because that seemed to alleviate the pain. There was a cross incised into the keystone

of the arch. He stared at it until the pain re-
ceded. He put away the pistol, which, carelessly,
he was still holding, though the arch was deep
enough to hide him from the few pedestrians
who passed. He noticed weeds growing at the
foot of the gates, which were secured by a big
old-fashioned ball padlock, like the one that had
guarded the Marquesa's boathouse. This padlock was rusted. He went out into the street and
saw that the building's windows were shuttered
and barred. A watchtower rose above the building, and more weeds grew between the tower's
stones. The building was abandoned and no
more than forty paces from Nuñez's house. "Perfect," he said aloud, and a woman leading a goat
on a length of rope made the sign of the cross because she thought he was mad.

It was close to midday. He spent a long time
searching the streets for the merchant he
wanted, and had to bundle the filthy cloak and
hat under his arm before going into the shop,
where he bought a new padlock. The lock had
been made in Britain and had wards inside the
steel case to protect the levers from picks. The
shopkeeper charged him too much, probably because his customer was English, but Sharpe did
not argue. The money was not his, but had been

given him by Lord Pumphrey from the embassy's cash box.

He went back to the miraculous crucifix and settled on the steps under its stone canopy. He knew the three men would be back, or two of them would be back, but not until they had rousted up reinforcements, and he reckoned that gave him an hour or two. A dog investigated the interesting smells of his borrowed cloak, then pissed against the wall. Women came and went to the church and most dropped small coins into his bowl. Another beggar, a woman, whined at the far side of the steps. She tried to engage Sharpe in conversation, but all he would say was "Mother of God," and she abandoned her attempts. He just watched the house and wondered how he could ever hope to steal anything from inside, if indeed, the letters were even there. The place was plainly well guarded, and he suspected that the front door and the ground-floor windows had been blocked. A monk had been calling house to house, probably collecting for charity, and the man had hammered unavailingly on the door until the lantern-jawed priest had appeared from the alleyway. He shouted at the monk to go away. So the front door could not be opened, and that suggested it had been barricaded, as had the two barred windows. The French mortars fired twice more, but neither of the shells came anywhere near the street where Sharpe was waiting. He sat on the steps until the streets emptied as folk went for their siesta, then he shuffled back to the abandoned building where the three men had tried to rob him. He cracked the ball padlock with a loose cobblestone, unthreaded the chain, and went inside.

He found himself in a small cloistered courtyard. One part of the cloisters had collapsed and the stonework of the rest was scorched. There was a small chapel to one side and something had plunged through its roof and burned everything inside. A French mortar shell? Except, as far as Sharpe could see, the big French mortars did not have the range to reach this far into the city and, besides, this damage was old. There was mold growing on the scorch marks and weeds between the flagstones of the chapel floor.

He climbed the watchtower steps. The city's skyline was punctuated by the towers, close to two hundred of them, and Sharpe supposed they had been built so merchants could watch for their ships beating in from the Atlantic. Or perhaps the first of them had been built when Cádiz was young, when the Romans had garrisoned

the peninsula and watched for Carthaginian pirates. Then the Moors had taken Cádiz and they
had watched for Christian raiders, and when the
Spaniards at last took the city for themselves
they had watched for English buccaneers. They
had called Sir Francis Drake **el Draco,** and the
dragon had come to Cádiz and burned most of
the old city, and so the towers had been rebuilt,
tower after tower, because Cádiz was never short
of enemies.

This tower was six stories high. The top floor
was a roofed platform with a stone balustrade
and Sharpe eased his head over the parapet very
slowly so that no one watching would see a sudden movement. He peered eastward and saw he
had been right and that this was the perfect place
to watch Nuñez's house, which was just fifty
paces away and joined to the abandoned building by other houses, all with flat roofs. Most of
the city's houses had flat roofs, places to enjoy
the sun that rarely reached into the deep, narrow, balcony-blocked ravines of the streets. The
chimneys cast black shadows and it was in one of
those shadows that Sharpe saw the sentinel on
Nuñez's house: one man, dark cloaked, sitting
with a musket across his knees.

Sharpe watched for the best part of an hour

during which the man hardly moved. The French mortars had stopped firing, but far off to the south and east there was the bloom of gunsmoke beyond the marshes where the French besiegers faced the small British army that protected Cádiz's isthmus. The sound of the guns was muted, a mere grumble of distant thunder, and then that too died away.

Sharpe went back to the street where he closed the gates, put the chain back, and used his new padlock to secure it. He thrust the key into a pocket and walked east and south, away from Nuñez's house. He kept the ocean on his right, knowing that would bring him to the cathedral where he was to meet Lord Pumphrey. He thought about Jack Bullen as he walked. Poor Jack, a prisoner, and he remembered the burst of smoke from Vandal's musket. There was a revenge waiting. His head hurt. Sometimes a stab of pain blackened the sight in his right eye, which was odd, because the wound was on the left side of his scalp. He arrived early at the cathedral, so he sat on the seawall and watched the great rollers come from the Atlantic to break on the rocks and suck back white. A small band of men was negotiating the jagged reef that extended west from the city and ended in a lighthouse. He could see they were carrying burdens, presumably fuel for the fire that was lit nightly on the lighthouse platform. They hesitated between rocks, jumping only when the sea drew back and the white foam drained from the stones.

A clock struck five and he walked to the cathedral, which, even unfinished, loomed massively above the smaller houses. Its roof was half covered in tarpaulins so it was hard to tell what it would look like when it was complete, but for now it looked ugly, a brutal mass of gray-brown stone broken by few windows and spidery with scaffolding. The entrance, which fronted onto a narrow street piled with masonry, was approached by a fine flight of stairs where Lord Pumphrey waited, fending off the beggars with an ivory-tipped cane. "Good God, Richard," His Lordship said as he greeted Sharpe, "where did you get that cloak?"

"Off a beggar."

Lord Pumphrey was soberly dressed, though a smell of lavenders wafted from his dark coat and long black cloak. "Have you had a useful day?" he asked lightly, as he used the cane to part the beggars and reach the door.

"Maybe. All depends, doesn't it, whether the letters are in that newspaper place?"

"I trust it doesn't come to that," Lord Pumphrey said. "I trust our blackmailers will contact me."

"They haven't yet?"

"Not yet," Pumphrey said. He dipped a forefinger in the stoup of holy water and wafted it across his forehead. "I'm no papist, of course, but it does no harm to pretend, does it? The message hinted that our opponents are willing to sell us the letters, but only for a great deal of money. Isn't it ghastly?" This last question referred to the cathedral interior, which did not seem ghastly to Sharpe, just splendid and ornate and huge. He was staring down a long nave flanked by clusters of pillars. Off the side aisles were rows of chapels bright with painted statues, gilded altars, and candles lit by the faithful. "They've been building it for ninety-something years," Lord Pumphrey said, "and work has now more or less stopped because of the war. I suppose they'll finish it all one day. Hat off."

Sharpe snatched off his hat. "Did you write to Sir Thomas?"

"I did." Lord Pumphrey had promised to

write a note requesting that Sharpe's riflemen be kept on the Isla de León rather than be put on a ship heading north to Lisbon. The wind had gone southerly during the day and some ships had already headed north.

"I'll fetch my men tonight," Sharpe said.

"They'll have to be quartered in the stables," Pumphrey said, "and pretend to be embassy servants. We are going to the crossing."

"The crossing?"

"The place where the transept crosses the nave. There's a crypt beneath it."

"Where Plummer died?"

"Where Plummer died. Isn't that what you wanted to see?"

The farther end of the cathedral was still unbuilt. A plain brick wall rose where, one day, the sanctuary and high altar would stand. The crossing, just in front of the plain wall, was an airy high space with soaring pillars at each corner. Above Sharpe now was the unfinished dome where a few men worked on scaffolding that climbed each cluster of pillars and then spread about the base of the dome. A makeshift crane was fixed high in the dome's scaffolding and two men were hauling up a wooden platform loaded with masonry. "I thought you said they'd stopped building," Sharpe said.

"I suppose they must do repairs," Lord Pumphrey said airily. He led Sharpe past a pulpit behind which an archway had been built into one of the massive pillars. A flight of steps disappeared downward. "Captain Plummer met his end down there." Lord Pumphrey gestured at the steps. "I try to feel sorrow at his passing, but I must say he was a most obnoxious man. You wish to descend?"

"Of course."

"I very much doubt they will choose this place again," His Lordship said.

"Depends what they want," Sharpe said.

"Meaning?"

"If they want us dead then they'll choose this place. It worked for them once, so why not use it again?" He led the way down the stairs and so emerged into an extraordinary chamber. It was circular with a low-domed ceiling. An altar lay at one end of the chamber. Three women knelt in front of the crucifix, beads busy in their fingers, staring up at the crucified Christ as Pumphrey tiptoed to the crypt's center. Once there he put a finger to his lips and Sharpe assumed His Lordship was being reverent, but instead Pumphrey rapped his cane sharply on the floor and the sound echoed and reechoed. "Isn't it amazing?" Lord Pumphrey asked. "Amazing," the echo said, and then again, and again, and again. One of the women turned and scowled, but His Lordship just smiled at her and offered an elegant bow. "You can sing in harmony with yourself here," Pumphrey said. "Would you like to try?"

Sharpe was more interested in the archways leading from the big chamber. There were five. The center one led to another chapel, which had an altar lit by candles, while the remaining four were dark caverns. He explored the nearest one and discovered a passage leading from it. The passage circled the big chamber, going from cavern to cavern. "Clever bastards, aren't they?" he said to Lord Pumphrey who had followed him.

"Clever?"

"Plummer must have died in the middle of the big chamber, yes?"

"That's where the blood was, certainly. You can still see it if you look carefully."

"And the bastards must have been in these side chambers. And you can never tell which one they're in because they can go around the passage. There's only one reason for meeting in a

place like this. It's a killing ground. You're negotiating with the bastards? You tell them to meet
us in a public place, in daylight."

"I suspect we have reason to indulge them,
rather than the other way around."

"Whatever that means," Sharpe said. "How
much money are we talking about?"

"At least a thousand guineas. At least. Probably much more."

"Bloody hell!" Sharpe said, then gave a hu-
morless laugh. "That'll teach the ambassador to
choose his women more carefully."

"Henry paid the three hundred guineas that
Plummer lost," Pumphrey said, "but he can well
afford it. The man who stole his wife had to pay
him a fortune. But from now it will be the government's money."

"Why?"

"Because once our enemies published a letter
it became a matter of public policy. This business
is no longer about Henry's unfortunate choice of
bedmate, but about British policy toward Spain.
Perhaps that's why they printed the one letter. It
put up the price and opened His Majesty's purse
strings. If that was their motive, then I must say
it was rather clever of them."

Sharpe walked back to the central chamber.

He imagined enemies hidden all around, enemies who were moving through the hidden passage, enemies threatening from a new archway every few seconds. Plummer and his companions would have been like rats in a pit, never knowing which hole the terriers would come from. "Suppose they do sell you the letters," he said. "What's to stop them keeping copies and publishing them anyway?"

"They will undertake not to. That is one of our immutable conditions."

"Immutable rubbish," Sharpe said scornfully. "You're not dealing with other diplomats, but with bloody blackmailers!"

"I know, Richard," Pumphrey said. "I do know. It is unsatisfactory, but we must do our best and trust that the transaction is attended by honor."

"You mean you're just hoping for the best?"

"Is that bad?"

"In battle, my lord, always expect the worst. Then you might be ready for it. Where's the woman?"

"Woman?"

"Caterina Blazquez, is that her name? Where is she?"

"I have no idea," Pumphrey said distantly.

"Is she part of it?" Sharpe asked forcefully. "Does she want guineas?"

"The letters were stolen from her!"

"So she says."

"You have a very suspicious mind, Richard."

Sharpe said nothing. He disliked the way Pumphrey used his Christian name. It denoted more than familiarity. It suggested Sharpe was a valued inferior, a pet. It was patronizing and it was false. Pumphrey liked to give the impression of frailty, lightness, and frivolity, but Sharpe knew there was a razor mind at work in that well-groomed head. Lord Pumphrey was a man at home in darkness, and a man who knew well enough that ulterior motives were the driving force of the world. "Pumps," he said, and was rewarded by a slight flicker of an eyebrow, "you know bloody well that they're going to cheat us."

"Which is why I asked for you, Captain Sharpe."

That was better. "We don't know the letters are at the newspaper house, do we?"

"No."

"But if they cheat us, which they will, then I'm going to have to deal with them. What's the object, my lord? To steal them, or to stop them from being published?"

"His Majesty's government would like both."

"And His Majesty's government pays me, don't they? Ten shillings and sixpence a day, with four shillings and sixpence deducted for mess costs."

"The ambassador, I'm sure, will reward you," Lord Pumphrey said stiffly.

Sharpe said nothing. He went to the center of the chamber where he could see the dried blood black between the flagstones. He slapped his toe on the floor and listened to the echo. Noise, he thought, noise and bullets. Scare the bastards to death. But perhaps Pumphrey was right. Perhaps they did intend to sell the letters. But if they chose this crypt for the exchange then Sharpe reckoned they wanted both letters and gold. He climbed the steps back to the cathedral's crossing and Lord Pumphrey followed. There was a door in the temporary brick wall and Sharpe tried it. It opened easily and beyond was the open air and great stacks of abandoned masonry waiting for work to resume on the cathedral. "Seen enough?" Lord Pumphrey asked.

"Just pray they don't want to meet us in the crypt," Sharpe said.

"Suppose they do?"

"Just pray they don't," Sharpe said, for he had

never seen a place so ideally suited for ambush and murder.

They walked silently through the small streets. A mortar shell exploded dully at the other end of the city and a moment later every church bell in the city sounded at once. Sharpe wondered if the clangor was a summons for men to extinguish a fire set by the shell. Then he saw that everyone on the street had stopped. Men took off their hats and bowed their heads. "The **oraciones,**" Lord Pumphrey said, taking off his own hat.

"The what?"

"Evening prayer time." The folk made the sign of the cross when the bells ended. Sharpe and Pumphrey walked on, but had to step into a shopfront to make way for three men carrying gigantic loads of firewood on their backs. "It's all imported," Lord Pumphrey said.

"The wood?"

"Can't get it from the mainland, can we? So it's fetched in from the Balearics or from the Azores. It costs a great deal of money to cook or stay warm in a Cádiz winter. Luckily the embassy gets coal from Britain."

Firewood and coal. Sharpe watched the men disappear. They gave him an idea. A way to save the ambassador if the bastards did not sell the letters. A way to win.

Father Salvador Montseny ignored the two men operating the printing press while they were only too aware of him. There was something very threatening in the priest's calmness. Their employer, Eduardo Nuñez, who had brought Montseny to the pressroom, sat on a high chair in the room's corner and smoked a cigar as Montseny explored the room. "The work has been well done," Montseny said.

"Except now we can't see." Nuñez waved at the brick rectangles where the two windows had been. "Light was bad anyway. Now we work in the dark."

"You have lanterns," Father Montseny observed.

"But the work is delicate," Nuñez said, pointing at his two men. One was inking the press's form with a sheepskin ball while the other was trimming a sheet of paper.

"Then do the work carefully," Montseny said sourly. He was satisfied. The cellar, where the two printing apprentices lived, had no entrance other than a trapdoor that let into the pressroom's floor, while the pressroom itself, which took up almost all the ground floor, was now only accessible by the door that led from the courtyard. The first story was a storeroom, crammed with paper and ink, that could only be reached by an open stair beside the trapdoor. The second and third stories were Nuñez's living quarters, and Montseny had blocked the stairway leading to the flat roof. A guard was up on that roof at all hours, climbing to his post by a ladder from the balcony of Nuñez's bedroom. Nuñez did not like the arrangements, but Nuñez was being well paid in English gold.

"Do you really believe we shall be attacked?" Nuñez asked.

"I hope you're attacked," Montseny said.

Nuñez made the sign of the cross. "Why, Father?"

"Because then the admiral's men will kill our enemies," Montseny said.

"We are not soldiers," Nuñez said nervously.

"We are all soldiers," Montseny said, "fighting for a better Spain."

He had nine guards to keep the press safe. They lived in the storeroom upstairs and cooked their meals in the courtyard beside the latrine. They were solid oxlike men with big hands stained by years spent in the tarred rigging of warships, and they were all familiar with weapons and all ready to kill for their king, their country, and their admiral.

There was one small room off the pressroom. It was Nuñez's office, a charnel house of old bills, papers, and books, but Montseny had turfed Nuñez out, replacing him with a creature supplied by the admiral; a miserable creature, a whining, smoke-ridden, alcohol sodden, sweat-stinking excuse for a man, a writer. Benito Chavez was fat, nervous, peevish, and pompous. He had made his living writing opinions for the newspapers, but as the land ruled by the Spanish shrank, so the newspapers that would accept his opinions vanished until he was left only with **El Correo de Cádiz,** but that, at least, now promised to pay him well. He glanced around as Montseny opened the door. "Magnificent," he said, "quite magnificent."

"Are you drunk?"

"How can I be drunk? There's no liquor here! No, the letters!" Chavez chuckled. "They are magnificent. Listen! 'I cannot wait to caress your . . .' "

"I have read the letters," Montseny interrupted coldly.

"Passion! Tenderness! Lust! He writes well."

"You write better."

"Of course I do, of course. But I would like to meet this girl"—Chavez turned a letter over— "this Caterina."

"You think she would want to meet you?" Montseny asked. Benito Chavez was corpulent, his clothes were unkempt, and his graying beard speckled with scraps of tobacco. There was a bucket beside him and it was almost filled with cigar stubs and ash. Two half-smoked cigars were in a saucer on the table. "Caterina Blazquez," Montseny said, "serves only the best clients."

"She certainly knows how to wear out a mattress," Chavez said, ignoring Montseny's scorn.

"So make your copies," Montseny said, "and do your work."

"No need for copies," Chavez said. "I shall just rewrite everything and we can print it all at once."

"All at once?"

Chavez picked up one of the cigars, relit it from a candle, then scratched at an itch on his belly. "The English," he said, "provide the funds that keep the Regency going. The English supply the muskets for our army. The English give us the powder for the cannon on the city walls. The

English have an army on the Isla de León that protects Cádiz. Without England, Father, there is no Cádiz. If we annoy the English sufficiently, then they will persuade the Regency to shut the newspaper, and what use are the letters then? So fire all our ammunition at once! Give them a volley that will finish them. All the letters, all the passion, all the sweat on the sheets, all the lies I shall write, all at once! Blast them in one edition. Then it does not matter if they do close the newspaper."

Montseny stared at the miserable creature. There was some sense there, he allowed. "But if they do not close the newspaper," he pointed out, "then we shall have no more letters."

"But there are other letters," Chavez said enthusiastically. "Here"—he sorted through the sheets of paper—"there's a reference to His Excellency's last letter and it isn't here. I assume this marvelous creature still has some?"

"She does."

"Then get them," Chavez said, "or don't, as you please. It doesn't matter. I am a journalist, Father, so I make things up."

"Publish them all at once," Montseny said thoughtfully.

"I need a week," Chavez said, "and I shall

rewrite, translate, and invent. We shall say the English are sending muskets to the rebels in Venezuela, that they plan to impose the Protestant heresies on Cádiz"—he paused, sucking on the cigar—"and we shall say"—he went on more slowly, thoughtfully—"that they are negotiating a peace with France that will give Portugal its independence at the price of Spain. That should do it! Give me a week!"

"Ten days," Montseny snorted. "You have five."

Chavez's broad face took on a sly look. "I work better with brandy, Father." He gestured at the empty hearth, "and it is cold in here."

"After five days, Chavez," Montseny said, "you shall have gold, you shall have brandy, and you shall have all the fuel you can burn. Until then, work." He closed the door.

He could taste victory already.

The new south wind had loosed a dozen ships on their voyages to Portugal. Sergeant Noolan and his men had left, ordered aboard a naval sloop that was carrying dispatches to Lisbon, but Lord Pumphrey's note to Sir Thomas Graham had been sufficient to keep Sharpe's riflemen on the Isla de León. That evening Sharpe went to look for them in the tent lines. He had changed back into his uniform, then borrowed one of the embassy's horses. It was dark by the time he reached the encampment where he discovered Harper trying to revive a dying fire. "There's rum in that bottle, sir," Harper said, nodding at a stone bottle at the tent door.

"Where are the others?"

"Where I'll be in ten minutes. In a tavern, sir. How's your head?"

"It throbs."

"Are you keeping the bandage wet, like the surgeon said you must?"

"I forgot."

"Sergeant Noolan and his men are gone," Harper said. "Took a sloop of war to Lisbon. But we're staying, is that it?"

"Not for long," Sharpe said. He slid clumsily out of the saddle and wondered what the hell he was to do with the horse.

"Aye, we got orders from Lieutenant General Sir Thomas Graham himself," Harper said, relishing the rank and title, "delivered to us by Lord William Russell, no less." He gave Sharpe a quizzical look.

"We've got a job, Pat," Sharpe said, "some bastards in the city who need thumping."

"A job, eh?" There was a touch of resentment in Harper's voice.

"You're thinking of Joana?"

"I was, sir."

"Only be a few days, Pat, and there might be some cash in it." It had occurred to him that Lord Pumphrey was right and that Henry Wellesley could well be generous in his reward if the letters were retrieved. He stooped to the fire and warmed his hands. "We have to get you all some civilian clothes, then move you into Cádiz for a day or two, and after that we can go home. Joana will wait for you."

"She will, I hope. And what are you doing with that horse, sir? It's wandering off."

"Bloody hell." Sharpe retrieved the mare. "I'm going to take it to Sir Thomas's quarters. He'll have stables. And I want to see him anyway. Got a favor to ask him."

"I'll come with you, sir," Harper said. He abandoned the fire and Sharpe realized Harper had been waiting for him. The big Irishman retrieved his rifle, volley gun, and the rest of his equipment from the tent. "If I leave anything here, sir, the bastards will steal it. There's nothing but bloody thieves in this army." Harper was happier now, not because Sharpe had returned, but because his officer had remembered to ask about Joana. "So what's this job, sir?"

"We've got to steal something."

"God save Ireland. They need us? This camp is full of thieves!"

"They want a thief they can trust," Sharpe said.

"I suppose that's difficult. Let me lead the horse, sir."

"I need to talk to Sir Thomas," Sharpe said, handing over the reins. "Then we'll join the others. I could do with a drink."

"I think you'll find Sir Thomas is busy, sir. They've been running around all evening like starlings, they have. Something's brewing."

They walked into the small town. The streets of San Fernando were much more spacious than the alleys of Cádiz and the houses were lower. Lamps burned on some corners and light spilled from the taverns where British and Portuguese soldiers drank, watched by the ever-present provosts. San Fernando had become a garrison town, home to the five thousand men sent to guard the isthmus of Cádiz. Sharpe asked one of

the provosts where Sir Thomas's quarters were
and was pointed down a lane that led to the
quays beside the creek. The creek made the isthmus into an island. Two large torches flamed
outside the headquarters, illuminating a group
of animated officers. Sir Thomas was one of
them. He was standing on the doorstep and it
was clear that Harper had been right: something
was brewing and the general was busy. He was
giving orders, but then he saw Sharpe and broke
off. "Sharpe!" he shouted.

"Sir?"

"Good man! You want to come? Good man!
Willie, look after him." Sir Thomas said nothing
more, but turned brusquely away and, accompanied by a half dozen officers, strode toward the
creek.

Lord William Russell turned to Sharpe.
"You're coming!" Lord William said. "Good!"

"Coming where?" Sharpe asked.

"Frog-hunting, of course."

"Do I need a horse?"

"Good God, no, not unless it can swim?"

"Can I stable it here?"

"Pearce!" Lord William shouted. "Pearce!"

"I'm here, Your Lordship, I'm here, ever
present and correct, sir." A bowlegged cavalry

trooper who appeared old enough to be Lord William's father appeared from the alley beside the headquarters. "Your Lordship's forgotten Your Lordship's saber."

"Dear God, have I? So I have, thank you, Pearce." Lord William took the proffered saber and slid it into its scabbard. "Look after Captain Sharpe's gee-gee, will you, Pearce? There's a good fellow. Sure you don't want to come with us?"

"Have to get Your Lordship's breakfast."

"So you do, Pearce, so you do. Beefsteak, I hope?"

"Might I wish Your Lordship good hunting?" Pearce said, flicking a speck of dust from one of Lord William's epaulettes.

"That's uncommonly kind of you, Pearce, thank you. Come on, Sharpe, we can't dillydally. We have a tide to catch!" Lord William set off after Sir Thomas at a half run. Sharpe and Harper, still bemused, followed him to a long wharf where, in the small moonlight, Sharpe could see files of redcoats clambering into boats. General Graham was dressed in black boots, black breeches, red coat, and a black cocked hat. He had a claymore at his belt and was talking to a naval officer, but stopped long enough to greet Sharpe again. "Good man! How's your head?"

"I'll live, sir."

"That's the spirit! And that's our boat. In you get."

The boat was a big, flat-bottomed lighter, manned by a score of sailors with long sweeps. It was a short jump down onto the wide aft deck. The boat's hold was already occupied by grinning redcoats. "What the hell are we doing?" Harper asked.

"Damned if I know," Sharpe said, "but I need to talk to the general and this looks like as good a chance as I'll get."

Four other lighters lay astern and all were slowly filling with redcoats. An engineer officer threw a coil of quick match down onto the rearmost barge. Then a file of his men carried kegs of powder to the hold. Lord William Russell jumped down beside Sharpe, while General Graham, almost alone on the quay now, walked above the lighters. "No smoking, boys!" the general called. "We can't have the French seeing a light just because you need a pipe. No noise, either. And make damned sure your guns aren't cocked. And enjoy yourselves, you hear me? Enjoy yourselves." He repeated the injunctions to the men in each of the barges, then clambered down onto the foremost lighter. The spacious afterdeck had room for a dozen officers to stand or sit and still leave space for the sailor who wielded the long tiller. "Those rogues," Sir Thomas said to Sharpe, gesturing at the redcoats crouched in the lighter's hold, "are from the 87th. Is that who you are, boys? Damned Irish rebels?"

"We are, sir!" two or three men called back.

"And you'll not find better soldiers this side of the gates of hell," Sir Thomas said, loud enough for the Irishmen to hear. "You're most welcome, Sharpe."

"Welcome to what, sir?"

"You don't know? Then why are you here?"

"Came to ask a favor of you, sir."

Sir Thomas laughed. "And I thought you wanted to join us! Ah well, the favor must wait, Sharpe, it must wait. We have work to do."

The lighters had cast off and were now being rowed down a channel through the marshes that edged the Isla de León. Ahead of Sharpe, north and east, the long, low black silhouette of the Trocadero Peninsula just showed in the night. Sparks of light betrayed where the French forts lay. Lord William told him there were three forts.

The farthest away was the Matagorda, which lay closest to Cádiz, and it was the giant mortar in the Matagorda Fort that did most damage to the city. Just to its south was the Fort San José and, farther south still and closest to the Isla de León, was the Fort San Luis. "What we're doing," Lord William explained, "is rowing past San Luis to the river just beyond. The river mouth is a creek, and once we're in that creek, Sharpe, we'll be plumb between the San Luis and the San Jose. Enfiladed, you might say."

"And what's in the creek?"

"Five damned great fire rafts." Sir Thomas Graham had heard Sharpe's question and now answered it. "The bastards are just waiting for a brisk northerly wind to set them loose on our fleet. Can't have that." The fleet, mostly small coasters with a few larger merchantmen, was assembling to take Graham's men and General Lapeña's Spanish army south. They would land on the coast, then march north to assault the siege lines from the rear. "We plan to burn the rafts tonight," Sir Thomas went on. "It'll be past midnight before we get there. Perhaps you'll do the 87th the honor of joining them?"

"With pleasure, sir."

"Major Gough! You've met Captain Sharpe?"

A shadowy officer appeared at Sir Thomas's side. "I have not, sir," Gough said, "but I remember you from Talavera, Sharpe."

"Sharpe and his sergeant would beg the privilege of fighting with your boys tonight, Hugh," Sir Thomas said.

"They'll be most welcome, sir." Gough spoke in a soft Irish accent.

"Warn your boys they have two stray riflemen, will you?" Sir Thomas said. "We don't want your rogues shooting two men who captured a French eagle. So there you are, Sharpe. Major Gough is landing his lads on the south side of the creek. There are some guards there, but they'll be easy enough to take care of. Then I imagine the French will send a relief party from the San Luis fort so it should all become fairly interesting."

Sir Thomas's plan was to land two lighters on the southern bank and two on the northern, and the men would disembark to drive off the French guards, then defend the creek against the expected counterattacks. Meanwhile the fifth lighter, which carried engineers, would row to the fire rafts that were just upstream of the twin French encampments, capture them, and set their explosives. "It should look like Guy Fawkes Night," Sir Thomas said wolfishly.

Sharpe settled on the deck. Lord William Russell had brought cold sausage and a flask of wine. The sausage was chopped into slices and the flask handed around as the sailors heaved on the great sweeps and the lighter steadily butted its way through the small choppy waves. A Spaniard stood beside the steersman. "Our guide," Sir Thomas explained. "A fisherman. A good fellow."

"He doesn't hate us, sir?" Sharpe asked.

"Hate us?"

"I keep being told how the Spanish hate us, sir."

"He hates the French, like I do, Sharpe. If there is one constancy in this vale of tears, it is to always hate the damned French, always." Sir Thomas spoke with a real vehemence. "I trust you hate the French, Sharpe?"

Sharpe paused. Hate? He was not sure he hated them. "I don't like the bastards, sir," he said.

"I used to," Sir Thomas said.

"Used to?" Sharpe asked, puzzled.

"I used to like them," Sir Thomas said. The general was staring ahead at the small lights showing through the embrasures of the forts. "I liked them, Sharpe. I rejoiced in their revolution.

I believed it was a dawn for mankind. Liberty. Equality. Fraternity. I believed in all those things and I believe in them still, but now I hate the French. I've hated them, Sharpe, since the day my wife died."

Sharpe felt almost as uncomfortable as when the ambassador had confessed his foolishness in writing love letters to a whore. "I'm sorry, sir," he muttered.

"It was nineteen years ago," Sir Thomas said, apparently oblivious of Sharpe's inadequate sympathy, "off the southern coast of France. June twenty-sixth, 1792, was the day my dear Mary died. We took her body ashore and we placed it in a casket, and it was my wish that she should be buried in Scotland. So we hired a barge to take us to Bordeaux where we might find a ship to take us home. And just outside Toulouse, Sharpe"—the general's voice was turning into a growl as he told the tale—"a rascally crowd of half-drunk Frenchmen insisted on searching the barge. I showed them my permits, I pleaded with them, I entreated them to show respect, but they ignored me, Sharpe. They were men wearing the uniform of France, and they tore that coffin open and they molested my dear Mary in her shroud, and from that day, Sharpe,

I have hardened my heart against their damned race. I joined the army to get my revenge and I pray to God daily that I live long enough to see every damned Frenchman scoured off the face of this earth."

"Amen to that," Lord William Russell said.

"And tonight, for my Mary's sake," Sir Thomas said with relish, "I'll kill a few more."

"Amen to that," Sharpe said.

A small wind came from the west. It threw up tiny waves in the Bay of Cádiz across which the five lighters crawled slow, low and dark against the black water. It was chilly, not truly cold, but Sharpe wished he had worn a greatcoat. Five miles to the north and off to his left the lights of Cádiz glimmered against white walls to make a pale streak between the sea and sky, while closer, perhaps a mile to the west, yellow lantern light spilled from the stern windows of the anchored ships. Yet here, in the belly of the bay, there was no light, just the splash of black-painted oar blades. "It would have been quicker"—Sir Thomas broke a long silence—"to have rowed from the city, but if we'd have put lighters against the city wharves then the French would have

known we're coming. That's why I didn't tell you
about this little jaunt last night. If I'd said a word
of what we were planning, then the French
would have known it all by breakfast time."

"You think they have spies in the embassy, sir?"

"They have spies everywhere, Sharpe. Whole
city is riddled with them. They get their messages out on the fishing boats. The bastards already know we're sending an army to attack their
siege lines and I suspect Marshal Victor knows
more about my plans than I do."

"The spies are Spanish?"

"I assume so."

"Why do they serve the French, sir?"

Sir Thomas chuckled at that question. "Well,
some of them think as I used to think, Sharpe,
that liberty, equality, and fraternity are fine
things. And so they are, but God knows not in
French hands. And some of them just hate the
British."

"Why?"

"They've got plenty of reasons, Sharpe. Good
Lord, it was only fourteen years ago we bombarded Cádiz! And six years ago we broke their
fleet at Trafalgar! And most merchants here believe we want to destroy their trade with South
America and take it for ourselves, and they're

right. We deny it, of course, but we're still trying to do it. And they believe we're fomenting rebellion in their South American colonies, and they're not far wrong. We did encourage rebellion, though now we're pretending we didn't. Then there's Gibraltar. They hate us for being in Gibraltar."

"I thought they gave it to us, sir."

"Aye, so they did, by the Treaty of Utrecht in 1713, but they were raw damn fools to sign that piece of paper and well they know it. So enough of them hate us, and now the French are spreading rumors that we'll annex Cádiz as well! God knows that isn't true, but the Spanish are willing to credit it. And there are men in Spain who fervently believe a French alliance would serve their country better than a British friendship, and I'm not sure they're wrong. But here we are, Sharpe, allies whether we like it or not. And there are plenty of Spaniards who hate the French more than they dislike us, so there's hope."

"There's always hope," Lord William Russell said cheerfully.

"Aye, Willie, maybe," Sir Thomas said, "but when Spain is reduced to Cádiz and Lord Wellington only holds the patch of land around Lisbon, it's hard to see how we'll drive the damn

French back to their pigsties. If Napoleon had a scrap of sense he'd offer the Spanish their king back and make peace. Then we'd be properly cooked."

"At least the Portuguese are on our side," Sharpe said.

"True! And fine fellows they are. I've got two thousand of them here."

"If they'll fight," Lord William said dubiously.

"They'll fight," Sharpe said. "I was at Bussaco. They fought."

"So what happened?" Sir Thomas asked, and the telling of that story carried the lighter close to the reed-thick shore of the Trocadero Peninsula. The Fort of San Luis was close now. It stood two or three hundred paces inland, where the marshes gave way to ground firm enough to support the massive ramparts. Beyond the fort's flooded ditch Sharpe could just see a small glow of light above the glacis. That was a mistake by the French. Sharpe suspected that the sentries had braziers burning on the firestep to keep themselves warm, and even the small light of the coals would make it difficult for them to see anything moving in the black shallows. Yet the greater danger was not the fort's sentries, but guard boats, and Sir Thomas whispered that they were to keep a good lookout. "Listen for their oars," he suggested.

The French evidently possessed a dozen guard boats. They had been seen in the dusk as they patrolled the Trocadero's low coast, but there was no sign of them now. Either they were deeper in the bay or, more likely, their crews had been driven back to the creek by the chill wind. Sir Thomas suspected the crews of the boats were soldiers rather than sailors. "Bastards are shirking, aren't they?" he whispered.

A hand touched Sharpe's shoulder. "It's Major Gough," a voice said from the darkness, "and this is Ensign Keogh. Stay with him, Sharpe, and I'll warrant we won't shoot you."

"We probably won't." Ensign Keogh corrected the major.

"He probably won't shoot you." Major Gough accepted the correction.

There was light ahead now, just enough for Sharpe to see that Ensign Keogh was absurdly young with a thin and eager face. The light came from campfires that burned perhaps a quarter mile ahead. The five boats were turning into the creek, creeping through the water to avoid the withies that marked the shallow channel, and the campfires burned where the French sentries guarded the fire rafts. The lighters' black oars scarce touched the water now. The naval officer who led the boats had timed the expedition to arrive just as the tide finished its flood and so the rising water carried the lighters against the river's small current. By the time the raid was over the tide should have turned and the ebb would hurry the British away. Still no Frenchman saw the boats, though the sentries were certainly on duty, for Sharpe could see a blue uniform with white crossbelts beside one of the fires. "I hate them," Sir Thomas said softly, "God, how I do hate them."

Sharpe could see the dim trace of light leaking over the glacis of Fort San Jose. It looked about half a mile away. Long cannon shot, he thought, especially if the French used canister, but the southernmost fort, San Luis, was much closer, close enough to shred the creek with rounds of canister, which were missiles of musket balls encased in tin cylinders that burst apart at the cannon's muzzle. The balls, hundreds of them, spread like duck shot. Sharpe hated canister. All infantrymen did. "Buggers are asleep," Lord William murmured.

Sharpe was suddenly struck by guilt. He had arranged to meet Lord Pumphrey at midday to discover whether the blackmailers had sent any message, and though he doubted there would be any word he knew his place was in Cádiz, not here. His duty was to Henry Wellesley, not to General Graham, yet here he was and he could only pray that he was not gutted by canister fired in the night. He touched his sword hilt and wished he could have sharpened the blade before he came. He liked to go into battle with a sharpened blade. Then he touched his rifle. Not many officers carried a longarm, but Sharpe was not like most officers. He was gutter-born, gutter-bred, and a gutter fighter.

Then the lighter's bows ran softly onto the mud.

"Let's kill some bastards," Sir Thomas said vengefully.

And the first troops went ashore.

Chapter 5

Sharpe jumped from the lighter into water that came over his boot tops. He waded ashore, following Ensign Keogh whose cocked hat looked as though it had belonged to his grandfather. It had exaggeratedly hooked points from which hung skimpy tassels and at its crown was a massive blue plume that matched the facings of the 87th's red coats. "Follow, follow, follow," Keogh hissed, not at Sharpe, but at a big sergeant and a score of men who were evidently his responsibility this night. The sergeant had become entangled in a wicker fish trap and was cursing as he tried to kick it free of his boots. "Do you need help, Sergeant Masterson?" Keogh asked.

"Jesus no, sir," Masterson said, trampling on the trap's remnants. "Bloody thing, sir."

"Fix bayonets, boys!" Keogh said. "Do it quietly now!"

It seemed extraordinary to Sharpe that four or five hundred men could disembark so close to the twin encampments on the creek's banks and not be noticed, but the French were still oblivious of the attackers. Sharpe could see small tents in the firelight, and among the tents were crude shelters made of branches thatched with reeds. A stand of muskets stood outside one sagging tent and Sharpe wondered why in God's name the French had provided tents. The men were supposed to be guarding the rafts, not sleeping, but at least a few of the sentries were still awake. Two men wandered slowly across the encampment, muskets slung, suspecting nothing as a second lighter disgorged another company of redcoats alongside the men of the 87th. Two more companies were wading ashore on the northern bank.

"For a balla, boys," Major Gough appeared to say softly and urgently just behind Keogh's men, "for a balla!"

"For a what?" Sharpe whispered to Harper.

"**Faugh a ballagh,** sir. Clear the way, it means. Get out of our path because the Irish are coming." Harper had drawn his sword bayonet.

He was evidently reserving the seven bullets in the volley gun for later in the fight. "We bloody well are coming too," he said, and clicked the sword's brass hilt over his rifle's muzzle so that the barrel now held twenty-three inches of murderous steel.

"Forward now!" Major Gough reverted to English, but still spoke quietly. "And slaughter the bastards. But do it softly, boys. Don't wake the little darlings till you have to."

The 87th started forward, their bayonets glinting in the small light of the fires. Clicks sounded as men cocked their muskets and Sharpe was certain the French must hear that noise, but the enemy stayed silent. It was a sentry on the northern bank who first realized the danger. Perhaps he saw the dark shape of the lighters in the creek, or else he glimpsed the glimmering blades coming from the west, but whatever alarmed him prompted a strangled cry of astonishment followed by a bang as he fired his musket.

"**Faugh a ballagh!**" Major Gough yelled. "**Faugh a ballagh!** Hard at them, boys, hard at them!" Gough, now that surprise was lost, had no intention of keeping his advance slow and disciplined. Sharpe remembered the battalion from Talavera, and he knew them to be a steady unit, but Gough wanted speed and savagery now. "Run, you rogues!" he shouted. "Take them fast! And give tongue! Give tongue!"

The men responded to this hunting command by screaming like banshees. They began running through the marsh, stumbling on tussocks, and jumping small ditches. Ensign Keogh, lithe and young, ran ahead with his slender-bladed infantry officer's sword held aloft. "**Faugh a ballagh!**" he shouted. "**Faugh a ballagh!**" Then he leaped a ditch, all sprawling legs and flapping scabbard, while his left hand clutched at his oversized hat to keep it from falling off. He stumbled, but Sergeant Masterson, who was almost as big as Harper, snatched the frail-looking ensign back to his feet. "Kill them!" Keogh screamed. "Kill them!" Muskets sparked among the campfires, but Sharpe neither heard a ball pass nor saw anyone fall. The French, scattered and dozy, were scrambling out of their tents and shelters. An officer, his sword reflecting the firelight, tried to rally his troops, but the screams of the attacking Irish were enough to drive the newly woken men into the farther darkness. There was a smattering of musket fire from Gough's Irishmen, but most of the work was done by the mere threat of their seventeen-inch bayonets. A woman, bare-legged, scooped up her bedding and sprinted after her man. Two dogs were running in circles, barking. Sharpe saw a pair of mounted men vanishing into the darkness behind him. He whirled, rifle raised, but the horsemen had galloped past the Irish flank into the dark toward the place where the lighters had grounded. Keogh had vanished ahead, followed by his men, but Sharpe held Harper back. "We've got green coats, Pat," he warned. "Someone will mistake us for Crapauds if we're not careful."

He was right. A half dozen men with yellow facings on their red jackets suddenly appeared among the fires and Sharpe saw a musket swing toward him. "Ninety-fifth!" he shouted. "Ninety-fifth! Hold your fire! Who are you?"

"Sixty-seventh!" a voice shouted back. The 67th was a Hampshire regiment and they had advanced more slowly than the Irishmen, but kept closer order. A captain now took them east and south to guard the captured camp's inland perimeter, while Major Gough was shouting at his Irishmen to move back through the tents and make a similar cordon on the bay side. Sharpe was thrusting his sword into the small tents as he and Harper walked toward Gough, and one such thrust elicited a yelp. Sharpe pulled the canvas flaps aside and saw two Frenchmen cowering inside. "Out!" he snarled. They crawled out and waited at his feet, shaking. "I don't even know if we're taking prisoners," Sharpe said.

"We can't just kill them, sir," Harper said.

"I'm not going to kill them," Sharpe snarled. "Get up!" He prodded the men with his sword, then drove them toward another band of prisoners being escorted by the Hampshire redcoats. One of those Hampshires was stooping by a French boy who did not look more than fourteen or fifteen. He had taken a bullet in his chest and was choking to death, his heels beating a horrid tattoo on the ground. "Be easy, boy," the Hampshire man said as he stroked the dying boy's cheek. "Be easy." The far bank sparked with a sudden flurry of musket shots that died away as quickly as they had risen, and it was evident that the redcoats there had been just as successful as the men on the southern shore.

"Is that you, Sharpe?" It was Major Gough's voice.

"It is, sir."

"That was damnably quick," Gough said, sounding disappointed. "The fellows just ran!

Didn't put up a fight at all. Will you do me the honor of reporting to General Graham that this bank is secure and that there's no counterattack in sight? You should find the general by the rafts."

"A pleasure, sir," Sharpe said. He led Harper back through the captured encampment.

"I thought we'd get some fighting," Harper said, sounding as disappointed as Gough.

"Buggers were asleep, weren't they?"

"I come all this way just to watch a bunch of Dubliners wake up some Crapauds?"

"Are Gough's men from Dublin?"

"That's where the regiment's raised, sir." Harper spotted a discarded French pack, scooped it up, and filleted inside. "Bugger all," he said and threw it away. "So how long do we stay here?"

"Long as it takes. An hour?"

"That long!"

"Engineers have a lot of work to do, Pat," Sharpe said, and suddenly thought of poor Sturridge who had trusted that Sharpe would keep him alive on the Guadiana.

They found General Graham on the bank where the fire rafts were moored. The fifth lighter, the one containing the engineers, had tied up on the nearest raft where two Frenchmen lay dead.

Each of the five rafts was a great square platform of timber with a short mast to which a scrap of sail could be attached. The French had been waiting for a dark night, a north wind, and an incoming tide to drive the rafts down onto the fleet waiting to take the army south. Volunteer crews would have manned the ponderous rafts, guiding them to within a quarter mile or so of the anchorage. Then they would have lit the slow matches and taken to their rowing boats to escape the inferno. If the rafts had ever succeeded in getting among the British and Spanish shipping they would have caused panic. Ships would have cut their anchor cables rather than be set afire and the wind would have driven the anchorless ships crashing into one another or onto the marshy shore of the Isla de León, and meanwhile the monster fire rafts would drift on, causing more chaos. Each was crammed with barrels of incendiaries and with baulks of firewood, and they were armed with ancient cannons at their perimeters. The cannons' touchholes were connected to the incendiary-filled barrels with slow matches. The cannons, some of which looked two hundred years old, were all small, but

Sharpe supposed they were loaded with grapeshot, round shot, and anything else the French could cram into their muzzles so that the blazing rafts would spit balls and shells and death as they lumbered into the tightly packed anchorage.

The engineers were setting their charges and running quick fuse to the southern bank where General Graham stood with his aides. Sharpe gave him Gough's message and Sir Thomas nodded an acknowledgment. "Evil bloody things, aren't they?" he said, nodding at the nearest raft.

"Balgowan!" a voice hailed from the northern bank. "Balgowan!"

"Perthshire!" Sir Thomas bellowed back.

"All secure on this side, sir!" the voice shouted back.

"Good man!"

"Balgowan, sir?" Sharpe asked.

"Password," Sir Thomas said. "Should have told you that. Balgowan is where I grew up, Sharpe. Finest place on God's earth." He was frowning as he spoke, staring south toward the San Luis fort. "It's all been too easy," he said, worried. Sharpe said nothing because Lieutenant General Sir Thomas Graham did not need his comments. "Bad troops." Sir Thomas spoke of the French who had supposedly been guarding the rafts. "That's what it is. Battalion level, that's where the rot starts. I'll wager your year's wages against mine, Sharpe, that the senior battalion officers are sleeping in the forts. They've got warm beds, fires in the hearth, and dairymaids between the sheets while their men suffer out here."

"I'll not take your wager, sir."

"You'd be a fool if you did," Sir Thomas said. In the light of the dying French campfires the general could see ranks of redcoats facing the fort. Those men would be silhouetted against the fires and thus be prime targets for the fort's artillery. "Willie," he said, "tell Hugh and Johnny to lay their men down."

"Aye aye, sir," Lord William said, dropping into naval jargon. He ran southward and Sir Thomas slopped through the mud and clambered on board the nearest raft.

"Come and have a look, Sharpe!" he invited.

Sharpe and Harper followed the general who used his heavy-bladed claymore to prize open the nearest barrel. The top came off to reveal a half dozen pale balls, each about the size of a nine-pounder round shot. "What the devil are those?" Sir Thomas asked. "They look like haggis."

"Smoke balls, sir," an engineer lieutenant said after taking a quick look at the balls. He and an engineer sergeant were replacing the slow matches in the cannons with quick match.

Sir Thomas lifted one smoke ball and prodded the mixture beneath it. "What's in the rest of the barrel?" he asked.

"Mostly saltpeter, sir," the lieutenant said, "probably mixed with sulfur, antimony, and pitch. It'll burn like hell."

Sir Thomas hefted the smoke ball. The case was pierced by a dozen holes and, when Sir Thomas tapped it, sounded hollow. "Papier-mâché?" the general guessed.

"That's it, sir. Papier-mâché filled with powder, antimony, and coal dust. Don't see many of those these days. Naval equipment. You're supposed to light them and hurl them through the enemy gunports, sir, where they choke the gunners. Of course you'll probably die doing it, but they can be nasty little chaps in confined spaces."

"So why are they here?" Sir Thomas asked.

"I suppose the frogs hoped they'd churn out a

cloud of smoke that would drift ahead of the rafts to hide them, sir. Now, if you'll excuse me, sir."

"Of course, man." The general stepped out of the lieutenant's way. He put the smoke ball back in the barrel and was about to replace the lid when Sharpe reached for the balls.

"Can I have those, sir?"

"You want them?" Sir Thomas asked, surprised.

"With your permission, sir."

Sir Thomas looked as though he thought Sharpe very strange, then shrugged. "Whatever you want, Sharpe."

Sharpe sent Harper to find a French haversack. He was thinking of the cathedral's crypt, and about the caverns and passages around the low chamber, and about men lurking in the dark with muskets and blades. He filled the haversack with the smoke balls and gave it to Harper. "Look after it, Pat. It could save our lives."

General Graham had jumped onto the next raft where a squad of engineers was putting new fuses to the loaded cannon and planting powder charges in the raft's center. "More smoke balls here, Sharpe," he called back.

"I've enough, sir, thank you, sir."

"Why do you need . . ." the general began asking, then stopped abruptly because a gun had fired from the Fort of San Luis. The garrison had at last woken up to what was happening in the marsh and, as the bellow of the gun faded, Sharpe heard musket balls whistle overhead. That meant the cannon had been loaded with canister or grapeshot. The sound of the cannon had scarcely gone silent when the smoke of its shot was lit by three violent explosions of red light as more guns slashed their shots from the embrasures. A round shot screamed just above the general's head and a swarm of musket balls seethed across the marsh. "They won't use shell," Sharpe told Harper, "because they don't want to set the rafts alight themselves."

"That's not much of a comfort, sir," Harper said, "considering they're aiming their guns straight at us."

"They're just firing at the camp," Sharpe said.

"And we happen to be in the camp, sir."

Then the guns of the San José Fort opened on the northern bank. They were much farther away and the grapeshot sighed in the dark rather than hissed or whistled. A round shot landed in the creek and splashed water over the nearest raft. The guns' flashes were to the north and south now, lighting the night with sudden lurid flares that glowed on the writhing smoke, then faded, but leaving Sharpe dazzled. He knew he should not have come, nor indeed should Sir Thomas have come. A lieutenant general had no business joining a raiding party that should have been led by a major or, at most, a lieutenant colonel. But Sir Thomas was plainly a man who could not resist danger. The general was gazing south, trying to see in the intermittent light of the cannons' muzzle flashes whether any French infantry had sallied from San Luis. "Sharpe!" he called.

"Sir?"

"Captain Vetch tells me the engineers are making fine time. Go back to the lighters, will you? You'll find a marine captain there, name of Collins. Tell him we'll be sounding the withdrawal in about twenty minutes. Maybe half an hour. Remember the password and countersign?"

"Balgowan and Perthshire, sir."

"Good man. Off you go. And I haven't forgotten you need a favor from me! We'll talk about it over breakfast."

Sharpe led Harper back along the creek. The marines challenged them with the password and Sharpe called the countersign. Captain Collins proved to be a stout man who looked askance at the score of prisoners who had been put under his charge. "What am I supposed to do with them?" he asked plaintively. "There's no room in the lighters to take them back."

"Then we'll leave them here," Sharpe said. He delivered the general's message, then stood beside Collins and watched the cannon flashes. One French round shot struck the remains of a campfire so that embers, sparks, and flames exploded thirty or forty feet into the air. Some burning shards landed on the tents and started small fires that illuminated the cumbersome rafts.

"Don't like fighting at night," Collins admitted.

"It's not easy," Sharpe said. Every shadow seemed to move and the marshland was full of shadows cast by the fires. He remembered the night before Talavera, and how he had discovered the French coming up the hill. That had been a mad night of confusion, but tonight, at least, the enemy seemed to be supine. The fortress artillery still fired, but the grape and round shot were now going well to Sharpe's left.

"Two of the buggers came here," Collins said. "Both on horseback! I know we haven't got any horses, but I still thought they might have been a pair of our lads who'd captured a couple. They rode up to me, calm as you like, and then galloped off. We never fired a shot. One of them even called good evening as he went, the insolent bastard."

So the French, Sharpe thought, knew that the lighters were well downstream of the camp, and knew, moreover, that they were lightly guarded by a small picquet of marines. "If you don't mind me suggesting it," Sharpe said, "I'd move the lighters upstream."

"Why?"

"Because there's a big gap between you and the Irish boys."

"We had to land here," Collins said. "We couldn't row right up to the camp, could we?"

"You could get up there now," Sharpe said, nodding at the sailors who waited on the thwarts.

"My job is to guard the boats," Collins said heavily. "I don't command them."

"So who does?"

A naval lieutenant commanded the lighters, but he had evidently gone upstream on board the fifth boat and was now with the engineers, and Collins, with no direct orders, would not risk moving the two lighters on his own initiative. He seemed insulted that Sharpe had even suggested it. "I shall wait for orders," he said indignantly.

"In that case we'll make a picquet for you," Sharpe said. "We'll be out there." He nodded southward. "Warn your lads not to shoot us when we come back."

Collins did not reply. Sharpe told Harper to drop the haversack of smoke balls in the general's lighter, then took him southward. "Keep a lookout, Pat."

"You think the French will come?"

"They can't just sit there and let us burn the rafts, can they?"

"They've been dozy so far, sir."

They crouched in the reeds. The small wind was coming from the far ocean and it brought the smell of salt from the pans across the bay. Sharpe could see the reflection of the city's lights winking and shaking on the water. The gunfire from the forts punctured the night, but from this distance it was hard to tell if the shots were doing any damage in the captured camps. It was hard to see anything. The men from Dublin and Hampshire were lying flat and the engineers were busy in the shadows on the rafts. "If I were the Crapauds," Sharpe said, "I wouldn't worry about the rafts. I'd come and take these lighters. That would strand us all here, wouldn't it? They'll pick up a couple of hundred prisoners including a lieutenant general. Not a bad night's work for a dozy pack of bastards, eh?"

"You're not the Crapauds, are you, sir? They're probably getting drunk. Letting their gunners do the work."

"They can afford to lose the fire rafts," Sharpe went on, "if they capture five lighters. They can use the lighters instead of the rafts."

"We'll be gone soon, sir," Harper said consolingly. "No need to worry."

"Let's hope so."

They fell silent. Marsh birds, woken by the firing, cried forlorn in the dark. "So what are we doing in the city?" Harper asked after a while.

"There's some bastards that have got some letters and we have to buy them back," Sharpe said. "Or at least we have to make sure no one does anything nasty while they are bought back, and if it all goes wrong, which it will, we're going to have to steal the bloody things."

"Letters? Not gold?"

"Not gold, Pat."

"And it will go wrong?"

"Of course it will. We're dealing with black-mailers. They never settle for the first payment, do they? They always come back for more, so we're probably going to have to kill the bastards before it's all over."

"Whose letters are they?"

"Some whore wrote them," Sharpe said vaguely. He supposed that Harper would learn the truth soon enough, but Sharpe liked Henry Wellesley enough not to spread the man's shame even wider. "It should be easy enough," he went on, "except that the Spaniards won't like what we're doing. If we get caught they'll arrest us. Either that or shoot us."

"Arrest us?"

"We'll just have to be clever, Pat."

"That's all right then," Harper said. "We don't have a problem, do we?"

Sharpe smiled. The wind stirred the reeds. The tide was still. The guns were firing steadily, their shots thumping in the marsh or churning the creek. "I wish the bloody 8th was here," Sharpe said softly.

"The Leather-hats?" Harper asked, thinking Sharpe meant a regiment from Cheshire.

"No. The French 8th, Pat. The bastards we met up the river. The ones that took poor Lieu-

tenant Bullen prisoner. They've got to be coming
back here, don't they? They can't reach Badajoz
now, not without a bridge. I want to meet them
again. That bloody Colonel Vandal. I'm going to
shoot him in the skull, the bastard."

"You'll find him, sir."

"Maybe. But not here. We'll be gone in a
week. But one day, Pat, I'll find that bastard and
murder him for what he did to Lieutenant
Bullen."

Harper did not respond. Instead he laid a
hand on Sharpe's sleeve and Sharpe, at the same
instant, heard the rustle of reeds. It was not the
sound of the small wind stirring the plants, but
more regular. Like footsteps. And it was close.
"See anything?" he whispered.

"No. Yes."

Sharpe saw them then. Or he saw shadows
running at a crouch. Then there was the glint of
reflected light from a piece of metal, perhaps a
musket muzzle. The shadows stopped so that
they melded into the darkness, but Sharpe saw
more men moving beyond. How many? Twenty?
No, double that. He leaned close to Harper.
"Volley gun," he breathed into the sergeant's ear.
"Then we go to the right. We run like hell for
thirty paces, then drop."

Harper raised the volley gun slowly, very slowly. Then, with the stock against his right shoulder, he cocked it. The lock's pawl made a click as it engaged and the sound carried to the Frenchmen and Sharpe saw the pale faces turn toward him and just then Harper pulled the trigger and the gun flooded the marsh with noise and lit it with the burst of muzzle flashes. Smoke hid Sharpe as he took off running. He counted the paces and, at thirty, dropped flat. He could hear a man moaning. Two muskets fired, then a voice shouted a command, and no more guns sounded. Harper dropped beside him. "Rifles next," Sharpe said. "Then we go to the boats."

He could hear the Frenchmen hissing to one another. They had been hit hard by the seven bullets and they were doubtless talking about their casualties, but then they fell silent and Sharpe could see them more clearly now for they were suddenly outlined against the muzzle flames of the cannons firing from the fort. He got to one knee and aimed his rifle. "Ready?"

"Yes, sir."

"Fire."

The two rifles spat toward the shadows. Sharpe had no idea if either bullet struck. All he knew was that the French were trying to take the lighters, they were perilously close to the creek, and the shots would have raised the alarm. He hoped the marine captain would have had the initiative to order the boats upstream. "Come on," he said, and they ran clumsily, half-tripping on tussocks, and he sensed that the French had cast caution away and were running to his right. "Move the boats!" Sharpe shouted at the marine picquet. "Move the boats!" His head was all pain, but he had to ignore it. French muskets crashed in the night. A bullet thumped into mud close to Harper's feet just as the marines fired a ragged volley into the dark.

The sudden outburst of musketry had alerted the sailors and they had cut the lines to the boarding grapnels they were using as anchors and then shoved the lighters away from the bank, but the ponderous boats moved painfully slowly. The one farthest from Sharpe made better progress, but the nearer one seemed to be half-grounded. More French muskets banged, coughing out smoke in which Sharpe saw the glint of bayonets. The outnumbered marines scrambled aboard the nearest lighter as the French reached the bank. A marine fired and a blue-coated Frenchman was hurled back and two others closed on the lighter and rammed their bayonets at sailors who were trying to pole the lighter off the bank with their oars. The attackers grabbed the oars. The French prisoners who had been under the guard were free now and, though unarmed, were also trying to board the lighter. A pistol fired, its report crisper than a musket. Then a dozen heavier crashes sounded and Sharpe guessed the sailors had been issued with the heavy pistols used by boarding parties. They had been issued with cutlasses too, though doubtless none had expected to use them, but now the sailors were hacking at men scrambling over the lighter's gunwale.

Sharpe was twenty yards away, crouching at the creek's edge. He told himself that this was not his fight, that his responsibility was back in the city whose lights shimmered across the wide bay. But he had six smoke balls aboard that threatened lighter and he wanted them, and besides, if the French took even one lighter then it would make Sir Thomas's withdrawal almost impossible. "We're going to have to drive the buggers away from the boat," Sharpe said.

"There must be fifty of the bastards, sir. More."

"Plenty of our lads still fighting," Sharpe said. "We'll just scare the buggers. Maybe they'll run." He stood, slung the unloaded rifle on his back, and drew his sword.

"God save Ireland," Harper said.

Army regulations decreed that Sharpe, as a skirmishing officer, should be armed with a cavalry saber, but he had never liked the weapon. The saber's curve made it good for slashing, but in truth most officers wore the blades as mere decoration. He much preferred the heavy cavalry trooper's sword that was one of the longest manufactured. The blade was straight, almost a yard of Birmingham steel. The cavalry complained constantly of the weapon. It did not keep an edge, it was too heavy in the blade, and the asymmetrical point made it ineffective. Sharpe had ground down the back blade to make the point symmetrical and he liked the weapon's weight that made the sword into an effective club. He and Harper splashed into the creek's shallows and came at the French from their left. The blue-coated men were not expecting an attack and may even have thought the two dark-uniformed men were French, for none turned to oppose them. These men were the French laggards, those unwilling to plunge into the creek and fight against the marines and sailors, and none wanted a fight. Some were reloading their muskets, but most just watched the struggle for the lighter as Sharpe and Harper hit them. Sharpe lunged the sword at a throat and the man fell away, his ramrod clattering in his musket's barrel. Sharpe struck again. Harper was thrusting the sword bayonet and bellowing in Gaelic. A French bayonet glinted to Sharpe's right and he swung the sword hard, thumping its blunt edge against a man's skull, and suddenly there was no immediate enemy in front, just a stretch of water and a knot of Frenchmen trying to board the lighter's bows that was being defended by marines with cutlasses and bayonets. Sharpe waded into the creek and thrust the sword at a man's spine, and knew he had taken too big a chance because the men assailing the lighter turned on him ferociously. A bayonet slashed into his jacket and became entangled there. He cut sideways just as Harper arrived beside him.

Harper was screaming incoherently now. He drove his rifle butt into a man's face, but more Frenchmen were coming and Sharpe dragged Harper back from their blades. Four men were attacking them and these were not the laggards. These were men who wanted to kill and he could see their bared teeth and their long blades. He swept the sword in a massive haymaking blow that deflected two bayonet thrusts, then stepped back again. Harper was beside him, and the Frenchmen pressed hard, thinking they had easy victims. At least, Sharpe thought, the enemy had no loaded muskets. Just then a gun went off and the muzzle flash blinded him and thick smoke engulfed him. But the bullet went God knows where, and Sharpe instinctively twitched from it and fell sideways into the creek. The French must have thought he was dead because they ignored him and lunged at Harper who thrust his sword bayonet hard into a man's eyes just as the Irish struck.

Major Gough had brought his company back to the creek and the first Sharpe knew of their coming was a volley that drowned the marsh in noise. After that came the screams of the attacking redcoats. They came with bayonets and fury. **"Faugh a ballagh!"** they shouted, and the French obeyed. The attack on the lighter shredded under the assault of the 87th. A Frenchman stooped to Sharpe, thinking him dead and presumably wanting his sword, and Sharpe punched the man in the face, then came out of the water, sword swinging, and he slashed it across the man's face. The Frenchman ran. Sharpe could see Ensign Keogh cutting his

straight sword at a much bigger enemy who
flailed at the thin officer with his musket. Then
the big Sergeant Masterson drove his bayonet
into the man's ribs. The Frenchman went down
under Masterson's weight. Keogh sliced his
sword at the fallen man and wanted more. He
was screaming a high-pitched scream and he saw
the two dark figures in the creek's shallows and
turned to attack, shouting at his men to follow.

"**Faugh a ballagh!**" Harper roared.

"It's you!" Keogh stopped at the water's edge.
He grinned suddenly. "That was a proper fight."

"It was bloody desperate," Harper muttered.

Major Gough was shouting at his men to form
line and face south. Sergeants pulled redcoats
away from the enemy corpses they were plundering. The surviving marines were clubbing the few
remaining Frenchmen off the lighter, but Captain Collins, a cutlass in his hand, was dead. "He
should have moved the bloody boats, sir," a marine sergeant said as he greeted Sharpe. The sergeant spat a dark stream of tobacco juice onto a
French corpse. "You're soaked through, sir," he
added. "Did you fall in?"

"I fell in," Sharpe said, and the first explosion
split the darkness.

The explosion came from one of the five fire

rafts. A spire of flame, brilliantly white, shot into the sky, then red light followed, flashing outward in a ring that flattened the marsh grass. The night was flooded with fire. Later it was decided that an errant spark from a fire in one of the captured French camps had somehow ignited a quickfuse. The charges had already been laid and the engineers were stringing the last of the fuses when one saw the bright fizz of a burning quick match. He shouted a warning, then jumped off the raft just as the first powder keg exploded. All across the rafts now the fuses sparked and smoked like wriggling snakes of fire.

The white spire twisted and dimmed. The rumble of the explosion faded across the marshland as a bugle sounded, ordering the British troops back to the lighters. The bugle was still calling when the next charges exploded, one after the other, their fire pounding toward the clouds and their noise punching across the marshes where the reeds and grasses bent again to the warm and unexpected winds. Smoke began to boil from the rafts where the French-laid incendiaries caught the fire and their flames illuminated the French troops who had retreated from the lighters. "Fire!" Major Gough roared, and his company of the 87th loosed a volley, and still the charges exploded and the rafts burned. The cannons at the rafts' perimeters began to fire, the balls and grapeshot whistling across the creek and marsh.

"Back! Back!" Sir Thomas Graham was roaring. The bugle sounded again. Redcoats were streaming back from the camp, their work done. Some were being helped by comrades. At least the fort's cannon fire had stopped, presumably because the gunners were watching the fireworks in the creek. Flaming scraps of wood whirled in the air, new pulses of fire pierced the night, and another cannon exploded. Sharpe stumbled on a Frenchman's body half sunk at the creek's edge.

"Count them in!" Major Gough shouted. "Count them in!"

"One, two, three!" Ensign Keogh was touching men on the shoulder as they clambered aboard. A sailor retrieved one of the oars snatched by the French. A crackle of musketry sounded from the marsh and a man of the 87th fell face forward in the mud. "Pick him up!" Keogh shouted. "Six, seven, eight, where's your musket, you rogue?"

The Hampshire men were boarding the other lighter. General Graham, with his two aides and a group of engineers, was waiting to be the last aboard. The rafts were infernos now. They would never leave the creek. The smoke boiled hundreds of feet into the night sky, but there was enough flame feeding that smoke to illuminate the marsh, and the gunners of San Luis could see the redcoats grouped on the creek bank and they must have known the lighters were there, and suddenly the cannons started firing again. Now they used shell as well as round shot. One shell exploded on the far bank while another, the trail of its fuse a crazed streak of spinning red in the flame-shot night, plunged into the creek. A round shot crashed through the Hampshire's ranks.

"All here!" Keogh shouted.

"Sir Thomas!" Major Gough yelled. An exploding shell threw up mud, reeds, and a French musket. An ancient cannon banged from the closest raft and Sharpe saw the ball skipping along the water. "Sir Thomas!" Major Gough bellowed again, but Sir Thomas was waiting to make sure all the Hampshires had embarked, and only then did he come to the lighter. A shell exploded just paces behind him, but miraculously the scraps of casing whistled harmlessly past him. Sailors thrust the lighter off the bank and the ebbing tide took it out toward the bay. The fire rafts were now a huge incandescent blaze beneath a thundercloud of smoke. The reflections of their flames rippled on the water, then were broken by a round shot that hurled up a great splash to soak men on the two lighters leaving the northern bank. The fifth lighter was in mid-creek, its sailors heaving on their oars to escape the gunfire.

"Row!" a naval officer shouted in Sharpe's boat. "Row!"

Three guns fired at once from the San Luis and Sharpe heard a shot rumble overhead. Musket fire flickered in the marsh and some redcoats stood up in the belly of the lighter and fired back. "Hold your fire!" Gough shouted.

"Row!" the naval officer called again.

"Not quite the orderly withdrawal I anticipated," Sir Thomas said. A shell, fuse whipping the dark with its thread of frantic red light, slapped into the creek. "Is that you, Sharpe?"

"Yes, sir."

"You're wet, man."

"Fell in the water, sir."

"You'll catch your death! Strip off. Take my cloak. How's your head? I forgot you were wounded. I should never have asked you to come."

Two more guns fired, then two more from the San José Fort to the north, but every pull of the great oars took the lighters away from the flames and into the blackness of the bay. Wounded men moaned in the lighters' holds. Other men talked excitedly, and Gough allowed it. "What's your butcher's bill, Hugh?" Sir Thomas asked the Irishman.

"Three men dead, sir," Gough said, "and eight wounded."

"But a good night's work," Sir Thomas said, "a very good night's work."

Because the fleet was safe and Sir Thomas, when the Spaniards were at last ready, could take his small army south.

Sir Thomas Graham's quarters in San Fernando were modest. He had commandeered a boat builder's workshop that had whitewashed stone walls. He had furnished it with a bed, a table, and four chairs. The workshop had a great hearth in front of which Sharpe's clothes were put to dry. Sharpe had put his rifle there too, with its lock plate removed so that the heat of the fire could reach the mainspring. He himself was swathed in a shirt and cloak that General Graham insisted on lending him. The general, meanwhile, was dictating his report. "Breakfast soon," the general said in between sentences.

"I'm starving," Lord William Russell observed.

"Be a good fellow, Willie, see what's keeping it," the general said, then dictated lavish praise of the men he had led to the creek. Dawn was outlining the inland hills, but still the glow of the burning rafts was vivid in the dark marshlands, while the plume of smoke must have been visible in Seville over sixty miles away. "You want me to mention your name, Sharpe," Sir Thomas asked.

"No, sir," Sharpe said. "I didn't do anything, sir."

Sir Thomas gave Sharpe a shrewd look. "If you say so, Sharpe. So what's this favor I can do for you?"

"I want you to give me a dozen rounds of shell, sir. Twelve-pounders if you've got them, but nine-pounders will do."

"I've got them. Major Duncan does, anyway. What happened to your jacket? Sword cut?"

"Bayonet, sir."

"I'll have my man sew it up while we have breakfast. Twelve rounds of shell, eh? What for?"

Sharpe hesitated. "Probably best you don't know, sir."

Sir Thomas snorted at that answer. "Write that up, Fowler," he said to the clerk, dismissing him. He waited for the clerk to leave, then went to the fire and held his hands to its warmth. "Let me guess, Sharpe, let me guess. Here you are, orphaned from your battalion, and suddenly I'm commanded to keep you here rather than send you back where you belong. And meanwhile Henry Wellesley's love letter is amusing the citizens of Cádiz. Would those two things be connected?"

"They would, sir."

"There are more letters?" Sir Thomas asked shrewdly.

"There are plenty more, sir."

"And the ambassador wants you to do what? Find them?"

"He wants to buy them back, sir, and if that doesn't work he wants them stolen."

"Stolen!" Sir Thomas gave Sharpe a skeptical look. "Had any experience in that business?"

"A bit, sir," Sharpe said and, after a pause, realized the general wanted more. "It was in London, sir, when I was a child. I learned the business."

Sir Thomas laughed. "I was once held up by a footpad in London. I knocked the fellow down. Wasn't you, was it?"

"No, sir."

"So Henry wants you to steal the letters and you want a dozen of my shells? Tell me why, Sharpe."

"Because if the letters can't be stolen, sir, they might be destroyed."

"You're going to explode my shells inside Cádiz?"

"I hope not, sir, but it might come to that."

"And you'll expect the Spanish to believe it was a French mortar bomb?"

"I hope the Spanish won't know what to think, sir."

"They're not fools, Sharpe. The dons can be bloody uncooperative, but they're not fools. If they discover you exploding shells in Cádiz they'll have you in that pestilential prison of theirs before you can count to three."

"Which is why it's best you don't know, sir."

"Breakfast is coming," Lord William Russell burst into the room. "Beefsteak, fried liver, and fresh eggs, sir. Well, almost fresh."

"I suppose you'll want the things delivered to

the embassy?" Sir Thomas ignored Lord William and spoke to Sharpe.

"If it's possible, sir, and addressed to Lord Pumphrey."

Sir Thomas grunted. "Come and sit down, Sharpe. You're partial to fried liver?"

"Yes, sir."

"I'll have the things boxed up and delivered today," Sir Thomas said, then shot Lord William a reproving look. "No good looking curious, Willie. Mister Sharpe and I are discussing secret matters."

"I can be the very soul of discretion," Lord William said.

"You can be," Sir Thomas agreed, "but you very rarely are."

Sharpe's coat was taken away to be mended. Then he sat to a breakfast of beefsteak, liver, kidneys, ham, fried eggs, bread, butter, and strong coffee. Sharpe, though he was only half dressed, enjoyed it. It struck him, halfway through the meal, that one table companion was the son of a duke and the other a wealthy Scottish landowner, yet he felt oddly comfortable. There was no guile in Lord William, while it was plain Sir Thomas simply liked soldiers. "I never thought I'd be a soldier," he confessed to Sharpe.

"Why not, sir?"

"Because I was happy as I was, Sharpe, happy as I was. I hunted, I traveled, I read, I played cricket, and I had the best wife in the world. Then my Mary died. I brooded for a time and it occurred to me that the French were an evil presence. They preach liberty and equality, but what are they? They are degraded, barbarous, and inhuman, and it was borne upon me that my duty was to fight them. So I put on a uniform, Sharpe. I was forty-six years old when I first donned the red coat, and that was seventeen years ago. And on the whole, I must say, they have been happy years."

"Sir Thomas," Lord William remarked as he savaged the bread with a blunt knife, "did not just put on a uniform. He raised the 90th Foot at his own expense."

"And a damned expense it was too!" Sir Thomas said. "Their hats alone cost me four hundred and thirty-six pounds, sixteen shillings, and fourpence. I always wondered what the fourpence was for. And here I am, Sharpe, still fighting the French. Have you had enough to eat?"

"Yes, sir, thank you, sir."

Sir Thomas made a point of walking Sharpe to the stables. Just before they reached the building the general stopped Sharpe. "Play cricket, do you, Sharpe?"

"We used to play at Shorncliffe, sir," Sharpe said cautiously, referring to the barracks where the riflemen were trained.

"I need cricketers," the general said, then frowned in thought. "Henry Wellesley's a damned fool," he said, abruptly changing the subject, "but he's a decent damned fool. Know what I mean?"

"I think so, sir."

"He's a very good man. He deals well with the Spanish. They can be infuriating. They promise the world and deliver scraps, but Wellesley has the patience to treat with them, and the sensible Spaniards know they can trust him. He's a good diplomat and we need him as ambassador."

"I liked him, sir."

"But he made a bloody fool of himself over that woman. Does she have the letters?"

"I think she has some, sir."

"So you're looking for her?"

"I am, sir."

"You're not going to blow her up with my shells, are you?"

"No, sir."

"I hope not, because she's a pretty wee thing. I saw her with him once and Henry looked like a tomcat that had found a bowl of cream. She looked happy too. I'm surprised she betrayed him."

"Lord Pumphrey says it was her pimp, sir."

"And what do you think?"

"I think she saw gold, sir."

"Of course the thing about Henry Wellesley," Sir Thomas said, apparently ignoring Sharpe's words, "is that he's a forgiving sort of man. Wouldn't surprise me if he's still sweet on her. Ah well, I'm probably just blathering. I enjoyed your company last night, Mister Sharpe. If you finish your business quickly enough, then I hope you'll give us a game or two. I've a clerk who's a ferocious bowler, but the wretched man has sprained his ankle. And I trust you'll do me the honor of sailing south with us. We can bowl a few quick ones at Marshal Victor, eh?"

"I'd like that, sir," Sharpe said, though he knew there was no hope of it coming true.

He went to find Harper and the other riflemen. He found a slop shop in San Fernando and, with the embassy's money, bought his men civilian clothes and then, beneath the smoke of the burning rafts that hung above Cádiz like a great dark cloud, they went to the city.

In the afternoon the cloud was still there, and twelve common shells, boxed up and labeled as cabbages, had arrived at the embassy.

Chapter 6

Nothing happened in the next three days. The wind turned east and brought persistent February rain to extinguish the burning fire rafts, though the smoke from the rafts still smeared the Trocadero marshes and drifted across the bay toward the city where Lord Pumphrey waited for a message from whoever possessed the letters. The ambassador dreaded another issue of **El Correo de Cádiz**. None appeared. "It publishes rarely these days," James Duff, the British consul in Cádiz, reported to the ambassador. Duff had lived in Spain for nearly fifty years and had been consul for over thirty. Some folk reckoned Duff was more Spanish than the Spaniards and even when Spain had been at war with Britain he had been spared any insult and allowed to continue his business of buying and exporting wine. Now that the embassy had been driven to seek refuge in Cádiz, there was no need for a consul in the city, but Henry Wellesley valued the older man's wisdom and advice. "Nuñez, I think, is struggling," Duff said, speaking of the owner of **El Correo de Cádiz**. "He has no readership beyond the city itself now, and what can he print? News of the Cortes? But everyone knows what happens there before Nuñez can set it in type. He has nothing left except rumors from Madrid, lies from Paris, and lists of arriving and departing ships."

"Yet he won't accept money from us?" Wellesley asked.

"Not a penny," Duff said. The consul was thin, shrunken, elegant, and shrewd. He visited the ambassador most mornings, invariably complimenting Henry Wellesley on the quality of his sherry, which Duff himself sold to the embassy, though with the French occupying Andalusia the supply was running very short. "I suspect he's in someone else's pay," Duff went on.

"You offered generously?" the ambassador asked.

"As you requested, Your Excellency," Duff said. He had visited Nuñez on Wellesley's behalf and had offered the man cash if he agreed to publish no more letters. The offer had been refused, so Duff had made an outright bid for the newspaper itself, a bid that had been startlingly generous. "I offered him ten times what the house, press, and business are worth, but he would not accept. He would have liked to, I'm sure, but he's a very frightened man. I think he dares not sell for fear of his life."

"And he proposes publishing more of the letters?"

Duff shrugged, as if to suggest he did not know the answer.

"I am so sorry, Duff, to place you in this predicament. My foolishness, entirely my foolishness."

Duff shrugged again. He had never married and had no sympathy for the idiocies that women provoked in men.

"So we must hope," the ambassador went on, "that Lord Pumphrey is successful."

"His Lordship might well succeed," Duff said, "but they'll have copies, and they'll publish them anyway. You cannot depend on their honor, Your Excellency. The stakes are much too high."

"Dear God." Henry Wellesley rubbed his eyes, then swiveled in the chair to stare at the steady rain falling on the embassy's small garden.

"But at least," Duff said consolingly, "you will

then possess the originals and can prove that the **Correo** has changed them."

Henry Wellesley winced. It might be true that he could prove forgery, but he could not escape the shame of what was not forged. "Who are they?" he asked angrily.

"I suspect they are people in the pay of Cardenas," Duff said calmly. "I can smell the admiral behind this one, and I fear he is implacable. I surmise"—he paused, frowning slightly—"I surmise you have thought of more direct action to deter publication?"

Wellesley was silent for a few seconds, then nodded. "I have, Duff, I have. But I would sanction such action most reluctantly."

"You are wise to be reluctant. I have noted an increase in Spanish patrols around Nuñez's premises. I fear Admiral Cardenas has prevailed on the Regency to keep a watchful eye on the newspaper."

"You could talk to Cardenas," Wellesley suggested.

"I could," Duff agreed, "and he will be courteous, he will offer me excellent sherry, and he will then deny any knowledge of the matter."

Wellesley said nothing. He did not need to. His face betrayed his despair.

"Our only hope," Duff went on, "is if Sir Thomas Graham succeeds in lifting the siege. A victory of that sort will confound those who oppose a British alliance. The problem, of course, is not Sir Thomas, but Lapeña."

"Lapeña." Wellesley repeated the name dully. Lapeña was the Spanish general whose forces would accompany the British southward.

"He will have more men than Sir Thomas," Duff went on remorselessly, "so he must have command. And if he is not given command, then the Spanish will not commit troops. And Lapeña, Your Excellency, is a timid creature. We must all hope that Sir Thomas can inspire him to valor." Duff held his glass of sherry to the window light. "This is the '03?"

"It is."

"Very fine," Duff said. He got to his feet and, with the help of a cane, crossed to the table with the inlaid checkered top. He stared for a few seconds at the chess pieces, then advanced a white bishop to take a castle. "I fear that is check, Your Excellency. Doubtless by next week you will confound me."

The ambassador courteously walked Duff to the sedan chair waiting in the courtyard. "If they publish more," Wellesley said, holding an umbrella over the consul as they approached the chair, "I shall have to resign."

"It will not come to that, I'm sure," Duff said unconvincingly.

"But if it does, Duff, you'll have to shoulder my burden till a new man arrives."

"I pray you remain in office, your excellency."

"As do I, Duff, as do I."

Some kind of answer to the ambassador's prayers came on the fourth day after the fire rafts had been destroyed. Sharpe was in the stables where he struggled to keep his bored men busy by repairing the stable roof, a job they hated, but a better occupation than being drunk. Lord Pumphrey's servant found Sharpe handing tiles to Rifleman Slattery. "His Lordship requests your attendance, sir," the servant said, eyeing Sharpe's dirty overalls with distaste, "as soon as possible, sir," the servant added.

Sharpe pulled on Captain Plummer's old black jacket, donned a cloak, and followed the servant through the city's maze of alleys. He discovered Lord Pumphrey in the middle balcony of the church of San Felipe Neri. The church was an oval-shaped chamber with a floor tiled in bold black and white, above which three balconies punctuated the domed ceiling from which hung a tremendous chandelier that was unlit, but thick with stalactites of candle wax. The church was now home to the Cortes, the Spanish parliament, and the upper balcony, known as paradise, was where the public could listen to the speeches being given below. The middle balcony was for grandees, churchmen, and diplomats, while the lowest was where the deputies' families and friends gathered.

The church's huge altar had been draped in a white cloth, in front of which a portrait of Spain's king, now a prisoner in France, was displayed where the crucifix normally stood. In front of the concealed altar the president of the Cortes sat at a long table flanked by a pair of rostrums. The deputies were in three rows of chairs facing him. Sharpe slid onto the bench beside Lord Pumphrey who was listening to a speaker haranguing the church in shrill, passionate tones, but was plainly being dull, for deputies were slipping away from their chairs and hurrying out of the church's main door. "He is explicating," Lord Pumphrey whispered to Sharpe, "the crucial role played by the Holy Spirit in the governance of Spain."

A priest turned and scowled at Pumphrey who smiled and waggled his fingers at the offended man. "It is a pity," His Lordship said, "that they've draped the altar. It possesses a quite exquisite painting of the Immaculate Conception. It's by Murillo and the cherubs are enchanting."

"Cherubs?"

"Plump little darlings that they are," Lord Pumphrey said, leaning back. He smelled of rosewater today, though thankfully he had resisted wearing his velvet beauty patch and was soberly dressed in plain black broadcloth. "I do think cherubs improve a church, don't you?" The priest turned and demanded silence and Lord Pumphrey raised an eyebrow in exasperation, then plucked Sharpe's elbow and led him around the balcony until they were directly above the altar and so facing the three rows where the remaining deputies sat. "Second row back," Pumphrey whispered, "right-hand side, four chairs in. Behold the enemy."

Sharpe saw a tall thin man in a dark blue uniform. He had a stick propped between his knees and he looked bored for his head was tilted back and his eyes were closed. His right hand opened and closed repeatedly over the stick's head. "Admiral the Marquis de Cardenas," Lord Pumphrey said.

"The enemy?"

"He has never forgiven us for Trafalgar. We lamed him there and took him prisoner. He was well enough looked after in a very decent house in Hampshire, but he hates us all the same and that, Sharpe, is the man rumored to be paying **El Correo de Cádiz.** Do you have a spyglass?"

"Mine's at the embassy," Sharpe said.

"Fortunately I possess all the essential accoutrements of a spy," Lord Pumphrey said and gave Sharpe a small telescope with an outer barrel sheathed in mother-of-pearl. "You might care to look at the admiral's coat?"

Sharpe opened the glass and trained the lens, focusing it on the admiral's blue jacket. "What am I looking at?"

"The horns," Lord Pumphrey said, and Sharpe edged the glass right and saw one of the horned brooches pinned to the dark cloth. The mark of **el Cornudo,** the enemy's mocking badge. Then he raised the glass and saw that the admiral's eyes were now open and were staring straight up at him. A hard face, Sharpe thought, hard and knowing and vengeful. "What do we do about the admiral?" he asked Lord Pumphrey.

"Do?" Pumphrey asked. "We do nothing, of course. He's an honored man, a deputy, a hero of Spain and, publicly at least, a valued ally. In truth he's a sour creature, animated by hatred, who is probably negotiating with Bonaparte. I suspect that, but I can't prove it."

"You want me to murder the bastard?"

"That would certainly improve diplomatic relations between Britain and Spain, wouldn't it?" Pumphrey asked tartly. "Why didn't I think of doing that? No, Richard, I do not want you to murder the bastard."

The admiral had summoned a servant and now whispered to him, pointing up at Sharpe as he did. The servant hurried away and Sharpe collapsed the glass. "What did you say his name was?"

"The Marquis de Cardenas. He owns much land in the Guadiana valley."

"We met his mother," Sharpe said, "and she's a wicked old bitch. Well in bed with the French too."

"Literally?"

"No. But they haven't plundered her estate. And she summoned them when we arrived. Tried to have us taken prisoner. Bitch."

"Like mother like son," Pumphrey said, "and you're not to murder him. We must frustrate his knavish tricks, of course, but we must do it without anybody noticing. You look very dirty."

"We're mending the stable roof."

"That is hardly an officer's occupation."

"Nor is getting back blackmailer's letters," Sharpe said, "but I'm doing it."

"Ah, the messenger, I suspect," Lord Pumphrey said. He was looking at a man who had come onto the balcony and was sidling behind the benches toward them. The man wore the same small horned badge as the admiral.

"Messenger?" Sharpe asked.

"I was told to wait here. We are to have a meeting to discuss the purchase of the letters. I was afraid you would not arrive on time." Pumphrey went silent as the man edged behind him, then leaned down to His Lordship's ear. He spoke briefly and too quietly for Sharpe to hear, then moved on toward the balcony's second door.

"There is a coffeehouse opposite the church," Lord Pumphrey said, "and an envoy will meet us there. Shall we go?"

They followed the messenger down the stairs, emerging on the ground floor into a small antechamber where the admiral now stood. The Marquis de Cardenas was very tall and very thin and had a black wooden leg. He leaned on an ebony stick. Lord Pumphrey gave him a low and exquisite bow, which the admiral returned with a stiff nod before turning on his heel and limping back into the church. "Bugger's not bothering to hide from us," Sharpe said.

"He has won, Sharpe," Lord Pumphrey said. "He has won, and he gloats."

The wind was gusting in the narrow street, snatching at Lord Pumphrey's hat as he hurried through the cold drizzle to the coffeehouse. There were a dozen tables inside, most of which were taken by men who all seemed to be talking at once. They shouted at one another, ignored one another, and gesticulated extravagantly. One, to emphasize his argument, tore a newspaper into shreds and scattered the pieces on the table, then leaned back triumphantly. "The deputies of the Cortes," Lord Pumphrey explained. He looked around him, but saw no one who was obviously waiting and so threaded the noisy crowd to take one of the empty tables at the back of the café.

"Other chair, my lord," Sharpe said.

"You're fussy?"

"I want to face the door."

Lord Pumphrey dutifully moved and Sharpe sat with his back against the wall. A girl took an order for coffee and Pumphrey twisted to look at the customers who argued in the pall of cigar smoke. "Mostly lawyers," he said.

"Lawyers?"

"A large proportion of the deputies are lawyers," Pumphrey said, rubbing his thin face with both hands. "Slaves, liberals, and lawyers."

"Slaves?"

Lord Pumphrey gave an exaggerated shiver and drew his coat tighter about his thin shoulders. "There are, very crudely, two factions in the Cortes. One side are the traditionalists. They're comprised of the monarchists, the pious, and the old-fashioned. They're called the **serviles.** It's an insulting nickname, like calling a man a Tory. **Serviles** means the slaves, and they wish to see the king restored and the church triumphant. They are the faction of landlords, privilege, and aristocracy." He shivered again. "The **serviles** are opposed by the **liberales,**" he went on, "who are so called because they are forever talking about liberty. The **liberales** want to see a Spain in which the people's wishes are more influential than the decrees of a tyrannical church or the whims of a despotic king. His Brittanic Majesty's government has no official view in these discussions. We merely wish to see a

Spanish government willing to pursue the war against Napoleon."

Sharpe looked scornful. "You're on the side of the **serviles.** Of course you are."

"Oddly enough, no. If anything we support the **liberales,** so long, of course, as their wilder ideas are not exported to Britain, God forbid that. But either faction will suffice if they continue to fight Bonaparte."

"So where's the confusion?"

"The confusion, Sharpe, is that men on both sides dislike us. There are **serviles** and **liberales** who earnestly believe that Spain's most dangerous enemy is not France, but Britain. The leader of that faction, of course, is Admiral Cardenas. He's a **servile,** naturally, but if he can scare enough **liberales** into believing that we'll annex Cádiz, then he should get his way. He wants Spain under a Catholic king and with himself as the king's chief adviser, and to achieve that he has to make peace with France and then where will we all be?" Lord Pumphrey shrugged. "Tell me, why did the redoubtable Sir Thomas Graham send me a gift of artillery shells? Not that I'm ungrateful, of course I'm not, but curious, yes? Good God! What are you doing?"

The question was prompted by the sudden appearance of a pistol, which Sharpe laid on the table. Pumphrey was about to protest, then saw Sharpe was looking past him. He twisted to see a tall black-cloaked man coming toward them. The man had a long face with a lantern jaw that somehow seemed familiar to Sharpe.

The man took a chair from another table, swung it around, and sat between Sharpe and Pumphrey. He glanced at the pistol, shrugged, and waved at the serving girl. "**Vino tinto, por favor,**" he said brusquely. "I'm not here to fight," he said, speaking English now, "so you can put the gun away."

Sharpe turned it so the muzzle pointed directly at the man, who took off his damp cloak, revealing that he was a priest. "My name," he spoke to Lord Pumphrey now, "is Father Salvador Montseny. Certain persons have asked me to negotiate on their behalf."

"Certain persons?" Lord Pumphrey asked.

"You cannot expect me to reveal their identity, my lord." The priest glanced at Sharpe's pistol and it was then that Sharpe recognized him. This was the priest who had been at Nuñez's house, the one who had ordered him out of the alleyway. "I have no personal interest in this matter," Father Montseny went on, "but those who asked me to speak for them believed you would take confidence that they chose a priest."

"Do hide that gun, Sharpe," Lord Pumphrey said. "You're frightening the lawyers. They think you might be one of their clients." He waited as Sharpe lowered the flint and put the pistol under his cloak. "You speak excellent English, Father."

"I have a talent for languages," Montseny said modestly. "I grew up speaking French and Catalan. Then I learned Spanish and English."

"French and Catalan? You're from the border?"

"I am Catalonian." Father Montseny paused as coffee and a flask of red wine were placed on the table. He poured himself wine. "The price, I am instructed to tell you, is three thousand guineas in gold."

"Are you authorized to negotiate?" Lord Pumphrey asked.

Montseny said nothing. Instead of answering, he took a scrap of sugar from a bowl and dropped it into his wine.

"Three thousand guineas is risible," Pumphrey said, "quite exorbitant. But to end what is an embarrassment His Majesty's government is prepared to pay six hundred."

Father Montseny gave a slight shake of the

head as if to suggest the counteroffer was absurd, then took an empty glass from the next table and poured Sharpe a glass of wine. "And who are you?" he asked.

"I look after him," Sharpe said, jerking his head at Lord Pumphrey and wishing he had not because pain whipped through his skull.

Montseny looked at the bandage on Sharpe's head. He seemed amused. "They gave you a wounded man?" he asked Lord Pumphrey.

"They gave me the best they had," Pumphrey said apologetically.

"You hardly need protecting, my lord," Montseny said.

"You forget," Lord Pumphrey said, "that the last man to negotiate for the letters was murdered."

"That is regrettable," the priest said sternly, "but I am assured it was the fault of the man himself. He attempted to seize the letters by force. I am authorized to accept two thousand guineas."

"One thousand," Pumphrey said, "with an undertaking that no more will be published in **El Correo.**"

Montseny poured himself more wine. "My principals," he said, "are willing to use their influence on the newspaper, but it will cost you two thousand guineas."

"Alas," Pumphrey said, "we only have fifteen hundred left in the embassy's strongbox."

"Fifteen hundred," Father Montseny said, as if he was thinking about it.

"For which sum, Father, your principals must give us all the letters and an undertaking to publish no more."

"I think that will be acceptable," Father Montseny said. He gave a small smile, as if satisfied with the outcome of the negotiations, then leaned back. "I could offer you some advice that would save you the money, if you wish?"

"I should be most grateful," Pumphrey said with exaggerated politeness.

"Any day now your army will sail, yes? You will land your troops somewhere to the south and come north to face Marshal Victor. You think he doesn't know? What do you think will happen?"

"We'll win," Sharpe growled.

The priest ignored him. "Lapeña will have, what? Eight thousand men? Nine? And your General Graham will take three or four thousand? So Lapeña will have command, and he's an old woman. Marshal Victor will have just as many, probably more, and Lapeña will take fright. He'll panic, and Marshal Victor will crush him. Then you will have very few soldiers left to protect the city, and the French will storm the walls. It will take many deaths, but by summer Cádiz will be French. The letters won't matter then, will they?"

"In that case," Lord Pumphrey said, "why not just give them to us?"

"Fifteen hundred guineas, my lord. I am instructed to tell you that you must bring the money yourself. You may have two companions, no more, and a note will be sent to the embassy telling you where the exchange will be made. You may expect the note after today's **oraciones.**" Montseny drained his glass, stood, and dropped a dollar on the table. "There, I have discharged my function," he said, nodded abruptly, and left.

Sharpe spun the dollar coin on the table. "At least he paid for his wine."

"We can expect a note after the evening prayers," Lord Pumphrey said, frowning. "Does that mean he wants the money tonight?"

"Of course. You can trust the bugger on that," Sharpe said, "but on nothing else."

"Nothing else?"

"I saw him at the newspaper. He's up to his

bloody eyes in it. He's not going to give you the letters. He'll take the money and run."

Pumphrey stirred his coffee. "I think you're wrong. The letters are a depreciating asset."

"Whatever the hell that means."

"It means, Sharpe, that he's right. Lapeña will have command of the army. You know what the Spanish call Lapeña? **Doña Manolito.** The lady Manolito. He's a nervous old woman and Victor will thrash him."

"Sir Thomas is good," Sharpe said loyally.

"Perhaps. But Doña Manolito will command the army, not Sir Thomas, and if Marshal Victor beats Doña Manolito then Cádiz will fall, and when Cádiz falls the politicians in London will fall over one another in their race to the negotiating chamber. The war costs money, Sharpe, and half of Parliament already believe it cannot be won. If Spain falls, what hope is there?"

"Lord Wellington."

"Who clings to a corner of Portugal while Bonaparte bestrides Europe. If the last scrap of Spain falls, then Britain will make peace. If, no, when Victor defeats Doña Manolito the Spaniards won't wait for Cádiz to fall. They'll negotiate. They would rather surrender Cádiz than see the city sacked. And when they surrender, the letters won't be worth a tin penny. That is what I mean by describing them as a depreciating asset. The admiral, if it is the admiral, would rather have the money now than a few worthless love letters in a month's time. So, yes, they're negotiating in good faith." Lord Pumphrey added a few small coins to the priest's dollar and stood. "We must get to the embassy, Richard."

"He's lying," Sharpe warned.

Lord Pumphrey sighed. "In diplomacy, Sharpe, we assume that everyone lies all the time. That way we make progress. Our enemies expect Cádiz to be French within a few weeks so they want their money now because after those few weeks there will be no money. They make hay while the sun shines, it is as simple as that."

It was raining harder now and the wind was gusting strong. The signs over the shops were swinging wildly and a crash of thunder rumbled over the mainland, sounding uncannily like heavy artillery shots traveling overhead. Sharpe let Pumphrey guide him through the maze of narrow alleys to the embassy. They went through the arch that was guarded by a squad of bored Spanish soldiers and hurried across the courtyard, only to be checked by a voice from high above. "Pumps!" the voice called. "Up here!"

Sharpe, like Lord Pumphrey, looked up to see the ambassador leaning out of a window of the embassy's watchtower, a modest five-story structure at the edge of the stable yard. "Up here," Henry Wellesley called again, "and you, Mister Sharpe! Come on!" He sounded excited.

Sharpe emerged onto the roofed platform to see that Brigadier Moon was lord of the tower. He had a chair and a footstool, and beside the chair was a telescope, while on a small table was a bottle of rum and beneath it a chamber pot. This tower had been equipped with windows to protect the upper platform from the weather, and it was plain that Moon had adopted the aerie. He had got to his feet now and, resting on his crutches, was looking eastward with the ambassador. "The ships!" Henry Wellesley greeted Sharpe and Lord Pumphrey.

A whole host of small ships was scurrying through white-capped waves into the vast harbor of the Bay of Cádiz. They were odd-looking craft to Sharpe's eyes. They were single-masted and had one gigantic sail each. The sails were wedge-shaped, sharp at the front and massive at the stern. "Feluccas," the ambassador said, "not a word to attempt when drunk."

"Felucky to get here before the storm broke," the brigadier commented, earning a smile from Henry Wellesley.

The French mortars were trying to sink the feluccas but having no success. The sound of the guns was muted by the rain and wind. Sharpe could see the blossom of smoke from inside Fort Matagorda and Fort San José each time a mortar fired, but he could not see where the shells plummeted for the water was already too turbulent. The feluccas thrashed onward, heading for the southern end of the bay where the rest of the shipping was safely out of mortar range. They were pursued by dark squalls and seething rain as the storm spread southward. A lightning bolt cracked far away on the northern coast. "So the Spaniards kept their word!" Henry Wellesley said exultantly. "Those ships have come here all the way from the Balearics! A couple of days to provision them, then the army can embark." He was a man who looked as though his troubles were coming to an end. If the combined British and Spanish army could destroy the French siege works and drive Victor's forces away from Cádiz, then his political enemies would be neutered.

The Cortes and the Spanish capital might even move back to a recaptured Seville and there would be the rare taste of victory in the air. "The plan," Henry Wellesley said to Sharpe, "is for Lapeña and Sir Thomas to rendezvous with troops from Gibraltar, then march north, take Victor in the rear, hammer him, and drive his troops out of Andalusia."

"It's supposed to be a secret," the brigadier grumbled.

"Some secret," Lord Pumphrey said sourly. "A priest just told me all about it."

The ambassador looked alarmed. "A priest?"

"Who seemed quite certain that Marshal Victor is entirely apprised of our plans to assault his lines."

"Of course he's bloody apprised of them," the brigadier said. "Victor might have started his career as a trumpeter, but the man can count ships, can't he? Why else is the fleet gathering?" He turned back to watch the feluccas that were now out of range of the mortars that had fallen silent.

"I think, Your Excellency, that we should confer," Lord Pumphrey said. "I have a proposal for you."

The ambassador glanced at the brigadier who

was studiously watching the ships. "A useful proposal?"

"Most encouraging, Your Excellency."

"Of course," Henry Wellesley said and headed for the stairs.

"Come, Sharpe," Lord Pumphrey said imperiously, but as Sharpe followed His Lordship the brigadier snapped his fingers.

"Stay here, Sharpe," Moon ordered.

"I'll follow you," Sharpe told Pumphrey. "Sir?" he asked the brigadier when Wellesley and Pumphrey were gone.

"What the devil are you doing here?"

"I'm helping the ambassador, sir."

"Helping the ambassador, sir," Moon mimicked Sharpe. "Is that why you stayed? You were supposed to ship back to Lisbon."

"Weren't you supposed to as well, sir?" Sharpe asked.

"Broken bones heal better on land," the brigadier said. "That's what the doctor told me. Stands to reason when you think about it. All that lurching about on ship? Doesn't help a bone knit, does it?" He grunted as he lowered himself into his chair. "I like it up here. You see things." He tapped the telescope.

"Women, sir?" Sharpe asked. He could think

of no other reason why a man with a broken leg would struggle to the top of a watchtower, and the tower did give Moon views of dozens of windows.

"Mind your tongue, Sharpe," Moon said, "and tell me why you're still here."

"Because the ambassador asked me to stay, sir, to help him."

"Did you learn your impudence in the ranks, Sharpe? Or were you born with it?"

"Being a sergeant helped, sir."

"Being a sergeant?"

"You have to deal with officers, sir. Day in, day out."

"And you have no high opinion of officers?"

Sharpe did not answer. Instead he gazed at the feluccas that were rounding into the wind and dropping anchors. The bay was a turmoil of whitecaps and small angry waves. "If you'll excuse me, sir?"

"Is it anything to do with that woman?" Moon demanded.

"What woman, sir?" Sharpe turned back from the stairs.

"I can read a newspaper, Sharpe," Moon said. "What are you and that bloody little molly cooking up?"

"Molly, sir?"

"Pumphrey, you idiot. Or hadn't you noticed?" The question was a sneer.

"I'd noticed, sir."

"Because if you're too fond of him," the brigadier said nastily, "you've got a rival." Moon was delighted by the indignation on Sharpe's face. "I keep my eyes open, Sharpe. I'm a soldier. Best to keep your eyes open. You know who visits the molly's house?" he gestured through the window. The embassy was composed of a series of houses, gathered around two courtyards and a garden, and the brigadier pointed to a house in the smaller yard. "The ambassador, Sharpe, that's who! Sneaks into the molly's house. What do you think of that, then?"

"I think Lord Pumphrey is an adviser to the ambassador, sir."

"Advice that must be given at night?"

"I wouldn't know, sir," Sharpe said, "and if you'll excuse me?"

"Excused," Moon sneered, and Sharpe clattered down the tower stairs, going to the ambassador's study where he found Henry Wellesley staring into the garden where the rain crashed down. Lord Pumphrey was by the fire, warming his behind. "Captain Sharpe is of the opinion that Father Montseny was lying," Pumphrey told Wellesley as Sharpe entered.

"Are you, Sharpe?" Wellesley asked without turning.

"Don't trust him, sir."

"A man of the cloth?"

"We don't even know he's a real priest," Sharpe said, "and I saw him at the newspaper."

"Whatever he is," Lord Pumphrey said tartly, "we have to deal with him."

"Eighteen hundred guineas," the ambassador said, sitting at his desk, "good God." He was so appalled that he did not see the look Sharpe shot at Lord Pumphrey.

Pumphrey, his peculation inadvertently revealed by the ambassador, looked innocent. "I would suggest, Your Excellency, that the Spaniards saw the ships arriving before we did. They conclude that our expedition will sail in the next day or two. That means battle within a fortnight and they are entirely confident of victory. And if the forces defending Cádiz are destroyed, then the letters become irrelevant. They would like to profit from them before that happens and thus the acceptance of my offer."

"Eighteen hundred guineas, though," Henry Wellesley said.

"Not your guineas," Pumphrey said.

"Good God, Pumps, the letters are mine!"

"Our opponents, Your Excellency, by publishing one letter, have made the correspondence into instruments of diplomacy. We are therefore justified in using His Majesty's funds to render them ineffectual." Lord Pumphrey made a pretty gesture with his right hand. "I shall lose the money, sir, in the accounts. Not difficult."

"Not difficult!" Henry Wellesley retorted.

"Subventions to the guerrilleros," Lord Pumphrey said smoothly, "purchase of information from agents, bribes to the deputies of the Cortes. We expend hundreds, thousands of guineas on such recipients and the Treasury has never glimpsed a receipt yet. It's not difficult at all, Your Excellency."

"Montseny will take the money," Sharpe said stubbornly, "and keep the letters."

Both men ignored him. "He insists you make the exchange personally?" the ambassador asked Lord Pumphrey.

"I suspect it is his way of assuring me that violence is not contemplated," Lord Pumphrey said. "No one would dare murder one of His Majesty's diplomats. It would cause too much of a ruction."

"They killed Plummer," Sharpe said.

"Plummer was not a diplomat," Lord Pumphrey said sharply.

The ambassador looked at Sharpe. "Can you steal the letters, Sharpe?"

"No, sir. I can probably destroy them, sir, but they're too well guarded to steal."

"Destroy them," the ambassador said. "I assume that means violence?"

"Yes, sir."

"I do not, I cannot, countenance acts that might aggravate our relationship with the Spanish," Henry Wellesley said. He rubbed his face with both hands. "Will they keep their word, Pumps? No more letters published?"

"I imagine the admiral is content with the damage done by the first, my lord, and is eager for gold. I think he will keep his word." Pumphrey frowned as Sharpe made a noise of disgust.

"Then so be it," Henry Wellesley said. "Buy them back, buy them back, and I apologize for causing this trouble."

"The trouble, Your Excellency," Lord Pumphrey said, "will soon be done." He looked down at the ambassador's chess game. "We have come, I think," he said, "to the end of the matter. Captain Sharpe? I assume you will accompany me?"

"I'll be there," Sharpe said grimly.

"Then let us gather gold," Lord Pumphrey said lightly, "and be done with it."

The note came well after dark. Sharpe was waiting with his men in an empty stall of the embassy stables. His five men were all in cheap civilian clothes and looked subtly different. Hagman, who was thin anyway, looked like a beggar. Perkins resembled an unappealing street rat, one of the London boys who swept horse shit out of the way of pedestrians in hope of a coin. Slattery appeared menacing, a footpad who could turn violent at the slightest show of resistance. Harris looked like a man down on his luck, perhaps a drunken schoolmaster turned onto the streets, while Harper was like a countryman come to town, big and placid and out of place in his shabby broadcloth coat. "Sergeant Harper comes with me," Sharpe told them, "and the rest of you wait here. Don't get drunk! I might need you later tonight." He suspected this night's adventure would go sour. Lord Pumphrey might be optimistic about the outcome, but Sharpe wanted to be ready for the worst, and the riflemen were his reinforcements.

"If we're not to get drunk, sir," Harris asked, "why the brandy?"

Sharpe had brought four bottles of brandy from the ambassador's own supply and now he uncorked the bottles and poured their contents into a stable bucket. Then he added a jug full of lamp oil. "Mix all that up," he told Harris, "then put it back in the bottles."

"You're setting a fire, sir?"

"I don't know what the hell we're doing. Maybe we're doing nothing. But stay sober, wait, and we'll see what happens."

Sharpe had thought about taking all his men, but the priest had been insistent that Pumphrey only bring two companions, and if His Lordship arrived with more, then probably nothing would happen. There was a chance, Sharpe allowed, that Montseny was dealing honestly, and so Sharpe would give the priest that small chance in hope that the letters would be handed over. He doubted it. He cleaned the two sea-service pistols he had taken from the embassy's small arsenal, oiled their locks, then loaded them.

The clocks in the embassy struck eleven before Lord Pumphrey came to the stables. His

Lordship was in a black cloak and carried a leather bag. "It's the cathedral, Sharpe," Lord Pumphrey said. "The crypt again. After midnight."

"Bloody hell," Sharpe said. He splashed water on his face and buckled his sword belt. "Are you armed?" he asked Pumphrey, and his lordship opened his cloak to show a pair of dueling pistols stuck in his belt. "Good," Sharpe said, "because the bastards are planning murder. Is it still raining?"

"No, sir," Hagman answered. "Windy, though."

"Pat, volley gun and rifle?"

"And a pistol, sir," Harper said.

"And these," Sharpe said. He crossed to the wall where the French haversack hung and took out four of the smoke balls. He was remembering the engineer lieutenant describing how the balls could be nasty in tight places. "Anyone got a tinderbox?"

Harris had one. He gave it to Harper. "Maybe we should all come, sir?" Slattery suggested.

"They're expecting three of us," Sharpe said, looking at Pumphrey who nodded in confirmation, "so if they see more than three they'll probably vanish. They're going to do that anyway once they've got what's in that bag." He nodded at the leather valise that Lord Pumphrey carried. "Is that heavy?"

Pumphrey shook his head. "Thirty pounds," he guessed, hefting the bag.

"Heavy enough. Are we ready?"

The cobbled streets were wet, gleaming in the intermittent light of torches burning in archways or at street corners. The wind gusted cold, plucking at their cloaks. "You know what they're going to do?" Sharpe said to Pumphrey. "They'll have us hand over the gold, then they'll make themselves scarce. Probably fire a couple of shots to keep our heads down. You'll get no letters."

"You are extremely cynical," Pumphrey said. "The letters are of ever-lessening use to them. If they print more, then the Regency will close them down."

"They will print more," Sharpe said.

"They would rather have this," Lord Pumphrey said, raising the bag.

"What they'd rather have," Sharpe said, "is the letters and the gold. They probably don't want to kill you, considering that you're a diplomat, but you're worth fifteen hundred guineas to them. So they'll kill if they have to."

Pumphrey led them west toward the sea. The

wind was brisker and the night filled with the booming, slapping sound of the canvas covering the unfinished parts of the cathedral's roof. Sharpe could see the cathedral now, its vast gray wall flickering with patches of light thrown by torches in the nearby streets. "We're early," Lord Pumphrey said, sounding nervous.

"They'll already be here," Sharpe said.

"Maybe not."

"They'll be here. Waiting for us. And don't you owe me something?"

"Owe you?" Pumphrey asked.

"A thank you," Sharpe said. "How much is in the bag, my lord?" he asked when he saw Lord Pumphrey's puzzlement. "Eighteen hundred or fifteen?"

Lord Pumphrey glanced at Harper, as if to suggest Sharpe should not talk about such matters in front of a sergeant. "Fifteen, of course," Pumphrey said, his voice low, "and thank you for saying nothing in front of His Excellency."

"Doesn't mean I won't tell him tomorrow," Sharpe said.

"My work requires expenses, Sharpe, expenses. You probably have expenses too?"

"Don't count me in, my lord."

"I merely do," Lord Pumphrey said with fragile dignity, "what everyone else does."

"So in your world everyone lies, and everyone's corrupt?"

"It is called the diplomatic service."

"Then thank God I'm just a thief and a murderer."

The wind buffeted them as they left the last small street and climbed the steps to the cathedral's doors. Pumphrey went to the left-hand one that squealed on its hinges as he pushed it open. Harper, following Sharpe inside, made the sign of the cross and gave a brief genuflection.

Pillars stretched toward the crossing where small lights glimmered. More candles burned in the side chapels, all of the flames flickering in the wind that found its way into the vast space. Sharpe led the way down the nave, rifle in hand. He could see no one. A broom lay discarded against one pillar.

"If trouble starts," Sharpe said, "lie flat."

"Not just run away?" Lord Pumphrey asked flippantly.

"They're behind us already," Sharpe said. He had heard footsteps and now, glancing back, saw two men in the shadows of the nave's end. Then he heard the scratch and bang of bolts being shot home. They were locked in now.

"Dear God," Lord Pumphrey said.

"Pray he's on our side, my lord. There are two men behind us, Pat, guarding the door."

"I've seen them, sir."

They reached the crossing where the transept met the nave. More candles burned on the temporary high altar. Scaffolding climbed the four huge pillars, vanishing in the lofty darkness of the unfinished dome. Pumphrey had gone to the crypt steps, but Sharpe checked him. "Wait, my lord," he said, and he went to the door in the temporary wall built where the sanctuary would one day stand. The door was locked. There were no bolts on the inner side, no padlock and no keyhole, which meant it was secured on the outer side and Sharpe cursed. He had made a mistake. He had assumed the door would be bolted from the inside, but when he had explored the cathedral with Lord Pumphrey he had not checked, which meant his retreat was cut off. "What is it?" Lord Pumphrey asked.

"We need another way out," Sharpe said. He stared up into the tangled shadows of the scaffolding that surrounded the crossing. He remembered seeing windows up there. "When we come out," he said, "it's up the ladders."

"There won't be any trouble," Lord Pumphrey said nervously.

"But if there is," Sharpe said, "then it's up the ladders."

"They will not dare attack a diplomat," Lord Pumphrey insisted in a hoarse whisper.

"For fifteen hundred beans I'd attack the king himself," Sharpe said, then led the way down the steps to the crypt. Candlelight glowed in the big round chamber. Sharpe went almost to the foot of the steps and crouched there. He thumbed back the rifle's flint and the small noise echoed back to him. To his right he could see the second flight of stairs. He could also see three of the cavern archways and he edged down another step until he could see the remaining two passageways to his left. No one was in sight, but a dozen candles burned on the floor. They had been arranged in a wide circle and there was something sinister about them, as if they had been placed for some barbaric ritual. The walls were bare stone and the ceiling a shallow dome of rough masonry. There was no decoration down here. The chamber looked as bare and cold as a cave, which it was, Sharpe realized, for the crypt had been hacked out of the rock on which Cádiz was built. "Watch behind, Pat," he said softly, and his voice bounced back to him across the wide chamber.

"I'm watching, sir," Harper said.

Then something white flashed in the corner of Sharpe's vision and he twisted, rifle coming up, and saw it was a packet thrown from a passage on the far side. It landed on the floor and the sound of it hitting the stones reverberated in multiple echoes that did not fade until the package had slid to a stop almost in the center of the ring of candles. "The letters," Montseny's voice sounded from one of the dark passageways, "and good evening, my lord."

Pumphrey said nothing. Sharpe was watching the dark archways, but it was impossible to tell which cavern Montseny was speaking from. The echo blurred the sound, destroying any hint of its source.

"You will put down the gold, my lord," Montseny said, "then pick up the letters and our business is concluded."

Pumphrey twitched as if he was going to obey, but Sharpe checked him with the rifle barrel. "We have to look at the letters," Sharpe said loudly. He could see the package was tied with string.

"The three of you will examine the letters," Montseny said, "then leave the gold."

Sharpe could still not determine where Montseny was. He thought the packet had been thrown from the passageway nearest the other flight of steps, but he sensed Montseny was in a different chamber. Five chambers. A man in each? And Montseny wanted Pumphrey and his companions in the center of the floor where they would be surrounded by guns. Rats in a barrel, Sharpe thought. "You know what to do," he said softly. He lowered the flint so the rifle was safe. "Pat? Take His Lordship's arm, and when we go, we go fast." He trusted Harper to do the right thing, but suspected Lord Pumphrey would be confused. What was important now was to stay away from the packet of letters, because that was in the lit space, the killing place. Sharpe suspected Montseny did not want to kill, but he did want the gold and he would kill if he had to. Fifteen hundred guineas was a fortune. You could build a frigate with that money, you could buy a palace, you could bribe a church full of lawyers. "We go slow at first," he said very softly, "then fast."

He stood, walked down the last step, looked

as if he was leading his companions to the package in the floor's center, then swerved left, to the nearest passageway where a burly man stood just inside the masonry arch. The man looked astonished as Sharpe appeared. He was holding a musket, but he was plainly not ready to fire it, and he was still just gaping as Sharpe hit him with the rifle's brass butt. It was a hard hit, smack on the man's jaw, and Sharpe seized the musket with his left hand and wrenched it away. The man tried to hit him, but Harper was there now and the butt of the volley gun cracked on the man's skull and he went down like a slaughtered ox. "Watch him, Pat," Sharpe said, and he went to the back of the chamber where the passage linked the separate crypts. Some small light filtered back here and a shadow moved. Sharpe hauled back the rifle's flint and the sound made the shadow move away.

"My lord!" Montseny said sharply from the dark.

"Shut your face, priest!" Sharpe shouted.

"What do I do with this bugger?" Harper asked.

"Kick him out, Pat."

"Put the gold down!" Montseny called. He

did not sound calm now. Things were not going as he had planned.

"I must see the letters!" Lord Pumphrey called, his voice high.

"You may look at the letters. Come out, my lord. All of you! Come out, bring the gold, and inspect the letters."

Harper pushed the half-stunned man out into the light. He staggered there, then hurried across the chamber into one of the far passageways. Sharpe was crouching beside Pumphrey. "You don't move, my lord," Sharpe said. "Pat, smoke balls."

"What are you doing?" Pumphrey asked in alarm.

"Getting you the letters," Sharpe said. He slung the rifle and cocked the captured musket instead.

"My lord!" Montseny called.

"I'm here!"

"Hurry, my lord!"

"Tell him to show himself first," Sharpe whispered.

"Show yourself!" Lord Pumphrey called.

Sharpe had gone back to the dark passage leading around the outer rim of the chambers.

Nothing moved there. He heard the click of Harper's tinderbox, saw the flame spring up, then the sparking of the fuse of the first smoke ball.

"It is you who want the letters, my lord," Montseny called, "so come for them!"

The second, third, and fourth fuses were lit. The worms of fire vanished into the perforated balls, but then nothing seemed to happen. Harper edged away from them, as if fearing they would explode.

"You wish me to come and fetch the gold?" Montseny shouted, and his voice reverberated around the crypt.

"Why don't you?" Sharpe shouted. There was no answer.

Smoke began leaking from the four balls. It started thinly, but suddenly one of them gave a fizzing sound and the smoke thickened with surprising speed. Sharpe picked it up, feeling the warmth through the papier-mâché case.

"My lord!" Montseny shouted angrily.

"We're coming now!" Sharpe called, and he rolled the first ball into the big chamber. The other three balls were spewing foul-smelling smoke now and Harper tossed them after the first, and suddenly the big central crypt was no longer a well-lit place, but a dark cavern filling with a writhing, choking smoke that obliterated the light of the dozen candles. "Pat!" Sharpe said. "Take His Lordship up the stairs. Now!"

Sharpe held his breath, ran to the crypt's center, and scooped up the package. He turned back to the steps just as a man came through the smoke with musket in hand. Sharpe swept his own musket at him, ramming the muzzle into the man's eyes. The man fell away as Sharpe ran to the steps. Harper was near the top, holding Pumphrey's elbow. A musket fired in the crypt and the multiple echo made it sound like a batallion volley. The ball clipped the ceiling over Sharpe's head, striking off a chip of stone, and then Sharpe was up the steps and Harper was there, waiting for Sharpe, and there were two men with muskets halfway down the nave. Sharpe knew Harper was wondering whether to attack them and so escape out of the cathedral's main doors.

"Ladder, Pat!" Sharpe said. To go down the nave would be to allow Montseny and his men to fire at them from behind. "Go!" He pushed Pumphrey toward the nearest ladder. "Take him up, Pat! Go! Go!"

A musket fired from the nave. The shot went

past Sharpe and buried itself in a pile of purple cloths waiting to decorate the cathedral's altars during the coming season of Lent. Sharpe ignored the man who had fired, shooting his captured musket down the crypt stairs. Then he took the rifle off his shoulder and fired that as well. He heard men scrambling in the smoke below, heard them coughing. They expected a third shot, but none came because Sharpe had run for the scaffold and was climbing for his life.

Chapter 7

Sharpe scrambled up the ladder. A musket fired from the nave, its sound magnified by the cathedral walls. He heard the ball crack on stone and whine off into the transept. Then an enormous crash prompted a shout of alarm from his pursuers. Harper had thrown a block of building stone into the crossing and the limestone shattered there, skittering shards across the floor.

"Another ladder, sir!" Harper called from above and Sharpe saw the second ladder climbing into the upper gloom. Each of the massive pillars at the corners of the crossing supported a tower of scaffolding, but once the four flimsy towers reached the arches spanning the pillars the scaffolding branched and joined to encompass the walls climbing to the base of the dome. Another musket fired and the ball buried itself in a plank, starting dust that half choked Sharpe as he climbed the second ladder that swayed alarmingly. "Here, sir!" Harper reached out a hand. The Irishman and Lord Pumphrey were on the wide stone ledge of the tambour, a decorative shelf running around the middle of the pillar. Sharpe guessed he was forty feet above the cathedral floor now, and the pillar climbed that far again before the scaffolding spread out beneath the dome. There was a window high in the gloom. He could not see it, but he remembered it.

"What have you done?" Lord Pumphrey asked angrily. "We should have negotiated! We didn't even see the letters!"

"You can see them now," Sharpe said, and he thrust the packet into Pumphrey's hands.

"Do you know what offense this will cause the Spaniards?" Lord Pumphrey's anger was unassuaged by the gift of the packet. "This is a cathedral! They'll have soldiers here at any moment!"

Sharpe gave his opinion of that statement, then peered over the tambour's edge as he reloaded the rifle. They were safe enough for the moment because the stone ledge was wide and it protected them from any shots fired from the crossing's floor, but he guessed their enemies would soon try to climb the scaffold and attack them from the flanks. He could hear men talking below, but he could also hear something odd, something that sounded like battle. It was a booming sound like cannon fire. It crackled, rose, and fell, and Sharpe realized it was the wind tearing at the tarpaulins covering the unfinished roof. A louder grumble overlaid the booming, and that was thunder. Any noise of guns in the cathedral would be drowned by the storm and besides, Montseny had bolted the doors. The priest would send for no soldiers. He wanted the gold.

A volley of musketry cracked and echoed and the balls spattered all around the tambour. Sharpe guessed the shots must have been fired to protect someone climbing a ladder. He looked, saw the shadow on the opposite pillar, aimed the rifle, and pulled the trigger. The man was hurled sideways off the rungs and fell to the floor before crawling into the nave's choir stalls and so out of sight.

"You have a knife?" Pumphrey asked.

Sharpe gave him his pocketknife. He heard the string being cut, then the rustle of papers. "You want Sergeant Harper to strike a light?" he offered.

"No need," Pumphrey said sadly. He unfolded a large sheet of paper. Even in the semi-
darkness above the tambour, Sharpe could see
the package had not contained letters, but a
newspaper. Presumably **El Correo de Cádiz.**
"You were right, Sharpe," Pumphrey said.

"Fifteen hundred beans," Sharpe said, "one
thousand five hundred and seventy-five pounds.
A man could retire on that. You and me, Pat, we
could take the money"—Sharpe paused to bite
off the end of a cartridge—"we could sail off to
America, open a tavern, live well forever."

"Wouldn't need a tavern, sir, not with fifteen
hundred guineas."

"Be nice though, wouldn't it?" Sharpe said.
"A tavern in a town by the sea? We could call it
the Lord Pumphrey." He took a leather patch
from his cartridge pouch, wrapped the bullet,
and rammed it down the barrel. "But they don't
have lords in America, do they?"

"They don't," Lord Pumphrey said.

"So maybe we'll call it the Ambassador and
the Whore instead," Sharpe said, sliding the ramrod back into place beneath the barrel. He
primed and cocked the rifle. No one was moving
below, which suggested Montseny was considering his tactics. He and his men had learned to

fear the firepower above them, but that would not deter them for long, not when there were fifteen hundred golden English guineas to be won.

"You wouldn't do that, Sharpe, would you?" Pumphrey asked nervously. "I mean, you're not planning on taking the money?"

"For some reason, my lord, I'm a loyal bastard. God knows why. But Sergeant Harper is Irish. He's got plenty of cause to hate us English. One shot from that volley gun and you and I are dead meat. Fifteen hundred guineas, Pat. You could do a lot with that."

"I could, sir."

"But what we have to do now," Sharpe said, "is go to our left. We climb to that window." He pointed. His eyes had adjusted to the gloom and he could see a slight sheen betraying the window beneath the dome. "We break through. There's scaffolding on the outer wall. We go down that and we're off into the city like rats into a hole."

To get there they would have to climb the scaffold above the tambour, then cross a narrow plank and climb another ladder, which led to a rickety platform just beneath the window. The ladders, like the scaffolding poles, were tied in place with rope. It was not a long journey, no more than thirty feet upward, the same across, and half as much up again, but to make it they must expose themselves to the men below. Sharpe guessed there were eight or nine men there, all with muskets, and even a musket could hit at that distance. Once they left the shelter of the wide stone ledge, then one of them would surely be struck by a bullet. "What we have to do," he said, "is distract the bastards. Pity we don't have those other smoke balls."

"They worked fine, didn't they?" Harper said happily. Smoke was leaking out of the crypt stairways and spreading on the crossing floor, but there was not enough to obscure the high dome.

Sharpe crouched on the tambour, staring at the scaffolding all about the crossing. Montseny and his men were just out of sight in the nave. They were doubtless waiting for Sharpe to move off the safety of the stone ledge. Then they would fire a volley. So distract them, he thought, confuse them, but how? "You got any more stone, Pat?"

"There's a dozen blocks here, sir."

"Throw them down. Just to keep them happy."

"Can I use the volley gun, sir?"

"Only if you see two or three of them." The

volley gun was a vicious thing, but took so long to reload that it was useless once it was fired.

"What about you, sir?"

"I've got an idea," Sharpe said. It was a desperate idea, but Sharpe had seen the long rope that was tied to the base of the scaffold opposite. It climbed into the gloom, vanishing somewhere in the dome, then reappeared closer to him. There was a great iron hook on its end and that hook was tied to the scaffold to his right and on the next platform down. The rope was used to hoist the masonry blocks to the dome. "Give me back the knife," he said to Pumphrey. "Now, Pat!" he said, and Harper heaved a block of limestone into the transept. When it crashed onto the floor, Sharpe dropped down the ladder. He did not use the rungs, but went down it like a seaman using a companionway, hands and feet on the outer edge, and he swore as a splinter drove into his right hand. He hit the plank platform hard and felt it shake. A second stone banged onto the cathedral floor, and Montseny must have thought they were hurling the masonry because they had run out of ammunition, for he and three other men stepped out with muskets.

"God bless you," Harper said, and fired the volley gun. The sound was deafening, a massive explosion that reverberated around the cathedral as the seven bullets flayed the space between the choir stalls. A man cursed below as Sharpe reached the hook. A musket fired at him, but the shot came from the far transept and the ball missed by a yard. He seized the heavy hook and sawed through the rope lashing it in place, then carried the hook and its heavy line back along the plank, up the ladder, and onto the tambour just as another two shots cracked bright in the gloom below. He gave the hook to Harper. "Pull on it," he said. "Don't jerk it, just pull as hard as you can." He did not want the men below to understand what was happening, so the tension on the rope had to be gradual.

A faint squeal from the upper darkness betrayed that the rope went through a sheave up there. Sharpe saw the line tighten and heard Harper grunt. A shadow moved below and Sharpe snatched up his rifle, aimed too quickly, and fired. The shadow vanished. Harper was pulling with all his huge strength as Sharpe took out another cartridge.

"It's not moving," Harper said.

Sharpe finished reloading, then gave the rifle and his pistol to Lord Pumphrey. "Keep them amused, my lord," he said. Then he crouched by

Harper and both of them heaved on the rope. It did not budge an inch. The bitter end was tied to a scaffold pole and the pole seemed immovable. The knot had slid up to where a second pole was tied crosswise and it would move no farther. The angle was all wrong, too acute, but if Sharpe could just move that pole he might have his distraction.

Lord Pumphrey fired one of his dueling pistols, then the second one, and Sharpe heard a yelp from the nave. "Well done, my lord," he said. He decided to abandon caution now. "Jerk it," Sharpe told Harper, and they gave the rope a series of hard pulls. Sharpe thought the pole moved slightly, just a shudder, and the men below must have realized what they were doing for one of them ran out of the nave with a knife in his hand. Lord Pumphrey fired a sea-service pistol and the ball struck the flagstone floor and whipped away down the nave. The man had reached the scaffold and was climbing to cut the rope. "Pull!" Sharpe said, and he and Harper gave a huge heave. The scaffold pole bent outward. The scaffolding was old. It had been in place for almost twenty years and the lashings were frayed. Masonry blocks were piled on its platforms and some of them shifted. Once they began to move, they would not stop. "Pull!" Sharpe said again, and they tugged on the rope once more. This time the far scaffold pole snapped clean away from the rest of the structure. Stones began to crash through the planking. The man with the knife jumped for his life, and just then the rest of the scaffolding on the crossing's far side collapsed in a welter of noise and dust.

"Now," Sharpe said.

The noise was monstrous. The falling poles, planks, and stones crashed and tore, splintered and banged as almost a hundred feet of scaffolding cascaded into the crossing. Blocks of stone ripped through the poles and planks, but what was most useful was the dust. It was thicker than smoke, and amid the tumbling stones and timber it blossomed like a dark gray cloud to dim the small candlelight coming from the cathedral's chapels. The scaffolding that Sharpe was crossing began to shake as the destruction spread around the crossing. Then he pushed Pumphrey up the ladder. Harper was already at the top, using his volley gun's butt to smash open the window. "Use your cloak!" Sharpe shouted. He could hear someone screaming below.

Harper laid his cloak over the broken shards

of glass in the bottom of the shattered window and then unceremoniously hauled Pumphrey up beside him. "Come on, sir!" He reached for Sharpe's hand and grabbed it just as the planks slid out from under Sharpe's feet. The last of the scaffolding tumbled, filling the cathedral with more noise and dust.

They were now balanced precariously on the window's edge. The crossing behind them was boiling with dust through which the candlelight died, plunging the cathedral into utter darkness. "There's a drop, sir," Harper warned. Sharpe jumped, thought the drop would never end, and suddenly sprawled on a flat roof. Pumphrey came next, hissing with pain as he landed, and Harper followed. "God save Ireland, sir," the sergeant said fervently, "but that was desperate!"

"Have you got the money?"

"Yes," Pumphrey said.

"I enjoyed that," Sharpe said. His head hurt like the devil and his hand was bleeding, but there was nothing he could do about either. "I really enjoyed that," he said. The wind plucked at him. He could hear waves breaking nearby. When he went to the edge of the roof he saw the pale white fret of breakers beyond the seawall. It had begun to rain again, or perhaps it was sea spray driven on the wind. "Scaffolding's on the other side," he said.

"I think my ankle's broken," Lord Pumphrey said.

"No it's bloody not," Sharpe said, who did not know one way or the other, but this was no time for His Lordship to become feeble. "Walk and it'll get better."

The monstrous sails beat against the unfinished crown of the dome and above the unbuilt sanctuary. Sharpe blundered into one of the ropes securing them, then felt his way to the roof's edge. Just enough light came from a lantern in a courtyard below for him to see where the scaffolding was built. He could see other lanterns, bobbing as they were carried through the streets. Someone must have heard the shots in the cathedral despite the noise of the storm, but whoever went to investigate was going to the eastern facade with its three doors. No one was watching the cathedral's northern flank where Sharpe found the ladders. With Harper now holding the gold, they went down ladder after ladder. Thunder sounded overhead and a flash of lightning lit the intricate pattern of poles and planks down which they climbed. Lord Pumphrey almost kissed the cobblestones when they reached the bottom. "Dear God," he said. "It's just sprained, I think."

"Told you it wasn't broken," Sharpe said. He grinned. "It was all a bit hurried at the end, but otherwise it went well."

"It was a cathedral!" Harper said.

"God will forgive you," Sharpe said. "He might not forgive those bastards inside, but he'll forgive you. He loves the Irish, doesn't he? Isn't that what you keep telling me?"

It was not far to the embassy. They knocked on the gate and a sleepy doorkeeper pulled it open. "The ambassador's waiting?" Sharpe asked Pumphrey.

"Of course."

"Then you can give him His Majesty's money back," Sharpe said, "less six guineas." He opened the valise and found it filled with leather bags. He untied one, counted six guineas, and gave the rest to Pumphrey.

"Six guineas?" Lord Pumphrey asked.

"I might need to bribe someone," Sharpe said.

"I imagine His Excellency will want to see you in the morning," Pumphrey said. He sounded dispirited.

"You know where to find me," Sharpe said.

He walked toward the stables, but stopped under the arch and saw that Lord Pumphrey was not going toward the house where the embassy had its offices and Henry Wellesley had his quarters. Instead he went to the courtyard that led to the smaller houses, to his own house. He watched His Lordship disappear, then spat. "They think I'm daft, Pat."

"They do, sir?"

"They all do. Are you tired?"

"I could sleep for a month, sir, so I could."

"But not now, Pat. Not now."

"No, sir?"

"When's the best time to hit a man?"

"When he's down?"

"When he's down," Sharpe agreed. There was work to do.

Sharpe gave each of his riflemen a guinea. They had been fast asleep when he and Harper returned to the stables, but they woke up when Sharpe lit a lantern. "How many of you are drunk?" Sharpe asked.

The faces looked at him resentfully. No one spoke. "I don't care if you are," Sharpe said, "I just want to know."

"I had some," Slattery said.

"Are you drunk?"

"No, sir."

"Harris?"

"No, sir. Some red wine, sir, but not much."

Perkins was frowning at his guinea. He might never have seen one before. "What does m, b, f, et, h, rex, f, d, b, et, l, d, s, r, I, a, t, et, e mean," he asked. He had read the inscription on the coin and stumbled over the letters, half remembered from some long-ago schooling.

"How the hell would I know?" Sharpe asked.

"King of Great Britain, France, and Ireland," Harris said. "Defender of the Faith, Duke of Brunswick and Luneburg, Arch-Treasurer and Elector, of course."

"Bloody hell," Perkins said, impressed. "So who's that, then?"

"King George, you idiot," Harris said.

"Put it away," Sharpe told Perkins. He was not quite sure why he had given them the guineas, except that on a night when so much money had been treated so lightly he saw no reason why his riflemen should not benefit. "You're all going to need greatcoats and hats."

"Jesus," Harris said, "we're going out? In this storm?"

"I need the twelve-pounder shells," Sharpe said, "and the last two smoke balls. Put them in your packs. Did you fill the bottles with lamp oil and brandy?"

"Yes, sir."

"We need those too. And yes, we're going out." He did not want to. He wanted to sleep, but the time to strike was when the enemy was off balance. Montseny had taken at least six men, maybe more, to the cathedral, and those men were probably still entangled with the wreckage of the scaffolding and snared in the questions of the troops who had gone to discover the cause of the commotion. Did that mean the newspaper was unguarded? But guarded or not, the storm was a godsend. "We're going out," he said again.

"Here, sir." Hagman brought him a stone bottle.

"What's that?"

"Vinegar, sir, for your head, sir. Take off your hat." Hagman insisted on soaking the bandage with vinegar. "It'll help, sir."

"I stink."

"We all stink, sir. We're the king's soldiers."

The storm was worsening. The rain had started again and was coming harder, driven by a wind that pounded the city's ocean walls with heavy waves. Thunder rolled like cannon shots above the watchtowers and lightning ripped across the bay where the waiting fleet jerked at its anchor lines.

Sharpe guessed it was past two in the morning when he reached the abandoned building close to Nuñez's house. The rain was malevolent. Sharpe fumbled in his pocket for the key, opened the padlock, and pushed the door open. He had only got lost twice on the way here, and had eventually found the place by taking the route along the harbor wall. There had been Spanish soldiers there, sheltering by the cannons overlooking the bay's entrance, and Sharpe had feared being asked his business, so he had marched his five men as a squad. He reckoned the Spanish sentinels would assume the five men were a detail from the garrison, forced to endure the weather, and leave them alone. It had worked, and now they were inside the abandoned building. He closed the gates and locked them with the inside bolts. "You've got the lantern?" he asked Perkins.

"Yes, sir."

"Don't light it till you're inside the building," Sharpe said. Then he gave Harper careful orders

before taking Hagman to the watchtower. They
groped their way through the dark and up the
steps. Once at the top, it was hard to see anything because the night was so dark. Sharpe was
watching for a sentry on the roof of the Nuñez
house, but could see nothing. He had brought
Hagman because the old poacher had the best
eyesight of any of his riflemen.

"If he's there, sir," Hagman said, "he's staying
out of the wind and rain."

"Probably."

A shard of lightning lit the interior of the
watchtower. Then thunder echoed across the
city. The rain was pelting down, hissing on
the roofs below. "Do people live above the printers, sir?" Hagman asked.

"I think so," Sharpe said. Most of the houses
in the city seemed to have shops or workplaces
on the ground floor and living quarters above.

"Suppose there are women and children
there?"

"That's why I've got the smoke balls."

Hagman thought about that. "You mean
you'll smoke them out?"

"That's the idea, Dan."

"Only I wouldn't like to kill little ones, sir."

"You won't have to," Sharpe said, hoping he was right.

There was another flash of lightning. "There's no one there, sir," Hagman said, nodding toward the roof of Nuñez's house. "On the roof, sir," he added, realizing that Sharpe could not have seen the nod.

"They all went to the cathedral, didn't they?"

"They did, sir?"

"I'm talking to myself, Dan," Sharpe said, staring into the rain and wind. He had seen a sentry on the roof in daylight and he had assumed there would be a man there at night, but suppose that man was still in the cathedral? Or was he just keeping dry and warm inside the house? Sharpe had planned to drop the smoke balls down the chimneys. The smoke would drive whoever was inside the building out to the street. Then Sharpe would drop the shells down to wreak what damage they could. The idea of using the chimneys had come to him when he saw the firewood being carried through the city's streets, but suppose he could get inside Nuñez's house?

"When this is done, sir," Hagman asked, "do we go back to battalion?"

"I hope so," Sharpe said.

"I wonder who's commanding the company now, sir. Poor Mister Bullen isn't."

"Lieutenant Knowles, I should think."

"He'll be glad to see us back, sir."

"I shall be glad to see him. And it won't be long, Dan. There!" Sharpe had seen a glimmer of light immediately beneath the tower. It showed for a second, then vanished, but told Sharpe that Harper had found a way onto the roof. "Down we go."

"How's your head, sir?"

"I'll live, Dan."

Sharpe reckoned the flat roofs were a thief's dream. A man could walk all around Cádiz four stories above the streets, and few of those streets were too wide to be jumped. The storm was just as big a help. The rain and wind would drown any noise, though he still told his men to take off their boots. "Carry them," he said. Even with the storm the boots would make too much noise on the roofs of the houses between the watchtower and the newspaper.

There were low walls between the roofs, but it took less than a minute to cross them and so discover that there was no sentry on Nuñez's house. There was a trapdoor, but it was firmly bolted on the inside. Sharpe had seen the ladder climbing from the balcony on his first reconnaissance. He gave Perkins his boots, slung his rifle, and climbed down. The ladder went to the side of the balcony so the big wooden shutters covering the door had room to open. The shutters were closed and latched now. Sharpe groped for the place they joined, then put his knife between them. The blade slid easily because the wood had rotted. He found the latch, pushed it up, and one of the shutters caught the wind and swung violently, banging against the wall. The shutters had protected a half-glazed door that began to rattle in the wind. Sharpe put his knife into the gap between the doors, but this wood was solid. The shutter banged again. Break the glass, he thought. Easy. But suppose there were bolts at the foot of the door?

He was about to crouch and push against the foot of the door when he saw a glimmer of light from inside the room. For a heartbeat he thought he had imagined it, then wondered whether it was the reflection of distant lightning on the glass, but the glimmer showed again. It was a spark. He stepped to one side. The light vanished a second time, reappeared, and he reckoned someone inside had been sleeping.

They had been woken by the banging of the shutter and now they used a tinderbox to light a candle. The flame burned bright suddenly, then steadied as the candle was lit.

Sharpe waited, knife in hand. The rain was loud on his hat, the same hat he had bought from the beggar. He heard the bolts being drawn. Three bolts. Then the door opened and a man appeared in a nightshirt. He was an older man, in his forties or fifties, and had tousled hair and a bad-tempered face. He reached for the swinging shutter as the candle flickered in the wind behind him. Then he saw Sharpe and opened his mouth to shout. The blade touched his throat. **"Silencio,"** Sharpe hissed. He pushed the man inside. There was a rumpled bed, clothes heaped on a chair, a chamber pot, and nothing else. "Pat! Bring 'em down!"

The riflemen filled the room. They were dark figures, soaking wet, who now pulled on their boots. Sharpe closed the shutters and latched them. Harris, who spoke the best Spanish, was talking to the prisoner who gesticulated wildly as he spoke. "He's called Nuñez, sir," Harris said, "and he says there's two men on the ground floor."

"Where are the others?" Sharpe knew that there had to be more than two guards.

There was a flurry of Spanish. "He says they went out, sir," Harris said.

So Montseny had stripped the place of sentries in hope of making an ungodly profit. "Ask him where the letters are."

"The letters, sir?"

"Just ask him. He'll know."

A sly look flickered on Nuñez's face, then an expression of pure alarm as Sharpe turned on him with the knife. He stared into Sharpe's face and his courage fled. He spoke fast. "He says they're downstairs, sir," Harris translated, "with the writer. Does that make sense?"

"It makes sense. Tell him to be quiet now. Perkins, you're going to stay here and watch him."

"Tie him up, sir?" Harris suggested.

"And stop his mouth up too."

Sharpe lit a second candle and carried it into the next room where he saw a flight of stairs going up to the bolted trapdoor. Another flight went down to the second floor where there was a small kitchen and a parlor. A door opened onto the next stairway, which led to one huge storeroom, piled with paper. Light showed from the ground floor. Sharpe, leaving the candle on the stairs, went to the top of the open staircase and saw the press vast and black beneath him, and next to it a table on which playing cards had been discarded. A man was sleeping on the floor, while another, with a musket over his knees, was slouched in a chair. A huge pile of newly printed newspapers was stacked against the wall.

Henry Wellesley had been insistent that Sharpe should do nothing to upset the Spanish. They were prickly allies, he had explained, resentful that the defense of Cádiz needed British troops. "They must be handled with a very light rein," the ambassador had said. There must be no violence, Wellesley had declared. "Bugger that," Sharpe said aloud, and hauled back the flint of the rifle. The sound of it made the man in the chair start.

The man began to lift his musket, then saw Sharpe's face. He put it down and his hands trembled.

"You can come down, lads," Sharpe called back up the stairs. It was all so easy. Too easy? Except fifteen hundred guineas was a powerful incentive to carelessness and Father Montseny was doubtless still trying to explain the wreckage in the cathedral.

The two men were disarmed. Harper discovered two apprentice printers sleeping in the cellar and they were brought up and put into a corner with the guards while the writer, a wreck of a man with an unkempt beard, was dragged out of a smaller room. "Harris," Sharpe said, "tell that miserable bugger he's got two minutes to live unless he gives me the letters."

Benito Chavez yelped as Harris put a sword bayonet to his throat. Harris forced the wretched man against a wall and started questioning him as Sharpe explored the room. The door that led to the street was blocked up with rough masonry while the back door, which presumably led to the courtyard, was locked with big iron bolts. This meant that Sharpe and his men had the place to themselves. "Sergeant? All that paper on the first floor, throw it down here. Slattery? Keep one of those newspapers"—he pointed to the newly printed editions stacked against the blocked front door—"and scatter the rest. And I want the shells."

Sharpe put the shells on the bed of the press, then screwed down the platen so they were held as though in a vice. Harper and Hagman were chucking the paper onto the floor and Sharpe pushed crumpled sheets into the gaps between the shells so that the burning paper would light their fuses. "Tell Perkins to bring Nuñez down," Sharpe said.

Nuñez came down the stairs and immediately understood what Sharpe intended. He began pleading. "Tell him to be quiet," Sharpe told Harris.

"These are the letters, sir." Harris held out a sheaf of papers that Sharpe thrust into a pocket. "And he says there are more."

"More? So get them!"

"No, sir, he says the girl must have them still." Harris jerked a thumb at Chavez who was fumbling as he lit a cigar. "And he says he wants a drink, sir."

There was a half-empty bottle of brandy on the table with the playing cards. Sharpe gave it to the writer, who sucked on it desperately. Hagman was pouring the mix of brandy and lamp oil onto the paper covering the floor. The two remaining smoke balls were by the back door, ready to fill the house with smoke and impede any attempt to extinguish the blaze. The fire, Sharpe reckoned, would gut the whole house.

The lead letters, carefully racked in their tall cases, would melt, the shells would destroy the press, and the fire would climb the stairs. The stone side walls of the house should keep it confined and, once the roof burned through, the furious rain would subdue the flames. Sharpe had planned to just take the letters, but he suspected there might be copies. An intact press could still print the lies, so it was better to burn it all.

"Throw them out," he told Harper, gesturing at the prisoners.

"Out, sir?"

"All of them. Into the back courtyard. Just kick them out. Then bolt the door again."

The prisoners were all pushed through the door, the bolts were shot home, and Sharpe sent his men back up the stairs. He went to the foot of the stairs and used a candle to light the nearest papers. For a few seconds the flame burned low. Then it caught some sheets soaked in brandy and lamp oil and the fire spread with surprising speed. Sharpe ran up the steps, pursued by smoke. "Out the trapdoor onto the roof," he told his men.

He was the last to the trapdoor. Smoke was already filling the bedroom. He knew the smoke balls would be seething in the flames. Then it seemed the whole house shuddered as the first shell exploded. Sharpe clung to the trapdoor's edge as a succession of deep thumps and blasting smoke punched past him to announce that the rest of the shells had caught the fire. That, he thought, was the end of **El Correo de Cádiz,** and he slammed the trapdoor shut and followed Hagman across the rooftops to the empty church building. "Well done, lads," he said when they were back in the chapel. "Now all we have to do is get home," he told them, "back to the embassy."

A church bell was ringing, presumably summoning men to extinguish the flames. That meant there would be chaos in the streets and chaos was good because no one would notice Sharpe and his men in the confusion. "Hide your weapons," he told them, then led them across the courtyard. His head was throbbing and the rain was crashing down, but he felt a huge relief that the job was done. He had the letters, he had destroyed the press, and now, he thought, there was only the girl to deal with, but he saw no problem there.

He shot the heavy bolts and pulled at the gate. He only wanted to open it an inch, just enough to peer outside, but before it had moved even half an inch it was thrust inward with such force that Sharpe staggered back into Harper. Men suddenly crowded the gate. They were soldiers. Folk who lived in the street had lit lamps and opened shutters to see what happened at Nuñez's house. There was more than enough light for Sharpe to see pale blue uniforms and white crossbelts and half a dozen long bayonets that glinted bright as a seventh soldier appeared with a lantern. Behind him was an officer in a darker blue coat, his waist circled by a yellow sash. The officer snarled an order that Sharpe did not understand, but he understood well enough what the bayonets meant. He backed away. "No weapons," he told his men.

The Spanish officer growled a question at Sharpe, but again spoke too fast. "Just do whatever they want," Sharpe said. He was trying to work out the odds and they were not good. His men had guns, but they were concealed beneath cloaks or coats, and these Spanish soldiers looked efficient, wide awake, and vengeful. The officer spoke again. "He wants us in the chapel, sir," Harris translated. Two of the Spanish soldiers went first to make sure none of Sharpe's men produced a weapon once they were out of the rain. Sharpe thought of attacking those two men, chopping them down and then defending the chapel's doorway, but he abandoned the idea instantly. He doubted he could escape from the chapel, men would surely die, and the political fuss would be monstrous. "I'm sorry about this, boys," he said, not sure what he could do.

He backed toward the empty altar steps. The Spanish soldiers lined opposite, their faces grim and their bayonets held level. The lantern was put on the floor and in its light Sharpe could see that the muskets were cocked. He doubted the guns would fire. There had been too much rain, and even the best musket lock could not prevent heavy rain dampening the powder. "If the bastards pull a trigger," he said, "you can fight back. But not till then."

The officer looked to be in his twenties, perhaps ten years younger than Sharpe. He was tall and had a broad, intelligent face and a hard jaw. His uniform, wet as it was, betrayed that he was wealthy for it was beautifully tailored of rich cloth. He rattled a question at Sharpe, who shrugged. "We were sheltering from the rain, señor," Sharpe said in English.

The officer asked another question in impenetrable Spanish. "Just sheltering from the rain," Sharpe insisted.

"Their powder will be damp, sir," Harper said softly.

"I know. But I don't want any killing."

The officer had seen their weapons now. He snapped an order. "He says we're to put the weapons on the floor, sir," Harris said.

"Do it," Sharpe said. This was a bloody nuisance, he thought. The likelihood was that they would end up in a Spanish jail, in which case the important thing was to destroy the letters, but this was no place to try that. He laid his sword down. "We were just sheltering from the rain, señor," he said.

"No you weren't," the officer suddenly spoke in good English. "You were setting fire to Señor Nuñez's house."

Sharpe was so surprised by the abrupt change of language that he could find nothing to say. He was still half crouched, his hand on his sword.

"You know what this place is?" the Spaniard asked.

"No," Sharpe said cautiously.

"The Priory of the Divine Shepherdess. It used to be a hospital. My name is Galiana, Captain Galiana. And you are?"

"Sharpe," Sharpe said.

"And your men call you 'sir,' so I assume you have rank?"

"Captain Sharpe."

"**Divina Pastora,**" Galiana said, "the Divine Shepherdess. Monks lived here, and the poor could receive medical care. It was a charity, Captain Sharpe, a Christian charity. You know what happened to it? Of course you don't." He took a step forward and kicked the sword out of Sharpe's reach. "Your Admiral Nelson happened. It was in '97. He bombarded the city and this was the worst damage he did." Galiana gestured about the scorched chapel. "One bomb, seven dead monks, and a fire. The priory closed because there was no money to make the repairs. My grandfather founded the place and my family would have repaired it, but our fortune comes from South America and your navy ended that income. That, Captain Sharpe, is what happened."

"We were at war when it happened," Sharpe said.

"But we are not at war now," Galiana said. "We are allies. Or had that escaped your attention?"

"We were sheltering from the rain," Sharpe said.

"It was fortunate, then, that you discovered the priory unlocked?"

"Very fortunate," Sharpe said.

"But what of the misfortune of Señor Nuñez? He is a widower, Captain Sharpe, struggling to make a living, and now his business is in ruins." Galiana gestured to the chapel door, beyond which Sharpe could hear the commotion in the street.

"I don't know anything about Señor Nuñez," Sharpe said.

"Then I shall educate you," Galiana said. "He owns, or rather he did own, a newspaper called **El Correo de Cádiz.** It's not much of a news-paper. One year ago it was read all across Andalucía, but now? Now it sells a few copies only. He used to publish twice a week, but now he is lucky to find enough news for one issue a fort-night. He lists the ships arriving and departing the harbor and he describes their cargoes. He prints which priests will preach in the city churches. He describes the proceedings of the Cortes. It is thin fare, isn't that what you say? But in the last issue, Captain Sharpe, there was something much more interesting. A love letter. It was not signed. Señor Nuñez merely said it was a letter translated from the English and that he had found it lying in the street, and that if the true owner would like it then he should come to the newspaper. Is that why you were here, Captain? No! Please don't say you were sheltering from the rain."

"I didn't write any love letters," Sharpe said.

"We all know who wrote it," Galiana said scornfully.

"I'm a soldier. I don't deal with love."

Galiana smiled. "I doubt that, Captain, I do doubt that." He turned as a man came through the chapel door. A small crowd was braving the rain to watch the efforts to extinguish the fire and some, seeing the priory gates open, had come into the courtyard. One of them, a bedraggled, soaking-wet creature with a tobacco-stained beard, stepped into the chapel.

"It was him!" the man shouted in Spanish, pointing at Sharpe. It was the writer, Benito Chavez, who had managed to get another bottle of brandy. He was almost drunk, but not so helpless that he could not recognize Sharpe. "It was him!" he said, still pointing. "The one with the bandaged head!"

"Arrest him," Galiana ordered his men.

The Spanish soldiers stepped forward and Sharpe thought of trying to pick up his sword, but before he could move he saw that Galiana was gesturing at Chavez. The soldiers hesitated, unsure what their officer meant. "Arrest him!" Galiana said, pointing at Chavez. The writer yelped in protest, but two of Galiana's men thrust him against the wall and held him there. "He is drunk," Galiana explained to Sharpe, "and making damaging accusations against our allies, so he can spend the rest of the night contemplating his own foolishness in jail."

"Allies?" Sharpe was as confused as Chavez now.

"Are we not allies?" Galiana asked in mock innocence.

"I thought we were," Sharpe said, "but sometimes I'm not sure."

"You are like the Spanish, Captain Sharpe, confused. Cádiz is filled with politicians and lawyers and they encourage confusion. They argue. Should we be a republic? Or perhaps a monarchy? Do we want a Cortes? And if so, should it have one chamber or two? Some want a parliament like Britain's. Others insist that Spain is best ruled by God and by a king. They squabble about these things like children, but in truth there is only one real argument."

Sharpe understood now that Galiana had

been playing with him. The Spaniard truly was an ally. "The argument," Sharpe said, "is whether Spain fights France or not?"

"Exactly," Galiana said.

"And you," Sharpe said carefully, "believe Spain should fight against France?"

"You know what the French have done to our country?" Galiana asked. "The women raped, the children killed, the churches desecrated? Yes, I believe we should fight. I also believe, Captain Sharpe, that British soldiers are banned from entering Cádiz. They are not even allowed inside the city without their uniforms. I should arrest you all. But I assume you are lost?"

"We're lost," Sharpe agreed.

"And you were merely sheltering from the rain?"

"We were."

"Then I shall escort you to your embassy, Captain Sharpe."

"Bloody hell," Sharpe said in relief.

It took a half hour to reach the embassy. The wind had died a little by the time they reached the gate and the rain had lessened. Galiana took Sharpe aside. "I was ordered to watch the newspaper," he said, "in case someone tried to destroy it. I believe, and I trust I am not deceiving myself, that by failing in that duty I have helped the war against France."

"You have," Sharpe said.

"I also believe you owe me a favor, Captain Sharpe."

"I do," Sharpe agreed fervently.

"I shall find one. Be sure of that, I shall find one. Good night, Captain."

"Good night, Captain," Sharpe said. The courtyard inside the embassy was dark, the windows showing no light. Sharpe touched the letters in his coat pocket, took the newspaper from Slattery, and went to bed.

Chapter 8

Henry Wellesley looked tired, and that was to be understood. He had been at a reception for the Portuguese ambassador half the night and had then been woken soon after dawn when an indignant delegation arrived at the British embassy. It was a measure of the urgency of their protest that the delegation had arrived so early in the morning, long before most of the city was stirring. The two elderly diplomats, each dressed in black, had been sent by the Regency, the council that ruled what was left of Spain, and the pair now sat very stiffly in the ambassador's parlor where a newly made fire smoked in the hearth behind them. Lord Pumphrey, hastily dressed and looking pale, sat to one side of Wellesley's desk while the interpreter stood on the other. "One question, Sharpe," Wellesley greeted the rifleman brusquely.

"Sir?"

"Where were you last night?"

"In bed, sir, all night, sir," Sharpe said woodenly. It was the tone of voice he had learned as a sergeant, the voice used to tell lies to officers. "Took an early night, sir, on account of my head." He touched his bandage. The two Spaniards looked at him with distaste. Sharpe had just been woken by an embassy servant and he had hurriedly pulled on his uniform, but he was unshaven, weary, dirty, and exhausted.

"You were in bed?" Wellesley asked.

"All night, sir," Sharpe said, staring an inch above the ambassador's head.

The interpreter repeated the exchange in French, the language of diplomacy. The interpreter was only there to translate Sharpe's words, because everyone else said what they had to say in French. Wellesley looked at the delegation and raised an eyebrow as if to suggest that that was as much as they could hope to learn from Captain Sharpe. "I ask you these questions, Sharpe," the ambassador explained, "because there was something of a small tragedy last night. A newspaper was burned to the ground. It was quite destroyed, alas. No one was hurt, fortunately, but it's a sad thing."

"Very sad, sir."

"And the newspaper's proprietor, a man called"—Wellesley paused to look at some notes he had scribbled down.

"Nuñez, Your Excellency," Lord Pumphrey offered helpfully.

"Nuñez, that's it, a man called Nuñez, claims that British men did it, and that the British were led by a gentleman with a bandaged head."

"A gentleman, sir?" Sharpe asked, suggesting that he could never be mistaken for a gentleman.

"I use the word loosely, Captain Sharpe," Wellesley said with a surprising asperity.

"I was in bed, sir," Sharpe insisted. "But there was lightning, wasn't there? I seem to remember a storm, or perhaps I dreamed that?"

"There was lightning, indeed."

"A lightning strike caused the fire, sir, most likely."

The interpreter explained to the delegation that there had been lightning and one of the visiting diplomats pointed out that they had found scraps of shell casing in the embers. The two men stared again at Sharpe as their words were translated.

"Shells?" Sharpe asked in mock innocence.

"Then it must have been the French mortars, sir."

That suggestion prompted a flurry of words, summed up by the ambassador. "The French mortars, Sharpe, don't have the range to reach that part of the city."

"They would, sir, if they double-charged them."

"Double-charged?" Lord Pumphrey inquired delicately.

"Twice as much powder as usual, my lord. It will throw the shell much farther, but at the risk of blowing up the gun. Or perhaps they've found some decent powder, sir? They've been using rubbish, nothing but dust, but a barrel of cylinder charcoal powder would increase their range. Most likely that, sir." Sharpe uttered this nonsense in a confident voice. He was, after all, the only soldier in the room and the man most likely to know about gunpowder, and no one disputed his opinion.

"Probably a mortar, then," Wellesley suggested, and the diplomats politely accepted the fiction that the French guns had destroyed the newspaper. It was plain they disbelieved the story and equally plain that, despite their indignation, they did not much care. They had protested because they had to protest, but they had no future in prolonging an argument with Henry Wellesley who, effectively, was the man who funded the Spanish government. The fiction that the French had contrived to extend their mortars' range by five hundred yards would suffice to dampen the city's anger.

The diplomats left with mutual expressions of regret and regard. Once they were gone Henry Wellesley leaned back in his chair. "Lord Pumphrey told me what happened in the cathedral. That was a pity, Sharpe."

"A pity, sir?"

"There were casualties!" Wellesley said sternly. "We don't know how many, and I daren't show too much interest in finding out. At present no one is directly accusing us of causing the damage, but they will, they will."

"We kept the money, sir," Sharpe said, "and they were never going to give us the letters. I'm sure Lord Pumphrey told you that."

"I did," Pumphrey said.

"And it was a priest who tried to cheat you?" Wellesley sounded shocked.

"Father Salvador Montseny," Lord Pumphrey said sourly.

Wellesley twisted his chair to look out the window. It was a gray day and a thin mist blurred the small garden. "I could, perhaps, have done something about Father Montseny," he said, still looking into the mist. "I could have brought pressure to bear, I might have had him posted to some mission in a godforsaken fever swamp in the Americas, but that's impossible now. Your actions at the newspaper, Sharpe, have made it impossible. Those gentlemen pretended to believe us, but they know damned well you did it." He turned back, his face showing a sudden anger. "I warned you that we must step carefully here. I told you to observe the proprieties. We cannot offend the Spanish. They know that the newspaper was destroyed in an attempt to stop the letters being published, and they will not be happy with us. They might even go so far as to make another press available for the men who have the letters! Good God, Sharpe! We have a house burned, a business destroyed, a cathedral desecrated, men wounded, and for what? Tell me that! For what?"

"For that, sir?" Sharpe said, and laid the copy of **El Correo de Cádiz** on the ambassador's desk. "I believe it's a new edition, sir."

"Oh, dear God," Henry Wellesley said. He

was blushing as he turned the pages and saw column after column filled with his letters. "Oh,
dear God."

"That's the only copy," Sharpe said. "I burned
the rest."

"You burned"—the ambassador began, then
his voice faltered because Sharpe had begun laying the ambassador's imprudent letters on top of
the newspaper, one after the other, as if he were
dealing cards.

"These are your letters, sir," Sharpe said, still
in his sergeant's tone of voice, "and we've ruined
the press that printed them, sir, and we've
burned their newspapers, and we've taught the
bastards not to take us lightly, sir. As Lord
Pumphrey told me, sir, we have frustrated their
knavish tricks. There, sir." He laid the last letter
down.

"Good God," Henry Wellesley said, staring at
the letters.

"Dear Lord above," Lord Pumphrey said
faintly.

"They might have copies, sir," Sharpe said,
"but without the originals they can't prove the
letters are real, can they? And, anyway, they
don't have a way of printing them now."

"Good God," Wellesley said again, this time looking up at Sharpe.

"Thief, murderer, and arsonist," Sharpe said proudly. The ambassador said nothing, just stared at him. "Have you ever heard of a Spanish officer called Captain Galiana, sir?" Sharpe asked.

Wellesley had looked back to the letters and seemed not to have heard Sharpe. Then he gave a start as if he had just woken. "Fernando Galiana? Yes, he was a liaison officer to Sir Thomas's predecessor. A splendid young man. Are those all the letters?"

"All they had, sir."

"Good God," the ambassador said, then stood abruptly, took hold of the letters and the newspaper, and carried them all to the fire. He threw them on the coals and watched them blaze bright. "How—" he began, then decided there were some questions better not answered.

"Will that be all, sir?" Sharpe asked.

"I must thank you, Sharpe," Wellesley said, still staring at the burning letters.

"And my men, sir, all five of them. I'll be taking then back to the Isla de León, sir, and we'll wait there for a ship."

"Of course, of course." The ambassador hurried across to his bureau. "Your five men helped?"

"Very much, sir."

A drawer was opened and Sharpe heard the sound of coins. He pretended not to be interested. The ambassador, not wanting his generosity or lack of it to be obvious, wrapped the coins in a piece of paper that he brought to Sharpe. "Perhaps you'd convey my thanks to your fellows?"

"Of course, sir, thank you, sir." Sharpe took the coins.

"But you rather look as if you should go back to bed now," Wellesley said.

"You too, sir."

"I'm well awake now. Lord Pumphrey and I will stay up. There's always work to do!" Wellesley was happy suddenly, suffused with relief and the realization that a nightmare was over. "And of course I shall write to my brother commending you in the very highest terms. Be certain I'll do that, Sharpe."

"Thank you, sir."

"Good God! It's over." The ambassador stared at the last small flames flickering above the blackened mess of the papers lying on the coals. "It's over!"

"Except the lady, sir," Sharpe said, "Caterina. She has some letters, doesn't she?"

"Oh no," the ambassador said happily, "oh no. It really is over! Thank you, Sharpe."

Sharpe let himself out. He went into the courtyard where he sniffed the air. It was a dull morning, exhausted after the night's rain. The weathervane on the embassy's watchtower betrayed that the wind was from the west. A cat rubbed itself against his ankles and he leaned down to stroke it, then unwrapped the coins. Fifteen guineas. He guessed he was supposed to give one each to his men and keep the rest. He pushed them into a pocket, not sure whether it was a generous reward or not. Probably not, he decided, but his men would be happy enough. He would give them two guineas apiece and that would buy them a lot of rum. "Go and find a mouse," he told the cat, "because that's what I'm doing."

He walked through the archway to the smaller courtyard where servants were sweeping steps and the embassy cow was being milked. The back door to Lord Pumphrey's house was open and a woman came down the steps to fetch milk. Sharpe waited till her back was turned, then ran up the steps and through the kitchen where the stove had just been relit. He took the next stairs two at a time and opened the door at the top to find himself in a tiled hallway. He climbed more stairs, these deep carpeted, past pictures of Spanish landscapes of white houses, yellow rocks, and blue skies. A white marble statue of a naked boy stood on the landing. The statue was life-size and had a cocked hat on its head. A door stood open and Sharpe saw a woman dusting a bedroom, which he supposed was His Lordship's. He crept past and she did not hear him. The next flight of stairs was narrower and led to a landing with three closed doors. The first opened onto another stairway, which presumably climbed to the servants' quarters. The second was the door to a box room that was heaped with unused furniture, valises, and hat boxes. The last door led into a bedroom.

Sharpe crept inside and closed the door. It took a moment for his eyes to adjust to the gloom, for the shutters on both tall windows were closed, but then he could see an empty tin bath in front of the hearth where the remnants of the night's fire smoldered. There was a bureau, two sofas, a great wardrobe with mirrored doors, and a four-poster bed that had its embroidered curtains drawn.

He crossed the deep rugs and pulled open the nearest shutters to find himself staring across the roofs to the Bay of Cádiz where errant slants of watery sunlight were finding their way through gaps in the cloud to silver the small waves.

Someone grunted in the bed, then moaned slightly, as if resenting being woken by the new light filtering past the bed's curtains. Sharpe went to the second window and opened its shutters. Arrayed on the window seat, mounted on mahogany stands, were six golden wigs. A blue dress had been discarded on one of the sofas along with a necklace of sapphires and a pair of sapphire earrings. The moan sounded again and Sharpe went to the bed and yanked back the curtains. "Good morning," he said cheerfully.

And Caterina Veronica Blazquez opened her mouth to scream.

"My name is Sharpe," Sharpe said before she could alarm the household.

Caterina closed her mouth.

"Richard Sharpe," he added.

She nodded. She was clutching the bedclothes to her chin. The bed was wide and it was plain a second person had occupied it through the night, for the pillows still showed the mark of his head. The ambassador's head, Sharpe was certain. Brigadier Moon had seen him come to the house, and Sharpe could not blame Henry Wellesley for being unable to surrender his whore because Caterina Blazquez was a beauty. She had short golden curls that were pretty even in disarray, wide blue eyes, a small nose, a generous mouth, and a smooth pale skin. In a land of dark-eyed, dark-haired, dark-skinned women she glowed like a diamond.

"I've been looking for you," Sharpe said, "and I'm not the only one."

She gave the smallest shake of her head, which, together with her scared expression, conveyed that she was frightened of whoever looked for her.

"You do understand me, don't you?" Sharpe asked.

A tiny nod of the head. She pulled the covers higher, covering her mouth. This was a good place to hide her, Sharpe thought. She was in no danger here, certainly in no danger from Lord Pumphrey, and she lived in the comfort that a man would want his mistress to enjoy. She was safe enough, at least until the servants' gossip betrayed her presence in Pumphrey's house. Caterina was examining Sharpe, her eyes traveling down his shabby uniform, seeing the sword, rising again to his face, and her eyes, if anything, were now slightly wider.

"I was busy last night," Sharpe said. "I was fetching some letters. Remember those letters?"

Another tiny nod.

"But I got them back. Gave them to Mister Wellesley, I did. He burned them."

She lowered the bedclothes an inch and rewarded him with a flicker of a smile. He tried to work out how old she was. Twenty-two? Twenty-three? Young, anyway. Young and flawless as far as he could see.

"But there are more letters, darling, aren't there?"

There was a slight rising of her eyebrows when he called her darling, then a barely discernible shake of her head.

Sharpe sighed. "I know I'm a British officer, darling, but I'm not daft. You know what daft means?"

A nod.

"So let me tell you a bedtime story. Henry

Wellesley wrote you a lot of letters that he shouldn't have written and you kept them. You kept them all, darling. But your pimp took most of them, didn't he? And he was going to sell them and share the money with you, but then he got murdered. Do you know who murdered him?"

She shook her head.

"A priest. Father Salvador Montseny."

The slight rise of eyebrows again.

"And Father Montseny murdered the man sent to buy them back," Sharpe went on, "and last night he tried to murder me, only I'm a much harder man to kill. So he lost the letters and he lost the newspaper that printed them and he's now a very angry priest, darling. But he knows one thing. He knows you didn't destroy all the letters. He knows you kept some. You kept them in case you needed the money. But when your pimp got murdered you became scared, didn't you? So you ran to Henry and told him a pack of lies. You told him the letters were stolen, and told him there weren't any more. But there are more, and you've got them, darling."

The tiniest and most unconvincing denial, just enough to shiver her curls.

"And the priest is angry, my love," Sharpe went on. "He wants those other letters. One way or another he'll find a printing press, but first he has to get the letters, doesn't he? So he's coming after you, Caterina, and he's a wicked man with a knife. He'll slit your pretty belly from bottom to top."

Another shiver of the curls. She pulled the bedclothes higher to hide her nose and mouth.

"You think he can't find you?" Sharpe asked. "I found you. And I know you've got the letters."

This time there was no reaction, just the wide eyes watching him. There was no fear in those eyes. This was a girl, Sharpe realized, who had learned the enormous power of her looks and she already knew that Sharpe was not going to hurt her.

"So tell me, darling," Sharpe said, "just where the other letters are, and then we'll be done."

Very slowly she drew the sheet and blankets down to uncover her mouth. She stared at Sharpe solemnly, apparently thinking about her answer, then she frowned. "Tell me," she said, "what did you do to your head?"

"It got in the way of a bullet."

"That was very silly of you, Captain Sharpe."

The smile flickered and was gone. She had a languorous voice, her vowels American. "Pumps told me about you. He said you're dangerous."

"I am, very."

"No, you're not." She smiled at him, then half rolled over to look at the face of an ornate clock that ticked on the mantel. "It's not even eight o clock!"

"You speak good English."

She lay back on the pillow. "My mother was American. Daddy was Spanish. They met in Florida. Have you heard of Florida?"

"No."

"It's south of the United States. It used to belong to Britain, but you had to give it back to Spain after the war of independence. There's nothing much there except Indians, slaves, soldiers, and missionaries. Daddy was a captain in the garrison at St. Augustine." She frowned. "If Henry finds you here he'll be angry."

"He's not coming back this morning," Sharpe said. "He's working with Lord Pumphrey."

"Poor Pumps," Caterina said. "I like him. He talks to me such a lot. Turn around."

Sharpe obeyed, then edged sideways so that he could see her in the mirrors of the wardrobe doors.

"And move away from the mirrors," Caterina said.

Sharpe obeyed again.

"You can turn around now," she said. She had pulled on a blue silk jacket that she laced to her chin, giving him a smile. "When they bring breakfast and water you'll have to wait in there." She pointed to a door beside the wardrobe.

"You drink water for breakfast?" Sharpe asked.

"It's for the bath," she said. She pulled on a ribbon that rang a bell deep in the house. "I'll have them revive the fire as well," she went on. "You like ham? Bread? If the chickens have laid then there'll be eggs. I'll tell them I'm very hungry." She listened until she heard footsteps on the stairs. "Go and hide," she ordered Sharpe.

He went into a small room filled with Caterina's clothes. A table with a mirror was cluttered with salves and cosmetics and beauty patches. Behind the mirror was a window and Sharpe, peering into the clearing air, could see the fleet weighing anchor and sailing north out of the bay. The army was on the move. He stared at the ships and thought his place was there, with men, muskets, cannons, and horses stalled in the holds. Men going to war, and here he was in a whore's dressing room.

The breakfast came a half hour later, by which time the fire was blazing and the bath filled with steaming water. "The servants hate filling the bath," Caterina said, sitting up on banked pillows now, "because it's so much work for them, but I insist on having a bath every day. The water will be too hot now, so it can wait. Have some breakfast."

Sharpe was ravenous. He sat on the bed and ate, and in between mouthfuls he asked questions. "When did you leave, what did you call it, Florida?"

"When I was sixteen, my mother died. Daddy had run away long before that. I didn't want to stay there."

"Why not?"

"Stay in Florida?" She shuddered at the thought. "It's just a hot swamp filled with snakes, alligators, and Indians."

"So how did you come here?"

"By ship," she said, her big eyes serious. "It was much too far to swim."

"By yourself?"

"Gonzalo brought me."

"Gonzalo?"

"The man who died."

"The man who was going to sell the letters?"
She nodded.

"And you've been working with Gonzalo ever since?"

She nodded again. "In Madrid, Seville, and now here."

"The same game?"

"Game?"

"Pretend to be well-born, get letters, sell them back?"

She smiled. "We made a lot of money, Captain Sharpe. More than you could ever dream of."

"I don't need to dream, darling. I once stole the jewels of an Indian king."

"So you're rich?" she asked, eyes brightening.

"Lost it all."

"Careless, Captain Sharpe."

"So what will you do without Gonzalo?"
She frowned. "I don't know."

"Stay with Henry? Be his mistress?"

"He's very kind to me," Caterina said, "but I don't think he'd take me back to London. And he will go back eventually, won't he?"

"He'll go back," Sharpe confirmed.

"So I'll have to find someone else," she said, "but not you."

"Not me?"

"Someone rich," she said with a smile.

"And you have to stay away from Father Salvador Montseny," Sharpe said.

She gave another shudder. "He is really a killer? A priest?"

"He's as nasty as they come, darling. And he wants your letters. He'll kill you to get them."

"But you want my letters too."

"I do."

"And Pumps says you're a killer."

"I am."

She seemed to consider her dilemma for a moment, then nodded at the bath. "It's time to get clean," she said.

"You want me back in that room?" Sharpe asked.

"Of course not. That bath's for you. You stink. Get undressed, Captain Sharpe, and I'll wash your back."

Sharpe was a good soldier. He obeyed.

"I like Henry Wellesley," Sharpe said.

"So do I," Caterina said, "but he is"—she paused, thinking—"earnest."

"Earnest?"

"Sad. His wife hurt him. Pumps says she was not beautiful."

"You can't trust everything Pumps says."

"But I think he is right. Some women are not beautiful yet they drive men mad. She has driven Henry sad. Are you going to sleep?"

"No," Sharpe said. The bed was the most comfortable he had experienced. A feather mattress, silk sheets, big pillows, and Caterina. "I have to go."

"Your uniform isn't dry." She had insisted on washing his uniform in the used bath water and it was now propped on two chairs before the fire.

"We have to go," Sharpe corrected himself.

"We?"

"Montseny wants to find you. And to get the letters he'll hurt you."

She thought about that. "When Gonzalo died," she said, "I came here because I was frightened. And because this is safe."

"You think Pumps will protect you?"

"No one would dare come in here. It's the embassy!"

"Montseny will dare," Sharpe said. "There's no guard on Lord Pumphrey's front door, is there? And if the servants see a priest they'll trust him. Montseny can get in here easily. I did."

"But if I go with you," she said, "how do I live?"

"Same as everyone else."

"I am not everyone else," she said indignantly, "and didn't you tell me you were sailing back to Lisbon?"

"I am, but you'll be safer in the Isla de León. Lots of British soldiers to defend you. Or you can come back to Lisbon with me." She rewarded that suggestion with a smile and silence. "I know," Sharpe went on, "I'm not rich enough. So why did you lie to Henry?"

"Lie to him?" She opened her eyes wide and innocent.

"When you came here, darling, you told him you had no letters. You told him you'd lost the ones Gonzalo didn't have. You lied."

"I thought perhaps if things went wrong," she began, then shrugged.

"You'd still have something to sell?"

"Is that bad?"

"Of course it's bad," Sharpe said sternly, "but it's bloody sensible. So how much do you want for them?"

"Your uniform is scorching," she said. She climbed out of bed and went to turn the jacket and overalls around. Sharpe watched her. A beauty. She would drive men mad, he thought. She came back to the bed and slid in beside him again.

"So how much?" he asked her.

"Gonzalo said he would make me four hundred dollars."

"He was cheating you," Sharpe said.

"I don't think so. Pumps said he couldn't get more than seven hundred."

It took Sharpe a moment to understand what she was saying. "Lord Pumphrey said that?"

She nodded very seriously. "He said he could hide the money in the accounts. He would say it was for bribes, but he could only hide seven hundred."

"And he'd give you that for the letters?"

She nodded again. "He said he would get seven hundred dollars, keep two, and give me five. But he had to wait till the other letters were found. Mine, he said, weren't valuable till they were the only letters left."

"Bloody hell," Sharpe said.

"You're shocked." Caterina was amused.

"I thought he was honest."

"Pumps! Honest?" She laughed. "He tells me

his secrets. He shouldn't, but he wants to know my secrets. He wants to know what Henry says about him so I make him tell me things first. Not that Henry tells me any secrets! So I tell Pumps what he wants to hear. He told me a secret about you."

"I've got no secrets with Lord Pumphrey," Sharpe said indignantly.

"He has one about you," she said. "A girl in Copenhagen? Called Ingrid?"

"Astrid."

"Astrid, that's the name. Pumps had her killed," Caterina said.

Sharpe stared at her. "He what?" he asked after a while.

"Astrid and her father. Pumps had their throats cut. He's very proud of it. He made me promise not to tell anyone."

"He killed Astrid?"

"He said she and her father knew too many secrets that the French would want to know, and he couldn't trust them to keep quiet, so he told them to go to England and they wouldn't so he had them killed."

It had been four years since Sharpe had been in Copenhagen with the invading British army.

He had wanted to stay in Denmark, leave the army, and settle with Astrid, but her father had forbidden the marriage and she was an obedient girl. So Sharpe had abandoned the dream and sailed back to England. "Her father used to send information to Britain," Sharpe said, "but he got upset with us when we captured Copenhagen."

"Pumps says he knew a lot of secrets."

"He did."

"He doesn't know any now," Caterina said callously, "nor does Astrid."

"The bastard," Sharpe said, thinking of Lord Pumphrey, "the bloody bastard."

"You mustn't hurt him!" Caterina said earnestly. "I like Pumps."

"You tell Pumps the price for the letters is a thousand guineas."

"A thousand guineas!"

"In gold," Sharpe said. "You tell him that, and tell him he can deliver the money to you in the Isla de León."

"Why there?"

"Because I'll be there," Sharpe said, "and so will you. And as long as I'm there you'll be safe from that murderous priest."

"You want me to leave here?" she asked.

"You've got the letters," Sharpe said, "so it's time you made money on them. And if you stay here someone else will make the money. And like as not they'll kill you to get the letters. So you tell Pumps you want a thousand guineas, and that if you don't get it you'll tell me about Astrid."

"You were in love with her?"

"Yes," Sharpe said.

"That's nice."

"Tell Lord Pumphrey that if he wants to live he should pay you a thousand guineas. Ask for two thousand and maybe you'll get it."

"What if he doesn't pay?"

"Then I'll slit his throat."

"You're a very nasty man," she said, putting her left thigh across his legs.

"I know."

She thought for a few seconds, then made a rueful face. "Henry likes having me here. He'll be unhappy if I go to the Isla de León."

"Do you mind that?"

"No." She looked searchingly into Sharpe's face. "Will Pumps really pay a thousand guineas?"

"He'll probably pay more," he said, then kissed her nose.

"So what do you want?" she asked.

"Whatever you want to give me."

"Oh, that," she said.

The fleet left, all except the Spanish feluccas that could not beat against the monstrous waves that were the remnant of the storm, so they returned to the bay, pursued by the futile splashes of the French mortar shells. The larger British ships drove through the heavy seas and then went south, a host of sail skirting Cádiz to disappear beyond Cape Trafalgar. The wind stayed in the west and the next day the Spaniards found kinder seas and followed.

San Fernando was empty with most of the army gone. There were still battalions on the Isla de León, but they were manning the long defense works on the marshy creek that protected the island and the city from Marshal Victor's army, though that army left their siege lines two days after the Spanish feluccas sailed. Marshal Victor knew full well what the allies planned. General Lapeña and General Graham would sail their troops south and then, after landing close to Gibraltar, would march north to attack the French siege works. Victor had no intention of allowing his lines to be assailed from the rear. He took most of his army south, looking for a place where he could intercept the British and Spanish forces. He left some men to guard the French lines, just as the British had left some to protect their own batteries. Cádiz waited.

The wind turned north and cold. The Bay of Cádiz was mostly deserted of shipping, except for the small fishing craft and the mastless prison hulks. The French forts on the Trocadero fired desultory mortar shells, but with Marshal Victor gone the garrisons seemed bereft of enthusiasm. The wind stayed obstinately north so that no ships could sail for Lisbon. Sharpe, back on the Isla de León, waited.

A week after the last of the allied ships had sailed, and a day after Marshal Victor had marched away from the siege works, Sharpe borrowed two horses from Sir Thomas Graham's stable and rode south along the island's coast where the sea broke white on endless sand. He had been invited to ride to the beach's end and he was accompanied by Caterina. "Put your heels down," she told him. "Put your heels down and hold your back straight. You ride like a peasant."

"I am a peasant. I hate horses."

"I love them," she said. She rode like a man,

straddling the horse, the way she had been taught in Spanish America. "I hate riding sidesaddle," she told him. She wore breeches, a jacket, and a wide-brimmed hat that was held in place by a scarf. "I cannot abide the sun," she said. "It makes your skin like leather. You should see the women in Florida! They look like alligators. If I didn't wear a hat I'd have a face like yours."

"Are you saying I'm ugly?"

She laughed at that, then touched her spurs to the mare's flanks and turned into the sea's fretted edge. The hooves splashed white where the waves seethed up the beach. She circled back to Sharpe, her eyes bright. She had arrived in San Fernando the day before. She had come in a coach hired from the stables just outside the city, close to the Royal Observatory, and behind the coach three ostlers led packhorses piled with her clothes, cosmetics, and wigs. Caterina had greeted Sharpe with a demure kiss, then gestured at the coachmen and ostlers. "They need paying," she said airily before stepping into the house Sharpe had rented. There were plenty of empty houses now that the army was gone. Sharpe had paid the men, then looked ruefully at the few coins he had left.

"Is the ambassador unhappy with you?" Sharpe had asked Caterina when he joined her in the house.

"Henry is quiet. He always goes quiet when he's unhappy. But I told him I was frightened to stay in Cádiz. This is a sweet house!"

"Henry wanted you to stay?"

"Of course he wanted me to stay. But I insisted."

"And Lord Pumphrey?"

"He said he would bring the money." She had given him a dazzling smile. "Twelve hundred guineas!"

Sergeant Harper had watched Caterina's arrival with an expressionless face. "On the strength is she now, sir?"

"She'll stay with us awhile," Sharpe said.

"Isn't that a surprise."

"And if that bloody priest shows his face, kill him."

Sharpe doubted Montseny would come near the Isla de León. The priest had been beaten and if the man had any sense he would give up the fight. The best hope for his faction now was that Marshal Victor would beat the allied army, for then Cádiz must inevitably fall and the politicians in its walls would want to make peace with France before that disaster occurred.

That was other men's business. Sharpe was riding on a long sea-beaten beach. To his east were sand dunes and, beyond them, the marshes. To his west was the Atlantic and to the south, where the beach ended at a river's mouth, were Spanish soldiers in their sky blue uniforms. From far off across the marshes came the grumble of gunfire, the sound of French cannons bombarding the British batteries guarding the Isla de León. The sound was fitful and faint as distant thunder.

"You look happy," Caterina said.

"I am."

"Why?"

"Because it's clean here," Sharpe said. "I didn't like Cádiz. Too many alleys, too much darkness, too much treachery."

"Poor Captain Sharpe." She mocked him with a brilliant smile. "You don't like cities?"

"I don't like politicians. All those bloody lawyers taking bribes and making pompous speeches. What's going to win the war is that." He nodded ahead to where the blue-coated soldiers labored in the shallow water. Two feluccas

were anchored in the river's mouth and longboats were ferrying soldiers to the beach beyond.
The feluccas were loaded to the gunwales with
baulks of timber, anchors and chains, and piles
of planks, the materials needed to make a bridge
of boats. There were no proper pontoons, but
the longboats would serve, and the resultant
bridge would be narrow, though if it was properly anchored it would be safe enough.

Captain Galiana was among the officers. It
was Galiana who had invited Sharpe to the
beach's end and he now rode out to greet the rifleman. "How is your head, Captain?"

"It's getting better. It doesn't hurt so much as
it did. It's vinegar that cures it. May I present the
Señorita Caterina Blazquez? Captain Fernando
Galiana."

If Galiana was surprised that a young woman
would have no chaperone he hid it, bowing instead and giving Caterina a welcoming smile.
"What we're doing," he said in answer to her first
question, "is making a bridge and protecting it
by building a fort on the other bank."

"Why?" Caterina asked.

"Because if General Lapeña and Sir Thomas
fail to reach the French siege works, señorita,
they will need a bridge back to the city. I trust

the bridge will not be needed, but General Lapeña thought it prudent to make it." Galiana gave Sharpe a rueful look as though he deplored such defeatism.

Caterina thought about Galiana's answer. "But if you can build a bridge, Captain," she asked, "why take the army south on boats? Why not cross here and attack the French?"

"Because, señorita, this is no place to fight. Cross the bridge here and there is nothing but beach in front of you and a creek to your left. Cross here and the French would trap us on the beach. It would be a slaughter."

"They sailed south," Sharpe told her, "so they can march inland and take the French from the rear."

"And you wish you were with them?" Caterina asked Sharpe. She had heard envy in his voice.

"I wish I was," Sharpe said.

"Me too," Galiana put in.

"There's a regiment in the French army," Sharpe said, "that I've got a quarrel with. The 8th of the line. I want to meet them again."

"Perhaps you will," Galiana said.

"No, I'm in the wrong place," Sharpe said sourly.

"But the army will advance from over there"—Galiana pointed inland—"and the French will march to meet them. I think a determined man could ride around the French army and join our forces. A determined man, say, who knows the country."

"Which is you," Sharpe said, "not me."

"I do know the country," Galiana said, "but whoever commands the fort here will have orders to stop unauthorized Spanish troops from crossing the bridge." He paused, looking at Sharpe. "But they will have no orders to stop Englishmen."

"How many days before they get here?" Sharpe asked.

"Three? Four?"

"I'm under orders to take a ship to Lisbon."

"No ships will be sailing for Lisbon now," Galiana said confidently.

"The wind might turn," Sharpe said.

"It's nothing to do with the wind," Galiana said, "but with the possibility that General Lapeña is defeated."

From what Sharpe had heard, everyone expected Lapeña, Doña Manolito, to be thrashed by Victor. "And if he is defeated?" he asked tonelessly.

"Then they will want every available ship ready to evacuate the city," Galiana said, "which is why no ship will be permitted to leave until the thing is decided."

"And you expect defeat?" Sharpe asked brutally.

"What I expect," Galiana said, "is that you will repay the favor you owe me."

"Get you across the bridge?"

Galiana smiled. "That is the favor, Captain Sharpe. Get me across the bridge."

And Sharpe thought he might yet meet Colonel Vandal again.

Part Three
The Battle

Chapter 9

It was chaos. Bloody chaos. It was infuriating. "It is," Lord William Russell said calmly, "entirely to be expected."

"God damn it!" Sir Thomas Graham exploded.

"In each and every particular," Lord William said, sounding far wiser than his twenty-one years, "precisely what we expected."

"And damn you too," Sir Thomas said. His horse pricked back its ears at its master's vehemence. "Bloody man!" Sir Thomas said, slapping his right boot with his whip. "Not you, Willie, him. Him! That bloody man!"

"What bloody man is that?" Major John Hope, Sir Thomas's nephew and senior aide, asked solemnly.

Sir Thomas recognized the line from **Mac-**

beth, but was in too much of a temper to acknowledge it. Instead he put spurs to his horse, beckoned to his aides, and started toward the head of the column where General Lapeña had called yet another halt.

It should all have been so simple. So damned simple. Land at Tarifa and there meet the British troops sent from the Gibraltar garrison, and that had happened as planned, at which point the whole army was supposed to march north. Except they could not leave Tarifa because the Spanish had not arrived, and so Sir Thomas waited two days, two days of consuming rations that were supposed to be reserved for the march. And when Lapeña's troops did arrive, their boats would not risk crossing the surf on the beach, so the Spanish troops had been forced to wade ashore. They landed soaking, shivering, and starving, in no condition to march, and so another day was wasted.

Yet still it should have been easy. There were just fifty miles to march, which, even with the guns and baggage, should not have taken more than four days. The road went northward, following a river beneath the Sierra de Fates. Then, once out of those hills, they should have crossed the plain by a good road that led to Medina

Sidonia where the allied army would turn west to attack the French siege lines that were anchored on the town of Chiclana. That is what should have happened, but it did not. The Spaniards led the march and they were slow, painfully slow. Sir Thomas, riding at the head of the British troops, which formed the rearguard, noted the boots that had torn themselves to pieces and been discarded beside the road. Some weary Spaniards had fallen out of their ranks, joining the broken boots, and they just watched the red-coated and green-jacketed men march by. And maybe that would not have mattered if enough Spaniards, barefoot or not, had reached Medina Sidonia to chase out whatever garrison the French had placed in the town.

General Lapeña had seemed as eager as Sir Thomas when the march started. He understood the necessity of hurrying north and turning west before Marshal Victor could find a place to make a stand. The allied army was supposed to erupt like a storm on the unprotected rear of the French siege lines. Sir Thomas envisaged his men rampaging through the French camps, ravaging the artillery parks, exploding the magazines, and harrying the broken army out of its earthworks and onto the guns of the British line protecting the Isla de León. All it needed was speed, speed, speed, but then, on the second day, Lapeña had decided to rest his footsore troops and instead march through the next night. And even that might have served, except that the Spanish guides had become lost and the army wandered in a great circle under the hard brightness of the stars. "God damn it!" Sir Thomas had exclaimed. "Can't they see the North Star?"

"There are marshes, Sir Thomas," the Spanish liaison officer had pleaded.

"God damn it! Just follow the road!"

But the road had not been followed and the army wandered, then halted, and men sat in fields where some tried to sleep. The ground was damp and the night surprisingly cold, so very few managed any rest. The British lit short clay pipes and the officers' servants walked their masters' horses up and down while the guides argued until finally some gypsies, woken from their encampment in a grove of cork oaks, pointed the way to Medina Sedonia. The troops had marched for twelve hours and, by the time they bivouacked at midday, had covered only six miles, though at least the King's German Legion cavalry, who served under Sir Thomas's command, had managed to surprise a half battalion of foraging French infantry and had killed a dozen enemy and captured twice as many.

General Lapeña, in a fit of energy, had then proposed marching again that same afternoon, but the men were exhausted from a wasted night and the rations were still being distributed. So he had agreed with Sir Thomas to wait until the men were fed, and then he decided they should sleep before they marched at dawn, yet at dawn Lapeña himself was not ready. It seemed that a French officer, one of those captured by the German cavalry, had revealed that Marshal Victor had reinforced the garrison in Medina Sidonia so that now it numbered more than three thousand men. "We cannot go there," Lapeña had declared. He was a lugubrious man, slightly stooped, with nervous eyes that were rarely still. "Three thousand men! We can beat them, but at what cost? Delay, Sir Thomas, delay. They will hold us up while Victor maneuvers around us!" His hands had made extravagant gestures describing an encirclement, and finished by crushing together. "We shall go to Vejer. Today!" He made the decision with a fine forcefulness. "From Vejer we can assail Chiclana from the south."

And that was a viable plan. The captured

French officer, a bespectacled captain called Brouard, drank too much of General Lapeña's wine and cheerfully revealed that there was no garrison in Vejer. Sir Thomas knew that a road went north from the town, which meant the allied army could come at the French siege works from the south, rather than from the east, and though he was not happy with the decision, he recognized the sense in it.

So, by the time the orders had been changed, it was almost midday before they marched and now the army was in chaos. It was infuriating. It was incompetence.

Vejer was visible across the plain, a town of white houses atop a sudden hill on the northwestern horizon, yet the guides had begun by marching the army southeast. Sir Thomas had ridden to Lapeña and, at his most diplomatic, had indicated the town and suggested it would be better to head in that direction. After a long consultation, Lapeña had agreed, and so the army had reversed itself, and that took time because the Spanish vanguard had to march back along a road crowded with stalled troops. But at last they had been going in the right direction and now they had stopped again. Just stopped. No one moved. No messages came back down the column explaining the halt. The Spanish soldiers fell out and lit their paper rolls of damp tobacco.

"Bloody man!" Sir Thomas said again as he rode to find General Lapeña. When the halt occurred he had been at the rear of the column because he liked to ride up and down his troops. He could tell a lot about his men from the way they marched, and he was pleased with his small force. They knew they were being ill led, they knew they were in chaos, but their spirits were high. The Cauliflowers were last in the column, more formally known as the second battalion of the 47th Regiment of the line. Their red coats were faced with the white patches that gave them their nickname, though the Cauliflowers' officers preferred to call the Lancashire men "Wolfe's Own" to remember the day they had turned the French out of Canada. The Cauliflowers, a staunch battalion from the Cádiz garrison, were reinforced by two companies of the Sweeps, green-jacketed men from the third battalion of the 95th. Sir Thomas raised his hat to the officers, then again to the men of the two Portuguese battalions who had sailed from Cádiz. They grinned at him, and he doffed his hat again and again. He noted approvingly that the Portuguese cacadores, light infantry, were in fine spirits. One of their chaplains, a man in a mud-stained cassock with a musket and a crucifix slung about his neck, demanded to know when they could start killing Frenchmen. "Soon!" Sir Thomas promised, hoping that was true. "Very soon!"

Ahead of the Portuguese was the Gibraltar Flanker battalion. That was a makeshift unit, formed by the light companies and grenadier companies of three battalions from the Gibraltar garrison. Prime troops, all of them. Two companies from the 28th, a Gloucestershire regiment, two from the 82nd, which was from Lancashire, and the two flank companies of the 9th, Norfolk lads and known as the Holy Boys because their shako plates, decorated with a picture of Britannia, was taken by the Spanish as an image of the Virgin Mary. Wherever the Holy Boys marched in Spain, women would genuflect and make the sign of the cross. Beyond the Gibraltar Flankers were the Faughs, the 87th, and Sir Thomas touched his hat in response to Major Gough's greeting. "It's chaos, Hugh, chaos," Sir Thomas admitted.

"We'll make sense of it, Sir Thomas."

"Aye, that we will, that we will."

Ahead of the 87th was the second battalion of the 67th, men from Hampshire, newly come from England, and unblooded until the night they had assailed the fire rafts. A good regiment, Sir Thomas reckoned, as were the remaining eight companies of the 28th who waited in front of them. The 28th was another solid county regiment from the shires. They had come from the Gibraltar garrison and Sir Thomas was pleased to see them because he remembered the men of Gloucestershire from Corunna. They had fought hard that day and had died hard too, belying their nicknames, the Dandies or the Silver Tails. Their officers insisted on wearing extra long tails to their coats, and the coattails were lavishly embroidered with silver. The 28th preferred to be known as the Slashers in solemn memory of the day they had sliced off the ears of an irritating French lawyer in Canada. The Slasher's lieutenant colonel was talking with Colonel Wheatley, who commanded all the troops on the road behind and Wheatley, seeing Sir Thomas ride by, called for his horse.

Major Duncan and his two batteries of artillery, five guns in each, waited on the road ahead of the Silver Tails. Duncan, resting against a limber, raised his eyebrows as Sir Thomas passed and was rewarded with a quick shrug. "We'll untangle the mess!" Sir Thomas called, and again hoped he was right.

In front of the guns was his first brigade, and he knew how fortunate he was to have such a unit under his command. It was only two battalions, but each was strong. The rearmost was another composite battalion, this one made up of two companies of Coldstreamers, two more of riflemen, and three companies of the Third Foot Guards. Scotsmen! The only Scottish infantry under his command and Sir Thomas took his hat off to them. With Scotsmen, he reckoned, he could break down the gates of hell, and he had a lump in his throat as he passed the blue-faced redcoats. Sir Thomas was a sentimental man. He loved soldiers. He had once thought all men who wore the red coat were rogues and thieves, the scourings of the gutter, and since he had joined the army he had discovered he was right, but he had also learned to love them. He loved their patience, their ferocity, their endurance, and their bravery. If he should die prematurely, Sir Thomas often thought, and join his Mary in her Scottish heaven, then he wanted to die among these men as Sir John Moore, another Scotsman, had died at Corunna. Sir Thomas kept Moore's red sash as a memento of that day, the weave stained dark with his hero's blood. A soldier's death, he thought, was a happy one, because a man, even in the throes of awful pain, would die in the best company in the world. He twisted in the saddle to look for his nephew. "When I die, John," he said, "make sure you take my body back to join your Aunt Mary."

"You won't be dying, sir."

"Bury me at Balgowan," Sir Thomas said, and touched the wedding ring he still wore. "There's money to pay for the costs of moving my corpse home. You'll find there's money enough." He had to swallow as he rode past the Scotsmen to where the second battalion of the First Foot Guards led his column. The First Footguards! They were called the Coal Heavers because, years before, they had carried coal to warm their officers in a freezing London winter, and the Coal Heavers were as fine a battalion as any that marched the earth. All the Guardsmen were led by Brigadier General Dilkes who touched the tip of his cocked hat and joined Colonel Wheatley to follow Sir Thomas past the Spanish troops to where General Lapeña sat, disconsolate and helpless, in his saddle.

Lapeña looked heavily at Sir Thomas. He

sighed as though he had expected the Scotsman's arrival and thought it a nuisance. He gestured toward distant Vejer, which glowed white on its hill. "**Inundación,**" Lapeña said slowly and distinctly, then made circling gestures with his hand as if to suggest that all was hopeless. Nothing could be done. Failure had been decreed by fate. It was over.

"The road, Sir Thomas," the liaison officer translated unnecessarily, "is flooded. The general regrets it, but it is so." The Spanish general had expressed no such regrets, but the liaison officer thought it prudent to suggest as much. "It is sad, Sir Thomas. Sad."

General Lapeña stared mournfully at Sir Thomas, something in his expression seeming to suggest it was all the Scotsman's fault. "**Inundación,**" he said again, shrugging.

"The road," Sir Thomas agreed in Spanish, "is indeed flooded." The drowned stretch was where the road crossed a marsh bordering a lake and, though the road was built on a causeway, the heavy rains had raised the water level so that now the marsh, the causeway, and a quarter mile of the road were underwater. "It is flooded," Sir Thomas said patiently, "but I dare say, señor, that we shall find it passable." He did not wait for Lapeña's response, but spurred his horse onto the causeway. The horse splashed, then waded as the water rose. It grew nervous, tossing its head and rolling its eyes white, but Sir Thomas kept firm control as he followed the line of withies stuck into the causeway's verges. He curbed the horse halfway through the flood, by which time the water was over his stirrups, and shouted back to the eastern bank in a voice honed by hallooing across windy Scottish hunting fields. "We should keep going! You hear me? Press on!"

"The guns cannot make it," Lapeña said, "and they cannot go around the flood." He gestured sadly to the north where marshes stretched beyond the flood's margin.

This was repeated to Sir Thomas when he trotted back. He nodded in acknowledgment, then shouted for Captain Vetch, the engineer officer who had burned the fire rafts and who had been posted with the advance guard to make just such assessments. "Make a reconnaissance, Captain," Sir Thomas ordered, "and tell me if the guns can use the road."

Captain Vetch rode his horse across the flooded stretch and came back with a confident report that the road was eminently passable, but

General Lapeña insisted that the causeway might have been damaged by the water and that it must be properly surveyed and, if necessary, repaired before any cannons could be drawn across the lake. "Then at least send the infantry across," Sir Thomas suggested, and after a while it was tentatively agreed that perhaps the infantry could risk the crossing.

"Bring your boys up," Sir Thomas said to Brigadier General Dilkes and Colonel Wheatley. "I want both your brigades close to the bank. Don't want them strung along the road." There was no danger in having his brigades tailing away into the distance, but Sir Thomas hoped that under the eyes of the British and Portuguese troops the Spaniards would show some alacrity.

The two brigades closed onto the lake bank, leaving the guns on the highway, but the arrival of Sir Thomas's men had no effect on the Spaniards. Their soldiers insisted on stripping off their boots and stockings before stepping cautiously onto the flooded road. Most of Lapeña's officers had no horses, for few mounts had been shipped in the feluccas, and those unmounted officers demanded to be carried by their men. They all went painfully slowly, as if they feared the ground would give way beneath them and

the waters engulf them. "God in his heaven," Sir
Thomas groused as he watched a small group
of mounted Spanish officers who were halfway across and nervously probing the hidden
road with long sticks. "John"—he turned to his
nephew—"my compliments to Major Duncan.
Tell him I want the guns here now and I want
them across this damned lake by mid-af-
ternoon."

Major Hope rode to fetch the guns. Lord
William Russell dismounted, took a telescope
from his saddlebag, and rested it on his horse's
back as he searched the northern landscape. It
was low country, edged on the horizon by bare
hills on which white villages reflected the winter
sun. The plain was dotted with strange ever-
greens that looked for all the world like a child's
drawing of what a tree should be. They were lofty
trees with a black bare trunk and a dark puff of
foliage spreading wide above. "I like those trees,"
he said, still staring through his glass.

"**Sciadopitys verticillata**," Sir Thomas said
casually, then saw Lord William look at him with
awe and astonishment. "My dear Mary took a
fancy to them on our travels," Sir Thomas explained, "and we tried planting a stand in Balgowan, but they didn't take. You'd think pines

would grow well in Perthshire, wouldn't you? But these didn't. Died the very first winter." He sounded relaxed, but Lord William could see the general's fingers drumming impatiently on his saddle pommel. Lord William looked back through the glass, edging the lens past a small village half hidden by the tracery of a winter olive grove, and then the glass stopped. He stared.

"We're being watched, Sir Thomas," he said.

"Aye, I should imagine so. Marshal Victor's no fool. Dragoons, are they?"

"A troop of them." Lord William twitched the long barrel to bring the lens into finer focus. "There's not a lot of them. Maybe twenty." He could see the horsemen's green uniforms against the white walls of the houses. "They're dragoons, sir, yes, and they're in a village between two low hills. Three miles off." A flash of light showed from a roof and Lord William guessed that a Frenchman was staring back through another telescope. "They're just watching us, it seems."

"Watching and reporting back," Sir Thomas said gloomily. "They'll have no orders to trouble us, Willie, just to keep a sharp eye on us, and I'll

wager your father's dukedom to one of my game-
keeper's cottages that Marshal Victor's already
marching."

Lord William searched the hills on either side
of the village, but no enemy showed on those low
heights. "Should we tell Doña Manolito?" he
asked.

Sir Thomas, for once, did not object to the
mocking nickname. "Leave him in peace," he
said softly, glancing at the Spanish general. "If
he knows there are green men stalking him he'll
like as not turn and run. You'll not repeat that,
Willie."

"Soul of discretion, sir," Lord William said,
then collapsed the glass and put it back into his
saddlebag. "But if Victor's marching, sir—" he
added, thinking about the implications, but leaving the question unfinished.

"He'll bar our road!" Sir Thomas said, at last
sounding cheerful, "and that means we have to
fight. And we need to fight. If we just run away
then those bastard lawyers in Cádiz will say the
French can't be beaten. They'll sue for peace,
then they'll throw us out of Cádiz and invite the
French in. We have to fight, Willie, and we have
to show the Spaniards we can win. Look at those
troops." He pointed to where his redcoats and

greenjackets waited. "Finest men in the world, Willie, finest in the world! So let's force a battle, eh? Let's do what we came to do!"

The Spanish infantry waiting to cross the causeway had to hurry off the road to let the two batteries of British guns pass. Those guns came in a rattling jangle of trace chains and a clatter of hooves. General Lapeña, seeing his men scatter, spurred to Sir Thomas and indignantly demanded to know why the ten cannons, with their limbers and caissons, had broken the order of march.

"You need them on the far bank," Sir Thomas said encouragingly, "in case the French come while your brave men are crossing." He waved the leading gun onto the causeway. "And go hard," he told the officer commanding the gun. "Force those buggers to hurry!"

"Yes, sir," the lieutenant said as he grinned.

A company of riflemen were sent to escort the guns. They stripped off their cartridge boxes and waded onto the causeway where they lined the verges, their presence intended to calm the horse teams. The first battery, under Captain Shenley, made fine time. The water came above the guns' axles, but four nine-pounder cannons and a five-

and-a-half-inch howitzer, each weapon pulled by eight horses, made the crossing without mishap. The limbers had to be emptied so that the water would not ruin the twenty-powder charges they each carried. The charges were placed on one of the battery's wagons that stood high enough to keep the charges dry and carried another hundred rounds of spare ammunition besides. "Now the second battery!" Sir Thomas ordered. He was in a fine mood now because Shenley's battery, chains jingling and wheels throwing up cockscombs of spray, had harried the laggard Spaniards to the far bank. There was suddenly a sense of urgency.

Then the leading gun of the second battery slewed off the causeway. Sir Thomas did not see what happened. Later he learned that one of the horses had stumbled, the team veered left, the drivers had hauled them back, and the gun, swinging behind its limber, had skidded off the road, bounced across the verge, then slammed down into the flood, spilling the gunners off the limber and bringing the horses to a sudden, sodden halt.

General Lapeña turned his head very slowly to give Sir Thomas an accusing look.

The gunners whipped the horses, the horses pulled, and the gun would not move.

And across the plain, beyond the long stretch of marshes, a glint of sun reflected from metal.

Dragoons.

It was over that night, all except for the fighting that would determine whether Cádiz would survive or fall. But the treacherous part ended when Lord Pumphrey came to the house Sharpe had rented in San Fernando. He came after dark, carrying the same bag he had taken to the cathedral crypt, and it seemed to Sharpe that His Lordship was even more nervous than when he had gone down the steps to where Father Montseny had waited in the dark. Pumphrey edged into the room and his eyes widened slightly when he saw Sharpe sitting by the hearth. "I thought you might be here," he said. He forced a smile for Caterina, then looked around the room. It was small, sparsely furnished with a dark table and high-backed chairs. The walls were lime washed and hung with portraits of bishops and with an old crucifix. The light came from a small fire and from a flickering lantern hanging under one of the black beams that crossed the ceiling. "This isn't the comfort you like, Caterina," Pumphrey said lightly.

"It's heaven compared to the home where I grew up."

"There is that, of course," Lord Pumphrey said. "I forget you grew up in a garrison town." He gave a worried glance at Sharpe. "She tells me she can geld hogs, Sharpe."

"You should see what she can do to men," Sharpe said.

"But you'd be much more comfortable back in the city," Pumphrey said to Caterina, ignoring Sharpe's sour words. "You have nothing to fear now from Father Montseny."

"I don't?"

"He was injured when the scaffolding fell in the cathedral. I hear he won't ever walk again, not ever." Pumphrey looked again at Sharpe, waiting for a reaction. He got none so he smiled at Caterina, put the bag on the table, drew a handkerchief from his sleeve, dusted a chair, and sat. "So your reason for leaving the city, my dear, no longer applies. Cádiz is safe."

"What about my reasons for staying here?" Caterina asked.

Pumphrey's eyes rested briefly on Sharpe. "Those reasons are your affair, my dear. But do come back to Cádiz."

"Are you Henry's procurer?" Sharpe asked scornfully.

"His Excellency," Pumphrey said with assumed dignity, "is in some ways relieved that Señorita Blazquez is gone. He feels, I think, that an unfortunate chapter in his life is now over. It can be forgotten. No, I merely wish Caterina to return so I can enjoy her company. We are friends, are we not?" He appealed to Caterina.

"We're friends, Pumps," she said warmly.

"Then as a friend I have to tell you that the letters no longer have value." He smiled at her. "They ceased to have value the moment Montseny was crippled. I only learned of that unfortunate outcome this morning. No one else, I assure you, will try to publish them."

"So why did you bring the money, my lord?" Sharpe asked.

"Because I had withdrawn it before I heard the sad news about Father Montseny, and because it is safer with me than left in my house, and because His Excellency is willing to pay a smaller sum for the return of the letters."

"A smaller sum," Sharpe repeated tonelessly.

"Out of the kindness of his heart," Lord Pumphrey said.

"How small?" Sharpe asked.

"One hundred guineas," Pumphrey proposed. "It is really very generous of His Excellency."

Sharpe stood and Lord Pumphrey's hand twitched toward the pocket of his coat. Sharpe laughed. "You've brought a pistol! You really think you can fight me?" Lord Pumphrey's hand went very still and Sharpe walked behind him. "His Excellency doesn't know a damn bloody thing about these letters, my lord. You didn't tell him. You want them for yourself."

"Don't be absurd, Sharpe."

"Because they'd be valuable, wouldn't they? A small lever to hold over the Wellesley family forever? What does Henry's oldest brother do?"

"The Earl of Mornington," Pumphrey said very stiffly, "is foreign secretary."

"Of course he is," Sharpe said, "and a useful man to have indebted to you. Is that why you want the letters, my lord? Or do you plan to sell them to His Excellency?"

"You have a fertile imagination, Captain Sharpe."

"No. I've got Caterina, and Caterina has the letters, and you've got money. Money's easy for you, my lord. What did you call it? Subventions to the guerrilleros and bribes for the deputies? But the gold is for Caterina now, which is a hell of a better cause than filling the purses of a pack of bloody lawyers. And there's one other thing, my lord."

"Yes?" Lord Pumphrey asked.

Sharpe laid a hand on Pumphrey's shoulder, making His Lordship shiver. Sharpe bent down to whisper hoarsely in His Lordship's ear. "If you don't pay her, then I'll do to you what you ordered done to Astrid."

"Sharpe!"

"Throat cut," Sharpe said. "It's harder than gelding hogs, but just about as messy." He drew a few inches of his sword, letting the blade scrape against the scabbard's throat. He felt a quiver in Lord Pumphrey's shoulder. "I ought to do it to you, my lord, for Astrid's sake, but Caterina doesn't want me to. So, are you paying her the money?"

Pumphrey stayed very still. "You won't cut my throat," he said with surprising calm.

"I won't?"

"People know I'm here, Sharpe. I had to ask two provosts where you were billeted. You think they'll forget me?"

"I take risks, my lord."

"Which is why you are valuable, Sharpe, but you are not a fool. Kill one of His Majesty's diplomats and you will die yourself. Besides, as you say, Caterina won't let you kill me."

Caterina said nothing. Instead she just shook her head slightly, though whether that was a denial of Lord Pumphrey's confident assertion or a sign that she did not want him killed, Sharpe could not tell.

"Caterina wants money," Sharpe said.

"A motive I entirely comprehend," Pumphrey said, and pushed his bag into the center of the table. "You have the letters?"

Caterina gave the six letters to Sharpe, who showed them to His Lordship, then carried them to the fire.

"No!" Pumphrey said.

"Yes," Sharpe said, and threw them on the burning driftwood. The letters flared up, sudden and bright, filling the room with a flickering glow that lit Lord Pumphrey's pale face. "Why did you kill Astrid?" Sharpe asked.

"To preserve Britain's secrets," Pumphrey said harshly, "which is my job." He stood abruptly, and there was a sudden air of authority in his frail figure. "You and I are alike, Captain

Sharpe, we know that in war, as in life, there is only one rule. To win. I am sorry about Astrid."

"No, you're not," Sharpe said.

Pumphrey paused. "You're right. I'm not." He smiled suddenly. "You play the game very well, Captain Sharpe, I congratulate you." He blew a kiss to Caterina, then left without another word.

"I do like Pumps," Caterina said when his lordship had gone, "so I'm glad you didn't kill him."

"I should have done."

"No," she said firmly. "He's like you, a rogue, and rogues should be loyal to each other." She was putting guineas into piles, playing with the coins, and the light from the lamp hanging from the beam reflected from the gold to shine yellow on her skin.

"You'll go back to Cádiz now?" Sharpe asked.

She nodded. "Probably," she said, and spun a coin.

"Find a man?"

"A rich man," she said, watching the spinning coin. "What else can I do? But before I find him I would like to see a battle."

"No!" Sharpe said. "It's no place for a woman."

"Maybe," she shrugged, then smiled. "So how much do you want, Richard?"

"Whatever you want to give me."

She pushed a generous pile across the table. "You are a fool, Captain Sharpe."

"Probably. Yes."

And somewhere to the south two armies were marching. And Sharpe reckoned there was a chance he might be able to join them, and gold would be no good to him there, but the memory of a woman was always a comfort. "Let's take the money upstairs," he suggested.

So they did.

One of General Lapeña's aides had seen the dragoons. He was watching them file out of the far olive grove toward the troops waiting at the causeway's far end. General Lapeña borrowed a telescope and made an aide stand his horse beside him so he could rest the barrel on the aide's shoulder. "**Dragons**," he said balefully.

"Not many of them," Sir Thomas said brusquely, "and a damned long way off. Good God, can't they shift that gun?"

They could not. The cannon, a nine-pounder

with a six-foot-long barrel, was stuck fast. Most of the gun was underwater so that only the tip of its left wheel and the top of the breech were visible. One horse was flailing as a gunner tried to keep its head above water. The riflemen posted to guard the causeway's edges were holding the other horses, but the beasts were getting increasingly fearful and the panicking horse threatened to jar both gun and limber farther down the flooded embankment. "Detach the limber, man!" Sir Thomas roared and, when his injunction failed to have an immediate effect, he spurred his horse onto the causeway. "I want a dozen more fellows!" he shouted at the nearest infantry.

A squad of Portuguese infantrymen followed Sir Thomas who curbed his horse beside the stricken cannon. "What's the problem?" he asked brusquely.

"There seems to be a culvert down here, sir," a lieutenant said. He was clinging to the drowned wheel and plainly feared the whole heavy weapon would tip onto him. "The wheel's caught in the culvert, sir," the lieutenant added. A sergeant and three gunners were heaving at the gun, attempting to lift the trail-plate eye that attached the cannon to its limber, and every heave jarred the cannon slightly deeper, but at last they succeeded in raising the eye free of the pin so that the limber shot out onto the road in a flurry of splashing hooves. The gun stayed behind but lurched dangerously, and the lieutenant's eyes widened in fear before the weapon settled, though now the breech was entirely submerged.

Sir Thomas unbuckled his sword belt and threw it with his scabbard and pouches to Lord William who had dutifully followed his master onto the causeway. Sir Thomas gave the aide his cocked hat too, so that the small wind stirred his white hair. Then he slid from the saddle, plunging up to his chest into the gray water. "Not nearly as cold as the River Tay," he said. "Come on, boys."

The water was now up to Sir Thomas's armpits. He put his shoulder to the wheel while grinning riflemen and Portuguese privates joined him. Lord William wondered why Sir Thomas had allowed the gun to be released from its horse team, then understood that the general did not want the freed gun to leap ahead and crush a man under its wheel. Slow and steady would do this job.

"Put your backs into it!" the general shouted

to the men around him. "Heave on it! Come on now!"

The gun moved. The breech reappeared, then the top of its right wheel showed above water. A rifleman lost his footing, slipped under, flailed his way back, and hauled on a wheel spoke. The gunners on the road had attached a strap to the trail and were pulling like men in a tug-of-war.

"Here she comes!" Sir Thomas shouted triumphantly, and the cannon lurched up the verge and rolled onto the causeway. "Hook her up!" Sir Thomas said. "And let's get moving!" He wiped his hands on his drenched jacket as the trail-plate eye was reconnected. There was the crack of a whip and the gun was on its way again. A Portuguese sergeant, seeing that the general was having trouble mounting his horse because of the weight of his wet clothes, hurried to help and heaved Sir Thomas upward. "Obliged to you, obliged," Sir Thomas said, giving the man a coin before settling himself in the saddle. "That's the way to do it, Willie."

"You'll catch your death, sir," Lord William said with genuine concern.

"Aye, well, if I do, Major Hope knows what to do with my corpse," Sir Thomas said. He was wet through, but grinning broadly. "That water was cold, Willie! Damned cold! Make sure those infantrymen get a change of clothes." He laughed suddenly. "When I was a lad, Willie, we chased a fox into the Tay. I was just a boy and the hounds were doing nothing except bark at the thing, so I drove my horse into the river and caught the beast with my bare hands. I thought I was a hero! My uncle gave me a whipping for that. Never do the hounds' work, he told me, but sometimes you have to, sometimes you just have to."

The dragoons had swerved northward, never coming within a mile of the troops crossing the causeway, and when the light cavalry of the King's German Legion trotted toward them the dragoons galloped fast away. The rest of the Spanish infantry crossed, still going with painful slowness, so that it was dusk before Sir Thomas's two brigades came across the causeway, and full dark before the army marched again. The road climbed steadily and undramatically toward the lights of Vejer that flickered and twinkled on the hilltop beneath the stars. The army marched north of the town, following a road that led to a midnight bivouac in a spread of olive groves where Sir Thomas at last rid himself of his damp clothes and crouched over a fire to get warm.

Foraging parties went out the next day, returning with a herd of skinny bullocks and a flock of pregnant ewes and fractious goats. Sir Thomas fretted, eager to be moving, and, for want of other activity, he rode with a squadron of German cavalry to find that the hills north and east were lively with enemy horsemen. A troop of Spanish cavalry cantered down a stream bank to join Sir Thomas's men. Their commander was a captain who wore yellow breeches, a yellow waistcoat, and a blue jacket with red facings. He touched his hat to Sir Thomas. "They're watching us," he spoke in French, assuming that Sir Thomas could not speak Spanish.

"That's their job," Sir Thomas answered in Spanish. He had taken care to learn the language when he was first posted to Cádiz.

"Captain Sarasa." The Spaniard named himself, then took a cigar from his saddlebag. One of his men struck a light with a tinderbox and Sarasa bent over the flame until the cigar was drawing properly. "I have orders," he said, "not to engage the enemy."

Sir Thomas heard the sullen tone and understood that Sarasa was frustrated. He wanted to take his men up to the crests of the low hills and match them against the French vedettes. "You have orders?" Sir Thomas inquired tonelessly.

"General Lapeña's orders. We are to protect the forage parties, no more."

"You would rather fight?"

"Is that not why we are here?" Sarasa asked truculently.

Sir Thomas liked Sarasa. He was a young man, probably not yet thirty, and he had a belligerence that encouraged Sir Thomas, who believed that the Spaniards would fight like devils if they were given a chance and, perhaps, some leadership. At Bailén, three years before, a Spanish force had outfought a whole French corps and forced a surrender. They had even taken an eagle so they could fight well enough and, if Captain Sarasa was an example, they wanted to fight, but for once Sir Thomas found himself agreeing with Lapeña. "What's across the hill, Captain?" he asked.

Sarasa stared at the nearest crest where two vedettes were visible. A vedette was a sentry post of cavalrymen who were posted to watch an enemy. There were twelve men in the two vedettes while Sir Thomas, reinforced now by Sarasa's swordsmen, had more than sixty. "We don't know, Sir Thomas," he admitted.

"There's probably nothing across the hill," Sir Thomas said, "and we could chase those fellows off, and if we did we'd see them on a farther hill and we'd think there's no harm in chasing them off that, and so it would go on until we're five miles north of here and the forage parties are dead."

Sarasa drew on his cigar. "They offend me," he said vehemently.

"They disgust me," Sir Thomas said, "but we fight them where we choose or where we must, not always when we want."

Sarasa gave a quick smile as if to say he had learned his lesson. He tapped ash from his cigar. "The rest of my regiment, Sir Thomas," he said, "is ordered to reconnoiter the road to Conil." He spoke very flatly.

"Conil?" Sir Thomas asked and Sarasa nodded. The Spaniard was still watching the distant dragoons, but he was very aware as Sir Thomas took a folded map from his saddlebag. It was a bad map, but it did show Gibraltar and Cádiz, and between them it marked Medina Sidonia

and Vejer, the town which lay just to the south.
Sir Thomas drew a finger westward from Vejer
until he reached the Atlantic coast. "Conil?" he
asked again, tapping the map.

"Conil de la Frontera." Sarasa confirmed the
location by giving the town its full name. "Conil
beside the sea," he added in an angrier voice.

Beside the sea. Sir Thomas stared at the map.
Conil was indeed on the shore. Ten miles north
of it was a village called Barrosa, and from there
a road led east to Chiclana, which was the base
of the French siege lines, but Sir Thomas already
knew that General Lapeña had no intention of
using that road, because, just a couple of miles
north of Barrosa was the Rio Sancti Petri where,
supposedly, the Spanish garrison was making a
pontoon bridge. Cross that bridge and the army
would be back on the Isla de León, and another
two hours' marching would have Lapeña's men
back in Cádiz and safe from the French. "No,"
Sir Thomas said angrily and his horse stirred
nervously.

The road north from Vejer was the one to
take. Break through the French cordon of
vedettes and march hard. Victor would be defending Chiclana, of course, but by skirting east
of the city the allied army could maneuver the

French marshal out of his prepared position and force him to fight on ground of their own choosing. But instead the Spanish general was thinking of a stroll by the sea? He was thinking of retreating to Cádiz? Sir Thomas could hardly believe it, but he knew that an attack on Chiclana from Barrosa was untenable. It would be an advance over poor country tracks against an army in prepared positions and Lapeña would never contemplate such a risk. Doña Manolito just wanted to go home, but to get home he would march his army along a coastal road and all the French needed to do was advance on that road to trap the allies against the sea. "No!" Sir Thomas said again, then turned his horse toward the distant encampment. He spurred away, then abruptly curbed the stallion and turned back to Sarasa. "You're not to engage, those are your orders?"

"Yes, Sir Thomas."

"But of course, if those bastards threaten you, then your duty is to kill them, isn't it?"

"Is it, Sir Thomas?"

"Assuredly yes! And I am sure you will do your duty, Captain, but don't pursue them! Don't abandon the foragers! No further than the skyline, you hear me?" Sir Thomas spurred on and reckoned that if one Frenchman of the vedette even raised a hand, then Sarasa would attack. So at least some enemy would die, even if Doña Manolito apparently wanted the rest to live forever. "Bloody man," Sir Thomas growled to himself, "bloody, bloody man," and rode to save the campaign.

"I saw your friend last night," Captain Galiana said to Sharpe.

"My friend?"

"Dancing at Bachica's."

"Oh, Caterina?" Sharpe said. Caterina had returned to Cádiz, traveling there in a hired carriage and with a valise filled with money.

"You didn't tell me she was a widow," Galiana said reprovingly. "You called her señorita!"

Sharpe gaped at Galiana. "A widow!"

"She was dressed in black, with a veil," Galiana said. "She didn't actually dance, of course, but she watched the dancing." He and Sharpe were on a patch of shingle at the edge of the bay. The north wind brought the stench of the prison hulks moored off the salt flats. Two guard boats rowed slowly down the hulks.

"She didn't dance?" Sharpe asked.

"She's a widow. How could she? It is too soon. She told me her husband has only been dead for three months." Galiana paused, evidently remembering Caterina riding on the beach where her dress and demeanor had been anything but bereaved. He decided to say nothing of that. "She was most gracious to me," he said instead. "I like her."

"She's very likable," Sharpe said.

"Your brigadier was also there," Galiana said.

"Moon? He's not my brigadier," Sharpe said, "and I don't suppose he was dancing either."

"He was on crutches," Galiana said, "and he gave me orders."

"You! He can't give you orders!" Sharpe spun a stone into the water, hoping it would skip across the small waves, but it sank instantly. "I hope you told him to go to hell and stay there."

"These orders," Galiana said, taking a piece of paper from his uniform pocket and handing it to Sharpe to whom, surprisingly, the orders were addressed. The paper was a dance card and the words had been carelessly scrawled in pencil. Captain Sharpe and the men under his command were to post themselves at the Rio Sancti Petri until further orders or until the forces presently under the command of Lieutenant

General Graham were safely returned to the Isla de León. Sharpe read the scrawled note a second time. "I'm not sure Brigadier Moon can give me orders," he said.

"He did, though," Captain Galiana said, "and I, of course, will come with you."

Sharpe returned the dance card. He said nothing, just skimmed another stone that managed one bounce before vanishing. Grazing, it was called. A good artilleryman knew how to skip cannon balls along the ground to increase their effective range. The balls grazed, kicking up dust, coming flat and hard and bloody.

"It is a precaution," Galiana said, folding the card.

"Against what?"

Galiana selected a stone, threw it fast and low, and watched as it skipped a dozen times. "General Zayas is at the bridge across the Sancti Petri," he said, "with four battalions. He has orders to stop anyone from the city crossing the river."

"You told me," Sharpe said, "but why stop you?"

"Because there are folk in the city," Galiana explained, "who are **anfrancesado.** You know what that is?"

"They're on the French side."

Galiana nodded. "And some, alas, are officers in the garrison. General Zayas has orders to stop such men offering their services to the enemy."

"Let the buggers go," Sharpe said. "Have fewer mouths to feed."

"But he won't stop British troops."

"You told me that, too, and I said I'd help you. So why the hell do you need orders from bloody Moon?"

"In my army, Captain," Galiana said, "a man cannot just take it upon himself to do whatever he wants. He requires orders. You now have orders. So, you can take me over the river and I shall find our army."

"And you?" Sharpe asked. "Do you have orders?"

"Me?" Galiana seemed surprised at the question, then paused because one of the great French mortars had fired from the forts on the Trocadero. The sound came flat and dull across the bay and Sharpe waited to see where the shell would fall, but he heard no explosion. The missile must have plunged into the sea. "I have no orders," Galiana admitted.

"Then why are you going?"

"Because the French have to be beaten," Galiana said with a sudden vehemence. "Spain must free herself! We must fight! But I am like your brigadier, like the widow—I cannot join the dance. General Lapeña hated my father and he detests me and he does not want me to distinguish myself, so I am left behind. But I will not be left behind. I will fight for Spain." The grandiosity of his last words were touched by passion.

Sharpe watched the cloud of smoke left by the mortar's firing drift and dissipate across the distant marshes. He tried to imagine himself saying he would fight for Britain in that same heartfelt tone, and could not. He fought because it was all he was good for, and because he was good at it, and because he had a duty to his men. Then he thought of those riflemen. They would be unhappy at being ordered away from the taverns of San Fernando, and so they should be. But they would follow orders. "I"—he began and immediately fell silent.

"What?"

"Nothing," Sharpe said. He had been about to say that he could not order his riflemen into a battle that was none of their business. Sharpe would fight if he saw Vandal, but that was personal, but his riflemen had no ax to grind and their battalion was miles away, and it was all too complicated to explain to Galiana. Besides, it was unlikely that Sharpe would travel to the army with Galiana. He might take the Spaniard across the river, but unless the allied army was within sight Sharpe would have to bring his men back. The Spaniard could ride across country to find Lapeña, but Sharpe and his men would not have the luxury of horses. "Did you tell Moon all that?" he asked. "About you wanting to fight?"

"I told him I wanted to join General Lapeña's army and that if I traveled with British troops then Zayas would not stop me."

"And he just wrote the orders?"

"He was reluctant to," Galiana admitted, "but he wanted something from me, so he agreed to my request."

"He wanted something from you," Sharpe said, then smiled as he realized just what that something must have been. "So you introduced him to the widow?"

"Exactly."

"And he's a rich man," Sharpe said, "very rich." He skimmed another stone and thought that Caterina would skin the brigadier alive.

Sir Thomas Graham discovered General Lapeña in an uncharacteristically cheerful mood. The

Spanish commander had taken a farmhouse for his headquarters and, because the winter's day was sunny and because the house sheltered the yard from the north wind, Lapeña was taking lunch at a table outside. He shared the table with three of his aides and with the French captain who had been captured on the way to Vejer. The five men had been served dishes of bread and beans, cheese and dark ham, and had a stone jug of red wine. "Sir Thomas!" Lapeña seemed pleased to see him. "You will join us, perhaps?" He spoke in French. He knew Sir Thomas could speak Spanish, but he preferred to use French. It was, after all, the language with which European gentlemen communicated.

"Conil!" Sir Thomas was so angry that he did not bother to show courtesy. He slid from his saddle and tossed the reins to an orderly. "You want to march to Conil?" he said accusingly.

"Ah, Conil!" Lapeña clicked his fingers at a servant and indicated that he wanted another chair brought from the farmhouse. "I had a sergeant from Conil," he said. "He used to talk of the sardine catch. Such bounty!"

"Why Conil? You're hungry for sardines?"

Lapeña looked sadly at Sir Thomas. "You have not met Captain Brouard? He has, of course, given us his parole." The captain, wearing his French blue and with a sword at his side, was a thin, tall man with an intelligent face. He had watery eyes, half hidden behind thick spectacles. He stood on being introduced and offered Sir Thomas a bow.

Sir Thomas ignored him. "What is the purpose," he asked, resting his hands on the table so that he leaned toward Lapeña, "in marching on Conil?"

"Ah, the chicken!" Lapeña smiled as a woman brought a roasted chicken from the farmhouse and placed it on the table. "Garay, you will carve?"

"Allow me the honor, Excellency," Brouard offered.

"The honor is all ours, Captain," Lapeña said, and ceremoniously handed the Frenchman the carving knife and a long fork.

"We hired ships," Sir Thomas growled, ignoring the chair that had been placed next to Lapeña's place at the table, "and we waited for the fleet to assemble. We waited for the wind to be in our favor. We sailed south. We landed at Tarifa because that gave us the ability to reach the rear of the French positions. Now we march to Conil? For God's sake, why did we bother with the fleet at all? Why didn't we just cross the Rio Sancti Petri and march straight to Conil? It would have taken a short day and we wouldn't have needed a single ship!"

Lapeña's aides stared resentfully at Sir Thomas. Brouard pretended to ignore the conversation, concentrating instead on carving the fowl, which he did with an admirable dexterity. He had jointed the carcass and now cut perfect slice after perfect slice.

"Things change," Lapeña said vaguely.

"What has changed?" Sir Thomas demanded.

Lapeña sighed. He hooked a finger at an aide who at last understood that his master wished to see a map. Dishes were put aside as the map was unfolded onto the table and Sir Thomas noted that the map was a good deal better than the ones the Spanish had supplied to him. "We are here," Lapeña said, placing a bean just north of Vejer, "and the enemy are here," he put another bean on Chiclana, "and we have three roads by which we may approach the enemy. The first, and longest, is to the east, through Medina Sidonia." Another bean served to mark the town. "But we know the French have a garrison there. Is that not right, monsieur?" he appealed to Brouard.

"A formidable garrison," Brouard said, separating the drumstick from the carcass with a surgeon's skill.

"So we shall find ourselves between Marshal Victor's army here"—Lapeña touched the bean marking Chiclana—"and the garrison here." He indicated Medina Sidonia. "We can avoid the garrison, Sir Thomas, by taking the second road. That goes north from here and will approach Chiclana from the south. It is a bad road. It is not direct. It climbs into these hills"—his forefinger tapped some hatch marks—"and the French will have picquets there. Is that not so, monsieur?"

"Many picquets," Brouard said, easing out the wishbone. "You should inform your chef, **mon général,** that if he removes the wishbone before cooking the bird, the carving will be made easier."

"How good to know that," Lapeña said, then looked back to Sir Thomas. "The picquets will apprise Marshal Victor of our approach so he will be ready for us. He will confront us with numbers superior to our own. In all conscience, Sir Thomas, I cannot use that road, not if we are to gain the victory we both pray for. But fortunately there is a third road, a road that goes along the sea. Here"—Lapeña paused, putting a fourth bean on the shoreline—"is a place called . . ." He hesitated, unsure what place the bean marked and finding no help from the map.

"Barrosa," an aide said.

"Barrosa! It is called Barrosa. From there, Sir Thomas, there are tracks across the heath to Chiclana."

"And the French will know we're using them," Sir Thomas said, "and they'll be ready for us."

"True!" Lapeña seemed pleased that Sir Thomas had understood such an elementary point. "But here, Sir Thomas"—his finger moved to the mouth of the Sancti Petri—"is General Zayas with a whole corps of men. If we march to . . ." He paused again.

"Barrosa," the aide said.

"Barrosa," Lapeña said energetically, "then we can combine with General Zayas. Together we shall outnumber the French! At Chiclana they have, what? Two divisions?" He put the question to Brouard.

"Three divisions," the Frenchman confirmed, "the last I heard."

"Three!" Lapeña sounded alarmed, then waved a hand as if dismissing the news. "Two?

Three? What does it matter? We shall assail them from the flank!" Lapeña said. "We shall come at them from the west, we shall destroy them, and we shall gain a great victory. Forgive my enthusiasm, Captain," he added to Brouard.

"You trust him?" Sir Thomas asked Lapeña, jerking his head at the Frenchman.

"He is a gentleman!"

"So was Pontius Pilate," Sir Thomas said. He thrust a big finger down onto the shoreline. "Use that road," he said, "and you place our army between the French and the sea. Marshal Victor is not going to wait at Chiclana. He's going to come for us. You want to see your men drowning in the surf?"

"So what do you suggest?" Lapeña asked icily.

"March to Medina Sidonia," Sir Thomas said, "and either crush the garrison"—he paused to eat the bean denoting that town—"or let them rot behind their walls. Attack the siege lines. Force Victor to march to us instead of us marching to him."

Lapeña looked wonderingly at Sir Thomas. "I admire you," he said after a pause, "I truly do. Your avidity, Sir Thomas, is an inspiration to us all." His aides nodded solemn agreement, and even Captain Brouard gave a polite inclination of his head. "But permit me to explain myself," Lapeña went on. "The French army, you will agree, is here." He had taken a handful of the beans and now arrayed them in crescent about the Bay of Cádiz, running from Chiclana in the south, around the siege lines, and finishing at the three great forts on the Trocadero marshes. "If we attack from here"—Lapeña tapped the road from Medina Sidonia—"then we assault the center of their lines. We shall doubtless make good progress, but the enemy will converge on us from both flanks. We shall run the risk of encirclement." He held up a hand to stop Sir Thomas's imminent protest.

"If we come from here," Lapeña continued, this time indicating the southern road from Vejer, "we shall, of course, strike at Chiclana, but there will be nothing, Sir Thomas, absolutely nothing, to stop the French marching onto our right flank." He scooped the beans into a small pile to show how the French might overwhelm his attack. "But from the east, from—" He hesitated.

"Barrosa, señor."

"From Barrosa," Lapeña went on, "we strike their flank. We hit them hard!" He smacked a fist into a palm to show the force with which he envisaged making the attack. "They will still try to march against us, of course, but now their men must get through the town! They will find that hard, and we shall be destroying Victor's forces while his reinforcements still thread the streets. There! Do I convince you?" He smiled, but Sir Thomas said nothing. It was not that the Scotsman had nothing to say, but he was struggling to say it with even a hint of courtesy. "Besides," Lapeña went on, "I command here, and it is my belief that the victory we both desire is best achieved by marching along the coast. We were not to know that when we embarked on the fleet, but it is the duty of a commander to be flexible, is it not?" He did not wait for a response, but instead tapped the empty chair. "Join us for some chicken, Sir Thomas. Lent starts on Wednesday, and then there'll be no more chicken till Easter, eh? And Captain Brouard has carved the fowl superbly."

"Bugger the fowl," Sir Thomas said in English and turned to his horse.

Lapeña watched the Scotsman ride away. He shook his head but said nothing. Captain Brouard, meanwhile, reached over and crushed the bean at Barrosa with his thumb, then smeared the pulp down the shore so that it looked reddish against the map. Blood in the surf. "How very clumsy of me," Brouard lamented. "I simply meant to remove it."

Lapeña was unworried by the small mess. "It is a pity," he said, "that God in his wisdom decreed that the English should be our allies. They are"—he paused—"so very uncomfortable."

"They are blunt creatures," Captain Brouard sympathized. "They lack the subtlety of the French and the Spanish races. Allow me to give Your Excellency some chicken? Does Your Excellency prefer breast?"

"You are right!" General Lapeña was delighted with the Frenchman's insight. "No subtlety, Captain, no finesse, no"—he paused, seeking the word—"no grace. The breast. How very kind of you. I am obliged."

And he was also determined. He would take the road that offered the shortest route home to Cádiz. He would march to Conil.

There was another argument in the afternoon. Lapeña wanted to march that night and Sir Thomas protested that they were close to the enemy now, and that the men should come to any encounter with the enemy fresh, not exhausted from a night groping through unfamiliar country. "Then we march this evening"—Lapeña generously yielded the point—"and bivouac at midnight. In the dawn, Sir Thomas, we shall be rested. We shall be ready."

Yet midnight passed, as did the rest of the night, and at dawn they were still marching. The column had become lost again. The troops had stopped, rested, been woken, had marched, stopped again, countermarched, turned around, rested for a few uncomfortable minutes, been woken, and then retraced their footsteps. The men were laden with packs, haversacks, cartridge boxes, and weapons and, when they stopped, they dared not unbuckle their equipment for fear they would be hurried on at any moment. None rested properly so that by dawn they were exhausted. Sir Thomas spurred past his men, his horse kicking up small gouts of sandy soil as he looked for General Lapeña. The column had stopped again. The redcoats were sitting by the track and they looked resentfully at the general as though it were his fault that they had been given no rest.

General Lapeña and his aides were on a small wooded rise where a dozen civilians were arguing. The Spanish general nodded a distant greeting to Sir Thomas. "They are not sure of the way," Lapeña said, indicating the civilians.

"Who are they?"

"Our guides, of course."

"And they don't know the way?"

"They do," Lapeña said, "but they know different ways." Lapeña smiled and shrugged as if to suggest such things were inevitable.

"Where's the sea?" Sir Thomas demanded. The guides looked solemnly at Sir Thomas and then all pointed westward and agreed that the sea lay that way. "Which would make sense," Sir Thomas said caustically, nodding toward the east where the sky was suffused with new light, "because the sun has a habit of rising in the east and the sea lies to the west, which means our route to Barrosa lies that way." He pointed north.

Lapeña looked offended. "At night, Sir Thomas, there is no sun to guide us."

"That's what happens when you march at night!" Sir Thomas snarled. "You get lost."

The march began again, now following tracks across an undulating heath dotted with pinewoods. The sea came into sight soon after the sun rose. The track led north above a long sandy beach where the surf broke and seethed before sliding back to meet the next crashing wave. Far out to sea a ship bore southward, only her topsails visible above the horizon. Sir Thomas, riding on the inland flank of his leading brigade, climbed a sandy hill and saw three watchtowers punctuating the coast ahead, relics of the days when Moorish pirates sailed from the Straits of Gibraltar to murder, rob, and enslave. "The nearest, Sir Thomas, is the tower at Puerco," his liaison officer told him. "Beyond that is the tower of Barrosa, and the furthest is at Bermeja."

"Where's Conil?"

"Oh, we skirted Conil in the night," the liaison officer said. "It is behind us now."

Sir Thomas glanced at his tired troops who marched with heads down, silent. He looked north again and saw, beyond the tower at Bermeja, the long isthmus leading to Cádiz that was a white blur on the horizon. "We've wasted our time, haven't we?" he said.

"Oh no, Sir Thomas. I am sure General Lapeña means to attack."

"He's marching for home," Sir Thomas said wearily, "and you know it." He leaned forward on his saddle pommel and suddenly felt every one of his sixty-three years. He knew Lapeña was hurrying for home now. Doña Manolito had no intention of turning east to attack the French; he just wanted to be in Cádiz where, doubtless, he would boast of having marched across Andalusia in defiance of Marshal Victor.

"Sir Thomas!" Lord William Russell spurred his horse toward the general. "There, sir."

Lord William was pointing north and east. He gave Sir Thomas a telescope and the general extended the tubes and, using Lord William's shoulder as a slightly unsteady rest, saw the enemy. Not dragoons this time, but infantry. A mass of infantry half hidden by trees.

"Those are the forces masking Chiclana," the liaison officer declared confidently.

"Or the forces marching to intercept us?" Sir Thomas suggested.

"We know they have troops at Chiclana," the liaison officer said.

Sir Thomas could not see whether the distant troops were marching or not. He collapsed the glass. "You will go to General Lapeña," he told the liaison officer, "and give him my compliments, and tell him there is French infantry on our right flank." The liaison officer turned his horse, but Sir Thomas checked him. The Scotsman was looking ahead and could see a hill just inland of Barrosa, a hill with a ruin on its summit and a place that would offer a position of strength. It was the obvious place to post men if the French were planning an attack. Make Victor's forces fight uphill, make them die on the slope, and, when they were beaten, march on Chiclana. "Tell the general," he told the liaison officer, "that we are ready to turn and attack on his orders. Go!"

The liaison officer spurred away. Sir Thomas looked again at the hill above Barrosa and reckoned that the brief and so far disastrous campaign could yet be saved. But then, from far ahead, came the crackle of gunfire. The sound rose and fell in the wind, sometimes almost drowned by the crash of the endless waves, but it was unmistakable, the thorn-burning snap and splintering noise of musket volleys. Sir Thomas stood in his stirrups and stared. He was waiting for the thick smoke of the powder to reveal where the fighting took place, and at last he saw it. It was smearing the beach beyond the third watchtower, but still short of the pontoon bridge that led back to the city. Which meant that the French had already cut them off and were now barring the road to Cádiz and, worse, much worse, were almost certainly advancing from the inland flank. Marshal Victor had the allied force exactly where he wanted it: between his army and the sea. He had them at his mercy.

Chapter 10

"It's not our fight, sir," Harper said.

"I know."

Sharpe's admission checked the big Irishman who had not expected such ready agreement. "We should be in Lisbon," he persisted.

"Aye, we should, and we will be, but there are no boats going to Lisbon, and there won't be, not till this lot's over." Sharpe nodded across the Sancti Petri. It was an hour or so after dawn and a mile down the beach beyond the river were blue uniforms. Not the light blue uniforms of the Spanish, but the darker blue of the French. The enemy had come from the inland heath and their sudden appearance had caused General Zayas's troops to form in battalions that now waited on the northern side of the river. The strange thing was that the French had not come to attack the makeshift fort built on the far side of the pontoon bridge, but were facing south, away from the fort. A cannon in the fort had tried a shot at the French troops, but the ball had plowed into the sand well short and the one failed shot had persuaded the fort's commander to save his ammunition.

"I mean, sir," Harper went on, "just because Mister Galiana wants to fight—"

"I know what you mean." Sharpe interrupted him harshly.

"Then, sir, just what the hell are we doing here?"

Sharpe did not doubt Harper's bravery; only a fool could do that. It was not cowardice that was provoking the big Irishman's protest, but a sense of grievance. The one explanation for the French having their backs to the river was that allied forces were farther south, and that implied that General Lapeña's army, far from marching inland to attack the French siege works from the east, had chosen to advance along the coast instead. So now that army faced what, to Sharpe, looked like four or five battalions of French infantry. And that was Lapeña's fight. If the fifteen thousand men under Doña Manolito's command could not crush the smaller force on the

beach, then there was nothing Sharpe and five riflemen could do to help. For Sharpe to risk those
five lives was irresponsible; that was what Harper
was saying, and Sharpe agreed with him. "I'll tell
you what we're doing here," Sharpe said. "We're
here because I owe Captain Galiana a favor. We
all owe him a favor. If it wasn't for Galiana we'd
all be in a Cádiz jail. So in return we see him
across the river, and once we've done that, we're
finished."

"Across the river? That's all, sir?"

"That's all. We march him over, tell any Spanish bugger who interferes to jump in the river,
and we're finished."

"So why do we have to see him over?"

"Because he asked. Because he thinks they'll
stop him if he's not with us. Because that's the
favor he asked us."

Harper looked suspicious. "So if we see him
across, sir, we can go back to the town?"

"You're missing the tavern?" Sharpe asked.
His men had been bivouacking at the beach's
end for two days now: two days of constant
grumbling at the Spanish rations that Galiana
had arranged and two days of missing the com-
forts of San Fernando. Sharpe sympathized, but
was secretly pleased that they were uncomfort-

able. Idle soldiers got into mischief and drunken soldiers into trouble. It was better to have them grumbling. "So once we've got him safe across," Sharpe said, "you can go back with the lads. I'll write you orders. And you can have a bottle of that **vino tinto** waiting for me."

Harper, given what he wanted, looked troubled. "Waiting for you?" he asked flatly.

"I won't be long. It should all be over by nightfall. So go on, tell the lads they can go back as soon as we've got Captain Galiana over the bridge."

Harper did not move. "So what will you be doing, sir?"

"Officially," Sharpe said, ignoring the question, "we're all ordered to stay here till Brigadier bloody Moon tells us otherwise, but I don't think he'll mind if you go back. He won't know, will he?"

"But why will you be staying, sir?" Harper insisted.

Sharpe touched the edge of the bandage showing under his shako. The pain in his head had gone and he suspected it was safe to take the bandage off, but his skull still felt tender so he had left it on and religiously soaked it with vinegar each day. "The 8th of the line, Pat," he said, "that's why."

Harper looked down the shoreline to where the French stood silent. "They're there?"

"I don't know where the buggers are. What I do know is that they were sent north and they couldn't get north because we blew up their damned bridge, so the odds are they came back here. And if they are here, Pat, then I want to say hello to Colonel Vandal. With this." He hefted the rifle.

"So you're—"

"So I'm just going to wander along the beach," Sharpe interrupted. "I'm going to look for him. If I see him I'll have a shot at him, that's all. Nothing more, Pat, nothing more. I mean it's not our fight, is it?"

"No, sir, it isn't."

"So that's all I'm doing, and if I can't find the bugger, then I'll come back. Just have that bottle of wine ready for me." Sharpe clapped Harper on the shoulder, then walked to where Captain Galiana was sitting on a horse. "What's happening, Captain?"

Galiana had a small telescope and was staring southward. "I don't understand it," he said.

"Understand what?"

"There are Spanish troops there. Beyond the French."

"General Lapeña's men?"

"Why are they here?" Galiana asked. "They should be marching on Chiclana!"

Sharpe gazed over the river and down the long beach. The French stood in three ranks, their officers on horseback, their eagles glinting in the early sun. Then, quite suddenly, those eagles, instead of being outlined against the sky, were wreathed in smoke. Sharpe saw the musket smoke blossom thick and silent until, a few seconds later, the sound crackled past him.

Then, after that first massive volley, the world went silent except for the call of the gulls and the seethe of the waves. "Why are they here?" Galiana asked again, and then the muskets fired a second time, more of them now, and the morning was filled with the sound of battle.

A hundred or so paces upstream of the pontoon bridge a small tidal creek branched south from the Rio Sancti Petri. The creek was called the Almanza and it was a place of reeds, grass, water, and marsh where herons hunted. The creek headed inland, thus dictating that an army coming north along the coast would find itself on a narrowing strip of land and beach that ended at the Rio Sancti Petri. The Almanza Creek was a mile long at low tide and twice that distance at high, and its presence made the narrowing funnel of sand into a trap if another army could get behind the first and drive it north toward the river. The trap would become even more lethal if another force could ford the creek and so block any retreat across the pontoon bridge.

The Almanza Creek was not much of a barrier, except at its mouth it could be waded almost anywhere along its length and, at nine o'clock the morning of March 5, 1811, the tide had only just begun to flood and so the French infantry could cross it easily. They splashed through the marshes, slid down the muddy bank, and waded the creek's sandy bed before climbing to the dunes and beach beyond. Yet, though the creek was no obstacle to men or to horses, it was impassable to artillery. The cannons weighed too much. A French twelve-pounder, the most common gun in the emperor's arsenal, weighed a ton and a half, and to get a cannon, its limber, its caisson and crew across the marsh would require engineers. When

Marshall Victor ordered General Villatte's division to ford the Almanza there was no time to summon engineers, let alone for those engineers to build a makeshift road across the creek, so the force Villatte led to block the retreat of Lapeña's army was infantry alone.

Marshal Victor was no fool. He had made his reputation at Marengo and at Friedland, and since coming to Spain he had beaten two Spanish armies at Espinosa and at Medellin. It was true he had taken a bloody nose from Lord Wellington at Talavera, but **le beau soleil,** the beautiful sun as his men called him, regarded that reverse as a whim of fickle fortune. "A soldier who has never been defeated," he liked to say, "has learned nothing."

"And what did you learn from Lord Wellington?" General Ruffin, a giant of a man who led one of Victor's divisions, had asked.

"Never to lose again, François!" Victor had said, then laughed. Claude Victor was a friendly soul, outgoing and genial. His soldiers loved him. He had been a soldier in the ranks himself once. True, he had been an artilleryman, which was hardly the same as an infantryman, but he knew the ranks, he loved them, and he expected them to fight hard just as he led them hard. He was, all French soldiers said, a brave and a good man. **Le beau soleil.** And he was no fool. He knew that Villatte's infantry, unsupported by close artillery, could not stand against the approaching Spaniards, but they could delay Lapeña. They could hold Lapeña's forces on the narrowing beach while Victor's other two divisions, those of Leval and Ruffin, worked around their rear, and then the trap would be sprung. The allied army would be driven into the narrowing funnel that ended at the Rio Sancti Petri and, though Villatte's men would doubtless have to give way in front of the increasing pressure, the other two divisions would come from behind like avenging angels. Only a few Spaniards and Britons could hope to cross the pontoon bridge; the rest would be herded and slaughtered until, inevitably, the survivors surrendered. And it would be simple! The allied army, apparently oblivious of the fate that waited for it, was still in line of march, stretching for three miles along the straggling coast road. The marshal had watched their progress from Tarifa with growing astonishment; he had watched them haver and change course and stop and start and change direction again, and he came to understand that he was opposing enemy generals who did not know their business. It would all be so easy.

Now Villatte was across the creek and in place. He was the anvil. And the two sledgehammers, Leval and Ruffin, were ready to attack. Marshal Victor, from the summit of a hill on the inland heath, gave a last survey of his chosen battlefield and liked what he saw. On his right, closest to Cádiz, was the Almanza Creek, which he could cross with infantry but not with artillery, so he would let Villatte fight his battle there with musketry alone. In the center, south of the creek, was a stretch of heathland ending in a thick pinewood that hid his view of the sea. The enemy column, his scouts reported, was mostly strung along the track that ran inside that wood, so Marshal Victor would send General Leval's division to attack the pinewood and break through to the beach beyond. Such an attack would be threatened on its left flank by a hill that also hid the sea. It was not much of a hill—Victor guessed it rose no more than two hundred feet above the surrounding heath—but it was steep enough and it was crowned by a ruined chapel and a stand of wind-bent trees. The hill, astonishingly, was empty of troops, though Victor did not believe his enemies would be so foolish as to leave it unguarded. Occupied or not, the hill must be taken and the pinewood captured. Then Victor's two divisions could turn north up the shore and drive the remnants of the allied army to destruction in the narrowing space between the sea and the creek. "It will be a rabbit hunt!" Victor promised his aides. "A rabbit hunt! So hurry! Hurry! I want my bunnies in the pot by lunchtime!"

Sir Thomas had his eyes fixed on the hill crowned by a ruin. He galloped along the rough track that curled around the seaward side of the hill and discovered a Spanish brigade marching there. The brigade contained five battalions of troops and a battery of artillery, all of whom were under Sir Thomas's command because they followed the baggage and Lapeña had agreed that every unit behind the baggage would fall under Sir Thomas's authority. He ordered the Spaniards, both infantry and artillery, to the top of the hill. "You will hold there," he instructed their commander. The brigade was the nearest troops to the hill, an accident of where they happened to be when Sir Thomas decided to garrison the height, but the Scotsman was nervous of entrusting the army's rear to an unknown Spanish brigade. He turned his horse, its hooves kicking up sand, and found the battalion of flank companies from the Gibraltar garrison. "Major Browne!"

"At your service, Sir Thomas!" Browne swept off his hat. He was a burly man, red-faced, and eternally cheerful.

"Your fellows are stout, Browne?"

"Every man jack a hero, Sir Thomas."

Sir Thomas twisted in his saddle. He was on the coast road where it passed through a miserable village called Barroso. There was a watchtower there, built long ago to guard against enemies from the sea, and he had sent an aide to climb the tower, but it gave a poor view inland. Pinewoods edged the coast here and they hid everything to the east, but common sense told Sir Thomas that the French must attack the hill, which was the highest point on the coast. "The devils are out there somewhere," Sir Thomas said, pointing east, "and our lord and master tells me they're not coming here, but I don't believe it, Major. And I don't want the devils on that hill. You see those Spaniards?" He nodded

toward the five battalions toiling up the slope.
"Reinforce them, Browne, and hold the hill."

"It'll be held," Browne said cheerfully, "and
you, Sir Thomas?"

"We're ordered north." Sir Thomas pointed to
the next watchtower on the coast. "I'm told
there's a village called Bermeja under that tower.
We concentrate there. But don't leave the hill,
Browne, till we're all there." Sir Thomas
sounded sour. Lapeña was scuttling away and
Sir Thomas did not doubt that his two brigades
would be required to fight a rearguard action at
Bermeja. He would rather have fought here,
where the hill gave his troops an advantage, but
the liaison officer had brought Doña Manolito's
orders and they were specific. The allied army
was to retreat to Cádiz. There was no more talk
of striking inland to attack Chiclana; now it was
just an ignominious retreat. The whole campaign
was a waste! Sir Thomas was angry at that, but
he could not disobey a direct order, so he would
hold the hill to protect the army's rear while it
marched north to Bermeja. He sent aides to tell
General Dilkes and Colonel Wheatley to continue north along the track concealed in the
pinewoods. Sir Thomas followed, spurring out of

the village into the trees, while Major Browne took his Gibraltar Flankers to the top of the hill that was called the Cerro del Puerco, though neither Browne nor any of his men knew that.

The summit of the Cerro del Puerco was a wide shallow dome. On its seaward side was a ruined chapel and a stand of windswept trees. Browne discovered the five Spanish battalions lined just in front of the ruins. He was tempted to march past the Spaniards and take post on the right of their line, but he suspected their officers would protest if he took that place of honor, so he contented himself by putting his small battalion on the left of the line where the major dismounted and paced in front of his men. He had the grenadier and light companies from the 9th, 28th, and 82nd regiments, elite men from Lancashire, Silver Tails from Gloucestershire, and Holy Boys from Norfolk. The grenadier companies were the heavyweight infantry, big and hard men, selected for their height and fighting abilities, while the light companies were the skirmishers. It was an artificial battalion, put together for just this campaign, but Browne was confident of its abilities. He glanced at the Spaniards and saw that the battery of Spanish guns had deployed at the line's center.

The British and Spanish line, arrayed on the seaward crest of the Cerro del Puerco, was hidden from anyone inland; that meant the battalions could not see if any French troops approached from the east. Nor, of course, could they be bombarded by enemy cannon if the French did assault the hill, so Browne was content to let his Flankers stay where they were. But he wanted to see if anything threatened the hill and so he gestured to his adjutant and the two men picked their way across the coarse grass. "How are your boils, Blakeney?" Browne asked.

"Recovering, sir."

"Nasty things, boils. Especially bum boils. Saddles don't help them, I find."

"They're not too painful, sir."

"Have the surgeon lance them," Browne suggested, "and you'll be a new man. Good God."

The two men had reached the eastern crest and the great heath, undulating toward Chiclana, was visible beneath them. The major's last two words had been prompted by the sight of distant infantry. He could see the bastards half hidden by distant trees and hillocks, but where the blue-coated devils were going he could not work out. More immediately he could see three squadrons of French dragoons, green-coated devils, who were riding toward the hill. "You think those Frenchmen want to play with us, Blakeney?"

"They seem to be coming this way, sir."

"Then we must make them welcome," Browne said, and did a smart about-face and paced back toward the ruined chapel. In front of him now was a battery of five cannon and four thousand Spanish and British muskets. More than enough, he reckoned, to hold the hill.

A flurry of hooves to the south gave him a moment's alarm. Then he saw that allied cavalry had come to the hilltop. There were three squadrons of Spanish dragoons and two of the King's German Legion hussars, all under the command of General Whittingham, an Englishman in Spanish service. Whittingham rode to Browne who was still dismounted. "Time to go, Major," Whittingham said curtly.

"Go?" Browne thought he had misheard. "I'm ordered to hold this hill! And there are two hundred and fifty Crapaud dragoons down there," Browne said, pointing northeast.

"Seen them," Whittingham said. His face was deep-lined, shadowed by his cocked hat, beneath which he smoked a thin cigar that he kept tapping even though there was no ash to fall from its tip. "Time to withdraw," he said.

"I'm ordered to hold the hill," Browne insisted, "until Sir Thomas has reached the next village. And he hasn't."

"They're gone!" Whittingham pointed to the beach where the last of the baggage train was plodding well north of the Cerro del Puerco.

"We hold the hill!" Browne insisted. "Damn it, those are my orders!"

A cannon, not fifty paces off to Browne's right, suddenly fired, and Whittingham's horse skittered sideways and tossed its head frantically. Whittingham calmed the beast and moved it back to Browne's side. He dragged on his cigar and watched the dragoons who had appeared on the eastern skyline, or at least the helmeted heads of the leading squadron had shown over the crest and the Spanish artillerymen had greeted them with a round shot that screamed off into the eastern sky. A trumpeter sounded a call from the French ranks, but the man was so surprised or else so nervous that the fine notes cracked and he had to begin again. The trumpet did not prompt any extraordinary activity from the dragoons who, evidently surprised to see such a large force waiting for them, stayed just beneath the eastern crest. Two of the Spanish battalions put their skirmishers forward and those light infantrymen started a sporadic musket fire. "Range is much too long," Browne said scathingly, then frowned up at Whittingham. "Why don't you charge the buggers?" he asked. "Isn't that what you're supposed to do?" Whittingham had five squadrons while the French had only three.

"Stand here, Browne, and you'll be cut off," Whittingham said, tapping the cigar. "Cut off, that's what you'll be. Our orders are clear. Wait till the army's gone past, then follow."

"My orders are clear," Browne insisted. "I hold the hill!"

More Spanish skirmishers were sent forward. The apparent inactivity of the dragoons was encouraging the light companies. The French horsemen, Browne thought, must surely withdraw for they must realize they had no hope of chasing a whole brigade off a hilltop, especially when that brigade was reinforced by its own artillery and cavalry. Then some of the enemy horsemen cantered northward and drew carbines from their saddle holsters. "Buggers want to make a fight of it," Browne said. "By God, I don't mind! Your horse is pissing on my boots."

"Sorry," Whittingham said, kicking the horse a pace forward. He watched the Spanish light companies. Their musket fire was doing no evident damage. "Got orders to retreat," he said obstinately, "as soon as the army's passed the hill and that's what they've done, they've passed the hill." He sucked on the cigar.

"See that? The buggers want to skirmish," Browne said. He was looking past Whittingham to where at least thirty of the helmeted Frenchmen had dismounted and were advancing in a skirmish line to oppose the Spaniards. "Don't see that much, do you?" Browne asked, sounding as carefree as a man noticing some phenomenon on a country walk. "I know dragoons are supposed to be mounted infantry, but they mostly stay in the saddle, don't you find?"

"No such thing as mounted infantry, not these days," Whittingham said, ignoring the fact that the dragoons were disproving his point. "It doesn't work. Neither fish nor fowl. You can't stay here, Browne," he went on. He tapped again and at last some cigar ash dropped onto his boot. "Our orders are to follow the army north, not stand around here."

The Spanish gun that had fired was now reloaded with canister and its team trained the weapon around to face the dismounted dragoons who were advancing in skirmish order across the hilltop. The artillerymen dared not fire yet because their own skirmishers were in the way. The sound of the muskets was desultory. Browne could see two of the Spanish skirmishers laughing. "What they should do," he said, "is close on the bastards, hurt them, and provoke a charge. Then we could kill the whole damned lot."

The dismounted dragoons opened fire. It was only a smattering of musket balls that flicked across the hilltop and none of them did any damage, but their effect was extraordinary. Suddenly the five Spanish battalions were loud with orders. The light companies were called back, the gun teams were hurried forward, and, to Major Browne's utter astonishment, the guns and the five battalions simply fled. If he had been kind he might have called it a precipitate retreat, but he was in no mood to be kind. They ran. They went as fast as they could, tumbling down the seaward slope, skirting the hovels of Barrosa and heading north. "Good God," he said, "good God!" The enemy dragoons looked as astonished as Major Browne at the effect of their puny volley, but then the dismounted men ran back to their horses.

"Form square!" Major Browne shouted, knowing that a single battalion in a line of two ranks would make a tempting target for three squadrons of dragoons. The long, heavy, straight-bladed swords would already be whispering out of their scabbards. "Form square!"

"You mustn't stay here, Browne!" Whittingham shouted after the major. His cavalry had followed the Spaniards and the general now spurred after them.

"Got my orders! Got my orders! Form square, boys!" The Gibraltar Flankers formed square. They were a small battalion, numbering just over five hundred muskets, but in square they were safe enough from the dragoons. "Pull up your breeches lads," Browne shouted, "and fix bayonets!"

The dragoons, all mounted again, came over the crest. Their swords were drawn. Their guidons, small triangular flags, were embroidered with a golden **N** for Napoleon. Their helmets were polished. "Fine looking beggars, aren't they, Blakeney?" Browne said as he hauled himself back into his saddle. General Whittingham had disappeared, Browne did not see where, and it seemed the Flankers were alone on the Cerro del Puerco. The front rank of the square knelt. The dragoons had formed three lines. They were watching the square, knowing its first volley would cut down their leading rank, but wondering whether they could break the redcoats apart anyway. "They want to die, boys," Browne shouted, "so we shall oblige them. It is our God-given duty."

Then, from behind the ruined chapel, came a single squadron of King's German Legion hussars. They rode in two ranks, wore gray overalls, blue coats, and polished helmets, and carried sabers. They rode tight, boot to boot, and as they passed the corner of Browne's square the front rank spurred into the gallop. They were outnumbered by the dragoons, but they charged home and Browne heard the clangor of saber against sword. The dragoons, who had not started their advance, were pushed back. A horse fell, a dragoon spurred out of the fight with a face cut to the skull, and a hussar rode back toward the square with a sword piercing his belly. He fell from his saddle fifty yards from Browne's front rank and his horse immediately turned back to the fight that was a confusion of men, horses, and dust. The hussars, having hurled the first line of dragoons back, turned away and the French came after them, but then the trumpet threw the second line of Germans against the French and the dragoons were pounded back a second time. The first troop re-formed, the riderless horse taking its place in the rank. A sergeant and two men of the Holy Boys had fetched the wounded hussar into the square. The man was plainly dying. He stared up at Browne, muttering in German. "Pull the damned sword out!" Browne snapped to the battalion's surgeon.

"It will kill him, sir."

"What if it stays in?"

"He'll die."

"Then pray for the poor bugger's soul, man!" Browne said.

The hussars had come back now. The dragoons had retreated, leaving six bodies on the hill. They might have outnumbered the single squadron of Germans, but so long as the Germans stayed near the red-coated infantry, the dragoons were vulnerable to volley fire and so their commander took them down the hill's slope to wait for reinforcements.

Browne waited. He could hear musketry far to the north. It was volley fire, but it was someone else's fight so he ignored the sound. He was commanded to hold the hill and he was a stubborn man, so he stayed under the pale sky in which the wind brought the smell of the sea. The leader of the hussar squadron, a captain, politely requested to enter the square and touched the brim of his helmet to Browne. "The dragoons, I think, will not bother you now," he said.

"Obliged to you, Captain, obliged I'm sure."

"I am Captain Dettmer," the captain said.

"Sorry about this fellow," Browne said as he nodded at the dying hussar.

Dettmer stared at the hussar. "I know his mother," he said sadly, then looked back to Browne. "There is infantry coming to the hill," he went on. "I saw it when we were fighting."

"Infantry?"

"Too many," Dettmer said.

"Let's look," Browne said, and he ordered two files to leave the square, then led Captain Dettmer through the gap. The two men trotted to the hill's eastern edge and Browne stared down at approaching disaster. "Dear God," he said, "that's not pretty."

When he had last looked the heath was a wilderness of sand, grass, pines, and thickets. He had seen infantry in the distance, but now the whole heath was covered in blue. The whole wide world was a mass of blue coats and white crossbelts. He could see battalion after battalion of Frenchmen, their eagles shining in the morning sun as their army advanced on the sea. "Dear God," Browne said again.

Because only half the French army was marching on the pinewood that hid them from the sea. The other half was coming for Browne and his five hundred and thirty-six muskets.

Coming straight for him. Thousands.

Sharpe climbed the tallest sand dune in sight and leveled his telescope across the Rio Sancti Petri. He could see the backs of the Frenchmen on the beach and the musket smoke dark around their heads, but the image wavered because the glass was unsteady. "Perkins!"

"Sir?"

"Bring your shoulder here. Be useful."

Perkins served as a telescope rest. Sharpe stooped to the eyepiece. Even with the telescope held steady it was hard to tell what was happening because the French were in a line of three ranks and their powder smoke concealed everything beyond them. They were firing continually.

He could not see all the French line, for dunes hid their left flank, but he was watching at least a thousand men. He could see two eagles and suspected there were at least two more battalions hidden by the dunes.

"They're slow, sir." Harper had come to stand behind him.

"They're slow," Sharpe agreed. The French were firing as battalions, which meant that the slowest men dictated the rate of fire. He guessed they were not even managing three shots a minute, but that seemed sufficient because the French were taking very few casualties. He edged the telescope very slowly along their line and saw that only six bodies had been dragged behind the ranks to where the officers rode up and down. He could hear, but not see, the Spanish muskets and once or twice, as the smoke thinned, he had a glimpse of the Spanish in their lighter blue, and he reckoned their line was a good three hundred paces from the French. Might as well spit at that distance. "They're not close enough," Sharpe muttered.

"Can I look, sir?" Harper asked.

Sharpe bit back a sour comment to the effect that this was not Harper's fight, and instead yielded his place at Perkins's shoulder. He turned and looked out to sea where the waves fretted about a small island crowned by the ancient ruins of a fort. A dozen fishing boats were just beyond the line of surf that ran toward the beach. The fishermen were watching the fight, and more spectators, attracted by the crackle of musketry, were riding from San Fernando. No doubt there would soon be curious folk arriving from Cádiz.

Sharpe took the telescope back from Harper. He collapsed it, his fingers running over the small brass plate let into the largest barrel that was sheathed in walnut. IN GRATITUDE, AW, SEPTEMBER 23RD, 1803, the plate said, and Sharpe remembered Henry Wellesley's flippant line that the telescope, which was a fine instrument made by Matthew Berge of London, was not the generous gift Sharpe had always supposed it to be, but instead a spare glass that Lord Wellington had not wanted. Not that it mattered. 1803, he thought. That long ago! He tried to remember that day when Lord Wellington, Sir Arthur Wellesley back then, had been dazed and Sharpe had protected him. He thought he had killed five men in the fight, but he was not sure.

The Spanish engineers were laying the chesses over the last thirty feet of the pontoon bridge.

Those planks, which formed the roadway, were kept on the Cádiz bank to stop any unauthorized crossing of the bridge, but evidently General Zayas now wanted the bridge open and Sharpe saw, with approval, that three Spanish battalions were being readied to cross the bridge. Zayas had evidently decided to attack the French from their rear. "We'll be going soon," he said to Harper.

"Perkins," Harper growled, "join the others."

"Can't I look through the telescope, Sergeant?" Perkins pleaded.

"You're not old enough. Move."

It took a long time for the three battalions to cross. The bridge, constructed from longboats rather than pontoons, was narrow and it rocked alarmingly. By the time Sharpe and his men had joined Captain Galiana, there were almost a hundred curious onlookers arrived from San Fernando or Cádiz and some were trying to persuade the sentries to let them cross the bridge. Others climbed the dunes and trained telescopes on the distant French. "They're stopping everyone crossing the bridge," Galiana said nervously.

"They're not going to let civilians across, are they?" Sharpe said. "But tell me something, what are you going to do on the other side?"

"Do?" Galiana said, and plainly did not know the answer. "Make myself useful," he suggested. "It's better than doing nothing, isn't it?" The last Spanish battalion had crossed now and Galiana spurred forward. He dismounted well short of the bridge, preparing to lead his horse over the uncertain footing of the chesses, but before he reached the roadway a squad of Spanish soldiers pulled a makeshift barricade across the approach. A lieutenant held a warning hand toward Galiana.

"He's with me," Sharpe said before Galiana could speak. The lieutenant, a tall man with a burly, unshaven chin, looked at him pugnaciously. It was plain he did not understand English, but he was not going to back down. "I said he's with me," Sharpe said.

Galiana spoke in rapid Spanish, gesturing at Sharpe. "You have your orders?" he switched to English, looking at Sharpe.

Sharpe had no orders. Galiana spoke again, explaining that Sharpe was charged with delivering a message to Lieutenant General Sir Thomas Graham, and the orders were in English, which, of course, the lieutenant spoke? Galiana himself, the Spanish captain explained, was Sharpe's liaison officer. By now Sharpe had produced his ration authorization, permitting him to draw beef, bread, and rum for five riflemen from the headquarters stores at San Fernando. He thrust the paper at the lieutenant who, faced with hostile riflemen and the emollient Galiana, decided to yield. He ordered the hurdles pulled aside.

"I did need you after all," Galiana said. He held the reins very close to the mare's head and continually patted her neck as she made her cautious way across the plank roadway. The bridge, much less robust than the one Sharpe had destroyed on the Guadiana, quivered underfoot and bowed upstream under the pressure of the flooding tide. Once safe on the far bank, Galiana mounted and led Sharpe southward past the sandy ramparts of the temporary fort made to protect the pontoons.

General Zayas had formed his three battalions in a line across the beach where they were now marching slowly forward. The right-hand files were having their boots sporadically washed by the incoming surf. Sergeants bellowed at men to keep their dressing. The Spanish colors were bright against the pale sky. From far off came the report of a cannon, a deeper sound than musketry, a pounding in the air. It died away, but over the constant snap of the nearer muskets Sharpe thought he could hear other muskets firing, but much farther off. "You can go back now," he told Harper.

"Let's just see what these lads do first," Harper said, nodding at the three Spanish battalions.

The lads needed to do nothing except appear. General Villatte, seeing that his men were about to be assailed from the rear, ordered them to withdraw east across the Almanza Creek. They carried their wounded away. The Spaniards, seeing them go, gave a cheer of victory, then wheeled up the dunes to harry the retreating French who were now outnumbered almost two to one. Galiana, standing in his stirrups, was exultant. Surely the combined Spanish forces, joining from north and south, could now pursue the French across the creek and drive them far back along the tracks to Chiclana, but just then artillery opened fire from the Almanza's far bank. A battery of twelve-pounders had been placed on the firm ground to the east and their first salvo was of common shell that exploded in gouts of sand and smoke. The Spanish advance

checked as men took cover behind dunes. The
guns fired a second time and round shot slashed
through files slow to find shelter. The last of the
French infantry had waded the creek now and
were making a new line to face the Spaniards
across the incoming tide. The guns went silent as
their smoke drifted across the slowly rising water. The French were content to wait now. Their
force that had blocked the allied army's retreat
had been thrust aside, but their guns could still
hurl shell and round shot at any force marching
toward the bridge. They brought up a second
battery and waited for the rout to begin from the
south while the Spanish battalions, content to
have cleared the enemy off the beach, settled
among the dunes.

Galiana, disappointed that the pursuit had
not been pressed across the Almanza, had ridden
to a group of Spanish officers and now came
back to Sharpe. "General Graham is to the
south," he said, "with orders to bring the rear
guard here."

Sharpe could see a mist of musket smoke
drifting away from a hill two or more miles
southward. "He's not coming yet," he said, "so
I might go and meet him. You can go back
now, Pat."

Harper thought about it. "So what are you do-ing, sir?"

"I'm just taking a walk on the beach."

Harper looked at the other riflemen. "Does anyone here want to take a walk on a beach with me and Mister Sharpe? Or do they want to go back and talk their way past that nasty lieutenant on the bridge?"

The riflemen said nothing until another can-non sounded far to the south. Then Harris frowned. "What's happening down there?" he asked.

"Nothing to do with us," Sharpe said.

Harris could be a barrack room lawyer at times, and he was about to protest that the fight was none of their business. Then he caught Harper's eye and decided to say nothing. "We're just taking a walk on the beach," Harper said, "and it's a nice day for a walk." He saw Sharpe's quizzical look. "I was thinking of the Faughs, sir. They're up there, they are, all those poor wee boys from Dublin, and I thought they might like to see a proper Irishman."

"But we're not going to fight?" Harris de-manded.

"What do you think you are, Harris? A bloody soldier?" Harper asked caustically. He took care not to catch Sharpe's eye. "Of course we're not going to fight. You heard Mister Sharpe. We're going for a walk on the beach, that's all we're bloody doing."

So they did. They went for a walk on the beach.

Sir Thomas, certain that his rear was well protected by the brigade posted on the Cerro del Puerco, was encouraging his troops along the road that led through the long pinewood edging the beach. "Not far, boys!" Sir Thomas called as he rode down the line. "We've not far to go! Cheer up now!" He glanced to his right every few seconds, half expecting the appearance of a cavalryman bringing news of an enemy advance. Whittingham had undertaken to post vedettes on the inland edge of the wood, but none of those men appeared and Sir Thomas supposed the French were content to let the allied army retreat ignominiously into Cádiz. The firing ahead had stopped. A French force had evidently blocked the beach, but had now been chased away, while the firing from the south had also died. Sir Thomas reckoned that had been mere bickering, probably a cavalry patrol coming too close to the big Spanish brigade on the summit of the Cerro del Puerco.

He paused to watch the redcoats march past and he noted how the tired men straightened their backs when they saw him. "Not far, boys," he told them. He thought how much he loved these men. "God bless you, boys," he called, "and it's not far now." Not far to what, he wondered sourly. These bone-weary soldiers had been marching all night, laden with packs and haversacks and weapons and rations, and it was all for nothing, all for a scuttling retreat back to the Isla de León.

There was a flurry of shouts to the north. A man called a challenge and Sir Thomas stared down the track, but saw nothing and heard no shots. A moment later a mounted officer of the Silver Tails came pounding back down the track with two horsemen close behind. They were civilians armed with muskets, sabers, pistols, and knives. Partisans, Sir Thomas thought, two of the men who made life such hell for the French armies occupying Spain. "They want to talk to you, sir," the Silver Tail officer said.

The two partisans spoke at once. They spoke

fast, excitedly, and Sir Thomas calmed them. "My Spanish is slow," he told them, "so speak to me slowly."

"The French," one of them said and pointed eastward.

"Where have you come from?" Sir Thomas asked. One of the men explained that they had been part of a larger group that had shadowed the French for the last three days. Six men had ridden from Medina Sidonia and these two were the only ones left alive because some dragoons had caught them soon after dawn. The two had been chased toward the sea and they had just ridden across the heath. "Which is full of Frenchmen," the second man said earnestly.

"Coming this way," the first man added.

"How many French?" Sir Thomas asked.

"All of them," the two men said together.

"Then let us look," Sir Thomas said, and he led the two men and his aides inland through the pines. He had to duck under the branches. The wood was wide and deep, thick and shadowed. Pine needles overlay the sandy soil, muffling the sound of the horses' hooves.

The wood ended abruptly, giving way to the undulating heath that stretched away under the morning sun. And there, filling the wide world, were white crossbelts against blue coats.

"Señor?" one of the partisans said, gesturing at the French as though he had produced them himself.

"Dear God," Sir Thomas said softly. Then he said nothing more for a while, but just stared at the approaching enemy. The two partisans thought the general was too shocked to speak. He was, after all, watching disaster approach.

But Sir Thomas was thinking. He was noticing that the French marched with muskets slung. They could not see enemy troops to their front and so, instead of marching into battle, they were marching to battle. There was a difference. Men marching to battle might have loaded muskets, but the muskets would not be cocked. Their artillery was undeployed, and it took time for the French to deploy guns because the cannons' heavy barrels had to be lifted from the travel position to the firing position. In short, Sir Thomas thought, these Frenchmen were not ready for a fight. They were expecting a fight, but not yet. Doubtless they believed they must first pass the pinewood, and only then would they expect the killing to begin.

"We should follow General Lapeña," the liaison officer said nervously.

Sir Thomas ignored the man. He was thinking still, his fingers tapping the saddle pommel. If he continued north, then the French would cut off the brigade on the hill above Barrosa. They would wheel right and attack up the beach, and Sir Thomas would be forced to try a makeshift defense with his left flank open to attack. No, he thought, better to fight the bastards here. It would not be an easy fight, it would be a damned scramble, but better that than continuing north and turning the sea's edge red with his blood.

"My lord"—he was uncharacteristically formal as he glanced at Lord William Russell—"my compliments to Colonel Wheatley, and he is to bring his brigade here and face down these fellows. Tell him to send his skirmishers as fast as he can! I want the enemy engaged by the light bobs while the rest of his brigade comes up. Guns are to come here. Right here," he stabbed a hand at the ground on which his horse stood. "Hurry now, no time to lose!" He beckoned to another aide, a young captain in the blue-faced red coat of the First Foot Guards. "James, compliments to General Dilkes, and I want his brigade here," he gestured to the right. "He's to take position between the guns and the hill. Order him to send his skirmishers first! Quick now! Quick as he can!"

The two aides vanished into the trees. Sir Thomas lingered a moment, watching the approaching French who were now less than half a mile off. He was taking a vast gamble. He wanted to hit them while they were unprepared, but he knew it would take time to bring his battalions through the thick trees, which is why he had asked for the light companies to come first. They could make a skirmish line on the heath, they could begin to kill the French, and Sir Thomas could only hope that the skirmishers would hold the French long enough for the rest of the battalions to arrive and begin their deadly volley fire. He looked at the liaison officer. "Be so good," he said, "as to ride to General Lapeña and tell him the French are moving on the pinewood and that it is my intention to engage them and would be honored"—he was choosing his words carefully—"if the general could lead men onto the right flank of the enemy."

The Spaniard rode away and Sir Thomas looked back east. The French were coming in two huge columns. He planned to face the northern column with Wheatley's brigade, while

General Dilkes and his guardsmen would confront the column closest to the Cerro del Puerco. And that made him think of the Spaniards on the hill. The French would surely send their southern column to take that hill and they must not be allowed to do so, or else they could sweep down from its summit to attack the right flank of his hasty defense. He turned south, leading his remaining aides toward the Cerro del Puerco.

That hill, he thought as he rode back into the pines, was his one advantage. There were Spanish cannons on the summit, and those guns could fire down on the French. The hill was a fortress protecting his vulnerable right flank, and if the French could be held on the plain then the brigade on the hill could be used to make an attack on the enemy's flank. Thank God, he was thinking as he rode out of the trees, that the hill was his.

Except it was not. The Cerro del Puerco had been abandoned and, even as Sir Thomas had ridden south, the first French battalions were climbing the hill's eastern slopes. The enemy now held the Cerro del Puerco and the only allied troops in sight were the five hundred men of the Gibraltar Flankers. Instead of holding the high ground, they were forming into a column of march at the hill's foot. "Browne! Browne!" Sir Thomas shouted as he cantered toward the column. "Why are you here? Why?"

"Because I've got half the French army climbing the damned hill, Sir Thomas."

"Where are the Spaniards?"

"They ran."

Sir Thomas stared at Browne for a heartbeat. "Well, it's a bad business, Browne," he said, "but you must instantly turn around again and attack."

Major Browne's eyes widened. "You want me to attack half their army?" he asked incredulously. "I saw six battalions and a battery of artillery coming! I've got only five hundred thirty-six muskets." Browne, deserted by the Spaniards, had watched the mass of infantry and cannon approaching the hill, and had decided that retreat was better than suicide. There were no other British troops within sight, he had no promises of reinforcement, and so he had led his Gibraltar Flankers north, off the hill. Now he was being told to go back, and he took a deep breath, as if steeling himself for the ordeal. "If we must," he said, stoically accepting his fate, "then we will."

"You must," Sir Thomas said, "because I need

the hill. I'm sorry, Browne, I need it. But General Dilkes is coming. I'll bring him up to you myself."

Browne turned to his adjutant. "Major Blakeney! Skirmish order! Back up the hill! Drive the devils away!"

"Sir Thomas?" an aide interrupted, then pointed to the hill's summit, where the first French battalions were already appearing. Blue coats were showing at the skyline, a great array of blue coats ready to come down the slope and scour their way along the pinewood.

Sir Thomas gazed at the French. "Light bobs won't stop them, Browne," he said. "You'll have to give them volley fire."

"Close order!" Browne shouted at his men who had started to deploy into skirmish order.

"They have a battery of cannon up there, Sir Thomas," the aide said quietly.

Sir Thomas ignored the news. It did not matter if the French had all the emperor's artillery on the hilltop, they still had to be attacked. They had to be thrown off the hill, and that meant the only available troops must climb the slope and make an assault that would hold the French in place until General Dilkes's guardsmen came to assist them. "God be with you, Browne," Sir

Thomas said too quietly for the major to hear. Sir Thomas knew he was sending Browne's men to their deaths, but they had to die to give the Guards time to arrive. He sent an aide to summon Dilkes's men. "He's to ignore my last order," Sir Thomas said, "and to bring his men here with the utmost speed. The utmost speed! Go!"

Sir Thomas had done what he could. The coastline between the villages of Barrosa and Bermeja was two miles of confusion into which two French attacks were developing, one against the pinewood while the other had already captured the crucial hill. Sir Thomas, knowing that the enemy was on the brink of victory, must gamble everything on his men's ability to fight. Both his brigades would be outnumbered, and one must attack uphill. If either failed, the whole army would be lost.

Behind him, in the open heath beyond the pinewood, the first rifles and muskets fired.

And Browne marched his men back up the hill.

Chapter 11

Sharpe and his riflemen, still accompanied by Captain Galiana, walked through the Spanish army that mostly seemed to be resting on the beach. Galiana dismounted when they reached the village of Bermeja and led his horse through the hovels. General Lapeña and his aides were there, sheltering from the sun under a framework on which fishing nets hung to dry. There was a watchtower in the village, and its summit was crowded with Spanish officers staring south with telescopes. The sound of musketry came from that direction, but it was very muffled, and no one in the Spanish army seemed particularly interested. Galiana remounted when they left the village. "Was that General Lapeña?" Sharpe asked.

"It was," Galiana said sourly. He had walked the horse to avoid being noticed by the general.

"Why doesn't he like you?" Sharpe asked.

"Because of my father."

"What did your father do?"

"He was in the army, like me. He challenged Lapeña to a duel."

"And?"

"Lapeña wouldn't fight. He is a coward."

"What was the argument about?"

"My mother," Galiana said curtly.

South of Bermeja the beach was empty except for some fishing boats drawn up on the sand. The boats were painted blue, yellow, and red and had large black eyes on their bows. The musketry was still muffled, but Sharpe could see smoke rising beyond the pine trees that ran thick behind the dunes. They walked in silence until, perhaps half a mile beyond the village, Perkins claimed to have seen a whale.

"What you saw," Slattery said, "was your bloody rum ration. You saw it and drank it."

"I saw it, I did sir!" He appealed to Sharpe, but Sharpe did not care what Perkins had or had not seen and ignored him.

"I saw a whale once," Hagman put in. "It were dead. Stinking."

Perkins was gazing out to sea again, hoping to see whatever it was he had taken to be a whale.

"Maybe," Harris suggested, "it was backed like a weasel?" They all stared at him.

"He's being clever again," Harper said loftily. "Just ignore him."

"It's Shakespeare, Sergeant."

"I don't care if it's the Archangel bloody Gabriel, you're just showing off."

"There was a Sergeant Shakespeare in the 48th," Slattery said, "and a proper bastard he was. He choked to death on a walnut."

"You can't die from a walnut!" Perkins said.

"He did. His face turned blue. Good thing too. He was a bastard."

"God save Ireland," Harper said. His words were not prompted by Sergeant Shakespeare's demise, but by a cavalcade storming down the beach toward them. The baggage mules, which had been retreating down the beach rather than on the track in the pinewood, had bolted.

"Stand still!" Sharpe said. They stood in a tight group as the mules split to pass on either side. Captain Galiana shouted at passing muleteers, demanding to know what had happened, but the men kept going.

"I didn't know you were in the 48th, Fergus," Hagman said.

"Three years, Dan. Then they went to Gibraltar, only I was sick so I stayed at the barracks. Almost died, I did."

Harris snatched at a passing mule that evaded his grip. "So how did you join the Rifles?" he asked.

"I was Captain Murray's servant," Slattery said, "and when he joined the Rifles, he took me with him."

"What's an Irishman doing in the 48th?" Harris wanted to know. "They're from Northamptonshire."

"They recruited in Wicklow," Slattery said.

Captain Galiana had succeeded in stopping a muleteer and got from the fugitive a confused tale of an overwhelming French attack. "He says the enemy has taken that hill," Galiana said, pointing to the Cerro del Puerco.

Sharpe took out his telescope and, again using Perkins as a rest, he stared at the hilltop. He could see a French battery at the crest and at least four blue-coated battalions. "They're up there," he confirmed. He turned the glass toward the village between the hill and the sea and saw Spanish cavalry there. There were also Spanish infantry, two or three thousand of them, but they had marched a small way north and were now resting among the dunes at the top of the beach.

Neither the cavalry nor the infantry seemed concerned by the French possession of the hill and the sound of the fighting did not come from its slopes, but from beyond the pinewood on Sharpe's left.

Sharpe offered the glass to Galiana who shook his head. "I have my own," he said, "so what are they doing?"

"Who? The French?"

"Why don't they attack down the hill?"

"What are those Spanish troops doing?" Sharpe asked.

"Nothing."

"Which means they're not needed. Which probably means there's a lot of men waiting for the Crapauds to come down the hill, and meanwhile the fighting's over there"—he nodded toward the pinewood—"so that's where I'm going." The panicked mass of mules had gone by. The muleteers were still hurrying north, scooping up the loaves of hard bread jolted out of the animals' panniers. Sharpe picked one up and broke it in half.

"Are we looking for the 8th, sir?" Harper asked him as they walked toward the pines.

"I am, but I don't suppose I'll find them," Sharpe said. It was one thing to declare an ambition to find Colonel Vandal, but in the chaos he doubted he would be successful. He did not even know if the French 8th were here, and if they were they might be anywhere. He knew some Frenchmen were behind the creek where they threatened the army's route to Cádiz. There were plenty more on the distant hill, and plainly others were beyond the pinewood. That was where the guns sounded so Sharpe would go that way. He walked to the top of the beach, scrambled up a sandy bluff, then plunged into the shade of the pines. Galiana, who seemed to have no plan except to stay with Sharpe, dismounted again because the pine branches hung so low.

"You don't have to come, Pat," Sharpe said.

"I know that, sir."

"I mean we've got no business here," Sharpe said.

"There's Colonel Vandal, sir."

"If we find him," Sharpe said dubiously. "Truth is, Pat, I'm here because I like Sir Thomas."

"Everyone speaks well of him, sir."

"And this is our job, Pat," Sharpe said more harshly. "There's fighting and we're soldiers."

"So we do have business here?"

"Of course we bloody do."

Harper walked in silence for a few paces. "So you never were going to let us go back, were you?"

"Would you have gone?"

"I'm here, sir," Harper said as if that answered Sharpe. The musketry from their front was heavier. Till now it had sounded like skirmish fire, the thorn-splintering snap of light infantry firing independently, but the heavier noise of volley fire was punching through the trees now. Behind it Sharpe could hear the fine flurry of trumpets and the rhythm of drums, but he did not recognize the tune, so knew it must be a French band playing. Then a series of louder crashes announced that cannons were firing. Balls whipped through the trees, bringing down needles and twigs. The French were firing canister and the air smelled of resin and powder smoke.

They came to a track rutted by the wheels of gun carriages. A few mules were picketed to the trees, guarded by three redcoats with yellow facings. "Are you the Hampshires?" Sharpe asked.

"Yes, sir," a man said.

"What's happening?"

"Don't know, sir. We were just told to guard the mules."

Sharpe pushed on. The cannons were firing

constantly, the volley fire was crashing rhythmically, but the two sides had not come to close
quarters because the skirmishers were still deployed. Sharpe could tell that by the sound.
Musket and canister balls flicked through the
trees, twitching the branches like a sudden wind.
"Buggers are firing high," Harper said.

"They always do, thank God," Sharpe said.
The sound of battle became louder as they
neared the edge of the wood. A Portuguese rifleman, his brown uniform black with blood, lay
dead by a pine trunk. He had evidently crawled
there, leaving a trail of blood on the needles.
There was a crucifix in his left hand, the rifle still
in his right. A redcoat lay five paces beyond,
shuddering and choking, a bullet hole dark on
his jacket's yellow facing.

Then Sharpe was out of the trees.

And found slaughter.

Major Browne climbed the hill on foot, leaving
his horse tied to a pine trunk. The major sang as
he climbed. He had a fine voice, much prized in
the performances that whiled away the time in
the Gibraltar garrison. "Come cheer up, my
lads!" he sang. "'Tis to glory we steer, to add

something more to this wonderful year; to honor we call you, not press you like slaves, for who are so free as the sons of the waves?" It was a naval song, much sung by the ships' crews ashore in Gibraltar, and he knew it was not quite appropriate for this attack up the Cerro del Puerco's northern slope, but the major liked "Heart of Oak." "Let me hear you!" he shouted, and the six companies of his makeshift battalion sang the chorus. "Heart of oak are our ships, heart of oak are our men," they sang raggedly. "We always are ready; steady, boys, steady! We'll fight and we'll conquer again and again."

In the brief silence after the chorus, the major distinctly heard the clicking sound of dogheads being pulled back at the hill's summit. He could see four battalions of French infantry up there and suspected there were others, but the four he could see were cocking their muskets, readying to kill. A cannon was being manhandled forward so that its barrel could point down the hill. A band was playing on the hill's summit. It played a jaunty song, music to kill by, and Browne found himself tapping his fingers on his sword hilt to the rhythm of the French tune. "Filthy French noise, lads," he shouted, "take no note of it!" Not long now, he thought, not long at all, wishing he had his own band to play a proper British tune. He had no musicians, so instead he boomed out the last verse of "Heart of Oak." "We'll still make them fear, and we'll still make them flee, and drub them on shore as we've drubbed them at sea. Then cheer up, my lads! And with one heart let's sing, our soldiers, our sailors, our leaders, our king!"

The French opened fire.

The crest of the hill vanished in a great gray-white rill of choking powder smoke, and in the center, where the battery was deployed, the smoke was thicker still, a sudden explosion of churning darkness, streaked through with flame in the midst of which the canisters shredded apart and the balls whipped down the hill and it looked to Browne, following close on his men's heels, that almost half of them were down. He saw a mist of blood over their heads, heard the first gasps, and knew the screaming would start soon. Then the file-closers, sergeants, and corporals were shouting at the men to close on the center. "Close up! Close up!"

"Up, boys, up!" Browne shouted. "Give them a drubbing!" He had started with 536 muskets. Now he had a little over 300. The French had at least a thousand more and Browne, stepping over a thrashing body, saw the enemy ramrods flicker in the thinning smoke. It was a miracle, he thought, that he was alive. A sergeant reeled past him, his lower jaw shot away and his tongue hanging in a dripping beard of blood. "Up, boys," Browne called, "up to victory!" Another cannon fired and three men were snatched back, slamming into the ranks behind and smearing the grass with thick gouts of blood. "To glory we steer!" Browne shouted, and the French muskets started firing again and a boy near him was clutching his belly, eyes wide, blood oozing between his fingers. "On!" Browne shouted. "On!" A ball snatched at his cocked hat, turning it. He had his sword drawn. The French were firing their muskets as soon as they were reloaded, not waiting for the orders to fire in volleys, and the smoke pumped out on the hilltop. Browne could hear the balls striking home in flesh, rapping on musket butts, and he knew that he had done his duty and he could do no more. His surviving men were taking shelter in the slightest dips of the slope or behind thickets, and they were firing back now, serving as a skirmish line, and that was all they could be. Half his men were gone—they were stretched on the hill or limping back down, or bleeding to death, or weeping in agony—and still the musket balls buzzed and whistled and slashed into the broken ranks.

Major Browne walked up and down behind the line. It was not much of a line. Ranks and files were gone, blown to ragged ruin by the artillery or blasted by the musket balls, but the living had not retreated. They were shooting back. Loading and firing, making small clouds of smoke that hid them from the enemy. Their mouths were sour from the saltpeter of the gunpowder and their cheeks burned by sparks from the locks. Wounded men struggled up to join the line where they loaded and fired. "Well done, my boys!" Browne shouted. "Well done!" He expected to die. He was sad about that, but his duty was to stay on his feet, to walk the line, to shout encouragement, and to wait for the canister or musket ball that must end his life. "Come cheer up, my lads!" he sang. "'Tis to glory we steer, to add something more to this wonderful year; to honor we call you, not press you like slaves, for who are so free as the sons of the waves?" A corporal fell back, brains spilling from his forehead. The man must have been dead, but his mouth still moved compulsively until Browne leaned down and pushed the chin gently up.

Blakeney, his adjutant, was still alive and, like Browne, miraculously unwounded. "Our brave allies," Blakeney said, touching Browne's elbow and gesturing back down the hill. Browne turned and saw that the Spanish brigade that had fled from the hill was resting not a quarter mile away, sitting in the dunes. He turned away. They would either come or not, and he suspected they would not. "Should I fetch them?" Blakeney asked, shouting over the noise of the guns.

"You think they'll come?"

"No, sir."

"And I can't order them," Browne said. "I don't have the rank. And the bastards can see we need help and they ain't moving. So let the buggers be." He walked on. "You're holding them, boys!" he shouted. "You're holding them!"

And that was true. The French had broken Browne's attack. They had shattered the red ranks, they had ripped the Gibraltar Flankers apart, but the French were not advancing down the slope to where Browne's survivors would have made easy meat for their bayonets. They fired instead, tearing more bullets into the broken battalion while the redcoats, the men from Lancashire and the Holy Boys from Norfolk and the Silver Tails from Gloucestershire, shot back.

Major Browne watched them die. A boy from the Silver Tails reeled back with his left shoulder torn away by the razor-edged remnants of the canister's casing so that his arm hung by sinews and broken ribs poked white through the red mess of his shattered chest. He collapsed and began to gasp for his mother. Browne knelt and held the boy's hand. He wanted to stanch the wound, but it was too big, so the major, not knowing how else to comfort the dying soldier, sang to him.

And at the foot of the hill, where the pine tree wood straggled to its end, General Dilkes's brigade formed in two ranks. There was the second battalion of the First Foot Guards, three companies of the second battalion of the 3rd Foot Guards, two companies of riflemen, and half of the 67th Foot, which had somehow got tangled with Dilkes's men and, rather than try to rejoin the rest of their battalion, had stayed to fight with the guardsmen and sweeps. General Dilkes drew his sword and twisted its tasseled pendant about his wrist. His orders were to take the hill. He looked up and saw the slope crawling with wounded men from Browne's command. He also saw that his men were frighteningly outnumbered and he doubted that the French could be driven from the summit, but he had his orders. Sir Thomas Graham, who had given those orders, was close behind the bright colors of the 3rd Foot Guards, the Scotsmen, and now looked anxiously at Dilkes as if suspecting that he was delaying the order to attack. "Take them forward!" Dilkes said grimly.

"Brigade will advance!" the brigade major bellowed. A drummer boy gave a tap, then a roll, took a deep breath, and began beating the time. "By the center!" the brigade major shouted. "March!"

They climbed.

General Leval, while his colleague, General Ruffin, attacked the hill, advanced toward the pinewood. He had six battalions that, between them, had four thousand men who marched on a wide front. Leval kept two battalions behind the four who advanced in columns of divisions. French battalions had only six companies, and a column of divisions was two companies broad and three deep. Their drummers beat them on.

Colonel Wheatley had two thousand men to fight the four thousand and he began in disarray. His units had been in march order when the order to turn right and prepare to fight arrived, and there had been confusion among the pines. Two companies of Coldstream Guards were marching among Wheatley's men, but there was no time to send them south to join Dilkes's units, where they belonged, so they marched to battle under Wheatley. Half of the 67th from Hampshire was missing. Those five companies had found themselves under Dilkes's command, while the remaining five companies were in their rightful place with Wheatley. It was, in short, chaos, and the thickness of the pines meant that battalion officers were unable to see their men, but the company officers and sergeants did their job and took the redcoats east through the trees.

The first to emerge from the pines were four hundred riflemen and three hundred Portuguese skirmishers who came at the run. Many of their officers were on horseback and the French, astonished to see an enemy come from the wood, thought cavalry was about to attack. That impression was strengthened when ten gun teams, totaling eighty horses, burst from the trees on the left of the French front. They followed a track that led to Chiclana, but once out of the trees they slewed hard right to throw up sand and dust. The nearest two French battalions, seeing only horses in the dust, formed square to repel cavalry.

The gunners jumped off the limbers, lifted the cannon trails, and aimed the barrels as the horses were taken back to the cover of the pines. "Use shell!" Major Duncan shouted. Shells were brought from limbers, and officers cut the fuses. They cut them short because the French were close. The French were also in sudden confusion. Two battalions had formed square, ready-to-receive, nonexistent cavalry, and the rest were hesitating when the British guns opened fire. Shells screamed across the three hundred yards of heath, each leaving its small wavering trail of fuse smoke, and Duncan, sitting his horse well to the side of the batteries so that their muzzle smoke did not hide his view, saw the blue-uniformed men knocked violently aside by the shells, then the explosions in the hearts of the squares. "Good! Good!" he shouted, and just then the skirmish line of riflemen and cacadores opened fire, their rifles and muskets crackling, and the French seemed to recoil from the fusillade. The front ranks of the columns returned the fire, but the skirmishers were scattered across the whole French front and were small targets for clumsy muskets, while the French were in close order and the rifles could hardly miss. The twin batteries on the right of the British line fired again. Then Duncan saw French horse teams being whipped across the heath. He counted six guns. "Load round shot!" he called. "Traverse right!" Men levered the cannon trails with handspikes to change their aim. "Hit their guns!" Duncan ordered.

The French were recovering now. The two battalions in square had realized their mistake and were deploying back into columns. Aides were galloping among the battalions, ordering them to march on, to fire, to break the thin skirmish line with concentrated volleys of musket fire. The drums began again, beating the **pas de charge** and pausing to let the men shout "**Vive l'empereur!**" The first effort was feeble, but officers and sergeants bellowed at the men to shout louder, and the next time the war cry was firm and defiant. "**Vive l'empereur!**"

"**Tirez!**" an officer shouted, and the front ranks of the 8th of the line poured a volley at the Portuguese skirmishers on their front. "**Marchez! En avant!**" Now was the time to accept the casualties and crush the skirmishers. The British cannon had switched their fire to the French battery, so no more shells slammed into the ranks. **"Vive l'empereur!"** The eight ranks behind the leading men of each column stepped over the dead and dying. **"Tirez!"** Another blast of musketry. Four thousand men were marching toward seven hundred. The French battery fired canister across the front of the columns and the grass bowed violently as though it were being swept by a sudden gust of wind. Portuguese cacadores and British riflemen were scooped up, bloodied and thrown down. The skirmish line was retreating now. The French muskets were too close and the six enemy cannon enfiladed them. There was a brief respite as the French gunners, about to be masked by the advancing columns, seized the drag ropes and, despite the round shot slamming about them, dragged their guns a hundred paces forward. They fired again and more skirmishers were turned to bloody rags. The French scented victory and the four leading battalions hurried. Their fire was ragged because it was hard to load while marching, and some men fixed bayonets instead. The British skirmishers ran back, almost to the wood's edge. Duncan's two left hand guns, seeing the danger, slewed around and blasted canister across the face of the nearest French battalion. Men in its leading ranks went down in a bloody haze as though a giant reaper's hook had savaged them.

Then, suddenly, the wood's edge was thick with men. The Silver Tails were on the left of Wheatley's line and next to them were the two orphaned companies of Coldstreamers. Gough's Irish were on the right of the Guards, then the remaining half of the 67th, and last, next to the guns, two companies of the Cauliflowers, the 47th.

"Halt!" The shouts echoed along the tree line.

"Wait!" a sergeant bellowed. Some men had raised their muskets. "Wait for the order!"

"Form on your right! On your right!"

It was a confusion of voices, of officers shouting from their horses, of sergeants reordering ranks tumbled by the chaotic rush through the trees. "Look at that, boys! Look at that! Joy in the morning!" Major Hugh Gough, mounted on a bay gelding from County Meath, rode behind his battalion of the 87th. "We've got target practice, my lovelies," he shouted. "Wait a while, though, wait a while."

The newly arrived battalions recovered their dressing. "Take them forward! Take them forward!" Wheatley's aides shouted, and the two-deep line paced onto the heath toward the dead and dying skirmishers. A French round shot skimmed through the 67th, cutting one man almost in half, spraying twelve others with the dead man's blood, and taking the arm of a man in the rear rank. "Close up! Close up!"

"Halt! Present!"

"Vive l'empereur!"

"Fire!"

The inexorable rules of mathematics now imposed themselves on the fight. The French outnumbered the British by two to one, yet the leading four French battalions were in columns of divisions, which meant that each battalion was arrayed in nine ranks and had, on average, about seventy-two men in a rank. Four battalions with leading ranks of seventy-two men made a frontage of fewer than three hundred muskets. True, the men in the second rank could fire over their comrades' shoulders, but even so, Leval's four thousand men could only use six hundred muskets against the British line in which every man could fire, and Wheatley's line was now fourteen hundred men strong. The skirmishers, who had done their job of delaying the French advance, ran to the flanks. Then Wheatley's line fired.

The musket balls smacked into the heads of the French units. The redcoats were hidden by smoke behind which they reloaded. "Fire by platoons!" officers called, so now the rolling volleys would begin, half a company firing at once, then the next half, so that the bullets never stopped.

"Fire low!" an officer shouted.

Canister slashed through the smoke. A man reeled away, an eye gone, his face a mask of blood, but there was much more blood in the French battalions where the bullets were turning the front ranks into charnel rows.

"Bloody hell," Sharpe said. He had emerged from the wood at the right-hand side of the British line. Ahead of him, to his right, were Duncan's guns, each one bucking back three or more paces with every shot. Beside the guns were the remnants of the Portuguese skirmishers, still firing, and to his left was the redcoat line. Sharpe joined the brown-coated Portuguese. They looked haggard. Their faces were powder stained and eyes white. They were a new battalion and had never been in battle before, but they had done their job and now the redcoats were firing volleys, yet the Portuguese had suffered horribly and Sharpe could see too many brown-coated bodies lying in front of the French battalions. He could also see greenjackets there, all on the left of the British line.

The French battalions were spreading their fronts. They were not doing it well. Each man tried to find a place to fire his musket, or else tried to find shelter behind braver colleagues, and sergeants were pushing them out in any order. Canister howled around Sharpe and he instinctively looked behind to make sure none of his men was hit. They were all safe, but a crouching Portuguese skirmisher close to Sharpe tipped onto his back with his throat torn open. "Didn't know you were with us!" a voice called, and Sharpe turned to see Major Duncan on horseback.

"I'm here," Sharpe said.

"Can your rifles discourage gunners?"

The six French cannon were to the front. Two were already out of action, struck by Duncan's round shot, but the others were flailing the left of the British line with their hated canister. The problem of shooting at cannon was the vast cloud of filthy smoke that lingered after every shot, and the problem was made worse by the distance. It was long range, even for a rifle, but Sharpe pulled his men forward to the Portuguese and told them to fire at the French artillerymen. "It's a safe job, Pat," he told Harper, "not really fighting at all."

"Always a pleasure to murder a gunner, sir," Harper said. "Isn't that right, Harris?"

Harris, who had been most vocal about not joining any fight, cocked his rifle. "Always a pleasure, Sergeant."

"Then make yourself happy. Kill a bloody gunner."

Sharpe stared toward the French infantry, but could see little because the smoke of the muskets drifted across their front. He could see two eagles through the smoke, and beside them the small flags mounted on the halberds carried by the men charged with protecting the eagles. He could hear the drummer boys still beating the **pas de charge** even though the French advance had stopped. The real noise was of musketry, the pounding cough of volley fire, the relentless noise, and if he listened hard he could hear the balls striking on muskets and thumping into flesh. He could also hear the cries of the wounded and the screams of officers' horses put down by the balls. And he was amazed, as he always was, by the courage of the French. They were being struck hard, yet they stayed. They stayed behind a straggling heap of dead men, they edged aside to let the wounded crawl behind, they reloaded and fired, and all the time the volleys kept coming. Sharpe could see no order among the enemy. The columns had long broken into a thick line that spread wider as men found space to use their muskets, but even so the makeshift line was still thicker and shorter than the British line. Only the British and Portuguese fought in two ranks. The French were supposed to fight in three ranks when deployed in line, but this line was clumped together, six or seven men deep in some places.

A third French gun was struck. A round shot shattered a wheel and the gun tipped down as the gunners jumped out of the way. "Good shooting!" Duncan shouted. "An extra ration of rum for that crew!" He had no idea which of his guns had done the damage so he would give them all rum when the fighting was done. A gust of wind blew the smoke away from the French battery and Duncan saw a gunner rolling up a new wheel. Hagman, kneeling among the Portuguese, saw another gunner bring his linstock toward the closest French cannon, a howitzer. Hagman fired and the gunner vanished behind the short barrel.

The British had no music to inspire them.

There had been no space on the ships to bring instruments, but the bandsmen had come, armed with muskets, and now those men did their usual battle job of rescuing the wounded, taking them back to the trees, where the surgeons worked. The rest of the redcoats fought on. They did what they were trained to do, and what they did was fire a musket. Load and fire, load and fire. Take out a cartridge, bite off the top, prime the lock with a pinch of powder from the bitten end of the cartridge, close the frizzen to keep the pinch in place, drop the musket butt to the ground, pour the rest of the powder down the hot barrel, thrust the paper on top as wadding, ram it down, and inside the paper was the ball. Bring the musket up, pull back the cock, remember to aim low because the brute of a gun kicked like a mule, wait for the order, pull the trigger. "Misfire!" a man shouted, meaning his lock had sparked, but the charge in the barrel had not caught the fire. A corporal snatched the musket away from him, gave him a dead man's gun, then laid the misfired musket on the grass behind. Other men had to pause to change flints, but the volleys never stopped.

The French were becoming more organized, but they would never fire as fast as the redcoats.

The redcoats were professionals, while most of the French were conscripts. They had been summoned to their depots and given training, but were not permitted to practice with real gunpowder. For every three bullets the British fired in battle, the French fired two, so the rules of mathematics favored the redcoats again, but the French still outnumbered the British, and as their line spread, the gods of mathematics tipped the balance back toward the men in the blue coats. More and more of the emperor's soldiers brought muskets to bear, and more and more redcoats were carried back to the pinewood. On the left of the British line, where no artillery helped, the Silver Tails were being hit hard. Sergeants commanded companies now. They were opposed two to one, for Leval had sent one of his supporting battalions to add their fire and that new unit came into line and struck hard with fresh muskets. The fight now was like two boxers toeing the line and striking again and again, and every bare-knuckle blow started blood, and neither man moved, and it was a contest to see which could sustain the greatest pain.

"You, sir, you!" A voice snapped behind Sharpe and he turned, alarmed, to see a colonel on horseback, but the colonel was not looking at

Sharpe. He was glaring at Captain Galiana. "Where the devil are your men? Do you speak English? For Christ's sake, someone ask where his men are."

"I have no men," Galiana admitted hastily in English.

"For God's sake, why doesn't General Lapeña send us men?"

"I shall find him, señor," Galiana said and, with something useful to do, turned his horse toward the woods.

"Tell him I want them on my left," the colonel roared after him, "on my left!" The colonel was Wheatley, commanding the brigade, and he rode back to where the 28th, the Dandies, the Silver Tails, the Slashers, were being turned into dead and dying men. That suffering battalion was closest to the Spanish troops at Bermeja, but Bermeja was over a mile from the fighting. Lapeña had nine thousand men there. They sat on the sand, muskets stacked, and ate the last of their rations. A thousand of the Spaniards watched the French across the Almanza Creek, but those French were not moving. Any battle beside the Rio Sancti Petri had long died and the herons, encouraged by the silence between the armies, had come back to hunt among the reeds.

Sharpe had taken out his telescope. His rifle-men were still firing at the French gunners, but only one of the enemy cannon was still undamaged. That was the howitzer, and Duncan had shredded its crew with a finely judged burst of shrapnel. "Take these nearest bastards," Sharpe told his men, indicating the French line, and he now watched that line through the glass. The view was of smoke and blue coats. He lowered the telescope. He sensed that the battle had reached a pause. It was not that the killing had stopped, nor that the muskets had ceased firing, but that neither side was making a move to change the situation. They were thinking, wait-ing, killing while they waited, and it seemed to Sharpe that the French, despite being outfought by the musket fire of the redcoats, had gained the advantage. They had more men, so could af-ford to lose the musket duel, and their right and center were edging forward. It did not look like a deliberate move, but rather the result of pres-sure from the men in the rear ranks who were thrusting the French line toward the sea. The French left was stalled, for they were being flayed by Duncan's guns that had already knocked the French artillery out of the fight, but the French right and center were unaffected by the guns. They had already stepped over the line of dead men that was all that was left of their original front ranks and they were getting bolder. Their fire, inefficient though it was by redcoat standards, was taking its toll. With the widening of the French line and the commitment of one of their two reserve battalions, the laws of mathematics had tipped back to favor the French. They had taken the worst the British could give them, they had survived, and now they edged forward toward their weakened enemy.

Sharpe went back a few paces and looked behind the British line. No Spanish troops were in sight and he knew there were no British reserves. If the men on the heath could not do the job, then the French must win and the army would be turned into a rabble. He went back to his men who were now firing at the nearest French infantry. An eagle showed above them, and near the eagle was a group of horsemen. Sharpe leveled the glass again and, just before the musket smoke obscured the standard, he saw him.

Colonel Vandal. He was waving his hat, encouraging his men to advance. Sharpe could see the white pom-pom on the hat, could see the narrow black moustache, and he felt a surge of utter fury. "Pat!" he shouted.

"Sir?" Harper was alarmed by the tone of Sharpe's voice.

"Found the bastard," Sharpe said. He took the rifle from his shoulder. He had not fired it yet, but he cocked it now.

And the French sensed victory. It would be a hard-won triumph, but their drummers found new energy and the line lurched forward again. **"Vive l'empereur!"**

At least thirty officers had ridden south from San Fernando. They had stayed on the Isla de León when Sir Thomas's forces had sailed, and this Tuesday morning they had been woken by the sound of gunfire. Because they were off duty, they had saddled their horses and ridden south to discover what happened beyond the Rio Sancti Petri.

They went south along the Isla de León's long Atlantic beach, where they joined a crowd of curious horsemen from Cádiz who also rode to witness the fighting. There were even carriages being whipped along the sand. It was not every day that a battle was fought close to a city. The sound of gunfire rattling windows in Cádiz had prompted scores of spectators to head south along the isthmus.

The surly lieutenant guarding the pontoon bridge did his best to prevent those spectators from crossing the river, but he was effectively outgunned when a curricle was whipped along the track. Its driver was a British officer, his passenger a woman, and the officer threatened to use his whip on the lieutenant if the barricade was not removed. It was not so much the threat of the whip as the officer's lavish display of silver lace that persuaded the lieutenant to yield. He watched sourly as the curricle crossed the precarious bridge. He hoped a wheel would slip off the cresses and tip the passengers into the river, but the two horses were in expert hands and the light vehicle crossed safely and accelerated along the far beach. The other carriages were too big to cross, but the crowd of horsemen followed the curricle and spurred after it.

What they saw when they passed the makeshift Spanish fort guarding the pontoon bridge was a beach filled with resting Spanish soldiers. Cavalry horses were picketed while their riders rested with hats over their faces. Some played cards and cigar smoke drifted in the breeze. Far ahead was the hill above Barrosa and that was wreathed with a different smoke, and more smoke rose in a dirty plume above a pinewood to the east, but on the beach beside the river all was calm.

It was calm in Bermeja where General Lapeña took a lunch of cold ham with his staff. He watched in surprise as the curricle dashed past, its two wheels throwing up great sprays of sand from the track leading past the village church and the watchtower. "A British officer," he observed, "going the wrong way!"

There was polite laughter. Some of the general's staff, though, were embarrassed that they did nothing while the British fought, and that sentiment was felt most strongly by General Zayas, whose men had forced Villatte's division off the beach. Zayas had requested permission to take his troops farther south and join the fighting, a request that was strengthened when Captain Galiana arrived on a sweat-whitened horse with Colonel Wheatley's plea for help. Lapeña had curtly refused the request. "Our allies," he declared grandly, "are merely fighting a rearguard action. If they had followed orders, of course, no fighting would have been necessary, but now we must remain here to make certain they have a position to which they can retreat in safety." He had stared belligerently at Galiana. "And what business do you have here?" he had demanded angrily. "Are you not posted to the city garrison?" Galiana, whose nervousness at approaching Lapeña had made his request harsh, even peremptory, had not even deigned to answer. He just gave the general a look of utter scorn, then turned his tired horse and spurred back toward the pinewood. "His father was an insolent fool," Lapeña said harshly, "and the son's the same. He needs lessons in discipline. He should be posted to South America, somewhere where there's yellow fever."

No one spoke for a moment. Lapeña's chaplain poured wine, but General Zayas blocked his own glass by holding a hand over the rim. "At least let me attack across the creek." He pressed Lapeña.

"What are your orders, General?"

"I'm asking for orders," Zayas insisted.

"Your orders," Lapeña said, "are to guard the bridge, and that is your duty that you will do best by remaining in your present position."

So the Spanish troops stayed near the Rio Sancti Petri while the curricle sped southward. Its driver was Brigadier Moon who had hired the carriage from the posthouse stables just outside the city. He would have preferred to ride a horse, but his broken leg made that exquisitely painful. The curricle was only slightly more comfortable. Its springs were hard and, even though he had his broken leg propped on the dashboard that stopped most of the sand from the horses' hooves flying into his face, the mending bone still hurt. He saw a track slanting away from the beach into the pinewoods and he took it, hoping that the road would provide better footing for his horses. It did, and he bowled along smartly in the shade of the trees. His fiancée clung to the curricle's side and to the brigadier's arm. She called herself the Marquesa de San Augustin, the widowed Marquesa. "I won't take you where the bullets fly, my dear," Moon said.

"You disappoint me," she said. She wore a black hat from which a thin veil hung over her face.

"Battle's no place for a woman. Certainly no place for a beautiful woman."

She smiled. "I would like to see a battle."

"And so you shall, so you shall, but from a safe distance. I may limp up and lend a hand"— Moon slapped the crutches propped beside him—"but you're to stay with the curricle. Stay safe."

"I am safe with you," the Marquesa said. After marriage, the brigadier had told her, she would be Lady Moon. "**La Doña Luna,**" she said, squeezing his elbow, "will always be safe with you." The brigadier responded to her affectionate gesture with a guffaw of laughter. "What is that for?" La Marquesa asked, offended.

"I was thinking of Henry Wellesley's face when I introduced you last night!" the brigadier said. "He looked like a full moon!"

"He seemed very nice," the Marquesa said.

"Jealous, he was! I could tell! I didn't know he liked women. I thought that was why his wife bolted, but it was plain as a pikestaff that he liked you. Maybe I've got the fellow wrong?"

"He was most polite."

"He's a bloody ambassador, he bloody well ought to be polite. That's what he's for." The brigadier went silent. He had seen a track branching east through the wood and the turn was tight, but he could drive horses like a coachman and he took the bend in masterly fashion. The noise of battle was loud now, and not far ahead, so he gently pulled the reins to slow the horses. There were wounded men on either side of the track. "Don't look, my dear," he said. There was a man without trousers, writhing, his crotch a mass of blood. "Shouldn't have brought you," he said curtly.

"I want to know your world," she said, squeezing his elbow.

"Then you must forgive me its horrors," he said gallantly, and then pulled the reins again because he had emerged from the trees and the line of redcoats under their bullet-torn colors was only a hundred paces ahead. The ground between the curricle and the redcoats was a mess of dead men, injured men, discarded weapons, and scorched grass. "Far enough," the brigadier said.

The French had replaced the wheel of one twelve-pounder and now hauled the cannon back to its original position, but the battery commander knew he could not stay because the enemy guns had targeted him. He had been forced to abandon his one howitzer at the forward position, but he would not lose his last gun that was loaded with shell. He ordered the gun commander to fire the shell at the redcoats, then to retire smartly. The linstock touched the priming tube, the flame flashed to the breech, and the gun fired to leave a cloud of obscuring smoke behind which the battery commander could drag his last weapon to a safer position.

The shell crashed into the ranks of the 67th, where it disemboweled a corporal, took the left hand off a private, then fell to earth twenty paces behind the Hampshire men. The fuse smoked crazily as the shell spun on toward the pine trees. Moon saw it coming and urged the horses to their right, away from the missile. He put the reins into his right hand, which already held the whip, and placed his left arm around the Marquesa, sheltering her. Just then the shell exploded. Pieces of casing whipped over their heads, and one scrap drove bloodily into the belly of the nearside horse that took off as though the devil himself was under its hooves. The offside horse caught the panic and they both bolted. The brigadier hauled on the reins, but the noise and the pain and the stink of smoke were too much for the horses that ran obliquely right, white-eyed and desperate. They saw a gap in the British line and took it in a frantic gallop. The light curricle bounced alarmingly so that both the brigadier and the marquesa had to hold on for dear life. They shot through the gap. Ahead were smoke and bodies and open air beyond the smoke. The brigadier hauled again, using all his strength; the offside wheel struck a corpse and the curricle tipped. They were notorious vehicles for accidents; the Marquesa was spilled onto the ground and the brigadier followed, screaming abruptly as his splinted leg was struck by the curricle's rear rail. His crutches flew as the horses bolted on to disappear in the heath with the curricle breaking apart behind them. Moon and the woman he hoped would become the Doña Luna were left on the ground close beside the abandoned howitzer on the flank of the French column.

Which lurched forward and shouted, "**Vive l'empereur!**"

Chapter 12

Sir Thomas Graham blamed himself. If he had put three British battalions on the summit of the Cerro del Puerca, then it would never have fallen to the French. Now it had, and he had to trust Colonel Wheatley to hold the long line of the pinewood while Dilkes's men corrected Sir Thomas's mistake. If they failed, and if the French division came down the hill and swept northward, then they would be in Wheatley's rear and a massacre would follow. The French had to be driven off the hill.

General Ruffin had four battalions at the crest of the hill and held two specialist battalions of grenadiers in reserve. Those men no longer carried grenades; instead they were among the biggest men in the infantry and renowned for their fighting savagery. Marshal Victor, who knew as well as Sir Thomas Graham that the hill was the key to victory, had ridden to join Ruffin; from the summit, beside the ruined chapel, Victor could see Leval's division edging forward toward the pinewood. Good. He would let them fight on their own and bring Ruffin's men down to help them. The beach was mostly empty. A brigade of Spanish infantry was resting not far from the village, but, for some reason, they were taking no part in the fight while the rest of the Spanish army was a long way to the north and, as far as the marshal could see through his telescope, not bothering to stir themselves.

Ruffin's front line of four battalions numbered just over two thousand men. Like the Frenchmen on the heath they were in columns of divisions while beneath them on the hill were hundreds of bodies, the remnants of Major Browne's battalion. Beyond those corpses were redcoats who had evidently come to retake the Cerro del Puerco. "Fifteen hundred Goddamns?" Victor estimated the newcomers.

"I reckon so, yes," Ruffin said. He was a huge man, well over six feet tall.

"I do believe those are the English guards," Victor said. He was gazing at Dilkes's brigade through his telescope and could clearly see the blue regimental color of the First Foot Guards. "They're sacrificing their best," the marshal added cheerfully, "so let's oblige them. We'll sweep the bastards away!"

The bastards had begun to climb the hill. There were fourteen hundred of them, mostly guardsmen, but with half of the 67th on the right and, beyond the Hampshire men and closest to the sea, two companies of riflemen. They came slowly. Some had marched at the double for more than a mile to reach the hill's foot and, after a sleepless night on the move, were tired. They did not follow Major Browne's route to the top, but climbed closer to the beach where the hill was much steeper and the French cannons could not depress sufficiently to fire at them, at least not while they were on the lower slope. They came in a line, but this part of the hill was broken by trees and rough ground, and the line quickly lost its formation so that the British appeared to come in a formless straggle stretched about the hill's northwestern quadrant.

Marshal Victor accepted a drink of wine from an aide's canteen. "Let them get almost to the top," he suggested to Ruffin, "because the cannon can shred them there. Give them a gift of canister, a volley of musketry, then advance on them."

Ruffin nodded. It was exactly what he had planned to do. The hill was steep and the British would be breathless by the time they had climbed three-quarters of its flank, and that was when he would hit them with cannons and muskets. He would blast holes in their ranks, then release the four battalions of infantry down the hill with bayonets. The British would be swept away, and their fugitives would be in chaos by the time they reached the hill's foot, and then the infantry and dragoons could hunt them down the beach and through the pinewood. The grenadiers, he thought, could then be sent to assault the southern flank of the other British brigade.

The redcoats clambered upward. Sergeants made efforts to keep the line straight, but it was hopeless on such broken ground. French voltigeurs, the skirmishers, had come a small way down the hill and were firing at the attackers. "Don't return their fire!" Sir Thomas shouted. "Save your lead! We'll give them a volley when we reach the top! Hold your fire!" A voltigeur's bullet snatched Sir Thomas's hat clean off without touching his white hair. He kicked his horse on. "Brave boys!" he shouted. "Up we go!" He was riding among the rearmost men of the Third Foot Guards, his beloved Scotsmen. "This is our land, boys. Let's clear the rascals away!"

Major Browne's men, those who survived, were still on the hill and still firing upward. "Here come the Guards, boys!" Browne shouted. "Now I'll insure all your lives for half a dollar!" He had lost two-thirds of his officers and over half his men, but he shouted at the survivors to close up and join the flank of the First Foot Guards.

"They're fools," Marshal Victor said, more in puzzlement than in scorn. Fifteen hundred men hoped to take a two-hundred-foot hill garrisoned by artillery and by close to three thousand infantry? Well, their foolishness was his opportunity. "Give them your volley as soon as the artillery has fired," he told Ruffin. "Then run them down the slope with bayonets." He spurred across to the battery. "Wait till they're at half-pistol shot," he told the battery commander. At that range none of the guns could miss. It would be slaughter. "What are you loaded with?"

"Canister."

"Good man," Victor said. He was gazing at the

lavish regimental colors of the First Foot Guards, and he was imagining those two flags being paraded through Paris. The emperor would be pleased! To have the flags of the king of England's own guards! The emperor, he thought, would probably use the flags as table-cloths, or perhaps as sheets on which to bounce his new Austrian bride, and that thought made him laugh out loud.

The voltigeurs were scrambling uphill now because the British line was getting closer. Very nearly there, Victor thought. He would let them come almost to the top of the hill because that would bring the line right into the face of his six guns. He took a last glance north at Leval's men and saw they were pressing closer to the pinewood. In half an hour, he thought, this small British army would have collapsed. It would take at least another hour to re-form the troops, then they would assault the Spanish at the beach's end. How many flags would they send to Paris? A dozen? Twenty? Maybe enough to furnish all the emperor's beds.

"Now, sir?" The battery commander asked.

"Wait, wait," Victor said, and, knowing victory was his, turned and waved at the two grenadier battalions that he had held in reserve. "Forward!" he shouted to their general, Rousseau. This was no time to keep troops in reserve. Now was the moment to throw all his men, all three thousand of them, at fewer than half their number. He plucked an aide's elbow. "Tell the bandmaster I want to hear the 'Marseillaise'!" He grinned. The Emperor had banned the 'Marseillaise,' disliking its revolutionary sentiments, but Victor knew the song had retained its popularity and would inspire his soldiers to the slaughter of their enemies. He sang a line to himself, "**Le jour de gloire est arrivé**," then laughed aloud. The battery commander looked up at him with surprise. "Now," Victor said, "now!"

"**Tirez!**"

The guns fired, obliterating the view of the beach, of the sea, and of the distant white city in a bellying cloud of smoke.

"Now!" General Ruffin called to his battalion commanders.

Muskets hammered back into French shoulders. More smoke filled the sky.

"Fix bayonets!" the marshal shouted, and waved his white-plumed hat toward the cannon smoke. "And forward, **mes braves!** Forward!"

The band played, the drummers beat, and the French went to finish their job. The day of glory had arrived.

Colonel Vandal was some way north of Sharpe. The colonel was in the center of his battalion, which formed the left flank of the French line, and Sharpe, out by Duncan's guns, was at the right flank of the British line, which still overlapped the thicker, larger French formation. "This way," he shouted to his riflemen and ran behind the two companies of the 47th who were now down to one large company, and then behind the half battalion of the 67th until he was opposite Vandal.

"It's grim work!" Colonel Wheatley had again ridden up behind Sharpe. This time he was talking to Major Gough, who commanded the 87th that was now on Sharpe's left. "And no damned dons to help us," Wheatley went on. "How are your fellows, Gough?"

"My men are staunch, sir," Gough said, "but I need more of them. Need more men." He had to shout over the din of the volleys. The 87th had lost four officers and over a hundred men. The wounded were in the pines, and more were joining them as the French musket balls slammed home. The file-closers were shouting at men to close on the center and so the 87th shrank. They still fired back, but their muskets were being fouled with powder residue and every cartridge was harder to load.

"There are no more men," Wheatley said, "unless the Spanish come." He glanced along the enemy line. The problem was simple enough. The French had too many men and so they could replace their casualties while he could not. He could outfight them man to man, but the French advantage in numbers was starting to matter. He could wait in hope that Lapeña would send reinforcements, but if none came then he must inevitably be whittled down, a process that would go faster and faster as his line shrank.

"Sir!" an aide shouted, and Wheatley looked to see that the Spanish officer who had ridden to summon reinforcements was returning.

Galiana curbed his horse by Wheatley and, for a heartbeat, looked too upset to talk. Then he blurted out his news. "General Lapeña refuses to move," he said. "I'm sorry, sir."

Wheatley stared at the Spaniard. "Good God," he said in a surprisingly mild tone, then looked back to Gough. "I think, Gough," he said, "that we have to give them steel."

Gough looked at the throng of Frenchmen through the smoke. The 87th's colors just above the colonel's head were twitching as the bullets struck them. "Steel?" he asked.

"We have to do something, Gough. Can't just stand here and die."

Sharpe had lost sight of Vandal. There was too much smoke. He saw a Frenchman stoop to the body of a fallen Portuguese skirmisher and rummage through the dead man's pockets. Sharpe knelt, aimed, and fired. When the rifle smoke cleared he saw the Frenchman on all fours, head down. He reloaded. He was tempted to ram the ball down naked rather than wrapping it in its greased leather patch. He thought the French might charge at any moment and the thing to do now was to kill them fast, to pour fire at them, and a naked ball in a rifle was quick to load. At this distance the inaccuracy did not matter. But if he saw Vandal again he wanted to be sure of his shot and so he took a leather patch, wrapped the ball, and rammed it down the rifled barrel. "Look for their officers," he told his men.

A pistol sounded beside Sharpe and he looked to see that Captain Galiana had dismounted and was now reloading the small weapon. "Fire!" the lieutenant commanding the closest company of the 87th shouted and the muskets blasted out smoke. A man fell back from the front rank, a hole black in his forehead.

"Leave him be!" a sergeant shouted. "He's a dead 'un! Reload!"

"Fix bayonets!" the shout came from just behind the 87th and was repeated down the line, getting fainter as the order traveled north. "Fix bayonets!"

"God save Ireland," Harper said. "This is desperate."

"Not much choice," Sharpe said. The French were winning by sheer numbers. They were pressing forward, and Colonel Wheatley could either retreat or attack. To retreat was to lose, but to attack was at least to test the French.

"Swords, sir?" Slattery asked.

"Fix swords," Sharpe said. It was no time to worry about whether this was his fight or not. The battle trembled. Another French volley slammed into the red ranks. Then two gouts of canister slashed away the blue-coated men who had fired the shots. An Irish boy was screaming horribly, rolling in front of the ranks with bloody hands clutching his groin. A sergeant silenced

him with a merciful blow of a musket butt to the
skull.

"Forward now! Forward!" a brigade major
bellowed.

"The 87th will advance!" Gough shouted.
"Faugh a ballagh!"

"Faugh a ballagh!" the surviving men of the
87th responded, and went forward.

"Steady, boys!" Gough shouted. "Steady!"

But the 87th did not want to be steady. A
quarter of their number was either dead or
wounded, and they had a seething anger against
the men who had punished them in the last
hour, and so they went eagerly. The sooner they
were at the enemy, the sooner that enemy would
die, and Gough could not hold them. They began to run, and as they ran they sounded a high-
pitched scream, terrifying in itself, and their
seventeen-inch bayonets were bright in the sun,
which was almost at its winter zenith.

"Forward!" The men to Sharpe's right were
keeping pace with the 87th. Duncan's gunners
handspiked their cannon around to rake the
flank of the French line.

"And kill! And kill!" Ensign Keogh was shouting at the top of his voice. He carried his slim

sword in one hand and gripped his cocked hat in the other.

"**Faugh a ballagh!**" Gough bellowed.

French muskets roared horribly close and men were torn backward, blood spraying their neighbors, but the charge could not be stopped now. All along the line the redcoats were going forward with bayonets because to stay still was to die and to retreat was to lose. They numbered fewer than a thousand now, and they were attacking three times their number. "Get into them! Get into them!" an officer of the Cauliflowers shouted. "Kill them, kill them!"

The front rank of the French tried to step back, but the ranks behind thrust them on, and the redcoats struck. Bayonets rammed forward. Muskets fired at less than a yard's range. A sergeant of the 87th was chanting as though he were training men at the barracks. "Lunge! Recover! Stance! Lunge! Recover! Stance! Not in his ribs, you bloody fool! In his belly! Lunge! Recover! Stance! In the belly, boys, in the belly! Lunge!"

An Irishman's bayonet was trapped in the ribs of a Frenchman. It would not come out and in desperation he pulled his trigger and was surprised that the weapon was loaded. The blast of gas and ball jerked the bayonet free. "In the belly!" the sergeant shouted, for a bayonet was far less likely to be trapped in an enemy's stomach than in his ribs. Those officers still mounted were firing pistols over their men's shakos. Men lunged, recovered, lunged again, and some were so battle-maddened that they did not care how they fought and just clubbed with their musket butts. "Rip it out, boy!" the sergeant shouted. "Don't just prick the bastard! Do some damage! Lunge! Recover!"

They were the despised of England, Ireland, Scotland, and Wales. They were the drunks and the thieves, the scourings of gutters and jails. They wore the red coat because no one else wanted them, or because they were so desperate that they had no choice. They were the scum of Britain, but they could fight. They had always fought, but in the army they were taught how to fight with discipline. They discovered sergeants and officers who valued them. They punished them too, of course, and swore at them, and cursed them, and whipped their backs bloody and cursed them again, but valued them. They even loved them, and officers worth five thousand pounds a year were fighting alongside them now. The redcoats were doing what they did best, what they were paid a shilling a day less stoppages to do: they were killing.

The French advance was stopped. There was no edging forward now. Their front ranks were dying and the ranks behind were trying to escape the wild men with bloody faces, men who were screaming like fiends. **"Faugh a ballagh! Faugh a ballagh!"** Gough kicked his horse through his men and hacked down with his sword at a French sergeant. The color party was behind him, the ensigns carrying the two flags and the sergeants armed with nine-foot-long spontoons, razor-pointed pikes that were meant to protect the colors, though now the sergeants were on the offensive, savaging the French with the long narrow blades. Sergeant Patrick Masterson was one of the pikemen and he was almost as big as Harper. He thrust the spontoon into French faces, one after the other, driving them down where bayonets could kill them. He lunged a path through the first French rank, had the blade parried by a bayonet, withdrew it, lunged again, but at the last second dropped the spontoon's head so that it punched through cloth and skin and muscle into an enemy belly. The thrust was so hard that the blade sank to the crosspiece, which stopped an enemy's corpse, trapping itself on the shaft. He kicked the dying Frenchman off the blade and thrust again and redcoats cut their way into the gap he made. Some Frenchmen lay unwounded, their hands over their heads, just praying that the screaming fiends would spare them. Ensign Keogh sliced his sword at a mustachioed Frenchman, opening a slashing wound from one cheek to the other and almost hitting a redcoat beside him as the wild swing hissed backward. Keogh's hat was gone. He was shouting the 87th's war cry, **"Faugh a ballagh!"** Clear the way, and the blades were carving the way through the tight-packed French ranks.

All along the line it was the same. Bayonets against conscripts, savagery against sudden, bowel-loosening terror. The fight had been poised, it had even tilted toward the French as their greater numbers told, but Wheatley had made the move and the laws of mathematics had been taken over by the crueler laws of hardtraining and harder men. The redcoats were going forward, slowly forward because they were fighting against a press of enemy and were stumbling on the bodies they had put on the bloodslicked grass, but they were still going forward.

Then a curricle appeared at the tree's edge, and Sharpe saw Vandal again.

On the Cerro del Puerco the French advanced to take their victory. The four battalions that had lined the hill's summit came first, with the two grenadier battalions hurrying to join their left flank. The only worry of the general of the grenadiers, Rousseau, was that his men would arrive too late to share in the victory.

The British were still on the slope and their line was still ragged. They had been hit hard by the canister, though the French guns could no longer fire because the blue-coated infantry had advanced to mask the guns' red-coated targets. But Victor knew the guns would not be needed. The emperor's bayonets would seal this victory. The drummers beat the **pas de charge** and the eagles were lifted high as three thousand Frenchmen spilled over the northern crest of the hill and gave a cheer as they charged to victory.

They faced the British foot guards, half a battalion of men from Hampshire, two companies of riflemen, and the remnants of the flank companies who had marched to battle from Gibraltar. Those red- and green-coated men, outnumbered two to one, had marched all night and were downhill from the enemy.

"Present!" Sir Thomas Graham roared. He had miraculously survived the blast of canister that had snatched three Scotsmen from the ranks immediately in front of him. Lord William Russell had brought him back his battered hat and Sir Thomas now held it aloft, then brought it sharply down to point at the two unbroken columns that came charging from the hill with bayonets fixed. "Fire!"

Twelve hundred muskets and two hundred rifles fired. The range was mostly less than sixty paces, though it was a good deal more at the flanks, and the balls drove into the three hundred men in the leading rank of the French columns and stopped them. It was as though an avenging angel had struck the head of the French columns with a giant sword. Their front ranks were bloody and broken, and even men in the second ranks were down. The carnage was enough to halt the charge as men in the third and fourth ranks stumbled and fell on the dead and dying men in front of them. The redcoats could not see what their volley had done because the smoke of their own muskets shrouded them.

They expected the two columns to burst through that smoke with bayonets and so they did what they were trained to do: they reloaded. Ramrods scraped in barrels. The proper order of files and ranks had been broken by the climb and though some officers shouted at companies to fire as platoons, most men just fired for their lives. They did not wait for an officer or a sergeant to time the rolling volleys; they just reloaded, brought up the musket, pulled the trigger, and then reloaded again.

The drill books insisted on at least ten actions to charge a musket. It began with Handle Cartridge First Movement and ended with the command to fire. In some battalions the drill sergeants managed to find as many as seventeen different actions, all of which had to be learned and mastered and practiced. Some men, a few, came to the training with an understanding of firearms. They were mostly country boys who knew how to charge a fowling piece, but it all had to be unlearned. It might take a recruit a whole minute, even longer, to load a musket, but by the time they donned the red coat and were sent to fight for their king, they could do it in fifteen or twenty seconds. This was, above all other things, the necessary skill. The guards on the hill could look superb and there was no infantry unit that looked more splendid when taking post outside St. James's Palace or Carlton House, but if a man could not bite a cartridge, prime the lock, load the gun, ram it, and fire within twenty seconds, then he was not a soldier. There were nearly a thousand guardsmen still living on the hill, and they fired for their lives. They put shot after shot into the cloud of smoke and Sir Thomas Graham, mounted just behind them, could tell that they were hurting the French, not just hurting them but killing them.

The French had come in column again. They always came in column. This one was three hundred men wide and nine ranks deep, and that meant most of the French could not use their muskets while every redcoat and every green-jacket could fire his weapon. The balls converged on the French, they drove inward, and in front of the guards and in front of the men from Hampshire there were small flames in the grass where the wadding had started fires.

Sir Thomas held his breath. This was a moment, he knew, when orders would do nothing, when even to encourage the men would be a waste of breath. They knew what they were doing and they were doing it so well that he was even tempted to think he might snatch a victory from what had seemed like certain defeat. But then the crash of a well-orchestrated volley made him ride toward the right of his line and he saw the unbroken ranks of the French grenadiers coming downhill through the smoke of their opening volley. He saw the Scottish guards turning to take on this new enemy, and the riflemen, who were in more extended order around the seaward flank of the hill, drew closer together to pour their fire at the French reinforcements.

Sir Thomas still said nothing. He held his hat in his hand and he watched the grenadiers come down the slope. He saw how each man in the French ranks had a short saber as well as a musket. These were the enemy's elite, the men chosen to do the hardest work, and they were coming fresh to the fight, but again they came in a column, and the right of his own line, without any orders from Sir Thomas or anyone else, had half turned toward them to give them the benefit of their training. The half battalion of the 67th was right in front of the grenadiers who, unlike the first four battalions, were not checked by the first shots to hit them, but kept coming.

And this, Sir Thomas knew, was how a column should fight. It was a battering ram, and though the head of the column must suffer horribly, the momentum of its mass should take it through an enemy to bloody victory. On battlefield after battlefield across a suffering Europe the emperor's columns had taken their punishment and marched on to win. And this column, all of them elite troops, was coming downhill and getting ever closer. If it broke through the thin line of red and green, it would turn to its right and murder Sir Thomas's men with sabers and musket butts. And still it came. Sir Thomas rode behind the 67th, ready to slash with his sword and die with his men if the grenadiers succeeded. Then an officer shouted the command to fire.

Smoke billowed in front of Sir Thomas. Then more smoke. The 67th was firing platoon volleys now, and the Sweeps were up on their right, not bothering to wrap their bullets with leather because at this range they could not miss, and so their fire was almost as quick as the redcoats beside them. On Sir Thomas's left were his Scotsmen, and he knew they would not break. The noise of the musketry was like a great fire of dry wood. The air stank of rotten eggs. Somewhere a seagull cried, and far behind Sir Thomas the cannons crashed on the heath, but he could not spare a glance for what happened behind him. It was here and now that the battle would be decided. He suddenly realized he was holding his breath and he let it out, glanced at Lord William, and saw His Lordship staring wide-eyed and motionless into the musket smoke. "You can breathe, Willie."

"Dear Lord," Lord William said, letting out his breath. "You know there's a Spanish brigade behind us?" he asked Sir Thomas.

Sir Thomas turned and saw the Spanish troops on the beach. They made no move to reinforce him and even if he ordered them up the hill he knew they would arrive too late to be of any help. This fight could not last that long and so he shook his head. "Damn them, Willie," he said. "Just damn them."

Lord William Russell held a pistol, ready to shoot the first grenadier to come through the smoke, but the grenadiers had been stopped by the rifle and musket fire. Their front ranks were dead and the men behind were now trying to reload and fire back, but once a column stopped moving it became a giant target, and Sir Thomas's men were firing into its heart. Even though the grenadiers were elite troops, they could not fire as fast as the redcoats.

General Dilkes, his horse bleeding in the rump and shoulder, came to Sir Thomas's side. He said nothing, just stared, then glanced up the hill to where Marshal Victor sat on his horse with his white-plumed hat held low. Marshal Victor was watching three thousand men held by musket fire. He said nothing. It was up to his men now.

On the left of the British line, beyond the First Foot Guards, Major Browne fought his remnant of flankers. Fewer than half the men who had climbed the hill were still able to fire a musket, but they poured their volleys at the nearest French column and, in their eagerness, went higher up the hill to assail the column's flank.

"Don't you love the rogues?" Sir Thomas shouted at General Dilkes, and Dilkes was so surprised by the question that he gave a bark of laughter. "Time to give them the bayonet," Sir Thomas said.

Dilkes nodded. He was watching the red-coats fire their murderous volleys and he reckoned he had just watched his men perform a miracle.

"They'll run, I vouch," Sir Thomas said, and hoped he was right.

"Fix bayonets!" Dilkes found his voice.

"On to them, boys!" Sir Thomas waved his hat and galloped back behind the line. "On to them! Push them off my hill! Off my hill!"

And the redcoats, like hounds released, went uphill with bayonets. Marshal Victor, at the crest, heard the screams as the blades began their work. "For God's sake, fight!" he said to no one in particular, but his six battalions were recoiling. Panic had infected their ranks. The rearmost men, those least in danger, were edging back and the foremost ranks were being savaged by redcoats. The band, well behind the line and still playing the forbidden "Marseillaise," sensed the disaster coming and the music faltered. The bandmaster tried to rally his musicians, but the loudest noise now was the hoarse war cries of the British. Instead of playing, the band broke and ran. The infantry followed. "The guns," Victor said to an aide, "get the guns off the hill." It was one thing to lose a fight, but another to have the emperor's beloved guns captured, so the gunners brought up their teams and dragged four of the cannons eastward, off the hill. Two could not be saved because the redcoats were too close, so those guns were lost. Marshal Victor and his aides followed the four guns, and the remnants of his six battalions ran for their lives, ran across the hilltop and down its eastern face, and behind them the redcoats and greenjackets came with bayonets and victory.

General Rousseau, who had led the grenadiers, and General Ruffin, who had commanded the beaten division, were both wounded and left behind. Sir Thomas was told of their capture, but he said nothing; he just rode to the hill's inland crest from where he could see his beaten enemy running. He remembered that long-ago moment in Toulouse when the soldiers of France had insulted his dead wife and had spat in his face when he protested. Back then Sir Thomas had sympathized with the French. He had thought that their ideals of liberty, fraternity, and equality were beacons for Britain. He had loved France.

But that had been nineteen years ago. Nineteen years in which Sir Thomas had never forgotten the mockery given by the French to his dead wife, so now he stood in his stirrups and cupped his hands. "Remember me!" he shouted. He shouted in English, but that did not matter because the French were running too fast and were too far away to hear him. "Remember me!" he shouted again, then touched his wedding ring.

And south of him, beyond the pinewood, a cannon fired.

Sir Thomas turned and put spurs to his tired horse, because the battle was not yet won.

"Oh, bloody hell," Sharpe said. The curricle had bounced past him, wheels spinning as they left the ground, and it had dashed across the corner of the French column, then capsized twenty paces from the column's edge. The woman, black-veiled, was evidently uninjured for she was trying to help the brigadier to his feet, but a dozen Frenchmen from the column's rear ranks had seen the accident and also seen a profit there. A man festooned with lace could also be festooned with money, and so they darted from the column so that they could rifle the fallen man's pockets. Sharpe drew his sword and ran.

"We've got work, boys. Come on," Harper said.

The riflemen had been moving toward the column's flank. There was a foul battle going on between redcoats and Frenchmen, a battle of bayonet and musket butts, but Sharpe had seen Colonel Vandal on his horse. Vandal was in the press of Frenchmen, close to his regiment's eagle, and he was beating with his saber, not at red-coats, but at his own men. He was shouting at them to fight, to kill, and his passion was holding the men so that the French left flank alone was not retreating, but fighting stubbornly against the Irishmen who attacked from their front. Sharpe thought that by going to the column's side he might have a clear shot for his rifle, but now he had to rescue Brigadier Moon who was trying to protect the veiled woman. Moon hauled her down beside him and tried to find his pistol, but in his tumble from the curricle the weapon had fallen from his tail pocket. He drew his new saber, a cheap thing purchased in Cádiz, and found the blade was broken, and just then the widowed Marquesa screamed because the French were coming with bayonets.

Then a green-jacketed man came from Moon's left. The man carried a heavy cavalry sword, a weapon as brutal as it was clumsy, and his first stroke took a Frenchman in the throat. The blood sprayed higher than the eagle on its pole. The man's head flopped back as his body kept running. Sharpe turned, impaled a second man in the belly with the sword, twisted it fast to stop the flesh gripping the blade, then put his right boot on the man's belly to give him the leverage to rip the sword free. A bayonet went through his coat, but Captain Galiana was there and his slim sword pierced the Frenchman's side.

Brigadier Moon, his hand clutching the Marquesa's hand, just watched. Sharpe had killed one man and put another on the ground in the time it would take to swat a fly. Now two other Frenchmen came at Sharpe, and Moon expected the rifleman to step away from their frenzied attack, but instead he went to meet them and beat a bayonet aside with his sword before driving the blade up into the man's face. A boot into the crotch crumpled the man. The second lunged with his bayonet, and Moon thought Sharpe must be killed, but the rifleman had sidestepped the lunge with sudden speed and now turned on his attacker. Moon saw the ferocity on the rifleman's face and felt an unexpected pang of pity for the Frenchman who faced him. "Bastard," Sharpe snarled, and the sword lunged, hard and fast, and the Frenchman dropped his musket and clung to the blade impaling his belly. Sharpe ripped it out just as Perkins arrived to bayonet the man. Harper was beside Sharpe now and pulled the trigger of the volley gun, with the sound of a cannon firing. Two Frenchmen went backward, blood thick on their white crossbelts. The others had taken enough and were running back to the column.

"Sharpe!" Moon called.

Sharpe ignored the brigadier. He sheathed his sword and took the rifle from his shoulder. He knelt and aimed at Vandal. "You bastard," he said and pulled the trigger. The rifle's muzzle was lost in smoke, and when the smoke cleared Vandal was still alive, still on his horse, and still using the flat of his saber to drive his men onto Gough's Irish. Sharpe swore. "Dan," he called to Hagman, "shoot that bastard!"

"Sharpe," the brigadier called again, "the gun!"

Sharpe turned. He saw, without much surprise, that the veiled woman was Caterina and he wondered what kind of bloody fool the brigadier was to bring a woman into this carnage. Then he looked at the abandoned French howitzer and saw that a priming tube was still sticking out of the vent. That meant the short-barreled cannon was loaded. He looked on the scorched grass for the linstock, but could not see it. The half battalion of the 67th, the two companies of the Cauliflowers, and the survivors of the Portuguese cacadores were advancing beyond the gun, going to fight Leval's last reserve battalion that was hurrying toward the left flank of the beleaguered 8th. The cannon, Sharpe thought, might be more useful if it was aimed at that reserve battalion, but then he remembered poor Jack Bullen. "Sergeant! I want this bloody gun round!"

Harper, Galiana, Sharpe, and Harris lifted the trail and turned the howitzer so it pointed at the 8th of the line. "Here, Sharpe!" The brigadier tossed him a tinderbox.

"Out of the way!" Sharpe shouted to his other riflemen. Then he struck a light and blew the charred linen in the box so that it burst into flame. He took all the linen out of the box, scorching his fingers, and leaned over the gun's wheel to drop the burning mass onto the priming tube. He heard the powder fizz and ducked away.

The howitzer crashed back, its wheels leaping off the ground as it recoiled. It was a six-inch howitzer and it had been loaded with canister. The balls tore into the French flank with the force of a battalion volley. The cannon had been too close to spread the missiles wide, but where they struck they gouged a bleeding hole in the packed ranks and Sharpe, running aside, saw that Vandal had disappeared. Sharpe drew his sword again, then waited, wanting another sight of the colonel. Behind him the men of the 67th and the 47th and the 20th Portuguese started their volleys against the reserve battalion. Duncan's guns flayed it with shell and shrapnel. Somewhere a man howled like a dog.

Colonel Vandal was on the ground. His horse was dying, screaming as its head thrashed the sandy soil. Vandal himself was dazed, but he did not think he was wounded. He managed to stand, only to see that the redcoats were closing on his eagle. "Kill them!" he shouted, and the shout was a parched croak. A huge sergeant with a pike was slashing at the French sergeants protecting the standard. "Kill them!" Vandal shouted again, and just then a young and skinny redcoat officer leaped at the color and cut with his sword at Sous-Lieutenant Guillemain who had the honor of holding the emperor's eagle. Vandal thrust his saber at the thin officer and felt the blade's tip jar on the man's ribs. The redcoat ignored the thrust and, with his free hand, grabbed the eagle's pole and tried to pull it from Guillemain's grasp. Two French sergeants killed the man, piercing him with their long-bladed halberds, cursing him, and Vandal saw the life fade from the redcoat's eyes before he had even hit the ground. Then one of the French sergeants recoiled, his left eye nothing but a pit of jellied blood, and a huge voice shouted at the Frenchmen. **"Faugh a ballagh!"**

Sergeant Masterson had seen Ensign Keogh killed and now Masterson was angry. He had put down one of the killers with the spontoon's blade, and he slashed at the second, striking the man with the edge of the spear point. He brought it back and rammed the pike at Guillemain's throat. The lieutenant began gurgling, blood bubbling at his gullet, and Vandal reached for the eagle, but Masterson ripped the spontoon sideways so that Guillemain's dying body fell across the colonel. Then Masterson tore the eagle out of the Frenchman's grasp. Captain Lecroix shouted in incoherent rage and slashed his sword at Masterson, but a redcoat thrust his bayonet into Lecroix's ribs and another hit him on the skull with a musket. The last thing Lecroix saw in this world was the huge Irish sergeant flailing the precious standard. He was using the eagle to beat at the men trying to take it from him, and then a new rush of redcoats came on either side of Masterson and their bayonets went to work. "Lunge!" a sergeant was shouting in a high, cracked voice. "Recover! Stance! Lunge!"

A surge of Frenchmen tried to recover their eagle, but the Irish bayonets were in front of it now. "Lunge! Recover!" the sergeant was shouting, while behind him Masterson was bellowing incoherently and waving the eagle above his head. "Lunge! Recover! Do your work properly!"

Two men seized Vandal by his shoulders and pulled him away from the blood-spattered Irishmen. The colonel was not badly wounded. A bayonet had cut into his thigh, but he felt unable to walk, to speak, even to think. The eagle! It had a laurel wreath about its neck, a wreath of gilded bronze presented by the city of Paris to those regiments that had distinguished themselves at Austerlitz, and now some prancing fool was waving the eagle in the air! Vandal felt a surge of fury. He would not lose it! If he had to die in the attempt, he would take back the emperor's eagle. He screamed at the two men to drop him. He scrambled to his feet. **"Pour l'empereur!"** he shouted, and he ran toward Masterson, thinking to cut through the men barring his way. But suddenly there were more enemy to his left and he turned, parried a sword cut, lunged to kill the man, and saw, to his surprise, that it was a Spanish officer who, in turn, parried Vandal's lunge and riposted fast. More Frenchmen came to help their colonel. "Get the eagle!" he screamed at them, and he slashed at the Spaniard, hoping to drive the man away so he could join the attack on the redcoat who had his eagle. The slash ripped through coat and yellow sash to score a bloody wound on the Spaniard's belly, but just then the Spanish officer was thrust aside and a tall green-jacketed man beat down Vandal's saber with a huge blade, then simply reached out and gripped the collar of the colonel's coat. The green-jacketed man hauled Vandal out of the melee, tripped him, then kicked the colonel in the side of the head. Rifles fired, then a rush of Irishmen drove the last few Frenchmen back. Vandal tried to roll away from his attacker, but he was kicked again. When he looked up the big sword was at his throat.

"Remember me?" Captain Sharpe asked.

Vandal swung the saber, but Sharpe parried it with derisory ease. "Where's my lieutenant?" he asked.

Vandal still held the saber. He readied himself to sweep it up at the rifleman, but then Sharpe pressed the point of the heavy cavalry sword into the colonel's throat. "I yield," Vandal said.

The pressure relaxed. "Give me your saber," Sharpe said.

"I give my parole," Vandal said, "and under the rules of war I may keep my saber." The colonel knew his battle was finished. His men had gone and the Irish were harrying them farther east with bayonets. All along the line the French were running, and all along the line bloodied men were pursuing the enemy, though they did not pursue far. They had marched all night and fought all morning and they were bone tired. They followed the beaten enemy until it was certain that the broken army would not stop to re-form and then they sank down and marveled that they were still alive. "I give my parole," Vandal said again.

"I said give me the saber," Sharpe snarled.

"He can keep his weapon," Galiana said. "He's given his parole."

Brigadier Moon watched and flinched as Sharpe kicked the Frenchman again, then stabbed down with the heavy cavalry sword to cut the man's wrist. Vandal let go of the saber's snakeskin grip and Sharpe bent and picked up the fallen blade. He looked at the steel, expecting to see a French name engraved there, but instead it said Bennett.

"You stole this, you bugger," Sharpe said.

"I gave you my parole!" Vandal protested.

"Then stand up," Sharpe said.

Vandal, his sight blurred because of his tears that were caused not by physical pain but by the loss of the eagle, stood. "My saber," he demanded, blinking.

Sharpe threw the saber to Brigadier Moon, then hit Vandal. He knew he should not, but he was consumed by fury and so he hit him clean between the eyes. Vandal fell again, his hands clutching his face, and Sharpe bent over him. "Don't you remember, Colonel?" he asked. "War is war and there are no rules. That's what you told me. So where's my lieutenant?"

Vandal recognized Sharpe then. He saw the bandage showing under the ragged shako and remembered the man who had blown the bridge, the man he thought he had killed. "Your lieutenant," he said shakily, "is in Seville, where he is being treated with honor. You hear that? With honor, as you must treat me."

"Get up," Sharpe said. The colonel stood, then flinched as Sharpe dragged him around by tugging on one of his gilded epaulettes. Then

Sharpe pointed. "Look, Colonel," he said, "there's your bloody honor."

Sergeant Patrick Masterson, with a smile as broad as all Dublin, was parading the captured eagle. "By Jesus, boys," he was shouting, "I've got their cuckoo!"

And Sharpe laughed.

HMS **Thornside** cleared the Diamante rock off Cádiz and headed west into the Atlantic. Soon she would alter course for the mouth of the Tagus and for Lisbon. On shore a one-legged admiral watched her recede and tasted the bile in his throat. All Cádiz was praising the British now, the British who had taken an eagle and humiliated the French. No hope now of a new Regency in Spain, or of a sensible peace with the emperor, because the war fever had come to Cádiz and its hero was Sir Thomas Graham. The admiral turned away and stumped toward his home.

Sharpe watched the shore fade. He stood beside Harper. "I'm sorry, Pat."

"I know you are, sir."

"He was a friend."

"And that he was," Harper said. Rifleman

Slattery had died. Sharpe had not seen it happen, but while he and Galiana had run into the disintegrating column to find Vandal, a last errant musket shot had pierced Slattery's throat and he had bled to death on Caterina's skirts.

"It wasn't our fight," Sharpe said. "You were right."

"It was a rare fight, though," Harper said, "and you got your man."

Colonel Vandal had complained to Sir Thomas Graham. He protested that Captain Sharpe had wounded him after his surrender, that Captain Sharpe had insulted him and assaulted him, and that Captain Sharpe had stolen his saber. Lord William Russell had told Sharpe of the complaint and shaken his head. "I have to tell you it's serious, Sharpe. You can't upset a colonel, even a French one! Think what they'll do to our officers if they learn what we do to theirs?"

"I didn't do it," Sharpe had lied stubbornly.

"Of course you didn't, my dear fellow, but Vandal's made his complaint and I fear Sir Thomas insists there must be a court of inquiry."

But the inquiry had never taken place. Brigadier Sir Barnaby Moon had written his own report of the incident, saying that he had been within twenty paces of the colonel's capture, that he had seen every action taken by Captain Richard Sharpe, and that Sharpe had behaved as a gentleman and an officer. Sir Thomas, on receiving Moon's report, had apologized to Sharpe in person. "We had to take the complaint seriously, Sharpe," Sir Thomas said, "but if that wretched Frenchman had known there was a brigadier watching, he'd never have made up such a pack of lies. And, of course, Moon dislikes you—he's made that very clear— so he's hardly likely to exonerate you if there was even the smallest chance of making trouble for you. So you can forget it, Sharpe, and I have to say I'm glad. I didn't want to think you were capable of doing what Vandal claimed."

"Of course I'm not, sir."

"But Brigadier Moon, eh?" Sir Thomas had asked, laughing. "Moon and the widow! Is she a widow? A proper one, I mean, not just Henry's leavings?"

"Not that I know of, sir, no."

"Well, she's a wife now," Sir Thomas said, amused. "Let us all hope he never discovers who she really is!"

"She's a lovely lady, sir."

Sir Thomas had looked at him with some surprise. "Sharpe," he had said, "we should all be as generous as you. What a kind thing to say." Sir Thomas had thanked him effusively then, and Henry Wellesley had thanked him again that evening, an evening during which Lord Pumphrey found he had business away from the embassy.

Even Sir Barnaby Moon had thanked Sharpe, not just for the return of the precious saber, but for saving his life. "And for Lady Moon's life, Sharpe."

"That was an honor, sir."

"Her ladyship insists I must give your men some proper reward, Sharpe," Moon had said, and pressed coins into Sharpe's hand, "but I do it gladly on my own behalf as well. You're a brave man, Sharpe."

"And you're a lucky one, sir. Her ladyship is beautiful."

"Thank you, Sharpe," the brigadier had said, "thank you." His leg had been broken again in the fall from the curricle so he was staying a few more days in Cádiz, but Sharpe and his men were free to leave the city. And so they sailed to Portugal, to Lisbon, to the army, to the South Essex, and to the Light Company. They were sailing home.

Historical Note

I would hate anyone to think that Sergeant Patrick Masterson's feat in capturing the eagle of the 8th regiment was in any way due to Sharpe's help. Masterson and Ensign Keogh were wholly responsible and poor Keogh died in the attempt. Their eagle was the first to be captured by British troops in the Peninsular War (despite **Sharpe's Eagle**), and Masterson was rewarded with a battlefield commission. Another member of the family, a descendant, was awarded a VC at Ladysmith. Masterson's name is sometimes given as Masterman (I've seen it spelled both ways on the same page), but Masterson seems correct. He is usually quoted as saying, "Bejabbers, boys, I have their cuckoo." He did, too.

The colonel of the 8th was Colonel Autie and he died at Barrosa. I did not want to give a real man, who died heroically, my fictional villainy so I awarded the 8th to Vandal instead. Sous-Lieutenant Guillemain was the standard-bearer and he died trying to defend the eagle that was taken to London and presented, with great fanfare, to the prince regent. It was eventually lodged in the Royal Hospital, Chelsea, from where it was stolen in 1852. The staff is still there, but the eagle itself has never been recovered.

Sir Thomas Graham is one of the more likable generals of the Peninsular War. The story of his life sketched in **Sharpe's Fury** is true. Until the French insulted his dead wife, he had been a sympathizer with France and her revolution, but he became so convinced of the evil that the revolution's fine words disguised that he raised the 90th regiment with his own money and so joined the army. Barrosa was his finest achievement, a terrible battle in which the British infantry (greatly helped on the lower ground by Major Duncan's superb gunnery) gained an astounding victory. They were outnumbered, they were tired, they remained unsupported by General Lapeña's troops, and they won. Marshal Victor, after his defeat at Wellington's hands at Talavera, should have some idea of the destructive power of British musketry, yet once again he attacked in columns, thus denying most of his men the ability to discharge their muskets. Once again the two-deep British line proved the superior weapon. It was still a close-run thing and, at the end, the bayonet proved decisive.

The Spanish were mortified by General Lapeña's supine behavior. Their troops were more than capable of fighting, and of fighting well. They had proved that at Bailen where, in 1808, they had won an overwhelming victory against the French (and captured an eagle), and General Zayas and his men were to fight brilliantly at Albuera just two months after the battle of Barrosa. Zayas had wanted to help his allies at Barrosa, but Lapeña refused his permission. The Spanish government, realizing the service Graham had rendered, offered him the title of Duque del Cerro del Puerco, but Graham refused it, regarding it as a mere bribe that might persuade him to keep quiet about Lapeña's conduct. Lapeña's nickname was indeed Doña Manolito, so perhaps it should have been no surprise that he behaved so badly. One thing Graham did gain from the battle was a dog. General Rousseau, who was badly wounded when he led his grenadiers against the Guards, died of his wounds on the Cerro del Puerco. His dog, a poodle, found his dying master and refused to leave his side, or indeed, the grave where Rousseau was buried. Graham adopted the dog and sent him back to Scotland. "He seems to understand French best," he wrote home. Graham, after the battle, became Wellington's second in command for much of the Peninsular War. In time he was to become Lord Lynedoch. He lived to a great age and never remarried. His Mary was the love of his life. I strongly recommend Antony Brett-James's biography, **General Graham** (London, Macmillan, 1959), to anyone wishing to learn more about this extraordinary and most likeable Scot.

Henry Wellesley was also a most likeable man, probably the most amiable of the Wellesley brothers. I fear, by giving him an inappropriate love affair, I have traduced his memory. It is, nevertheless, true that he had suffered in love. His wife had left him for Henry Paget, 2nd Earl of Anglesey who, as the Marquess of Anglesey, was to lead Wellington's cavalry at Waterloo. The divorces of Henry Wellesley and Henry Paget (who divorced his first wife to marry Wellesley's wife) caused a great scandal, and I have no evidence whatsoever that Henry Wellesley was the cause of any more scandal. He was, however, an extremely able ambassador, and Britain needed such a man because the political situation in Spain (which meant, in 1811, Cádiz) was explosive. Britain and Spain, for reasons cited in the novel, were awkward allies, and there were influential Spaniards who wished to end the alliance and seek a rapprochement with Napoleon. That they failed is very much because of Henry Wellesley's calm wisdom and, of course, because of Sir Thomas Graham's victory at Barrosa.

The admiral, like Brigadier Moon and Caterina, is a fictional character. The action described at the start of the book, the attack on the pontoon bridge, is also fictional, though it is based on a very similar (and rather more successful) assault made by General Hill on the bridge over the Tagus at Almarez in May 1812. The attack on the fire rafts did occur, though much earlier than is implied in the novel, and General Graham took no part in that attack, but it proved a useful opportunity for Sharpe and him to meet, so I took liberties.

There is very little to be seen at Barrosa these days. The Spanish have no cause to remember the battle, and the village has now spread to become a pleasant seaside resort at the expense of the places where so many British, Portuguese, and French soldiers died. Marshal Victor began the battle with around seven thousand men and lost over two thousand killed and wounded, including General Rousseau who died on the day of the battle and General Ruffin who died of his wounds on board the ship taking him to England. Graham began with just over five thousand British and Portuguese, and lost fourteen hundred killed and wounded. The 28th had only two officers left at the battle's end. The First Foot Guards, the Coal Heavers, lost ten officers and 210 guardsmen. No unit suffered as much as John Browne's Flanker Battalion, which suffered at least 50 percent casualties. Major Browne, who did indeed sing "Heart of Oak" as he led them up the hill, miraculously survived. The 87th lost five officers (poor Keogh among them) and 168 men. Every unit suffered heavily, and all fought magnificently.

I must thank Johnny Watt who, at a time when ill health prevented me from traveling, reconnoitered the old city of Cádiz for me. He did a superb job and it was his enthusiasm for the crypt that led to so much murder and mayhem in the cathedral. Sharpe, I confess, had no business being at Barrosa, and if I had not gone to Johnny's brother's wedding in the nearby town of Jerez de la Frontera, I doubt my interest in the battle would have been piqued. But we were there and I could not resist seeing yet another peninsular battlefield, and so Sharpe was doomed to follow. He is now back in Portugal where, in 1811, he belongs, and Sharpe and Harper will march again.